Flatlanders

Mike Sherer

WolfSinger Publications ❧ Brackettville, TX

Thank you to the poets who graciously permitted the use of their works in this book.

'Base Eight In The Spring' and 'Index Theory',
by Dor Abrahamson.

'Monstrous Moonshine' and 'Heisenberg's Relations',
by Francesca Arici.

'Media Shower' and 'Fool Proof but Messy',
by Anna Bardone-Cone.

'The Dynamic Programming Principle',
by Samuel N. Cohen.

'Axiom of Choice',
by Jason Callahan.

'There's Not Enough Room',
by Christina Carol.

'Fibonacci',
by Benjamin Gaines.

'The Universe Is' and 'Primeval Silence',
by Radu Craiu.

'Surface Seeming Flat' and 'Cosecant, You Say'
and 'Suppose Humankind', by Kevin Farey.

--

"Grasshopper, not to understand a man's purpose does not make him confused." - a quote from episode 13 of season 3 ('The Vanishing Image' – written by Gustave Field) of the Kung Fu TV series produced by Warner Brothers Television for ABC that aired from 1972-1975. The series was created by Ed Spielman, Jerry Thorpe, and Herman Miller.

--

Cover Art created by Carol Hightshoe
using Midjourney Generative AI and stock photos

ISBN 978-1-944637-53-8

Bound and printed in the Unted States

Dedication

To my older brother Bob,
who instilled in me a love of science fiction.

PART ONE
FROM A DISTANT WORLD CLOSE BY

1.

No manuscript is as impressive as a blackboard smothered in mathematical calculations. This blackboard was a rectangular meter by a meter and a half. Its black surface was covered in scribblings done in white chalk that to an untrained eye appeared to be a foreign language, or one long forgotten. Here and there a familiar numeral emerged amid the entanglement of exotic symbols. A faint white blur of erased previous inscriptions existed beneath the bold white markings, much the way evidence of previous civilizations underlie the present-day world. On the tray at the bottom of the board were several well-used erasers and an array of white chalk nubs.

The small room, a little over two by three meters, contained little else. There were two worn easy chairs, a coffee table, and several folding chairs folded up against a wall. The bare wooden floor sported no rugs, the bare pale walls no paintings or pictures or posters or banners. There was one small window, but it was so securely blindered and heavily curtained that the time of day, or night, was indeterminable. Also, the room was poorly-lit. There was a spotlight clipped to the blackboard illuminating the work. The rest of the dim room was clean, in a sense. There were no food wrappers or drink cans or other detritus about, but then no janitorial effort had been squandered, either. Orderliness is revered by mathematicians; cleanliness, not so much.

About the easy chairs. They both were adorned with stickers. On one were images of cartoon mice, such as Mickey Mouse, Minnie Mouse, Mighty Mouse, Jerry (of Tom and Jerry fame), and Fievel Mousekovitz. On the other easy chair was a quote: 'George is *in* the engineering department. He is not *the* engineering department. He is merely in it.'

In the middle of the coffee table sat a laptop. Affixed to and nearly covering its lid was a sticker of a woman clad in a classical robe of antiquity. Although the laptop itself was nicked and coffee-stained, the glossy brightly-colored sticker appeared new. The laptop was open and music emanated. Electronica tunes blended seamlessly one into another and echoed about the hollow space.

Before the blackboard stood Mickey Haiku. Late twenties, short (a little more than one and a half meters) and skinny, dishwater-color hair of no discernable cut, wearing too-long pants rolled up at the cuffs and cinched tight with a too-long belt, a once white coffee-stained short sleeve button up shirt, and paper-thin double-knotted tennis shoes. As for his face, there was a hint of whiskers upon the lower half of a round pasty glob. Weak eyes squinted behind heavy industrial-strength glasses.

Mickey stood before the blackboard studying the computations. There was a footstool for him to reach the uppermost regions of the board. At the moment he was squatted down examining the bottom.

"Mick."

Mickey froze. Raised his head and looked around. No one else was present. He unsquatted and paused the electronica on his laptop. Total silence. He backed the track up and replayed it, listening closely. There was nothing in the music that sounded like someone saying his name. He paused the music once again and walked to a closed door and listened. No sounds from the other side. Mickey opened the door. In the small dark room a form could be seen in the invading light bundled up in a short bed. "George?"

"Mmphh?"

"Are you talking in your sleep?"

"If I was I'm not anymore."

"I thought I heard something."

"Are you having another nightmare?"

"I could be."

"Then wake up and leave me alone."

Mickey backed out, closing the door. He looked around the room. Shrugged. Then restarted the music on his laptop and returned to the chalkboard to squat where he had previously squatted.

2.

Mickey walked out the door of his brownstone apartment building onto a city sidewalk on an overcast chilly day carrying a folded sheet of plastic and his laptop. He had donned a Chicago Bulls cap and pulled on a torn and stained light jacket that retained a faded 'Pi' logo from Aranofsky's movie.

Turning the corner of his building, Mickey walked down a narrow alley and approached a human form huddled on the pavement beneath cardboard and plastic. Mickey stooped before it. "You doing okay, Ralph?"

A well-weathered stub of a head poked out from the plastic. "What happened to Gauss?"

Mickey glanced at the laptop he carried. "I had a dream about Hypatia."

"Dreams can be tricky, Haiku. You never know where they come from."

Mickey handed Ralph the plastic then fished a McDonalds gift card from his pocket, handing this to him, also. "Go buy something hot to eat. Get indoors for a while."

"Thanks, Haiku."

Mickey walked back out of the alley then continued several blocks to a small park. Passing a number of empty benches, he came to the one he had tagged. It was emblazoned with a formula— '6.62607004 x 10-34 m2 kg/s'. Mickey sat and opened his laptop. The faces of the most-tapped keys were worn off, and the entire keyboard was dusted in white chalk. His Mathematica program was open, and the exotic symbols on the screen matched the symbols that were on his blackboard. Joggers passed by, elders limped by, kids ran by, mothers pushed strollers by, scooters and skates and skateboards and bicycles rolled by. Mickey ignored them all, squinting at screen after screen of computations.

"Mickey."

Mickey jerked up and looked around. No one was near him, or paying any heed to his form slouched down into the bench. But it had been louder than last time, and this time he had discerned a feminine lilt. Only there were no women nearby.

Mickey rubbed his furrowed forehead to push back on an emerging headache. He clenched eyes and lips, massaging with one hand while keeping a firm grip on the laptop with the other. Did the boulders banging together inside his skull cause him to hear a woman call his name? Or did a woman calling his name bring on the boulders? These headaches were a recent development. They had begun about the same time as his wild nightmares. And both were getting worse.

3.

Mickey sat at a desk in an empty classroom on the Northwestern University campus in Evanston, on the shore of Lake Michigan thirty-two kilometers north of Chicago. His laptop was open and he was poring over his work. He had changed clothes at this point, but you couldn't tell it. His wad of hair remained as tangled. With the usual grimace it was difficult to tell if he was suffering a headache or not.

"Mickey Hi."

"Who are you?!" Mickey bellowed, looking all about the empty room.

Only it was no longer empty. A female form stood before him. Mickey jumped to his feet, yet kept a protective hand on his open laptop. Was this form real? A fiction from his worsening nightmares? The phantasm that had been calling his name?

The female form spoke. "I'm sorry."

Mickey decided since she didn't disappear and she spoke she was probably real. A skittish young woman dressed in jeans and tee shirt stood before a janitorial cart. The bright red scarf on her head caught his eye. He stepped up for a closer look.

The woman backed away, maneuvering the cart between them. "I thought this room was empty."

The bright red scarf was emblazoned with stark black numbers. He motioned to the faded symbol on his jacket hanging on the back of his chair. "Pi."

She touched the scarf, smiled.

"How many places is it solved to?" Mickey asked.

The woman shrugged. "It was a present from my mother."

"Did you call my name?"

"I don't know your name."

"Did you say hi to me?"

The woman retreated toward the door, pulling her cart along behind. "I can come back later." She backed out.

Mickey searched all the corners of the room. No one else was there. He collapsed into his chair, propping elbows on knees to grasp his lowered throbbing head. Why did the voice coincide with such headaches? Or did the headaches bring on the voice? Chicken or egg? Stupid question; the egg preceded the chicken by hundreds of millions of years.

4.

Mickey stood in the living room of his apartment looking from his open laptop on the coffee table to the crammed-full blackboard. On the screen of his laptop was mathematical haiku—Base Eight In The Spring, by Dor Abrahamson: 'I wrote a poem with/Seventeen syllables/Did I count right?'. Bicep played an electronica mix behind the poetry. Mickey shuffled from foot to foot to the soft beat of the music as he repeated the last line of haiku over and over. "Did I count right? Did I count right? Did I count right?"

"Forty-two."

Growing accustomed to real and immaterial female voices, Mickey forced himself not to overreact. He continued shuffling from foot to foot repeating his mantra, "Did I count right?", while looking around the room. This time no one was present. But the headache was. He stopped shuffling to rub his temples. Yet this didn't immobilize him. This he was getting used to, also.

Finally, he focused through blurry headachy eyes on the blackboard. Locked onto an equation. Carefully approached the board. Chalk marks could be squiggly, they were shape-shifters, could change their meaning in the blink of a sleep-starved eye. He zeroed in on the equation. Was that an empty spot? Black not scribbled over in white? Was there enough space? To inscribe? Two numerals? His nose was nearly touching the board. His trembling fingers picked up a sliver of chalk, barely a trace of chalk, and slowly, cautiously, scrunched the two numbers upon the little bit of bare black, forcing them to fit. Four. Two.

Mickey withdrew his nose. Mouthed the number. Forty-two. Sucked on the bit of chalk as he studied the equation. He stepped back, scanning the block of computation the equation was a part of. He stepped back further to scan the entire blackboard. Mickey began shuffling again, only more so than just from foot to foot; this could almost be interpreted as dancing. He began chanting. "Forty-two. Forty-two. Forty-two."

Mickey danced across the room to a closed door. "George! George!" Mickey flung the door wide.

"No."

"Forty-two!" Mickey danced into the dark room.

"Shut up."

"Forty-two!" Mickey danced up to the bed.

"Get out."

"Forty-two!" Mickey danced around the bed.

The bundled covers stirred. "I'll kill you."

Mickey stopped dancing. "Get up."

A fuzzy head emerged. "What time is it?"

"I have no idea." Mickey leaned in close. "I've got something to show you."

"What?"

"Forty-two. Arise and prepare to be astounded."

"Forty-two what?"

"I don't know. But the answer is forty-two."

"The answer to life, the universe, and everything?"

"Could be. Come check my math."

Fifteen minutes later George, wearing only undershorts, sat in the easy chair with the quotation affixed to it. Even in an irritable daze, he appeared exceptional. Early thirties, ruggedly handsome, his large muscular frame thickly-matted, while thick wild brown hair and full beard adorned his head. But there were conflicts. His eyes squinted, like Mickey's. His skin was sickly pale, like Mickey's.

Mickey restrained himself from dancing to the electronica still playing on his laptop, yet he seemed to quiver like Jell-o. "It's forty-two? Right?"

George turned from the blackboard to glare at his roommate. "You pulled me out of bed in the middle of the night…"

"It's not the middle of the night."

"Beyond the middle of the night…"

"It's almost morning."

"For this bad joke?"

"It's not a joke." Mickey pointed to the blackboard. "Do the math."

"You're an idiot." George stomped back into his bedroom.

Mickey followed George into the dark room and flipped on a light. This cell of a room was less than half the size of the living room. A narrow single bed, a chest of drawers, and a nightstand were the only furnishings crammed into it. No ornamentation whatsoever. Only books and journals and magazines and folders and binders and note-books and loose-leaf computer printout scattered everywhere. George moaned as he collapsed into the narrow single bed.

Mickey pursued him. "I didn't do an inverse operation. I didn't start with forty-two and work backwards."

George yanked up the covers and turned away.

Mickey hurried around to kneel at his side. "My equations just spit the number out."

George rolled over.

Mickey hurried around the foot of the bed to the other side to kneel before him again. "I've been working on this for years."

"For decades, centuries, millennia, millions of years."

"If you examined my work you wouldn't mock."

"The only thing I'm examining are the backs of my eyelids." George closed his eyes. "Cut the light off as you leave."

"This changes everything."

George opened his eyes, glancing at the table lamp on the nightstand next to his bed. "Or I smash the lamp."

"The higher dimensions are within reach now."

"Over your head."

"Mickey Haiku triumphant!" He resumed dancing, and recited a mathematical haiku poem ('Monstrous Moonshine', by Francesca Arici) — "'unexpected connections/symmetries and monstrous representations/are one under the moonshine'."

George reached for the lamp.

"That lamp is only a hologram," Mickey declared. "Like everything else."

"Want to test that theory?"

Mickey danced toward the door.

"Didn't think so. You're a theoretical physicist. You don't bother to test."

Mickey turned back at the open door. "I've rocked the world. And George sleeps." Mickey cut the light off and walked out.

A deep sigh of disgust issued from the darkness.

Mickey closed the door, as demanded. He touched his forehead, and smiled at the realization there was no headache. Must be the adrenaline. To continue his celebration, he resumed dancing and recited another mathematical haiku ('Heisenberg's Relations', by Francesca Arici): "'position and momentum/possess a non-trivial commutator/uncertainty relations'."

5.

The next day Mickey sat on his tagged bench in the city park with his laptop open and Mathematica running. He gazed at a cluster of equations in which the number '42' featured prominently. He rubbed his forehead, yet did not seem to be in serious distress.

A young female runner dressed in purple shorts, a tee shirt printed with an image of Frozen's Elsa, and exceptional running shoes approached. She was slender and shapeless, with skin stretched tight across sharp bones, and short chopped blond hair atop her tall frame. She slowed upon approaching the tagged bench. "Hi, Mickey."

Mickey looked up, fearful this was yet another manifestation of the disembodied female voice he had been hearing. He was pleasantly surprised to find a real woman standing before him, especially one he knew. He stopped rubbing his head. "Hi, Priscilla."

Priscilla stooped to look at the back of the laptop lid. "Who is this?"

"Hypatia."

"What did Gauss do to fall out of favor?"

Mickey shrugged. "Nothing. I just had a dream about Hypatia."

"A woman, no less." Mickey nodded. Priscilla sat next to Mickey. "She must be impressive to dispatch Gauss."

"Hypatia was the most famous female mathematician of the ancient world. She was born around 370 CE in Alexandria. At the time the city was a center of science and philosophy that rivaled Athens. She studied and taught at the Library. But the newly ascendant Christians hated her for her paganism, and also because she didn't behave as women of that time were supposed to behave. She gave public lectures all across Alexandria while wearing men's clothes. At one of those lectures a mob of Christian men dragged her into a church, where they stripped her naked and scraped the flesh from her bones with oyster shells. Her mutilated body was then burned, whether still alive or not I don't know. In the aftermath of her death, the Library of Alexandria was sacked and burned, and all other intellectuals and artists wisely fled the city."

Priscilla frowned. "Gruesome."

"She taught that Ptolemy was wrong. That the Earth wasn't the center of the Universe. About a thousand years before Copernicus."

"No wonder the Church tortured and killed her."

"There was no Church back then. Not an established Catholic Church, like today. Emperor Constantine had just converted, the Christians were just emerging from the shadows after being tortured and killed themselves for centuries by Romans. You can't blame the Church for what happened to Hypatia."

"So why the sudden interest?"

Mickey shrugged. "I don't know. I dreamed about her one night. Several nights." He closed his laptop. "Something big has happened."

Priscilla stood. "Can you run with me? I really want to get this run in."

Mickey stood and jogged alongside her through the park.

Priscilla ran slowly so Mickey could keep up. "So you've solved the Yang-Mills fields?"

"Re." Pant. "Nor." Pant. "Mal." Pant. "Lized."

"Renormalized by expanding them into higher dimensions?"

"Yes."

"How many dimensions are there?"

"Eleven."

"So where are they?"

"Curled up. At the time. Of the Big. Bang."

Priscilla pulled up before a large house.

Mickey stumbled to a halt, grabbing her to keep from falling. They were on a well-manicured side street lined with stately old homes several blocks off the Northwestern campus. He gasped on. "Most likely."

Priscilla started toward the house, but Mickey hung back, doubling over and sagging around his laptop. "My grandparents are in India," she said helpfully.

Mickey limped after her. "Good. They think I'm a vampire."

"They believe you believe you are a vampire."

"Same thing."

Arriving on the porch, Priscilla produced a key.

Mickey sniffed. "Garlic?" He glanced up at a clove hanging above the door.

"They are humoring you." Priscilla led Mickey into a well-furnished house which was a mishmash of American and Indian cultures. A statue of Ganesh was draped with an American flag. And so on. Priscilla led Mickey deep into the house. "Can we access these higher dimensions?"

"If they were connected. Through even higher dimensions. And they might be. By strings. Forty-two strings."

Priscilla ascended a staircase. "Forty-two. Where have I heard that number before?"

Mickey hauled himself up behind her with one hand pulling on the railing and his other hand clutching his laptop. "Douglas Adams. Hitchhiker's Guide. To The Galaxy."

Reaching the top, Priscilla peeled off her jersey, bringing a black sports bra into view. She glanced back to see Mickey stumble, staring, and nearly fall back down the steps. "I'm so sweaty I'm miserable. I've got to shower." She walked into her room, leaving the door open.

Mickey stopped at the open door. "Should I stay out here?"

"If you want."

Mickey hesitated a brief moment then limped into Priscilla's room. It was decorated in pinks and little girl princess motif. A poster of the Little Mermaid was on the wall, figurines of Aurora and Belle were displayed on a dresser top. Mickey's curious gaze settled upon the bathroom door, which was partway open. He sat on the edge of the bed covered with a Mulan sheet, laid aside his laptop, and stared in.

Priscilla's head appeared from behind the door. "Grandma thinks I'm still six." Her head was withdrawn from sight. Water began running in the shower. "So why forty-two?"

"No idea. I was hoping you'd go over my numbers."

"I can do that. But no theories?"

"Maybe it's a magic number."

"Like Ramanujan's twenty-four?"

Mickey craned his neck, trying to see further into the bathroom. No luck. "Yes. Plus two more dimensions of time and space. To make the twenty-six dimensions some string theorists believe exists. For the total number of spacetime dimensions possible."

"I thought you said eleven."

Mickey leaned far off the bed to peer into the bathroom. He could now see the drawn shower curtain. It was yellow, covered with Tinker Bells. "When the Ramanujan modular function is generalized, the number twenty-four is replaced by the number eight. The critical number for superstring theory. Plus the two physicists always add for spacetime. To make ten. Strings vibrate in ten, or some say eleven, dimensions because it requires these generalized Ramanujan functions to achieve symmetry."

"In other words you have no idea why ten and eleven and twenty-six dimensions are singled out."

"It's like some deep numerology is being manifested. These numbers keep popping up in equations." When the water was cut off, Mickey hastily scooted back on the bed so as not to appear to have been looking into the bathroom.

"And now your forty-two. Can you hand me a robe?"

"Sure." Mickey hopped up and went to her closet. There were

several long bulky robes, a long nightgown with Ariel on it, and one short flimsy pink robe. He selected the short flimsy pink robe. As Mickey handed it in to her, he looked through the half-open door at the bathroom mirror. It was fogged from the steam of the hot shower. Priscilla's arm extended from behind the door, and Mickey gave her the robe. He waited patiently, glancing hopefully at the fogged mirror. But it remained fogged.

The door swung all the way open and Priscilla appeared in the short flimsy pink robe. She wiped the fog from the mirror with a towel.

"*Now* you clean it."

She gave him an uncomprehending look then went to work on her hair.

6.

An hour later Priscilla, now dressed in baggy jeans and a baggy Snow White tee shirt that sagged off her long rail-thin frame, studied the blackboard in Mickey and George's apartment. Since there was company George had donned pants, but nothing else. He was seated in the easy chair with the quotation, while Mickey sat in the easy chair with the mouse stickers. They both studied Priscilla as she paced from side to side before the blackboard. Mickey's laptop with the large Hypatia sticker on the lid rested closed and silent on the coffee table.

At last, Priscilla stepped back, still staring. "You're right. It's forty-two."

"Forty-two what?" George demanded.

Mickey shrugged.

"Maybe the answer's in Ramanujan's lost notebooks," Priscilla suggested.

"Who?" George asked.

Priscilla turned from the blackboard to confront him. "The strangest man in all of mathematics, and you've not heard of him?"

"I'm not a math major teaching assistant to a physics professor." George glanced to Mickey. "Or a theoretical physicist grad student. Just a lowly mechanical engineer intern."

Priscilla slipped into professorial mode. "Srinivasa Ramanujan was born in India in eighteen-eighty-seven. With no formal training. With practically no contact with western science."

"He dreamed math," Mickey interjected.

"Over four-thousand formulas," Priscilla continued, "theorems of incredible power."

Mickey continued the tag team. "To protect conformal superstring symmetry from being destroyed by quantum mechanics, a number of mathematical identities must be miraculously satisfied."

Priscilla tagged back in. "These identities are precisely the identities of Ramanujan's modular functions. Who of course in his day had never heard of superstring theory or quantum mechanics."

Mickey tagged in. "The laws of nature simplify when self-consistently expressed in higher dimensions. This self-consistent restraint, or symmetry, forces us to use Ramanujan's modular functions, which fixes the dimensions of space-time to be eleven."

George was getting tennis-neck looking from one to the other.

"Being symmetric is that important?"

Mickey stood. He was growing too agitated to remain still. "Once we demand a unification of quantum theory and general relativity, God has no choice."

George pulled at his beard. "No choice in what?"

Mickey spread his arms wide. "Life, the Universe and everything. Self-consistency alone forced God to create the universe as he did."

Priscilla sat in Mickey's vacated chair. "I've always believed Douglas Adams' 'forty-two' was merely the reverse of Ramanujan's magic number, 'twenty-four'."

"Why don't you ask him?" George asked.

"People have," Mickey replied. "Douglas Adams won't say where the number forty-two came from."

Priscilla glanced back at the easy chair she was seated in. "Are you guys ever going to tell me about the chairs?"

"Sure. Since you agreed to look over my numbers." Mickey turned toward the chairs. "When George and I first moved in together we bought two new chairs for our new place. Somewhat new. The chairs, not the place." Mickey glanced around. "Well, this place is not too new, either."

"Anyway…" George prompted.

"Yes. Anyway. They were a set, which meant they looked alike. So we agreed each would decorate the other."

"Since, of course, being nerds, you each had to have your own chair," Priscilla commented.

"Of course," Mickey continued. "George went with the obvious. Since my name is Mickey, he went with all kinds of mice images. While I chose to be more obscure."

"It's a quote," George butted in.

"Of course it is," Mickey agreed. "But by who and from what?"

"Priscilla?" George looked hopefully at her.

"I have no idea. The only quote I know is 'et tu, Brute?'."

Mickey was surprised. "You read Shakespeare?"

"No. I do crossword puzzles. That quote gets used a lot, at least the 'et tu' part. So where does the quote on the chair come from?"

" 'Who's Afraid Of Virginia Woolf?'. An Edward Albee play. Also a good movie with Richard Burton and Elizabeth Taylor. Richard Burton's character was named George."

"Never heard of it." Priscilla stood and took out her phone. "Let's immortalize the moment."

Mickey stepped up alongside the blackboard, smiling.

Priscilla snapped a photo then busied herself with the keypad. "I sent it to you."

All three gathered around the coffee table as Mickey opened the laptop and displayed the photo that Priscilla had just taken. "True nerd."

"Nerds rule," George added.

"In all dimensions, however many there are." Smiling at Mickey, Priscilla continued, "Be sure to show this to your coffee group."

7.

One afternoon later that week Mickey sat at two scooted-together tables before a window of a coffee shop with his laptop open before him. Outside it was raining cats and dogs and other small animals. Inside, five others - a young couple, two middle-aged women, and an elderly man - sat with him looking at the photo Priscilla had taken that was now displayed on the laptop screen. Placed in the middle of the two tables was a placard: 'Phun with Physics'.

"So you are close to accessing a higher dimension?" Lucy, one of the two middle-aged women, asked.

Mickey sipped his coffee. "Closer than I was a week ago."

"Hurry," the elderly man said. "Some of us don't have long to learn the mysteries of life."

Mickey smiled. "Albert, there is nothing to suggest eternal life."

Miriam, the other middle-age woman, spoke up. "Forget eternal life. Do you think I want to get much older than this? I'm searching for the fountain of youth."

"You're in the wrong place for that," Stan, the ruggedly-handsome physically-fit male half of the young couple, said. "Isn't that somewhere in Florida?"

"Road trip," his ruggedly-attractive physically-fit wife Laurie suggested. "To Florida in search of the fountain of youth."

Lucy ignored their jesting. "Didn't you say time is a dimension? And the lower dimensions can be manipulated through the higher dimensions?"

"These are speculations, yes," Mickey said.

Laurie looked Mickey over. "I'd like to see Mickey on a Florida beach in a swim suit."

"He'd burn in sixty seconds," her husband Stan replied.

Mickey chuckled at the banter, oblivious to the look-over Laurie gave him.

Lucy was determined. "Like this." She took a pencil and made two dots on opposite corners of a sheet of paper. "This paper is two dimensional. It has length and width. But it can be bent through a third dimension, height." She picked up the sheet of paper and rolled it up so the two points were next to each other. "So that these two points, which were worlds apart, are now next to each other."

"Lucy, I'm honored," Mickey said. "You remember our discussions clearly."

Lucy frowned. "Don't patronize me, young man. Just because my eyesight is failing doesn't mean my mind is."

Albert touched her head then jerked his hand away, as if injured. "She's right. Sharp as a tack." He looked around the table. "Anyone have a band-aid?"

"So if time is a dimension..." Lucy pressed on.

Or tried to, until Miriam interrupted. "Duration? Didn't you say?"

"Yes. Duration." Mickey seemed accustomed to refereeing the two elderly women.

Lucy ignored both of them. "Then it can be bent through a higher dimension to bring any two points together."

"Theoretically," Mickey said.

Lucy held up her folded paper. "Then *theoretically* I could move through a higher dimension to encounter myself as a teenager."

Laurie smiled at Mickey in an unhealthy way. "I would enjoy meeting Mickey as a teenager."

Miriam smiled right back. "I'd take Stan just the way he is."

While the conversation between the five devolved further, Mickey looked out the window. It was raining so hard he could not see the city park with his tagged bench across the street from the coffee shop. Yet he spied something on that far side of the street. A hazy indistinct form stood on the sidewalk facing the coffee shop. Whether male or female, or much anything else, he couldn't make out. But the person didn't seem to be properly dressed for the rain. No umbrella, no raincoat, no shoes; in fact, the person didn't seem to be wearing much at all. A passing car splashed a quantity of water up on him or her, yet he or she didn't flinch.

"Mickey Haiku."

Mickey lunged to his feet. It was the female voice that had been calling his name. How could he hear her? Through the glass? From across the street? With all the traffic? In the storm? He stared out the window at the ephemeral vision in the pouring rain. Now the voice had a body. A bit of one.

Lucy was the first to comment on his discomposure. "Mickey? What's wrong?"

Mickey, afraid he'd lose sight of the strange woman if he looked away, merely shook his head. "You didn't hear her?" The five others, having fallen silent, stared blankly back. Mickey staggered away from the table toward the door.

"Mickey?" Lucy called with concern.

Mickey ran out into the storm. She was gone. He froze in the rain, searching. No sign of her. He splashed through the scant slow-moving traffic across the street to where she had been standing. Nothing but puddles. He cast frantic searching stares through the pelting rain up and down the street, into the city park. Hardly anyone but him was out in this downpour. Hoping she was still there, only he couldn't see her, like before, he cupped his hands to his mouth and screamed, "Who are you?!" Again and again, in all directions. "Who are you?!" No response.

At last, Mickey slogged back across the street into the coffee shop. He had never been so saturated. It felt like his clothes had absorbed ten pounds of water. He squished back to his table.

"What did it look like?" Albert asked. Getting nothing from Mickey except a dark glare and dripping water, he went on. "The ghost you just saw." He looked around at the others. "I see them all the time. People I've outlived. They're all over the place."

Mickey only shivered.

"You look like you *have* seen a ghost," Miriam said.

Lucy stood. "This meeting is over. Mickey needs to get dry."

"Right." Stan and his wife jumped up. "Next month, then? Same place, same time?" Mickey only shivered as the spooked couple rushed away.

"I'll sit a while," Albert said. "If I went out now I'd be likely to drown."

Miriam nodded in concurrence. "I'll sit with you, Albert."

"Mickey can't sit a while," Lucy insisted. "He'll catch pneumonia. I'll call a cab." She looked to Mickey. "I live less than a mile from here. You can dry off at my place."

"At your place?" Miriam screeched.

"He's had a shock," Lucy said. "Can't you see? He doesn't need to be alone right now. And he must get dry."

8.

Lucy took Mickey to her apartment. Her unit was tight and Spartan. What was unexpected were the decorations. Framed parchments displaying numbers in fantastic calligraphies. On flat surfaces, hanging on the walls, numerals of great imagination and beauty.

This sight brought Mickey out of his dark reverie. "These are beautiful, Lucy."

"Calligraphy is a hobby of mine, and I enjoy playing with numbers. I'm good at Sudoku and Numble." She ushered him into her bathroom. "I'll run your clothes through the dryer. I'll skip washing them, to save time. I'll just dry them. If that's alright." She held out both hands. "I promise I won't let anything happen to it."

Mickey handed the laptop he clutched with both hands to her, and in turn she handed him a towel. He closed the door. As he began peeling sodden clothes from his sodden body, he noticed the shower curtain. It appeared to have been purchased in Las Vegas. Sevens and elevens in all different sizes and colors and styles, such as on dice faces and slot machines displays and keno balls.

Was it a ghost haunting him, Mickey wondered, like Albert said? If so, who? Albert was nearly a hundred. He knew many people who had passed away. Who did Mickey know? He couldn't think of a single person he was acquainted with who had died. So who was haunting him? Whoever she was, it was getting worse. At first she was just in his nightmares. Then she called his name. That was bad enough, being personally addressed by a ghost. But then there was the '42' solution she had suggested. It worked! Now he was seeing her, at least vaguely.

"Mickey?" Lucy called out from the other side of the bathroom door. "Are you okay?"

"No." He pulled his undershorts off. "I'm embarrassed."

Lucy laughed. "Don't be. I'm old enough to be your grandmother. So let me be a grandmother."

Mickey handed his sopping clothes out to her and began drying off. Could it be his sub-conscious? Perhaps he had worked out the answer before he became consciously aware he had. So was he hearing his subconscious call out his name? Trying to get his attention? But had his subconscious constructed that specter in the rain, also? To what purpose? Maybe to let him know he was going insane. That's what this seemed like. He had struggled so hard on so difficult a problem for so long a time. But 42 worked! If losing his mind was what it took to prove inter-dimensional interaction was possible, so be it.

The towel was heavy by the time Mickey hung it up. He inspected the robe Lucy had given him. Pink, with slot machines. Another souvenir from Vegas? He slipped it on and looked himself over in the mirror. He was surprised by the fact it didn't feel too weird to have on a woman's robe. Should he worry about that? The fact he wasn't uncomfortable wearing women's clothes?

When Mickey emerged from the bathroom his first thought was to locate his laptop, which he spied on the coffee table in the living room. When he went to pick it up he noticed a physics textbook alongside. "Are you reading this?"

"I'm trying to."

Mickey picked the heavy tome up and opened the cover. He saw a Northwestern Bookstore stamp. "You bought this at the University?"

"No. A friend gave it to me."

"Bring it with you to our next meeting. If you are having trouble understanding something in it we can discuss it." Mickey set it back down and picked up his laptop. He joined Lucy at the kitchen table. Two cups of coffee and a half-dozen white chocolate macadamia nut cookies awaited.

"We didn't get to finish our coffee at the meeting," Lucy explained.

Mickey smiled his appreciation as he sat. He glanced to the closet where he could hear the dryer running.

"Let's give them another ten minutes," Lucy suggested. "They were pretty wet."

Mickey sipped his coffee. Strong and black. Lucy knew what he liked and how he liked it. A more calming and relaxing beverage had never been concocted. And the cookies were what he always ordered at the coffee shop. He sighed in relief.

"So Laurie wants to see you on a Florida beach in a swim suit," Lucy said.

Mickey was no longer so calm. "She was joking."

"I don't think so."

"Her husband was sitting right there."

"That didn't keep Laurie from flirting with you. The way she was looking you over was obscene."

"Laurie wasn't doing anything obscene."

Lucy laughed. "You've not had much experience with women, have you?"

Mickey joined in laughing, although his was more nervous. "That should be obvious."

"Maybe you should schedule a private Phun With Physics with Laurie."

"Enough about Laurie. She's married to an Army veteran who could snap my pencil neck with two fingers. She could probably do the same. She's an Army vet, too."

"Okay. I just wanted to make sure you are aware Laurie has her eye on you." Lucy picked up a cookie. "What happened today? You obviously saw something across the street that upset you."

Mickey picked up his second cookie. "My clothes should be dry enough. I don't want to impose."

Lucy spread her arms. "Does it look like you are keeping me from anything?" She lowered her arms. "You don't have to talk about it if you don't want to."

"I've been having bad dreams and terrible headaches. And hearing voices. Today is the first time I saw something that went along with the voice."

"You're not getting enough sleep. I can see it in your face."

"Sleep is a waste of time." Mickey picked up another cookie.

"Fooling with us old fogies is a waste of time."

"I enjoy it. It's good for me. Improves my communication skills." The dryer buzzed. Mickey crammed the rest of the cookie into his mouth.

"Take the rest with you."

He paused to ascertain if she was serious.

"I shouldn't eat them."

"Thank you."

Lucy went to check his clothes. "They are still damp. Another ten minutes." She started the dryer up again.

While she was busy, Mickey fetched his laptop. "Do you like poetry?"

"No." Lucy returned to the table.

"But you like numbers. This is mathematical haiku. The poetry of numbers." Mickey opened his laptop and brought up a page. "Here's one by Anna Bardone-Cone. 'Meteor shower/Vectors flying through the sky/Soft axis landing'."

Lucy scowled up from the screen. "It doesn't even rhyme."

Mickey closed his laptop with a shrug. "It's an acquired taste."

"Is that why your last name is Haiku? Because you like this stuff?"

"It's a nickname I've had for so long I can't remember what my real last name is."

"I don't believe that. Let's see your driver's license."

"I don't drive."

"Voter ID card? Credit card? Library card?"

"Don't vote, don't borrow money, and every book I want to read is on the Internet."

"Not even a Facebook page?"

"Of course I have a Facebook page, grandma. Registered to Mickey Haiku."

Lucy scowled at him from across the table. "You can call me grandma here, Mickey Haiku, or whoever you are, but I don't want to hear it at Phun With Physics."

9.

Mickey stood before the blackboard in his apartment sucking on a nub of chalk. His laptop was open upon the coffee table, from which Bicep's electronica played softly. He remained motionless, studying the white equations before him so intently he didn't notice a bedroom door open.

George emerged in his undershorts, more asleep than awake. Scratching, he paused to study Mickey, who still hadn't noticed him. George squeezed himself; he was obviously en route to the bathroom. He started to go on, keeping silent to not disturb his roommate's deliberations, then froze in mid-step. A shimmering white form appeared behind Mickey. It wasn't substantial, he could see through it, but it had a human shape. A female shape, in white, as if composed of chalk dust. She seemed to be hovering at his right shoulder. George squeezed harder. He was desperate to get to the bathroom, but he wanted to know what this thing was.

Mickey took the chalk from his lips and began writing on the blackboard. With his other hand he picked up an eraser. He choreographed equations across the board, erasing here, scribbling there, pausing to consider, then dancing before the board to erase and scribble some more. All the while the amorphous white chalky specter bobbed at his right shoulder.

George could wait no longer. He bolted across the room to the bathroom. His sudden movement made the phantasm disappear and Mickey snap to attention. "I'll be right back!" George yelled before closing the door. "Don't go anywhere."

When George emerged from the bathroom, he found Mickey standing before the blackboard studying his work. "What was that?"

Mickey turned dazed eyes to him. "What was what?"

"That thing behind you. It was like white fog. But it wasn't as solid as fog. I could see through it. But it was white. And it moved along with you."

"Sounds like you woke up from a bad dream."

"I woke up *to* a bad dream. What are you working on?"

"I'm just going over some stuff."

"You were working on something. You were erasing and writing stuff."

"No I wasn't."

"You were. I saw you."

"Where?" Mickey turned back to the blackboard. "Where was I working?"

George pointed out where Mickey had erased and inscribed.

Mickey studied that section of the board. "It's been changed." He turned his ire on George. "What did you do?!"

"*You* did it! I wouldn't touch your holy blackboard." Mickey turned back to stare at the altered work. After a minute of silence, George could stand it no longer. "Well? Is it ruined?"

"No."

"Does it still make sense?"

"Yes."

"Is Mickey Haiku triumphant?"

"Nearly."

George turned back to his room. Once Mickey was reduced to one word utterances conversation was futile. His mind was focused on physics. George closed the door and returned to bed. Maybe what he had seen hadn't really been there. His eyes weren't the best. And he had just awoken from a deep sleep. He would ask Mickey about it in the morning. If he remembered to.

10.

Mickey sat in the mouse chair staring at the blackboard. Motion-less, he seemed to be asleep with his eyes open. His laptop was open, displaying the photo Priscilla had taken and playing Bicep's electronica.

Chalk computations began to glow on the blackboard. They rose like a white mist from the black surface and formed a sphere in the air, whirling around faster and faster, compressing tighter and tighter, until the cloud was spinning and flashing like a pulsar. A spinning white flat ring expanded from the equator of the insanely rotating round mass to encompass Mickey. He remained perfectly still as he was engulfed in white.

Mickey found himself sitting on his tagged bench in the park. It was night. No one else was in sight. He looked down. Numbers and mathematical symbols written in chalk on the sidewalk were strung out in a single line away from him.

Mickey stood, studying the line of math as he followed it. Branches of figures diverged from the main trunk up trees and across benches and over fountains and statues. He followed the main trunk of equations out of the park onto the deserted city sidewalk and across the empty street to the dark coffee shop Phun With Physics met in. Chalk calculations spread out from there to cover the coffee shop plate glass window, the pavement, signs, billboards, and sides of other buildings.

The chalk figures began vibrating, squirming as if agitated by an electric current. They floated up off whatever surface they had been written upon to congeal in front of Mickey just above the pavement in the middle of the empty street. This reminded Mickey of the hazy form he had seen in the rain outside the coffee shop, only he couldn't see through it like then. This time the form was more substantial.

The glowing light resolved into a definite human shape. It resolved further into a female body. As the resolution grew ever sharper it became a young woman. It resolved no further; she remained diapha-nous. This ghost-like apparition wore the pink robe Mickey had selected for Priscilla after her shower. Yet she was the opposite of Priscilla. Where Priscilla was tall, she was short. Where Priscilla was thin and shapeless, she was full-bodied. Where Priscilla had short butchered blond hair, her full coal-black hair flowed down over her shoulders. She appeared terrified, hugging herself and squatting, as if trying to draw herself into a ball. "It's so big and empty."

Mickey recognized the ghost voice he had been hearing. "Why have you been calling my name?"

She closed her eyes. "I need a minute."

"What's the matter?"

"This is scary."

Mickey looked around. "What is?"

"Your world." She cracked her eyes to glance around.

"Was that you outside the coffee shop in the rain?"

"Yes. But I couldn't see so much then, in the rain. And I wasn't this far through."

"This far through to where?"

"Your dimension."

Mickey laughed. "The only place you've gotten through to is my dreams."

She opened her eyes half-way and focused on Mickey. "That was the only way I could contact you at first. In your dreams. But I keep projecting my hologram further and further through."

"If this is real, why is it real?"

"I'm here to help you find the way."

"To the higher dimensions?"

"Yes."

"Your forty-two works."

"Of course it works." She opened her eyes all the way. "How do you think Douglas Adams came up with it?"

"You contacted Douglas Adams?"

"I have helped others."

"Like Ramanujan? In his dreams?"

"He was too weak."

"He died of tuberculosis at thirty-three."

"You are stronger." She raised up out of her crouch, and seemed to be calming.

"You look familiar."

The woman made an unpleasant face. "That's funny. You look *very* familiar." She chanced quick glances from side to side. "I hope you are nicer than the man you resemble."

"I've seen *you* somewhere. I guess that's normal. To use people you know in your dreams." Mickey began rocking on his feet, something he did when nervous. "I haven't studied about dreams, so I don't really know."

The woman dropped her arms. She was now upright and casual. "Know this. This is no dream."

Mickey continued on unimpressed. "I've had weirder dreams. It must be the robe that makes you look familiar. I know the robe. I picked it out for Priscilla to wear."

The woman frowned as she looked the flimsy robe over. "I wish you'd picked out something more decent for *me* to wear."

Mickey smiled. "Since when did dreams have to be decent?"

A taxicab pulled up out of nowhere. It was numbered '1729'. "Seventeen twenty-nine," Mickey read. "The smallest natural number representable in two different ways as a sum of two cubes. Ramanujan."

The woman struggled to keep herself covered with the short robe as she climbed in the back of the cab.

Mickey leaned into the open back door. "Who are you?"

"My name is Eden." She closed the door and the cab drove away.

Mickey ran down the street after her. "Eden! EDEN!!"

"Mickey! MICKEY!!"

Mickey looked up from his easy chair. A blurry George in blurry undershorts shook him roughly. While hard rock music BLARED from the laptop. George, seeing Mickey's eyes had opened, rushed over to the laptop to stop the music. The room became stunningly quiet.

"Eden," Mickey mumbled.

George stumbled back to Mickey. "What?"

"I should write her name down. You forget details from dreams."

"So you were dreaming?"

"She is beautiful."

"At least you slept long enough to dream. You never sleep."

"She knows me. She wants to help me."

"Help you how?"

"Find my way to the higher dimensions."

George laughed. "A beautiful woman. Who somehow knows you. Scantily clad?" Mickey's expression remained noncommittal. "Offers to help you accomplish your life work. Sounds like a pretty good dream to me." He saw Mickey focus on the blackboard. "Why were you listening to that music? You never listen to that."

"Eden must like it." Mickey sprang from his chair to the blackboard. His nose was nearly pressed into the chalk as he scanned the entire surface. "Have you messed with my board again?"

George joined him at the blackboard. "I didn't mess with it before. I wouldn't. It'd be like defacing a work of art."

"It's different again." Mickey rushed to the coffee table to snatch up the laptop then rushed back to the blackboard to compare the splash screen displaying the photo Priscilla had taken to what was on the board. Changes had been made since the photo was taken.

"So you're working in your sleep now," George speculated. "With you, that's not beyond the realm."

Mickey jabbed a finger at a computation. "That's not my handwriting." He jabbed again. And again. "Or that. Or that."

George leaned in to look. "You're right. It's different."

"But it's marble."

"What?"

"Equations are either marble or wood. This is marble."

George stepped back as Mickey lunged from one change on his board to another. "You've lost me. As usual."

"Equations are either beautiful and symmetric, marble, or clumsy and clunky, wood. Relativity is marble. Quantum mechanics is wood. But there has to be a way to join the two."

"A Theory of Everything."

"Superstring theory, expressed in higher dimensions, has the best chance of doing that than anything we've come up with yet."

"So?"

"She said she'd help me." Mickey stepped back to examine the entire board. "She's helping me."

11.

Priscilla was seated before her computer at her desk in her office at Northwestern looking over turned in work when Mickey burst in. He appeared even more wildly unkempt than usual. "Have you got a minute?" Without waiting for a reply from a startled Priscilla, Mickey rushed to the blackboard and began scribbling as fast as his hand could move. "Eden changed this."

"Eden?"

"Which led me to do this. Which she corrected."

"Mickey? What is this?"

"A quantum version of Google Maps."

"I don't use Google Maps. I use Ways. Besides, quantum mechanics is beyond me."

"Numbers aren't beyond you. These are just numbers." Mickey stopped slashing with the chalk and stepped back. He had nearly filled one section of the blackboard with computations. "What do you think?"

Priscilla rose from her desk to examine the work. "I'm sorry, Mickey. I can't follow it."

Mickey laughed like a mad scientist from a 30's black and white Universal movie. "Eden is brilliant!"

Priscilla took a concerned step back from Mickey. "Who is Eden?"

"She's from a higher dimension. She's contacting me in my dreams. Like she did Ramanujan."

Priscilla took another step back. "Mickey, you're not making sense."

"We're this close, Priscilla." Mickey held up the nub of chalk he was using between his finger and thumb to emphasize how close he was. Then he smiled. "She's wearing your robe." Priscilla stared uncomprehending. "When she contacts me. She has your robe on. That one I picked out for you to put on."

"When you dream of her she's wearing my robe. Oh, Mickey." Priscilla placed a hand on his shoulder. "That's sweet. It's also kind of creepy. But from you it's sweet."

Mickey evaded her to snatch up an eraser and wipe the board clean.

"What are you doing?"

"This work is mine. And Eden's. No one else but you sees it." Mickey put the eraser down and turned toward Priscilla with a smile like that of a demented lab assistant from the same movie as before. "We are so close, Priscilla." He fled the room.

Priscilla examined the erased blackboard. She then pulled out her phone and snapped pictures of the faint traces of computations that remained.

12.

Mickey sat slumped in his easy chair with the mouse stickers staring at the blackboard while Bicep played on his laptop. He seemed exhausted yet energized at the same time, like a band that saves its best songs for the end of a three-hour concert. The blackboard was a mess. It had been scribbled on so much to be nearly illegible. Also, there were two distinct styles of handwriting, often merged together on the same lines.

Before the blackboard a soft white glow appeared. Eden emerged from out of the light as it faded away. Like before, she was dressed in Priscilla's little pink robe. She appeared more substantial in this manifestation—she could not be seen through—yet still extremely pale, as if coated with a light dusting of white chalk. The laptop drew a frown.

Mickey noticed. "Your music disturbs George."

"What you call music disturbs me." The frown intensified as she looked around the room. "This room is so tight it would give a sardine claustrophobia."

"That's a puzzler. Before you were upset by how big and open everything was."

"That was outside." She went to the window and pulled back the curtain. It was night, and she could see nothing but black. "What's out there?"

"An alley. Garbage cans. Rats. Ralph."

Her eyes grew wide, as if trying to pierce the darkness. "Ralph? His name is Ralph? What's he like?"

"Just some old homeless guy. We give him fresh cardboard and scraps of plastic whenever we order stuff. And gift cards, sometimes."

She let the curtain fall back in place and stared at Mickey. "Gift cards? Why not money?"

"If we gave him money he might spend it on drugs or alcohol. But a gift card from McDonalds means he'll get a hot meal."

"What's to stop him from selling the gift cards for money?"

Mickey stared at her, perplexed.

"Never thought of that? It's funny how intelligence can be so focused in one area that there is none to spare for the rest of existence." She glanced at the easy chairs. "Why is there a line from 'Who's Afraid Of Virginia Woolf' on that chair?"

Mickey was surprised. "You've seen it?"

"That's a paraphrase of what Martha says to George about his involvement with the history department of a small college."

"Your world must be identical to mine to contain the same literature."

"Similar. There are some minor differences." She picked up a bit of chalk and went to work. "We've got more important things to do than discuss old plays."

Mickey's eyes remained latched on her. "Is this a dream?"

Eden never stopped working. "What does it matter?"

"If this is real or not?"

"Dreams are real."

"The act of dreaming is real."

"So is their content."

"So if I dream about monsters from Mars?"

"Then there are monsters from Mars. At least inside your head. Which is real."

"So if I can conceive it then it's real?"

"Yes. But you cannot conceive of how limited people's conceptions are."

Mickey laughed. "This logic is getting too pretzelly."

"Let's simplify, then." Eden put down her chalk and turned toward Mickey. "Like this robe. Must this be what you dress me in?"

"If you don't like it why don't you take it off?" Mickey smiled. "That is something that would happen in my dreams. A beautiful woman presenting her naked body to me."

"I won't do that because you need to stay focused. Besides, I'm practically naked anyway in this thing. I wish you'd do something about it."

"You want *me* to change *your* clothes?"

"You picked this thing out of your memories. Pick something decent."

Mickey closed his eyes. Opening them, he saw Eden clad in the exercise clothes Priscilla had worn the last time he encountered her in the park—tee shirt with a print of Elsa from Frozen, purple shorts, and running shoes.

Eden looked the new outfit over. "Much better." She turned back to the blackboard. "Once we finish our work you can dress or undress me however you like."

"Once our work is done my figment will disappear."

"I hope that's not a consequence."

"Am I going mad?"

Eden pointed to the blackboard. "Does this look like the ravings of a mad man?"

"Yes."

Eden studied the blackboard, then laughed. "It does, doesn't it?"

"But it's not. It works. Somehow. Mitchell was intrigued."

Enraged, Eden pivoted back to Mickey. "WHO?!!"

Mickey cringed before her vehemence.

"YOU SWORE!! NOBODY SEES THIS!!"

"I showed it to Priscilla. She always looks over my work. I erased it after." Mickey ran his fingers through his hair. "Apparently I didn't erase it good enough. Somehow she copied it and showed it to Mitchell, the head of the physics department, the guy she works for." Mickey dropped his hand as his blathering sputtered out.

Eden threw her chalk at him. It struck him in the center of his forehead. "This is our work! After it's completed you can present it to the world. Submit papers, write best-selling books, go on world lecture tours. I don't care. After it's done. It's not ready yet."

"I don't understand how we're doing what we're doing." Mickey looked forlornly at Eden. "What are we doing?"

"Opening a gateway between dimensions."

"A gateway that's been closed since the Big Bang. Since Creation."

Eden pivoted back to the blackboard. "Just keep your mouth shut about it."

"What's going to come out of your dimension? Into ours?"

Eden worked at the blackboard without responding.

"Physicists opened up the atom and nuclear weapons spilled out. What will this lead to, Eden?"

"A Nobel Prize, for you. If you ever get up off your butt."

With a deep sigh, Mickey hauled himself to his feet. He changed the music on his laptop to heavy metal hard rock. "Just not so loud."

Eden gave Mickey a smile as he joined her at the blackboard. "Just you and me, Mickey. No one else."

"I'm not so sure there's a you."

"Are you sure there's a Mickey?"

"I used to be." He picked up from off the floor the piece of chalk he had been hit with and went to work.

13.

The next morning George trudged out of his room, as usual in his undershorts, to find Mickey slouched down in the mouse chair with caffeine jacked-open eyes locked on the blackboard. Hard rock played softly on his laptop. Shaking his head, George started toward Mickey, but halted half-way there and looked all around in wonder. Chalk computations were scribbled all over the walls.

"We ran out of room."

George saw Mickey's red-streaked eyes were focused on him. "Is this for real?" He started toward a block of computations on the wall before him.

"Watch where you step."

George stopped and looked down. There was chalk work on the floor before him. He tip-toed around it and continued to the wall to examine the equations. "This. Makes. Sense. Some of it. Sort of."

"It all makes sense. Are you going out today?"

George turned his puzzled gaze to Mickey. "At some point."

"Purchase some more blackboards."

George nodded yes as he returned his attention to the math on the wall.

"George."

George looked his way again.

"Is there chalk on my forehead?"

George avoided several blocks of work on the floor as he approached Mickey to stoop before him and look. "Yes."

Mickey released a deep sigh.

"There's chalk everywhere. So what?"

"She really hit me. With a piece of real chalk. I've really got real chalk on me. She's real."

George straightened with a grin. "Pissed her off? When do I get to meet this firebrand?"

Mickey struggled to his feet. "Soon. We're almost there." He picked up a scrap of chalk and squatted at a section of bare floor and went to work.

14.

Priscilla walked into the coffee shop Phun With Physics met at and searched the crowd. She saw Lucy wave at her from a table. Priscilla joined her. Before an empty chair were a coffee and two cookies. "Is someone else here?"

"That's for you." Lucy said. "Sumatra black and chocolate chunk."

Priscilla smiled with delight as she sat. "My favorites. Thank you."

"You've come to our group with Mickey twice. This is what you ordered both times."

Priscilla sipped her coffee. "I should come more often."

"You should. Mickey is fascinating. He's very good at explaining difficult things."

"He enjoys it. It's his public service, he says. And it's good for him. He's learning to communicate complex concepts in conversational English."

"I'm worried about Mickey."

Priscilla paused, cookie to lips.

"At our last meeting he ran out into the rain like he'd lost his mind. When he came back in he looked like he'd seen a ghost."

Priscilla put her cookie down. "He's been acting weird."

"He always acts weird. Why is he acting weirder?" Lucy took a sip of coffee. "Mitchell is worried about him, too."

"Mitchell? The head of the Physics Department at Northwestern? Talks to you about Mickey?"

Lucy dismissed the comment with the wave of her hand.

"I do work for Mitchell. He's never mentioned you," Priscilla said.

"He better not." She sipped her coffee. "Forget Mitchell. We were talking about Mickey."

"Did Mickey mention Eden?"

Lucy reacted as if slapped. "Who?!"

"Eden. Some woman he is working with."

Lucy struggled to her feet. She was pale as a ghost, but for such an elderly woman that wasn't much paler than usual. "Mickey is working with Eden? On his equations? On higher dimensions? Math?"

Priscilla sat dumbfounded. "Do you know her?" She watched Lucy walk out without saying another word.

15.

Mickey rambled through the park with his laptop in hand. He was off the pavement and on grass, cruising without a keel. Everything more than three meters away seemed out of focus. He approached his tagged bench. Once it came into focus he could see no cement or grass around it. Instead, there was dry dusty soil all about, while above the bench a large glowing orb hung low in the sky.

Eden dispelled the bizarre mirage by stepping into his zone of focus. Although so much of the rest of the world was blurry, she seemed more substantial than ever, every bit as substantial as Mickey. She was wearing the same outfit of Priscilla's running gear that he had dressed her in.

Mickey smiled. "Do you run?"

"Only in fear for my life. What are you doing?"

"Getting some fresh air."

"There's no time."

"One last jaunt through my world."

"Let's go." Eden held out her hand, and Mickey took it.

As they approached his apartment building, Mickey turned into the alley. When Eden refused to follow him, he cast a questioning look back.

"I'm not going in there," she said.

"Why not?"

"There could be Morlox."

"What?"

"Never mind. We don't have time for any more detours."

"I'll be quick." Mickey hurried down the alley. He found Ralph bundled up in his plastic and cardboard, as usual. "Ralph, I'm leaving."

His head poked out. "Where you going, Haiku?"

"I'm not sure. Here." Mickey dug several McDonalds gift cards out and handed them over. "All I've got left. Don't sell these for cash." He took off his Pi jacket and Bulls cap and handed them over, also. "You can have these, too."

"What size pants do you wear?"

"Sorry. I still need these." Mickey stepped back. "Let George know if you need anything."

"He's not going with you?"

"No. It's just me and Eden."

"She's the one you should give this jacket to. With her walking around in that little pink thing."

Mickey was amazed. "You've seen her?"

"Yes. She's brilliant. A lot smarter than you. I'd worry about that if I were you."

"How do you know her?"

"She's working for me. Same as you."

"Mickey!"

Mickey looked to see Eden waving at him from the entrance to the alley. He looked back at Ralph. "I don't think we are really having this conversation. I am imagining it in my head."

"Sure, Haiku. No way a homeless guy could be supreme leader." Ralph withdrew back into his shelter.

Mickey walked out of the alley to Eden. "I'm hallucinating. Worse than usual."

Eden snatched his hand and led him into the apartment. "This isn't a hallucination."

Mickey looked around, only mildly surprised the new blackboards George had brought in were already filled with computations. "We are really doing this?"

"And so much more. Are you ready?" After Mickey nodded, she said, "Put your laptop down."

"I don't go anywhere without it."

"It won't make it through." Eden took the laptop from him and placed it on the coffee table. She studied the closed lid. "Hypatia was a heroic figure. A martyr to science."

"I dreamed about her." Mickey frowned at Eden. "Probably because of you."

She smiled. "Of course because of me. Hypatia has always been one of my heroes." Eden's smile grew twisted. "Now focus."

They turned their attention to the array of blackboards. The chalk computations floated up off the boards, the walls, the floor. The chalk numbers coalesced around Mickey and Eden in a white cloud. Which grew thicker, opaque. The cloud swirled around and around. There were flashes within, as lightning within a storm cloud.

The flashes grew fainter, fewer, none. The chalk cloud slowed, thinned, dissipated. The white dust settled to the floor. All of the surfaces in the room had been wiped, leaving only smudges of the math. And standing where the cloud had been was only Mickey. Eden was gone.

Mickey looked around. Smiled. Then laughed. "Mickey Haiku triumphant indeed!"

PART TWO
A TALE OF TWO EARTHS

Earth

Priscilla froze upon entering Mickey and George's apartment. The blackboards and walls and floor had all been wiped. A thick coat of white chalk dust coated every flat surface. "George?! What happened?!"

George emerged from his room in his undershorts. "He's flipped. Again."

Priscilla was too surprised by what she saw to register his lack of pants. "What happened to all his work?"

"It's gone. Nearly." George stirred up a cloud of chalk dust when he kicked the floor. "No loss. It was all gibberish."

"It wasn't all gibberish." Priscilla dug several sheets of copy paper from her purse. "Mickey came to the college and filled a blackboard with his calculations. He never paused, he never corrected anything, he wrote it all out from memory. Then erased it." Priscilla handed George the papers then squinted at an erased black board. "But he didn't wipe it completely clean." She inspected another blackboard. "There were traces of his work left. So I photographed it. Resolved it enough in Photoshop that much of it was readable. Then showed it to Mitchell."

"What did Mitchell think?"

"Mickey was onto something."

"What?"

Priscilla stepped up to examine what was left of the math on a wall. Other surfaces had not been erased as completely as the black boards. She took out her phone and began photographing. "Plotting inter-dimensional connections."

"Yeah, right."

Priscilla moved on, photographing whatever she found containing traces of chalk. "Did you ever meet Eden?"

George snorted a laugh. "How could I? She's not real."

"She's real, alright. Lucy, a woman from his coffee group, knows her."

"Who is she?"

"Lucy didn't say." Priscilla indicated the section of wall she was photographing. "Mitchell says this is plausible."

"What do you think?"

"I don't know enough physics to have a valid opinion."

"You know numbers. What do you think of his numbers?"

Priscilla stopped photographing and put her phone away. "His numbers work. Where is he?"

"I was hoping you knew."

"If he comes in tell him to give me a call." Priscilla headed for the door.

"Are you going to look for him?"

"No. I've got more Photoshop work to do." Priscilla walked out.

George looked over the papers Priscilla had given him. "Where the hell are you, Mickey?"

Other Earth

Eden(Mickey) awoke to find himself in a spacious lecture hall. All around sat Einstein, Newton, Leibnitz, Gauss, Euler, Euclid, Archimedes, Pythagoras, Descartes, Riemann, and others. He moaned in several different languages. It felt like Wile E. Coyote had whacked him with a giant Acme hammer.

When Eden(Mickey)'s vision cleared enough for him to look around, he saw all the distinguished personages in the lecture hall were staring at him. "Is there a mathematicians' Ren Fair going on?" he asked, of no one in particular.

"Mick," came the response from some distant corner. Eden (Mickey) searched all around for the speaker. This was how it had begun before. With Eden saying 'Mick'. But it was a male voice this time. The large room was dark and gloomy, filled with unmoving bodies and shifting shadows. Eden(Mickey) could not locate the speaker.

Closer by, Leibnitz spoke, but it was in German. Since Eden (Mickey) didn't know German, he turned to Einstein. "Did you call out my name?" Einstein only stared. Eden(Mickey) tried a different tack. "Are you guys dressed up for some occasion?"

Einstein glanced down at his early twentieth century suit then looked back at Eden(Mickey). "What are you dressed up for, miss?"

Miss? From weird to weirder. Eden(Mickey) glanced down to check out the clothes Einstein was referring to. Sweat pants, and a white tee shirt stretched out over breasts. Sizeable breasts. He probed and prodded and squeezed the breasts. The breasts felt real. Eden(Mickey) screamed.

George ran into the lecture hall. "What's wrong?"

Eden(Mickey) stopped screaming to see George towering there. Mickey thought it was George. It looked like George, only this face was clean-shaven and not sporting glasses. Also, the body had clothes on instead of just undershorts, although not especially clean clothes. It appeared to be some kind of grease-stained work uniform. He only became convinced it was really George upon spying a patch with the name "George" sewn onto the shirt.

Excited by the scream and George's sudden entrance, the people in the lecture hall began jabbering in different languages.

"Shut up!" George yelled. They didn't. He turned back to Eden (Mickey). "Get rid of these guys."

Eden(Mickey) yelled, "Leave!" The famous mathematicians all stared back at him. He looked to George. "They won't leave."

George stared at him with concern. "Are you alright?"

"I doubt it."

"Clap your hands three times."

Eden(Mickey) merely stared. That made no sense at all. But then neither did these breasts or a lecture hall full of famous dead scientists. He clapped his hands three times. Einstein, Leibnitz, and all the rest disappeared. Only Eden(Mickey) and George remained in the lecture hall.

"What happened, Eden?"

Which 'what' was George referring to? The famous dead people who had just magically disappeared? The lecture hall? The breasts?

Eliciting nothing but a dumbfounded stare, George continued. "You screamed. Are you having a migraine?"

When Eden(Mickey) nodded yes, Wile E. whacked him again.

"They're getting worse," George said. "If you can't even remember how to run your holograms, I'm hooking you up to the hospital."

Eden(Mickey) tried to press trembling fingers through aching skull to massage the brain within. He was surprised to find his fingers entangled in long black hair. He tugged on it. It was firmly attached to the scalp. He peered up to George's concerned gaze. "Who do you see?"

"I'm in no mood for stupid games."

"WHO DO YOU SEE?!!"

"YOU!!"

"You who?!"

"You forgot the knock knock part."

"Who do you see, George?"

"Do I have to?"

"Yes."

"My sister Eden. Satisfied?"

Sister? Since when did George have a sister? He was an only child. Eden(Mickey) rose and stumbled around the room in a daze. "Where are we?"

"The lecture hall."

"What lecture hall? This doesn't look like any lecture hall at Northwestern."

"You are really out of it, sis."

"WHAT LECTURE HALL?!"

"The one you designed. Just like this tee shirt and sweat pants you designed."

"I design clothes?"

"You design holograms. We are standing in a hologram you designed. Those people who were here in the lecture hall were holograms you designed. You are wearing holograms you designed." Concern radiated from George's eyes. "I've got to get you hooked-up to the ER. You could be having a stroke."

Eden(Mickey) pinched tee shirt fabric between thumb and forefinger. "It feels real."

"Of course it does. No one alive can design holograms like you."

"The holograms are computer programs. Right?" George stared. He appeared agitated, but at least he wasn't yelling anymore. "How am I accessing these holograms?"

"We need to get you to a doctor now," George insisted.

"George, please. I'm not dying, just confused. These migraines are driving me nuts. Just help me clear my head. That would help me more than anything right now."

George reluctantly nodded.

"How am I creating these holograms?"

"The files are stored on your chip," George answered.

"What chip?"

"The chip in your head."

Eden(Mickey) grabbed his head with both hands, ignoring the long hair this time. Was that where the migraines were coming from? But Mickey had been having bad headaches for a while. There could possibly be a chip in Eden's head, but he knew there wasn't one in *his* head. Aha, a lapse in the dream logic! In this nightmare he had switched bodies with Eden. Eden had big breasts and long black hair. The last thing he remembered before this dream was being with Eden. She had said they were passing into another dimension. Had that been part of this dream? Or had the dream begun with him opening his eyes to Einstein and his buddies?

"Sis? Speak to me."

Why did George keep calling him sis? Must be part of the nightmare. Mickey decided to go along with it until he woke up. "You said I designed this lecture hall hologram." George nodded. Good, no yelling, and no mention of doctors or emergency rooms. "How do I make it go away? Like all those people went away."

"Clap your hands twice."

Eden(Mickey) clapped Eden's hands twice. The lecture hall faded away. It was replaced by a tiny room where Eden(Mickey) could reach out and nearly touch all four walls.

"Are we in jail?"

"My apartment."

"What happens if I clap once?"

"Don't do that!"

Eden(Mickey) did. The shirt and sweat pants disappeared. He stared down at Eden's naked body. Confronted with the undeniably real physical fact he possessed an actual physical female form, Eden(Mickey) passed out.

Earth

Priscilla, in Nemo and Dory pajamas, sat at a computer in her home office at her grandparents' house with Photoshop open. She was trying to improve the quality of the latest photos of Mickey's erased work she had loaded into the program. The doorbell rang. Priscilla rushed through several spacious rooms of the big house to open the front door. Mickey(Eden) looked ill. "Are you okay?"

"It's disorienting."

"You're confused?"

"Yes. I've been wandering around lost all day. And hungry." She sniffed. "Are you cooking? I smell garlic."

Priscilla beckoned her to enter. "You can cross the threshold, Mickey. I've invited you in before."

"So you think Mickey's a vampire?" Mickey(Eden) held out Mickey's arms to examine. "He's as pale as one."

"My grandparents think you think you're a vampire. I've told you that before." Priscilla led Mickey(Eden) back to her office.

Mickey(Eden) looked all around as they passed through the big house, fascinated with everything. "Why is Dumbo wearing a flag?"

"That's not Dumbo, it's Ganesh." Priscilla led Mickey(Eden) into her office. "Let me save this then we'll find something to eat."

"George said you wanted to see me."

Priscilla closed Photoshop. "You have a lot of people worried. Why did you erase all your work?"

"I finished."

"You copied it all down?"

"The work is backed up on the laptop."

Priscilla nodded as she turned away from her desk.

As soon as her back was turned, Mickey(Eden) pinched her butt. When Priscilla spun to confront her, she laughed. "I always wondered what that felt like. What the big deal was."

"Turn around and I'll show you."

Mickey(Eden) laughed. "I know what *that* feels like, believe me. Every time I venture out onto the plaza. I mean how it felt to *do* it. To a woman. As a man."

Priscilla's ire turned to concern.

"Never mind. Won't happen again. Promise."

Priscilla smiled. "You don't have to promise anything, Mickey. I'm not *that* mad at you for pinching me." Despite saying this, Priscilla covered up her butt with both hands as she led the way to the kitchen.

Other Earth

A spacious car showroom was filled with exotic sports cars. The expanse of tile floor was waxed to a high gloss, and the sweeping crystal-clear walls of windows gave a view outside to a large lot filled with many more sports cars. Sales award trophies sat upon the desks that lined the interior of the glass walls. Priscilla walked in, dressed in conservative office attire. "George?"

George, still in a grease-stained work coverall, emerged. "In here." He ducked back into an office.

Priscilla walked across the gleaming floor into the small office. She saw Eden(Mickey) stretched out on a couch under a sheet. "What's wrong with her?"

"I don't know. She passed out."

Priscilla stooped to peer into the lax face. "Did you hook her up to the emergency room?"

"Of course. They said she wasn't sick, just exhausted and severely stressed. They said the best thing for her was to sleep."

"What was going on before she passed out?"

"She woke up screaming from a nap. She was complaining about a migraine. And she couldn't remember how to do anything."

"What did she say?"

"She was talking out of her head. She didn't seem to know who she was or where she was. She kept staring at her breasts and touching them." George plopped down into an office chair. "I think she's cracked."

Priscilla frowned at him. "And what Internet university awarded you a degree in psychology?"

"You know what she's been like."

"She's been working way too hard. And the separation. And her migraines."

"At least she seemed to know who I was."

"That's encouraging." Priscilla kneeled beside the couch. "Eden? What's wrong?"

Eden's eyes fluttered open. Yet there was no other reaction, Eden(Mickey) merely stared.

"Talk to me, Eden."

"Too much. To process. Can't conceive. It really happened. How it happened."

Priscilla stroked Eden's long hair. "You've been working too hard."

"I don't think this is a dream. I need to think. Figure out what happened. How it happened." Eden(Mickey) focused his dazed gaze upon Priscilla. "Why are you dressed like that?"

Priscilla withdrew her hand. "Like what?"

Eden(Mickey) looked beyond Priscilla to George. "Why are you so filthy?"

"Because I've been too busy taking care of you to get cleaned up!"

"What were you doing?"

"Working!"

"In your office?"

"What office?!"

"The engineering firm you are interning at."

George and Priscilla gaped at each other.

"You're a mechanical engineer," Eden(Mickey) insisted.

"I'm a mechanic. I work on cars. Cars are greasy."

Eden(Mickey) focused on Priscilla. "And you? Where do you work?"

"I'm an administrative assistant."

"A secretary. Where?"

"At an actuarial firm."

Eden(Mickey) pulled the sheet up over Eden's face. "More information to process."

"Are you having a migraine?" Priscilla asked.

"Either that or Wile E. Coyote is setting off sticks of dynamite inside my head."

Priscilla pulled the sheet down. "Eden, we're worried."

"Don't be. I'll be okay. I just need time to think this through."

Still holding the sheet, Priscilla saw Eden(Mickey) was naked. "Why aren't you dressed?"

"She was wearing clothes," George butted in. "She took them off. That's when she passed out."

"I didn't take them off," Eden(Mickey) protested. "They disappeared."

Priscilla rearranged the sheet to decently cover her. "Can you put them back on?"

"I don't know."

"Try."

Eden(Mickey) closed Eden's eyes and furrowed her brow. Then opened her eyes. "It feels like I've got something on."

"Let's see." Priscilla turned to George. "George, turn your head. In case she doesn't."

"She's my sister, for Christ's sake." Despite the protestation he spun around in his office chair.

Eden(Mickey) raised the sheet to look. Eden's body was clad in the skimpy pink robe from Priscilla's closet.

"Interesting," Priscilla smiled. "You designed a robe just like one of mine."

Eden(Mickey) tossed the sheet aside and sat up. Immediately, he grabbed Eden's head with both hands and moaned, in Latin this time.

Priscilla sat beside him. "Have you taken anything for your migraine?"

Eden(Mickey) turned miserable eyes to Priscilla. "A guillotine might help."

George spun back around with his mouth agape. "Was that a joke? Did my sister just tell a joke?"

"I don't think so," Eden(Mickey) mumbled. "I don't hear anyone laughing."

"Another one! You haven't told two jokes in…let me think… ever."

"I just need peace and quiet to think. I'll be alright if I can concentrate." Eden(Mickey) sagged back down into the couch. "Do you have any Bicep?"

Priscilla shrugged, then rose. "What is that? Some kind of medicine?"

"It's music. It helps me focus."

"Is that some new heavy metal band?"

Eden(Mickey) sighed. "How about a piece of chalk?"

"I don't have any chalk in here," George said. "Why would I have any chalk?"

"What do you need chalk for?" Priscilla asked.

"To suck on." Seeing their worried gazes grow more worrisome, he continued. "It calms me." George and Priscilla had become statues. Eden(Mickey) stretched out and pulled the sheet back up.

"Are you cold?" Priscilla asked.

"No." Eden(Mickey) closed Eden's eyes. "In case my clothes go away if I fall back asleep."

Priscilla cast a curious glance to George. "Your hologram won't quit working unless you halt the program."

"Good." Eden(Mickey) tossed the sheet aside.

Priscilla motioned for George to follow her out of the office back onto the car showroom floor.

He closed the door to the office then faced her. "Has she flipped?"

"I don't know," Priscilla answered. "Keep an eye on her. If she's no better tomorrow we'll hook her up to a specialist."

"It's as if she recognizes us, but can't remember who we are."

"She could be having a breakdown. She's been under a lot of strain. Her work, her marital problems. Those migraines have been getting worse."

"And there's staying with me."

Priscilla smiled. "No, her big brother is the best thing she has going for her right now. She needs to stay with you until she makes up her mind if she's going to stay married or not." Priscilla walked across the car showroom to the door. "Take care of your little sister. I'll stop by tomorrow after work to see how she is. Call me if anything happens."

George nodded in agreement as Priscilla walked out.

Earth

Mickey(Eden) sat at the table in Priscilla's grandparents' kitchen wolfing down a six-egg omelet. "Your world is so huge! So open! It's scary."

Priscilla sat at the table in disbelief as she witnessed Mickey devour a six-egg omelet. "The house is big. Much bigger than my grandparents need."

Mickey(Eden) shrugged while chewing. "I've designed places bigger than this. I'm talking about outside." She motioned toward a window. "It's disorienting. You can't imagine the tight confines I grew up in. I need coordinates."

"I know you come from a small town."

Mickey(Eden) laughed, spitting food. "Small? The streets I walked today are deserted." She shoved some food she had spit out back into Mickey's mouth. "Sorry about that. I'm still learning how this body works." She smiled up at Priscilla with egg hanging off Mickey's lips. "I can't wait until I have to go to the bathroom."

"You know where it is, Mickey."

She put her fork down. "I don't know where anything is. I need coordinates. The only coordinates I have are for the apartment, the coffee shop, the park, the college, and here."

"You've been so focused. On your work. For years. It would be good for you to take a break. Get out of town. Take George up on that road trip he's been offering to take you on." Priscilla laughed when Mickey(Eden) released a belch. "Are you full? Finally?"

"Yes. Finally." Mickey(Eden) smiled up at Pricilla with egg stuck in Mickey's teeth. "I've had a big appetite lately." She stood. "Let's go exploring."

"It's the middle of the night." She glanced down at herself. "I'm in my pj's."

"Go get dressed. I'll clean up the kitchen." She began clearing dishes. "I need coordinates."

"Why do you keep saying that?"

"I need to know where I'm starting from in order to get where I'm going to. I've been exploring some, but there is so much space! Such empty volume! I get lost every time I turn around. I need a guide."

"Sounds like you need GPS."

Mickey(Eden) froze. "What?"

"Ways. Or Google Maps."

"Show me. Mine's not working."

"It's on your laptop. Where is your laptop? You never go anywhere without it."

"At the apartment, I guess." Mickey(Eden) put down the dishes and rushed from the room.

"Mickey! What are you doing now?"

"I've got to get my laptop and find this Google Ways." The front door slammed.

Priscilla laughed. "I hope his lapse of sanity is temporary." She got busy finishing the job of cleaning up the kitchen Mickey had started.

Other Earth

As he lay under a sheet on a couch in Eden's brother's office, Mickey began to come to grips with his situation. This was not a dream. Eden had sent him into her dimension. His consciousness, at least. This dimension was similar to his, but there were differences. The George in this dimension was an auto mechanic rather than a mechanical engineer, and this Priscilla was an admin at an actuarial firm rather than a math major and teacher's assistant for the head of the physics department of a major university. This George, apparently Eden's brother, dealt with mechanical principals, only on a baser level than his roommate. And this Priscilla dealt with statistics, a baser level of mathematics than what the Priscilla in his dimension was involved in. If Eden's dimension was a higher dimension, why would this be so? Maybe there wasn't a hierarchy of dimensions, Mickey speculated. Maybe there was a more linear distribution. So maybe this dimension wasn't more advanced than his, possibly *not* as advanced in some ways. Mickey needed to stop speculating and learn more about this world. To experiment, if he had to. It was time to get up off this couch and explore.

Eden(Mickey) sat up. So far, so good. That hadn't started the boulders to rolling about the interior of Eden's skull. Apparently, she suffered from migraines much worse than his. Mickey would continue using that. Blame the confusion and the blunders he was bound to make on the migraines.

Before exploring this new world, Mickey needed to explore his new body. He squeezed. Yep, the breasts were still there, and they still felt real. He assumed. It was not like he'd had a lot of experience with women's breasts. He dreaded what wasn't there. But he had to get it over with. He felt. There was nothing down there to squeeze. Easy, easy, Mickey told himself, take deep breaths. This wasn't permanent. He'd get his own body back when he got back to his own dimension.

As the sweat cooled on his forehead, Mickey considered his new body further. It shouldn't be too difficult to learn to operate it. Like riding a bike. There were different kinds of bicycles—some with hand brakes and some with coaster brakes, some with dozens of gears and some with only one, some on-road and some off-road—but they all operated on the same principles. Learn to ride one, and it wouldn't take much to learn to ride others. He had mastered his own body while a young child, so as an adult he was sure he could learn to operate this body. The most interesting thing—so far—was the chip in Eden's head. He had learned to manipulate the holograms while laying there. They were amazing! Eden had created hundreds.

Which led to the fact Eden was brilliant. Much more intelligent than him. And she had gotten a head start on him. She had passed into *his* dimension knowing exactly what was going on. Whatever her plans were, she was already advancing them. What were her plans? No idea, but he was certain they weren't good for him, and probably not good for his world. What were his plans? He was a scientist. He'd love to explore this new world. But not until he found out what Eden intended to do. She was out and about his world in his body doing god knew what harm to his world and his body, while he was wallowing in fear and confusion. Up on your feet, Mickey Haiku.

When Eden(Mickey) stood, he spied Hypatia on the lid of the laptop on a nearby table. That was definitely his laptop. Curious. Mickey's body hadn't made it through, but his laptop had. Eden had said his laptop wouldn't make it through, yet it had. He was overjoyed it had. Eden(Mickey) picked up his laptop. He felt better just holding it. He didn't like going anywhere without it, especially into a different body in a different dimension.

Eden(Mickey) emerged from the office onto the car showroom floor massaging Eden's forehead as if suffering from a headache. Mickey needed to play up the headache angle.

"How you doing, sis?"

Eden(Mickey) located George sprawled across a couch with a bag of chips and a can of beer watching a NASCAR race on a large wall-mounted TV. Mickey's roommate George liked NASCAR. Another connection between the two dimensions? People he knew populated both dimensions, but in different situations, yet deep down still much the same?

"I've got money on the Pauli car," this George said.

Eden(Mickey) stared at the screen in disbelief. "There's a Pauli NASCAR race team?"

"Yeah. It's going to *exclude* all the other cars from winning. Get it? Exclusion?"

Eden(Mickey) dropped down into a seat and massaged Eden's forehead. "You're making my head hurt worse."

George turned his attention back to the TV.

"What are you eating?"

"Chips." He offered the bag.

Eden(Mickey) took one chip and examined it. It looked like a potato chip. He chewed. Gagged. Spit it out.

George leaped to his feet. "What's the matter?"

Eden(Mickey) was gagging too much to speak.

"Here." George offered his beer.

Eden(Mickey) examined it. Then desperately gulped it down. It was beer, alright. Mickey hated beer. But it washed the horrid chip down. As the gags subsided, he hoped it was all going to stay down. Finally able to talk, Eden(Mickey) wheezed, "What the hell was that?"

"Stinky Socks. You like that flavor."

"Stinky socks flavored chips?"

"I've got Armpit Lick, if you'd rather."

Mickey recalled a game played with gross flavored jelly beans. But Eden actually liked this stuff? He had to be careful. No telling what she liked.

George glanced at the laptop Eden(Mickey) held. "Who is that broad in a toga?"

Eden(Mickey) examined the sticker. "It made it. But I didn't. My body didn't. But my laptop did."

"I wish I knew what you are talking about." George sat back down and returned his attention to the TV. "But then I never know what you are talking about. Get me a beer while you're up."

Eden(Mickey) ignored him, studying the laptop.

George crunched the empty can and belched. "What dimension are you lost in now, Sis? The fourth? The fifth? I often get lost in the fifth. The Johnny Walker dimension."

Eden(Mickey) looked at him in consternation.

"You never laugh at my jokes."

"Maybe if you gave me a hint. You know, nudge, nudge, wink, wink."

George rose from the couch. "I shouldn't ask, anyway. You're not supposed to discuss your work."

"I'm not?"

He stared at Eden(Mickey) with concern. "Can I call Priscilla and tell her you're okay? Or would that be lying?" He walked into the small office.

"I'll tell her myself." Eden(Mickey) walked across the spacious showroom floor toward the door.

George emerged from the office with another beer. "You're going out? In that outfit?"

Eden(Mickey) stopped to look Eden's body over. Mickey agreed with George. This little pink robe wasn't suitable to wear outside. Eden(Mickey) closed Eden's eyes and selected the tee shirt and sweat pants he had awakened in. He opened her eyes and checked to see what he had selected was actually on Eden's body. It was. He looked back to George. "How's this?"

He was still frowning. "Kind of slouchy for going out. But that's better than what you had on."

Eden(Mickey) turned to go.

"Sis? You still need shoes."

Eden(Mickey) glanced down to find bare feet. He closed Eden's eyes once more and located white tennis shoes and white crew socks. He opened her eyes to find Eden's feet was properly shod. "Am I presentable?"

George still appeared troubled. "Are you sure you're up to this?"

Without further ado, Eden(Mickey) headed for the door.

"Mickey."

That male voice again. Eden(Mickey) stopped to look all around the showroom. No one else was present. Was someone from yet another dimension trying to contact him, Mickey wondered? Like Eden had contacted him from her dimension? It had begun by her calling his name. But how did whoever it was know he was inside Eden's body? Another mystery to ponder.

Unable to locate the source of the voice, Eden(Mickey) continued out the front door of the car showroom.

Earth

George was sweeping up chalk dust from the living room floor when Mickey(Eden) walked into the apartment. "Where's my laptop?"

"You don't have it?" George asked, surprised.

Mickey(Eden) searched the living room.

"You always have it."

Mickey(Eden) went off into Mickey's bedroom.

"Don't tell me you've lost your laptop."

"I'll check the college," Mickey(Eden) called out.

"You left your laptop at the college? You never leave it anywhere. You sleep with it. I've seen you take it to the toilet with you."

Mickey(Eden) emerged from Mickey's bedroom. "What do you know about Google Ways?"

"I haven't used Google in years. I use Ways. I downloaded Tricky Dick."

Mickey(Eden) froze, while trying not to. Eden knew she shouldn't show surprise at anything she encountered in this primitive world. But a tricky dick? What the hell? "Can I get coordinates from Tricky Dick?"

"What do you need Ways for? You never go anywhere."

Mickey(Eden) exploded in laughter. "I've gone farther than you could ever imagine."

"Space, between Mickey's ears," George spoke in a solemn voice. "The final frontier. These are the voyages of Mickey Haiku."

At last, something Eden could relate to. Star Trek was interdimensional. "My continuing mission won't take five years." Mickey(Eden) rushed from the apartment. She had to locate that laptop. It held the inter-dimensional travel computations she and Mickey had stored on it.

Stepping outside, Mickey(Eden) noticed the homeless guy sheltering in the alley beneath cardboard and sheets of plastic. Mickey had mentioned his name was Ralph. Curious. But Eden had no time for curious. She had to find Mickey's laptop.

Mickey(Eden) rushed away down the sidewalk.

Other Earth

Eden(Mickey) stepped outside from the car showroom into pandemonium. A mass of flesh throbbed in all directions. No lanes, no lines, every single body slicing and sliding past other singular bodies, each intent on its own destination. No sidewalks, no roads, no vehicles, just a bare cement plaza overrun with people. Pushing, shoving, elbowing, shouldering others out of their paths.

The stink was stunning. So many bodies pressed so tightly together. The human aroma abused Eden's nasal passages. He tried taking shallow breaths, so not to taste the foul air entering her mouth.

The lack of noise was deafening. Only shallow breaths panting. As if people endeavored to keep their mouths closed in this miasmatic swamp. The huff of cautious lungs taking in as little of this fetid air as possible. No communication, no eye contact, no greeting, no threat, no whimper, no complaint, no soap box oratory.

The bodies in this mad commotion were all similar. Small, short, compact, same dull skin tone and same dull hair color, as if humanity had evolved to exist in this compressed space. But the clothes distinguished to compensate for this physical conformity. Some wore drab grey rags, some wore clean casual clothes, and some wore well-cut suits and stylish dresses, but many others were clad outlandishly as superheroes and super villains, characters from fantasy games, icons from the past such as Huns and Vikings, legends such as Knights of the Round Table, and mythological beings such as the gods and demigods of ancient Greece. A real world Comic-Con.

The crush was too much. Eden(Mickey) fought to go back the way he had come. But the car showroom wasn't there. The press of the mob had carried him away from the front door. He had to get back to safe ground. Then it dawned on him the car showroom had never been there, it was a hologram, like the lecture hall he had awakened in. The large car lot he had seen through the plate glass windows had merely been part of the hologram. Once outside of it, it no longer existed, at least not for him. Which meant he was totally lost. He had no idea what the exterior of George's place really looked like.

This was insanity. Eden(Mickey) struggled upstream against a stream flowing in all directions at once. In doing so, he felt grasping hands all over Eden's body, snatching at her legs, her breasts, her butt. In this swirling populace he could not tell which illicit fingers were grabbing at Eden's private parts. So this was what it felt like to be groped, Mickey thought. At least it didn't hurt, not like getting grabbed by the balls.

The insanity finally spit Eden(Mickey) out against the side of a building. Solid nondescript cement. He looked down to the cement below Eden's feet. He looked from side to side to other narrow cement structures lined side by side receding into the smog. He looked up. And up. The narrow cement structures rose countless stories to disappear high in the low clouds. Eden's knees buckled, and he slid down to the cement with her back pressed against the side of the building as the maddened throng swirled all around. He hugged her knees and dropped her head down to curl around the laptop into a protective ball.

"Mickey Haiku."

Eden(Mickey) jerked Eden's head up. Before him stood two hazy white forms. They appeared vaguely human. One of them had called him 'Mickey Haiku'. Mickey knew the body he inhabited did not look like Mickey. Yet they addressed it as Mickey. How could they know it was really Mickey within Eden's body?

Eden(Mickey) felt a hand on Eden's shoulder. He slapped the groping hand off.

But it was Priscilla. "George is a fool for letting you come out here by yourself. You are not well." She helped Eden(Mickey) up.

Eden(Mickey) looked all around at the hurried averted faces. The pair of white hazy forms were gone. If they had ever really been there.

"We'll go to my place." As Priscilla started to tow Eden(Mickey) along, she noticed him clutching the laptop with both hands. "What is that thing?"

Mickey's stunned mind could function well enough by this time to come up with a cover story. "I brought it home from work."

Priscilla recoiled in terror. "Then forget I asked!"

Earth

Mickey(Eden) searched high and low in the empty college classroom she recognized as the one Mickey always used. No laptop. Eden knew it couldn't have passed through with Mickey into her dimension. Nothing physical had been able to pass through. Not yet. She was about to fix that. But to do that she needed the laptop. What had happened to it?

The door opened and the cleaning woman, the same one as before, rolled a mop bucket in. Near the end of a hard night, her work uniform, and she, were tired and dirty. She froze at encountering the same unnerving young man as before. "I'm sorry. I thought this room was empty."

Mickey(Eden) froze upon hearing the eerily familiar voice. She charged up to the cleaning woman for a closer look. It was like looking into a mirror. Or it would have been if Eden was in her rightful body. This woman looked just like her. A carbon copy.

The cleaning woman was so startled by this sudden advance she overturned the bucket. Water flooded the floor.

"Is your name Eden?" Mickey(Eden) demanded, ignoring the puddle soaking into her shoes.

The harried woman ignored the question as she stooped to right the nearly empty bucket. "Do I know you?"

"No. But I certainly know you." Mickey(Eden) grabbed the mop and began cleaning up the spilled water.

"You don't have to do that," the distressed woman said. "That's my job."

Mickey(Eden) wrung the mop out then resumed mopping. "You clean the physics department?"

The woman watched, her hands twitching to reclaim the mop. "I work for the company that has the contract with the college." She lunged forward to wrest the mop from Mickey(Eden). "You shouldn't be doing that." She began to sling the mop about.

Mickey(Eden) stepped back to watch. "Your name is Eden."

"I prefer Edie." She glanced up from the floor. "How do you know me?"

"We're twins. Sort of."

Edie's mopping attained a manic pace. She wanted to clean up this spilled water and get away from this madman as quick as possible. "I don't have a twin."

"That you know about."

"I think I would know if I had a twin."

"Maybe that fairytale has a basis in reality, like many of them do. You know the one about twins separated at birth?" While Edie rushed to wring her mop out, Mickey(Eden) continued. "This could be the fact behind the fiction. Twins separated at birth. Maybe it happens to everyone. One goes into one dimension, the other into another."

Edie slung the mop about with abandon. "I forgot where I was at. The physics department."

Mickey(Eden) sat. She couldn't take Mickey's eyes off Eden's identical twin.

Edie noticed. She mopped faster. "What were you looking for?"

"A laptop. But that can wait. What's important is that I've found you." Mickey(Eden) sank into deliberation. *How* did I find her? Out of all the world? Could we have been drawn together? Could there be an attractive force passing between twins from different dimensions that pull them together? Or perhaps the topography of the inter-dimensional spacetime facilitates our collision with our twin?

Edie stopped mopping to glare at her. "I know you're a physicist. They warned me. Allowances are to be made. You are actually harmless. But you are scaring me."

Snap out of it, Eden. Don't frighten her away. This seemingly chance encounter with her twin in this dimension was too profound not to investigate. "Can I buy you breakfast? This is fascinating. Talking with you. With my twin." When Edie's glare became even more skeptical, she continued. "What time do you get off?"

Despite her apprehension, Edie didn't flee upon mopping up the last of the spill. She collapsed into a seat, keeping a curious eye on Mickey(Eden). "Seven."

Other Earth

Priscilla led a badly-shaken Eden(Mickey) into a tiny cell of a room similar to what Eden's brother George's apartment really looked like. She seated him in a small plastic chair at a small round plastic table. Eden(Mickey) doubled Eden's arms on the table and dropped her throbbing head down onto them. Priscilla gazed upon the lowered head with concern. "Do you need anything?"

"A new head. One without a train running through it."

"You've not taken your medication?"

"I don't want to take medication. I need a clear head so I can figure out what's going on."

"Will you start the holo? While I get out of these clothes."

Eden(Mickey) peeked to see Priscilla stepping out of her skirt. He stared, breathless, speechless.

Priscilla unbuttoned her blouse and pulled it off. "How about the holo?"

Eden(Mickey) raised Eden's head up from the tabletop and admired Priscilla in her underwear. They were yellow, with Snow White adorning the bra, while from the front of the panties the evil witch beckoned with a red apple. Eden(Mickey) reluctantly closed Eden's eyes to search the chip. There was one named Lecture Hall, another named Car Dealership. One file, Hide Holding, snagged his attention. Then he found one named Disney Castle. That had to be the one Priscilla wanted if, as her underwear suggested, this Priscilla was anything like the Priscilla in his dimension. Eden(Mickey) activated it.

When Eden(Mickey) opened Eden's eyes he saw the tiny cell had been transformed into a fairytale castle, and the small plastic chair he had sat in was now a lavish throne. He stared all around in wonder. Until his gaze fell upon Priscilla standing naked before him, her underwear piled on the floor with the rest of her clothes.

Priscilla smiled. "My gown, please."

Eden's jaw grew slack, slacker, slackest, as he stared. This was so much better than a fogged bathroom mirror.

"Eden," Priscilla pleaded. "Put my gown on me. This is starting to feel weird."

Eden(Mickey) yanked Eden's eyes closed and located a file named 'Cinderella's Gown'.

The blue gown from the animated classic appeared on Priscilla.

She smiled and spun, making the full-length skirt swirl about her. "Much better." She turned her smile upon Eden(Mickey) "Now you need to put on something nice."

"No. I'm good."

Priscilla frowned. "Those sweat pants are gross. Put on something nice."

Eden(Mickey) scanned the clothes files again, and located one named Hypatia.

Priscilla was pleased. "That's much better."

Eden(Mickey) found Eden's body garbed in a robe like the one Hypatia wore on the plastic sticker affixed to the laptop lid.

Priscilla sat on a sumptuous couch and removed the glass slippers. "I love the dress, but these are not practical." She looked up at Eden (Mickey). "Now what was so important you braved the mob to come see me about?"

"I'm so confused."

"At least you're up. You had me worried."

"It's been such a shock. Not how I was expecting my day to go at all this morning when I woke up. Help me figure this out."

"Me?"

"I always talk my work over with you."

Priscilla recoiled. "You never discuss your work with me. That I can remember. You said if you told me what you were doing the government would have to wipe my mind. Sometimes it feels like they already have. I mean, how would I know?"

Eden(Mickey) tried to reassure her. "You're right. I'm still confused. That was someone else I discuss my work with. Not you. You're a secretary. Right?"

"Administrative Assistant."

"But you work for actuaries."

Priscilla nodded yes.

"So you work with numbers."

Another cautious nod yes.

"There seems to be a connection between the same people in different dimensions. Both of you are involved with numbers, just at different levels of complexity. So try to help me. Please!"

"Both of who?"

Eden(Mickey) opened the laptop.

Priscilla shied away. "Eden! I don't have the clearance to see your work."

"You're right. You don't. I keep forgetting. Because you look so much like someone else."

"Who?"

"Cinderella?" Eden(Mickey) covered. He closed the laptop. "Let's just talk. Okay?"

Priscilla stared fretfully at him.

"You mentioned marital problems."

Priscilla nodded yes.

"So I'm married?"

Concern overwhelmed Priscilla's unease. "You don't remember? Eden. You have to see a doctor."

"I have to get back."

"Get back where?"

"To my own dimension! Eden and I have changed places. Sort of. I'm in her body. So she must be in mine. In my dimension. She tricked me. She didn't tell me this was going to happen. But if I got here then there has to be a way to get back." Eden(Mickey) looked at the closed laptop. "But if only our consciousness could pass between dimensions how did my laptop make it through?" He held it out to examine it from all angles. "It *is* my laptop, not a different version of it. I'm certain of that."

The door burst open! A half-dozen men in military uniforms charged into the castle hall. Priscilla screamed. Eden(Mickey) scanned the holo files on Eden's chip and located Hide Holding. He accessed the file and the laptop disappeared. He could still feel it in her hands. The hologram file had cloaked it. Eden(Mickey) slipped the invisible laptop beneath the large ornate chair he sat on.

Three of the guards seized Priscilla. The other three confronted Eden(Mickey), but seemed uncertain whether to grab him or not.

A man who looked like Mickey strode in. Only he was clad in an exquisite suit, and sported a neatly-trimmed corporate beard and moustache and was neatly coiffed. He smiled happily with perfect sparkling teeth. "Hello, Eden."

Eden(Mickey) stared back dumbstruck. He was gazing upon himself. A well-dressed well-manicured version of himself.

"Your brother called me. He's very concerned. He thinks you've had a breakdown."

"You've pushed her too hard, Mick," Priscilla said.

Mick looked around with distaste. "Can we dispense with the fairytale?"

Eden(Mickey) could only stare in wonder. This twin even sounded like him.

"Eden?"

An answer was expected. Eden(Mickey) had to snap out of it. He clapped twice. The castle disappeared, and the nine people found themselves squeezed up against each other in the tiny room.

This didn't displease Mick, as he was pressed up against Eden (Mickey) and could peer down the front of the loose toga. "A new holo?"

Priscilla looked past the three men holding her toward the busted door. "You better get my door fixed, Mick."

Mick turned toward her. "We'll fix your door, Priscilla. Among other things."

"Is that a threat? Are you going to wipe me?"

"Don't worry. It left no lasting damage last time." Mick signaled, and the three men holding Priscilla led her away. "But I don't know how many times a mind can tolerate it."

Priscilla screamed as she was drug outside.

Mick turned back to Eden(Mickey). "Let's get you home." He stepped up even closer, and the remaining three guards established a perimeter around them.

"Am I under arrest?" Eden(Mickey) asked.

"Of course not. I don't venture onto the plaza without an escort. You never should, either." The guards grasped batons, and the five advanced through the broken door.

"Are you taking me to your home?"

"Our home, dear. We can't let our marital problems interfere with our work. We need to get you well so you can complete the Crossover Project."

Eden(Mickey) was stunned. "I'm married. To you."

Mick smiled broadly. "That's the spirit. It's only a separation. We're still man and wife." He slipped his arm around a docile Eden(Mickey) as the three guards raised their batons to blaze a path through the mob.

Earth

Mickey(Eden) and Edie sat at a table in a small off-campus diner with coffees before them. It was early morning, and Edie was still in her work clothes since she had just finished her shift. Mickey(Eden) looked like she had been up for several days, which she had considering time spent in two different dimensions in two different bodies. "It's hard to explain," Mickey(Eden) said.

Edie frowned. "To a stupid person."

"To a person not conversant in math. But Abbott did a pretty good job."

"Abbott and Costello?"

"No. Edwin Abbott. He wrote Flatland. Ever read it?"

"Sounds familiar. I might have in school."

Mickey(Eden) turned over her paper place mat and took out a pen. "I saw Mickey do this once." She drew a square.

"Why did you just refer to yourself in the third person?"

Mickey(Eden) bored into Edie with barely-controlled exasperation. "I'm tired. Now. Flatland has two dimensions. Length and width. A denizen of Flatland could not comprehend us, who live in three dimensions, since we also possess height." Mickey(Eden) drew a line inside the square. "To a Flatlander, a cylinder in their world of two dimensions would appear merely as a straight line. No different from any other straight line."

"So you are saying a being from a higher dimension could be here right now and we wouldn't know it."

"We'd see something. But not what it really looked like."

Edie stared at the place mat. "It's starting to come back to me. I remember how confusing the book was."

"Yes. Now imagine a person in our three dimensional world. Abbott called it Spaceland."

"What did Costello call it?"

Mickey(Eden) frowned.

"Sorry."

"Comprehending a creature from a higher dimension would be impossible. No matter what they really looked like, all we could see of them would be the three dimensions of our world. Width, length, and height."

"There are other dimensions?"

"Ten or eleven, we believe."

Edie stared doubtfully. "Where are these other dimensions?"

"They could be all around us. We just can't experience them." Mickey(Eden) rolled up the placemat. "Or they could be rolled up. Tucked away in inaccessible corners of our world."

Edie stared dumbfounded.

"Shortly after the Big Bang."

Edie brightened. "I like that show. It's funny."

A waitress arrived with their plates. "Hello, Mickey."

Mickey(Eden) and Edie looked up in surprise.

"You don't recognize me in my waitress uniform? Laurie. From Phun With Physics."

Laurie? This was Laurie's twin? Damn Laurie! Mickey(Eden) struggled to cover her mounting anger. "It's been a long night."

Laurie cast a dark look at Edie. "I didn't know you had a girlfriend."

"He doesn't have a girlfriend," Edie replied, "if you are referring to me."

"We just met," Mickey(Eden) said.

Laurie's gaze flowed over Mickey(Eden) like liquid lust. "Good. That means you are still available." She glanced down at the scribbled-on placemat. "I heard you mention *Flatland*. My nephew's been talking about that book. He's studying it in school. He's been onto me to read it." She produced a paperback copy. "Would you autograph it? He'd love that, signed by a real physicist." She handed Mickey(Eden) a pen.

So the slut has a nephew, Mickey(Eden) fumed. "What's his name?"

"Oliver," Laurie answered.

Edie watched Mickey(Eden) autograph 'Flatland' — 'To Oliver, from Eden' —in a furious slashing script. Edie's face sparked. "Why did you sign my name to it? I go by Edie, but my real name is Eden." She snatched the book and examined the inscription. "That even looks like my handwriting." She gazed warily at Mickey(Eden) "How could you copy my handwriting so good? Have you studied my handwriting? Where did you get a copy of it? From my employment records at the college? Have you hacked my files?"

The table was heating up rapidly. Laurie got away with the signed book while the getting was good.

Edie scowled at Mickey(Eden). "Why did you sign that with my name and in my handwriting? Is this identity theft?"

Mickey(Eden) rubbed Mickey's aching forehead. "It's complicated."

"You bet it is," Edie said. She dug into the breakfast Laurie had delivered.

Mickey(Eden) watched Edie rip through the defenseless food on her plate. "I can explain everything."

"You bet you will."

Mickey(Eden) sighed, then joined Edie in consuming their now-silent meal.

Other Earth

Eden(Mickey) awoke in the living room of the apartment Mickey shared with George in Evanston. He was splayed out across the mouse chair. On one side stood the George and Priscilla from his dimension. Bearded mechanical engineer intern George was wearing only undershorts and mathematics major Priscilla was dressed in her flimsy pink robe. Eden(Mickey) looked hopefully from one to the other. "Am I back home?"

"You never left," Priscilla answered.

"Your body didn't," George said. "It's still back in your dimension. But your mind is in Eden's body. In Eden's dimension."

"Fool proof but messy/the quadratic formula/pick zeroes like fruit," Priscilla recited. "By Anna Bardone-Cone."

"A Dirac operator/recovers the manifold's topology/via its fredholm index," George recited. "Also by Francesca Arici."

Eden(Mickey) smiled. "I appreciate the poetry, guys, but what's going on?"

"We thought some mathematical haiku would calm you," George said.

Eden(Mickey) took a deep breath. "Okay. I'm calm. Can we talk now?"

"You two have made a huge mess," Priscilla said.

"Me and Eden?" Eden(Mickey) looked Eden's body over. It was still dressed in Hypatia's classical robes. "Are you referring to me? Inside Eden's body? Or to Eden, who must be inside my body since I'm inside hers? Or to two different individuals? Is there an Eden in my dimension, like there is a Mickey in this dimension? Like Eden's husband? Or since I am in Eden's body should I be referring to myself as Eden? But I think like Mickey. Does what you think define what you are? Could an AI become convinced it was human? And if so, would it be?" Sputtering to a close, Eden(Mickey) looked from the left to the right.

"Are you finished blathering?" George asked.

Eden(Mickey) nodded yes.

"We have got to get you two back to your proper dimensions," Priscilla said.

"And who is 'we'," Eden(Mickey) asked. "I am assuming you two aren't really the George and Priscilla I know."

"We are neither of the Georges or Priscillas you are aware of," George said.

"I only know the George and Priscilla from my world. From my dimension."

"As Mickey, yes," Priscilla said. "But Eden's body responds to the George and Priscilla, her brother and her best friend, from this dimension. That's why you don't freak out so much when you are with them. Both your mind and Eden's body recognize them, and are comfortable with them."

"I'm not comfortable with any of this," Eden(Mickey) said. "And I don't give a damn what Eden's body is comfortable with. Where am I?"

"Are you referring to spatially or dimensionally?" Priscilla asked.

"Can't you give me a straight answer?"

"There are no straight answers," George said.

"I am not in my apartment back on Earth," Eden(Mickey) insisted.

"You've never left Earth," Priscilla said.

Eden(Mickey) looked all around. "Is this a hologram?"

"Sort of," George said. "We recreated familiar surroundings to calm you. But we must get you back to reality soon. You must recover your laptop."

"There are files we loaded onto it that you need," Priscilla said.

"Like what files? To do what? That I need?"

"Eden!"

Eden(Mickey) looked up to see Mick approach with two cups of coffee. Mickey saw he was no longer in his basement apartment in Evanston. Instead, he saw he was seated at a desk before a computer. A game was running. On the screen cars, trucks and all manner of driverless vehicles raced up and down a city boulevard twenty lanes wide, while the Elvis Presley song 'Jailhouse Rock' played. Totally confused once again, he looked around searching for the third iteration of George and Priscilla he had been conversing with. They were gone. As was his living room. He was now in a walk-in closet size office, smaller even than his bedroom in the apartment he shared with George back on Earth. Or wherever.

Mick handed one cup to Eden(Mickey). "You're supposed to be resting. You shouldn't be playing a game." He glanced down at the screen. "What game is that? I've never seen it before. Did you download a new game onto my computer?"

Eden(Mickey) closed Eden's eyes and massaged her forehead, feigning a headache in order to gain time to compose himself. What had this third version of George and Priscilla been trying to tell him?

"Are you up to talking about it?"

Eden(Mickey) took his time closing the game. Just as he did a speeding driverless go cart was threading its way between semis. He concentrated on the fading images on the monitor so he didn't have to look up. Mickey didn't want to look at his twin. It was disconcerting. Not the talking to himself part. Mickey did that all the time. But it upset him to see himself talk back while he was talking to himself. He was never one for mirrors. Fitting, since he was accused of believing himself to be a vampire. Could he actually have some vampire blood in him? But the Mickey he stared at now was not staring back at him. This other Mickey was reacting to Eden. So Mickey was conversing with himself while himself was conversing with Eden. Damn! Maybe he could carry on a conversation with his twin if he started with something simple. "Imagine an old computer, Mickey." Eden(Mickey) said.

Mick frowned. "Why did you call me Mickey?"

That threw Mickey for a loop. Did he have a different name in this dimension? Or was Eden's husband expecting some term of endearment? "What should I call you?"

"What you've always called me. Mick."

Eden(Mickey) blurted out an honest question. "What's wrong with Mickey?"

"I prefer Mick. Like Mick Jagger. I detest Mickey. Like Mickey Mouse. You know this."

Eden(Mickey) shook Eden's head in irritation. What was so great about Jagger? "Okay. Mick. Now like I was saying. Imagine an old computer with an old operating system installed on it. Say DOS."

Mick pulled up a chair and sat at the desk with his coffee. "Okay. I remember reading about something like that. Only it was called DUM."

"DUM, DOS, whatever. Then a graphical user interface is installed on top of that. Say Windows."

Mick shook his head. "I remember something called Widows."

"Anyway, you now have two systems running on one computer. With the uppermost shell the dominant one."

"And this has to do with...?"

"Two operating systems can run on one computer, with the more complex system controlling the computer, the same way two dimensions can exist on one world, with the higher more complex system the dominant one." Mick nodded as if he understood what was being said, so Eden(Mickey) continued. "We've been probing the lower dimensions."

"But we can't pass through to one."

"We can't. But our calculations show that travel between dimensions might be possible if initiated from the more basic lower dimension."

"But no one in the lower dimensions is intelligent enough to accomplish this."

"That's why we've been trying to pass information down to a lower dimension that would aid someone who was intelligent enough."

"The closest we came was Ramanujan."

"And he died young."

"That is why the government is about to yank our funding."

"So we must work doubly hard while we still have a chance. I feel I am so close."

"But you've felt that way for a while. And you've been battling those headaches..."

Eden(Mickey) slammed Eden's fist down on the keyboard, wreaking havoc on the screen. "I must have more freedom! You have to stop shadowing me!"

"I'm worried about you."

"We must put our personal feelings aside! We must seize our opportunity!"

"Darling, you disappeared."

"This is our last chance, Mickey. I mean Mick. Everything else is secondary."

Mick leaned away, injured.

"We will have time later to work out our personal problems." Eden(Mickey) returned his attention to the computer. "But for now I need to focus."

"Certainly. What can I do?"

"Leave me alone. And grant me freedom."

"No matter how erratic your behavior?"

"Just for a while longer. I can do this."

"Of course you can." Mick stood. "Will you continue sleeping here?"

"I'd rather stay at George's. There are far less distractions at my brother's place."

"Of course."

Mick stooped to kiss Eden(Mickey). "Get to work." He turned to go.

Eden(Mickey) frowned as he discretely wiped the kiss from Eden's lips. *Some people would enjoy kissing themselves,* Mickey thought. *Then some people enjoy masturbation.* He returned his attention to the computer.

Mick stopped to speak quietly with the elderly guard stationed outside the room. "She's free to go as she wishes. Don't interfere. But don't let her out of your sight."

Earth

Mickey(Eden) hunkered down in fear as she and Edie walked out of the diner into a clear sunny morning.

Edie noticed. "What's wrong with you?"

"The world is so big." Mickey(Eden) looked all around. "What do you do with all this space?"

Edie looked around, also. "It seems crowded to me. It's a nice day and a lot of people are out."

Mickey(Eden) stared at her in disbelief. "You think this is crowded? Boy, I could show you crowded. How big is your plaza?"

"You mean city? Evanston is not that big, but Chicago is eight or nine million."

"In all this? Nine million? People?"

"How many people live in the city you come from?"

"One point one billion."

"No way. There is no city that big anywhere on Earth."

Mickey(Eden) began to shiver. "Can we get back indoors? This is too scary."

"We can go to my place." Edie took Mickey(Eden) by the hand. "Is that better?"

Mickey(Eden) clutched it like a mammogram vise. "Yes." She followed Edie's lead, her head swiveling like an IG-11 assassin droid.

Edie noticed the reactions of other pedestrians to the frantic actions of the man whose hand she was holding. "Will you calm down? You're making people nervous."

"I usually have an escort when I venture out at ground level."

"I'm escorting you."

"An armed escort."

"Is it that dangerous where you come from?"

"Yes. People are desperate from the pressures of the mob and fear of the Morlox. Desperate people do dangerous things." The two approached a small city park. Mickey(Eden)'s apprehension eased. "This looks familiar." She tugged Edie across the street into the park. "There's a certain bench where Mickey always sat."

"Is there another Mickey? Or are you talking about yourself again?"

"There's only one Mickey. Here. He's just mixed up right now." Mickey(Eden) found the tagged bench. "This is his bench."

Edie studied the inscription. "What do all these numbers and symbols mean?"

"It's the formula for Planck's Constant," Mickey(Eden) said. She smiled. "You know what Mickey did one time? He stood on one end of the bench, walked to the other end, then jumped off. I asked him what he was doing, and he said 'walking the Planck'."

Edie appeared perplexed. "Like in a pirate movie?"

"Yes. But it was P-l-a-n-c-k, Planck, not p-l-a-n-k, plank." She laughed. "It was so funny."

It was not difficult for Edie to refrain from laughing. "I guess I don't get physicist humor."

"Let's sit for a minute." Mickey(Eden) plopped down on the bench.

Edie sat next to him. "At least you're not so paranoid anymore."

Mickey(Eden) released Edie's hand and leaned back into the bench, looking around. "Mickey and I spent hours here."

Edie flexed feeling back into her crushed hand. "Sitting on a bench?"

"Working. Physicists can work anywhere. I can be cooking, cleaning blood off the side of my brother's building, dragging dead bodies out from in front of his door, designing holograms, and all the while I'll be thinking about whatever I'm working on. I've heard writers are that way, too. No matter what they're doing there is always a story percolating in the back of their mind."

"Whoa, whoa, back up there." Edie appeared alarmed. "What's this about blood and dead bodies?"

"George lives at ground level. That is a dangerous place. People get trampled by the mob. If a stampede starts they can get crushed against the sides of buildings. So I clean blood off his building and keep his doorway clear. To help out, since he's letting me stay there."

"You remove dead bodies from his doorstep?"

"If it's blocking the door."

"Otherwise, what, you step over it?"

Mickey(Eden) nodded yes.

"You just leave it lay there?"

"A vulture will pick it up."

"That would be one big vulture."

"Not a real vulture. A robot drone. They cruise around above the plaza. Whenever one detects a dead body it will swoop down to pick it up and fly it to the pit."

Edie shook her head. "I probably don't want to know what the pit is."

"The pit goes to the underground."

"So it's like a pit grave."

"No, it's not a grave. It's the underground."

"So what happens to the bodies in the underground?"

"The Morlox take care of them."

"The Morlox. Are they like undertakers?"

"Undertakers? I don't know that term. But the Morlox take things that come under, so maybe they are undertakers."

"What do the Morlox do with the dead bodies?"

"You don't want to know, and I don't like to think about it."

Edie scooted away from Mickey(Eden). "I've never heard of a country with such unusual customs."

"We're not that different from you. Only much more crowded." Mickey(Eden) stood. "A problem I am working to fix." She looked all around the park. "You have so much space here. Ten billion could come through right away and you wouldn't even notice."

"Ten billion people? There's not ten billion people on the whole planet."

"That's what you think." Mickey(Eden) leaped to Mickey's feet. "Let's get going. There's a world of adventure waiting for you, Edie. Several worlds."

Other Earth

As soon as Mick left the room, Eden(Mickey) looked around. *Come on, guys, he's gone, you can come back now.* But neither George nor Priscilla appeared.

Eden(Mickey) gave up and stood. The two had said he had to get his laptop back. He didn't need them to tell him that. He felt lost without his laptop. Besides, they said they had installed something on it he needed.

So it was off to retrieve Hypatia. Eden(Mickey) went to look out a window. To his surprise, he couldn't see the ground. He was far up in one of the skyscrapers. Up here the air was clearer, cleaner. This skyscraper, like the dozens of others all around, had pierced the noxious fog at ground level into a rarified atmosphere.

Eden(Mickey) emerged from the tiny office into an only-slightly larger living room. The elderly guard Mick had spoken to was lounging on the couch watching TV. Eden(Mickey) opened the sliding patio door to step out onto a sliver of a balcony. He looked down, but couldn't tell how high up he was. Ground level was shrouded in smog. Yet once in a while it would clear, and he could see he was several hundred floors above the ground. The mob broiled about the crammed plaza below like maddened ants whose hill had been disturbed. He looked up to see the skyscrapers all around receding into the clouds out of sight. A wave of vertigo overwhelmed him. Eden(Mickey) tilted back against the railing.

The guard grabbed Eden(Mickey) and pulled him back inside. The old man escorted him to an easy chair, then went back to close the patio doors. As the episode of vertigo passed, Eden(Mickey) focused on the guard. "Who are you?"

"Albert. I've been assigned to look after you."

"You look familiar."

"I should. I've been with Mick's family for decades."

"Albert?"

"Yes?"

"No, I mean Albert! You're Albert. From Phun With Physics."

"I don't think any of that stuff you do is fun."

"Never mind." Eden(Mickey) stood.

"You're not going back out on the balcony, are you? Mickey would turn me over to the Morlox if I let you fall off and splatter yourself."

"I need to go somewhere."

Albert stood, nodding. "I'll summon an escort."

"Really? I'm just going to Priscilla's place."

"She lives in a different 'scraper. You do not venture out onto the plaza without an escort. The mob is brutal. And the Morlox are getting more brazen. They've started grabbing people off ground level and dragging them down below."

"Down below where?"

"The underground." Receiving a blank stare, Albert sighed. "Mick said you weren't right in the head." He took a deep breath then continued in an irritated clipped voice. "These buildings extend down into the ground about half as far as they raise up into the sky. That's where the Morlox live, underground."

"So it's not just a book here." Receiving a blank stare, Eden (Mickey) continued. "'The Time Machine', by H. G. Wells."

Albert nodded at this. "HoGWells. Yes. A school for magicians. I've heard of that book."

Eden(Mickey) threw Eden's arms wide. "I give up. Let's go." Albert fell into step behind as he headed for the front door. "So it's just us two against the mob?"

Albert took his phone out. "Two more guards will meet us in the lobby." He stepped in front of Eden(Mickey) to open the door.

Eden(Mickey) glanced back at the TV. "Don't you want to cut that off?"

Albert sighed a sigh of the overburdened. "It will turn itself off." Seeing further explanation was required, he continued. "Once it senses no one is watching it."

"Smart TV," Eden(Mickey) said.

"Not that smart. Or it would make better programs."

"Wait. You mean the TV itself creates the programming it shows?"

"Of course." Albert stared. "Are you sure you didn't have a stroke?"

Eden(Mickey) shook Eden's head in dismay as he walked out. Albert explaining the world to *him*, Mickey thought. What a Bizarro world this was. He looked up and down the hall. "This is a good hologram. Did I design it?"

Albert gave him a curious look as he closed and locked the door behind them. "This is no hologram. The higher up you are, the more living space you are accorded."

"So Mickey's doing pretty good?"

Albert led the way to the elevators. "You both are. It's good to see you two back together."

"We are not back together. We are dimensions apart." Stopping before the elevators, Eden(Mickey) examined the huge banks of buttons. The uppermost button was listed '900'. "Wow. What's the nine-hundredth floor like?"

"I've never seen the top floor." Albert pushed the button for ground level. "But you might. If you succeed."

"What I'm doing is that big of a deal?"

"You could be the savior of our world." The doors opened, and the two stepped inside. As the doors closed Eden(Mickey) dreaded what was about to occur. Either the descent would take forever, or Eden's stomach would lurch up past her throat and smack on the ceiling of the car. The door slid open five seconds later with her stomach in its proper place. Apparently, they had traveled amazingly fast without suffering the ill effects. Technology, gotta love it.

Earth

Edie opened the door to her apartment and ushered Mickey (Eden) inside. The living room was tight and worn, but it was clean. Of course it was clean, Eden mused, it was the abode of a cleaning lady.

This cleaning lady turned on Mickey(Eden) the moment she closed the door. "Now tell me how you can sign my name in my handwriting. And why you want to."

Mickey(Eden) didn't back down. "Okay. If you'll tell me why you let me into your apartment if you suspect me of identity theft."

Edie shrank back. "Is that a threat?"

Mickey(Eden) dropped to a knee. "No! Just something I want you to think about."

Edie lost the struggle not to smile. "You're not proposing, are you?" After Eden shook Mickey's head no, Edie continued. "Then get up."

Mickey(Eden) rose. "I don't want you to feel in danger. I would never harm you. It would be like hurting myself."

Edie nodded as she turned away. "Does my little apartment look huge to you?"

"It's cramped." Mickey(Eden) roamed around looking at this and that.

Edie tracked his progress. "You don't make sense."

"I could design a country villa for you."

"If I could afford to live in a country villa I would be living in a country villa."

"It wouldn't cost you anything. I'd do it for free. For you." Mickey (Eden) stopped before a framed award hanging on the wall.

Edie noticed what Mickey(Eden) was looking at. "I won a math competition in elementary school."

"So you are good at math."

"I was."

"What happened?"

"I lost interest."

"You didn't have my mother. She pushed me hard. A tiger mom."

"My mother was like that, too. Until my father died."

"When you were in elementary school?"

"Fifth grade. It devastated my mother."

Mickey(Eden) stepped up to Edie. "Same ingredients, you and me.

Just cooked at different temperatures."

"I don't know what you are talking about. I haven't most of the time. But I enjoy listening to you anyway."

"There's a reason for that."

"I know. You're intelligent. So why bother with me? Why go to all the trouble of hacking my files and learning my handwriting?" Edie spread her arms wide, indicating her unimpressive apartment. "It's not like I have anything worth stealing."

"It's hard to explain."

"So explain later." Edie took Mickey(Eden) in her arms. "I feel so comfortable with you. So safe. So good." She kissed Mickey. "And I have no idea why." They both grew passionate.

Finally, Mickey(Eden) broke it off. "That was the most intense kiss I've ever had."

"Me too. Will you stay?" Edie stepped back, unbuttoning her work shirt. "I've got to shower. I've been cleaning up after physicist pigs all night."

"I'm not going anywhere."

Edie smiled, pulling off her shirt as she walked out of the room. "I'll be quick."

Mickey(Eden) glanced down at the bulge in the front of her pants. She rubbed it. "Oh wow." Mickey(Eden) looked around in wonder. Spying another frame on the wall, she walked up to look at it. It was a photograph of Edie and Lucy. "Oh my God!"

"What's wrong?!" Edie ran back into the room in her underwear.

Mickey(Eden) pointed to the photograph. "Who is this woman?"

"My mother. Do you know her?"

Totally unconvincing, "No."

Edie stared at Mickey(Eden), mystified.

Until Mickey(Eden) dissolved into nervous laughter. "I can believe she was a tiger mom."

Shaking her head, Edie walked back out.

Leaving Mickey(Eden) to stare in wonder at the photograph.

Other Earth

The two escorting guards were deployed in front, followed by Eden(Mickey), then Albert bringing up the rear. Their progress across the plaza was incremental. Most of the time the two guards shoved people out of the way. Occasionally, they swung their batons and clubbed people out of their way. Eden(Mickey) tripped once over a felled mobster, but Albert caught him.

After a tortuous trek, they arrived at the entrance to the building where Priscilla lived. Eden(Mickey) was distracted by the blood that had splattered on her once-white robe, and didn't notice the guards had parted to stand on either side of the door. Albert prompted. "The entrance code?"

Eden(Mickey) saw a keypad next to the door. He had no idea what the entrance code was. He pulled out a phone from a hidden pocket inside the robe. "I'll call her."

"Hello?"

"Priscilla? This is Eden. I'm at your building and need the entrance code."

"You forgot it?"

"Yeah. You know what kind of shape I've been in lately."

"Wait a minute. I've got it written down somewhere."

"*You* don't know it?"

"My mind is kind of fuzzy this morning. Here it is." She recited the code.

Eden(Mickey) punched it in, and the door swung open. He and Albert entered, while the two guards entered behind them, closed the door, then took up positions on either side. "They'll wait here for us," Albert said.

"Can't you wait with them?"

"I've instructions to keep a close watch on you."

Eden(Mickey) led Albert down a short hall to the door Priscilla had led Eden(Mickey) to the previous day. Priscilla, in sheer pajamas printed with an image of Jasmine from 'Aladdin', admitted them. She crossed her chest with her arms as she stepped back. "Oh. I thought it was just you."

With an iron will, Mickey averted Eden's admiring gaze and entered. Albert didn't bother to avert his as he stumbled in also. "Don't worry about Albert. He's a hundred years old."

"Eighty-nine." Albert corrected.

"What's the difference?"

"About ninety-two million breaths."

Eden(Mickey) turned to Priscilla. "Is he right?"

Priscilla stared back blankly with her arms still doubled across her chest.

"You work for actuaries. You should know if that number is correct or not."

"My mind's fuzzy this morning. I told you that. Didn't I?"

Eden(Mickey) looked around the room. It was as orderly as it had been prior to the raid. He examined the front door. "They fixed the door already. That was quick."

"What was wrong with it?" Priscilla asked.

Eden(Mickey) saw the puzzled look on Priscilla's face, then turned away. "It was squeaking." He scanned the room. "Did you find my laptop?"

"No."

Eden(Mickey) clapped Eden's hands once. The laptop appeared on the floor under the chair where he had hidden it.

"Eden!" Eden(Mickey) looked to see Priscilla squatting naked trying to cover herself up with her arms. "Why did you strip us naked?"

"Us?" Eden(Mickey) glanced down to see Eden's body was as naked as Priscilla's. This time Mickey didn't even bat an eye at the sight of Eden's bare body. He had something much better to bat Eden's eyes at. Mickey had never seen Priscilla naked with his own eyes, but this was the second time through Eden's eyes. There were advantages to being female. Also, Eden's eyesight was much keener than his.

Eden(Mickey) finally stuttered into action. "Sorry. I had to end the hologram that was hiding my laptop. I didn't realize it would end our holograms, too." Eden(Mickey) glanced to see Albert's eyes darting from Priscilla to him. "You could turn your head."

"That's not so easy for an eighty-nine year old man to do. I've got a stiff neck."

Eden(Mickey) looked back to Priscilla. It wasn't easy to do even with a limber neck. Yet he wasn't supposed to react like a man. Eden (Mickey) forced both eyes closed and searched the files on the chip. He selected Snow White's dress. "How's that?"

Priscilla rose upright, looking over the colorful yellow and blue garment. "Much better." She scowled at Albert. "You dirty old man."

"Am I a dirty old man simply because I'm not blind?"

Eden(Mickey) mentally fanned through a selection of dresses. That still seemed too weird, donning a dress, even though the body it would go on was female. So he merely replaced the blood-stained robe he'd been wearing with a clean version. He then picked up the laptop. "I'm sorry for getting you in trouble, Priscilla."

"Trouble?"

"I'd better go before getting you into more." Eden(Mickey) bolted for the door.

Priscilla blocked it. "Did they do it to me again?! Is that why I can't think straight this morning?!"

Mickey lowered Eden's eyes.

"I hate Mick!" Priscilla stepped away from her front door.

Thinking Priscilla was referring to Mickey, he started to protest. Then he realized she meant Mick from this dimension, Eden's estranged husband. "I don't care for Mick, either, but Mickey is not so bad."

Eden(Mickey) hurried out with the laptop before Priscilla could respond. Albert followed out and down the hall to the building's entrance where the other two guards awaited.

Earth

Mickey(Eden) dozed in a too-comfortable recliner. A book of fantastical images fashioned out of numbers she had been leafing through lay splayed face-down across Mickey's lap.

Edie walked in from the hall wearing a bathrobe. She gently lifted the book from Mickey's lap.

Mickey's eyes cracked open. "Interesting artwork."

"My mother's. She self-published." Edie set the book aside. "Did I take too long in the shower?"

"No." Mickey(Eden) dug into both eyes with knuckles.

"How about some coffee?" Edie walked away to the kitchen.

Mickey(Eden) righted the chair and stood. "I've had enough coffee. In fact, I've had too much."

"Bathroom's first door on the left."

"Have you ever wondered what it's like to pee with a penis?"

"Don't get weird on me again."

"I never thought much about it myself. Until recently." Mickey (Eden) walked into the bathroom, leaving the door open. "You can watch if you want. It's really amazing."

Edie closed the door.

Mickey(Eden) continued talking loudly through it. "Watching is not the same as doing it yourself, anyway. I've seen my brother pee. No big deal. But doing it yourself is so different. You can aim it, shake it off when you're done. A much better design."

When Mickey(Eden) emerged from the bathroom, she found Edie in the kitchen making coffee. "I told you I didn't need any more coffee. I had enough at the diner."

"You need coffee. You are starting to sound goofy again."

Mickey(Eden) walked up behind Edie and kissed her on the back of the neck. "I never realized how narcissistic I am."

"Wanting me to watch you pee makes you narcissistic?"

Eden wrapped Edie up in Mickey's arms. "No. Kissing you does." She nuzzled Edie's neck.

Edie relaxed into Mickey's embrace. "How does kissing me make you narcissistic?"

"It's hard to explain. It's like I'm kissing myself."

"Do you enjoy kissing men?"

"Of course," was Mickey(Eden)'s immediate response. Which she tried to cover up. "Not. I mean no. Of course not. I wouldn't kiss a man. Now."

Edie pulled away to turn and face her. "Not now? Does that mean you used to kiss men?"

"This is getting much too complicated."

Edie turned away to the drip coffee maker. "How do you like your coffee?"

"The same way you like yours."

Edie poured two cups. "I drink mine strong and black."

"Sounds perfect."

Edie handed a cup to her. "Now let's sit at the kitchen table so you can tell me why you are criminally interested in me."

They both sat. "You are my doppelganger."

"An explanation doesn't count if you give it in a foreign language."

"Doppelganger is German for 'double walker', or 'double goer'," Mickey(Eden) explained. "It doesn't just mean someone who resembles you. It refers to an exact double, right down to the way you walk, talk, act, and dress. And the way you sign your name."

Edie burst out laughing. "This obviously isn't the case here." When Mickey(Eden) didn't crack a smile, she continued. "We don't even look like fraternal twins. Go look in a mirror. You need a shave."

"That's because you can't see me. All you see is Mickey."

Edie shook her head with a relaxed smile on her lips.

"Now it's your turn."

Edie's smile dimmed as she focused on the man seated across the table.

"I just told you something freaky, and you just sit there smiling. Why don't you throw me out?"

"I'm getting used to your freaky ways."

"You shouldn't be. Encountering your doppelganger is an omen of your imminent death."

"Are you back to threatening me?"

"No. It would be like killing myself."

"Good. I was afraid you were about to propose a suicide pact."

"Never. But I do wonder what happens to the other when one of us dies. If we were born twins, does that mean since we entered our worlds at the same time we will leave our worlds at the same time? You know how nature loves symmetry. If we had simultaneous births will we then have simultaneous deaths?"

"You're right," Edie said. "I should throw you out. But I don't want to. Does that make me your double walker?"

"It makes you very special to me."

Edie set her empty cup down. "You better finish yours. You are going to need it."

She stood and walked out of the kitchen.

Mickey(Eden) watched her while gulping down the last drops. She nearly choked when Edie shed her bathrobe in the middle of the living room. She strode naked to the bedroom door, where she turned to beckon.

Mickey(Eden) lurched to Mickey's feet. "You are beautiful. You've taken much better care of yourself than I have."

"You don't look too bad yourself, Mickey," Edie said. "Just a little run down."

"You should see what I really look like." Mickey(Eden) relished Edie's beauty as she joined her in the bedroom doorway. "But you look so much better."

"If that's what you think then maybe you *don't* enjoy kissing men."

"Shut up." Mickey(Eden) took Edie in Mickey's arms and covered her with kisses.

Other Earth

Eden(Mickey) and his escorts left Priscilla's building in the same formation in which they arrived—the two guards in front, then Eden (Mickey), then Albert in back. As before, it was slow-going through the mob. The two guards abruptly stopped, causing Eden(Mickey) to bump into them. Albert caught her once again. Before she could ask why they stopped, a large drone swept down to snatch a body a few meters in front of them then fly away with it. Eden(Mickey) watched its progress through the sky. "Was that a vulture?"

"Yes," Albert answered.

"The man was still on his feet."

"The vultures are fast."

"Are you sure he was dead? It looked like he was kicking his legs while it was flying him away."

"Vultures hardly ever make mistakes."

"Hardly ever? You mean they do make mistakes?"

"Nobody's perfect."

The guards resumed moving forward, and the four staggered in lockstep through the mob. Eden(Mickey) shuffled on, until he felt Eden's butt get pinched. He glared back at Albert.

He grinned. "Did you get pinched?"

"Yes. Don't do it again."

"It wasn't me." He held up his right hand and waggled his fingers about. "I've got Dupuytren's contracture. I can't even get my finger and thumb to meet, let alone pinch anything."

"Oww." Eden(Mickey) scanned the nearby faces, but the mob was a throbbing tangle. No telling who had pinched Eden's butt.

"Let's tighten up the formation," Albert suggested. He urged Eden (Mickey) forward up against the two guards then stepped up directly behind him and spread his open hands out across Eden's bottom. When Eden(Mickey) scowled back at him, Albert gave a deadpan look. "For your protection."

The four staggered on in lockstep through the mindless milling bodies. Until a scream went up! The four were knocked backward by the mob surging back into them. "What's going on?" Eden(Mickey) demanded.

Albert grabbed Eden(Mickey) once again to keep him from falling. "I can't see from back here."

"Morlox!" one of the guards yelled.

As the mob in front of them thinned, Eden(Mickey) saw short squat pale bodies spewing up through an open manhole in the street before them. The two guards drew their batons and rained blows down on the closest. The press of bodies kept them from retreating quickly. Several people trampled by the crazed mob trying to get away were grabbed by Morlox and drug down through the open manhole.

Eden(Mickey) felt a cool clammy hand seize Eden's calf. He looked to see huge red eyes staring up from above a flat nose and a small thin mouth, all set in a smooth hairless head. The Morlox drug him toward an open manhole. Another Morlox grabbed him by the waist, nearly causing him to drop the laptop. Eden(Mickey) saw Albert watching from a safe distance. "Here!" He pitched the laptop to him. "Keep it safe!"

The pair of Morlox drug Eden(Mickey) down through the manhole out of sight into the underground.

Earth

Mickey(Eden) and Edie cuddled in bed in post-coital bliss. "I'm not like this," Edie murmured.

"I know exactly what you're like," Mickey(Eden) replied.

"Don't start with the double gang thing again."

"Then let's just call it gut instinct."

Edie stroked Mickey's stomach. "I like your gut." Her hand slid lower. "And other parts of your body."

Mickey(Eden) sighed with pleasure. "Ahh, what a toy to play with."

"Is that how you think of me? A toy?"

"No. I was referring to myself."

Edie stopped stroking. "You're confusing me. Again."

"So let's stop talking." Mickey(Eden) rolled over on top of her. "Already?"

Mickey(Eden) kissed her, caressed her. "My brand new toy. I had no idea."

Edie squirmed beneath Mickey's body, settling in for another bout. "We *can* try other positions. Besides me on my back and you on top of me."

"Okay. I'm always eager to learn." Mickey(Eden) rolled over onto Mickey's back, pulling Edie along over with her on top. "Some theoretical physicists enjoy experimenting."

"This isn't physics." Edie frowned. "And we're still staring at each other's face."

"I can't take my eyes off your face."

"I've noticed. You ignore my body. You're always staring me in the face."

"I thought women liked for men to maintain eye contact," Mickey (Eden) said.

Edie slipped into rhythm with her. "There's a time for everything."

"I like this position. I can reach your butt easier." Mickey(Eden) grabbed two handfuls.

"And I can beat you with my tits." Edie leaned over to gently batter Mickey's face.

"And I can still see your face."

Edie sighed. "Try closing your eyes for a change."

"I can't." Mickey(Eden) eased inside of her. "This is so intense. Watching myself being impaled. While I am the one impaling me.

Impaling you, I mean. At the same time."

"Shut up. You are confusing me." Edie closed her eyes, moving luxuriously upon Mickey. "This shouldn't be confusing."

Mickey(Eden) barked a laugh. "That's what you think!" They settled into serious love-making. "And my headaches are gone."

"I've cured your headaches?"

"Yesss."

Other Earth

"Wake up."

Eden(Mickey) opened Eden's eyes to total blackness. He felt something wriggling beneath him in the cool dankness. He felt something wriggling on top of him, too. And on either side. Eden(Mickey) became aware he was buried in a mass of twitching bodies. He thrashed madly in a panic trying to dig out.

"Calm down. It's just other people."

That was a female voice. It sounded like Priscilla? The new Priscilla? A hand poked him in the stomach. Eden(Mickey) screamed!

"Be quiet! Don't draw attention to yourself."

That was a male voice. It sounded like George? Someone grabbed Eden's leg. Eden(Mickey) kicked free and twisted all about trying to get clear of clutching hands and probing fingers.

"Stop it," Priscilla said. "People are just waking up and trying to figure out what's going on. Nobody is trying to hurt you. Not yet."

Several screams sounded out in the dark.

"The Morlox tossed you all into a pile," George said. "They'll come for the screamers first. So keep quiet."

Mickey clenched Eden's teeth as someone dug a knee into her back. Someone else jabbed an elbow into Eden's ribs. "Why did they grab me?"

"Ralph cut their food rations," Priscilla began.

George continued. "Belt-tightening, the dummy said, since the economy was tanking."

Eden's shoulder was clawed. Then someone bit Eden's butt. "Dammit!"

"Be quiet," Priscilla said.

"Someone just bit me in the butt."

"You need to get out of the flesh heap," George said. "Work your way to the right. Quietly." Mickey twisted over onto Eden's stomach and clawed his way through thrashing bodies in that direction, banging over heads and shoulders and elbows and knees.

"But the economy wasn't really tanking," Priscilla continued the tale. "The Supreme Leader and his cronies were skimming money and moving it to a secret off-floor account."

"The Morlox began snatching people from the surface to supplement their reduced food allotment," George said.

Eden(Mickey) knew George and Priscilla were trying to keep him calm by calmly talking to him. But how could he stay calm while entombed in living bodies? Yet with Eden's face pressed into what he hoped was someone's stomach he really didn't feel like talking. So Eden (Mickey) continued to just listen, following their directions as he wormed his way through the twitching flaccid flesh and stabbing bones.

"So Ralph restored full food allotments to the Morlox," Priscilla said.

"But it was too late," George said. "By then the Morlox discovered they liked the way people tasted."

Eden(Mickey) butted up against someone huge, and couldn't go any further. He succumbed to exhaustion.

"You're almost there, Mickey," Priscilla said.

"Another meter," George urged. "Go a little to your left, and up."

Gathering a lung full of foul bodily exhalations, Mickey kicked off against a head and a hip to propel Eden's body forward over the top of the obese man blocking his path. With a final grunt he thrust a hand free of flesh. Having touched empty air, Mickey clawed forward until, gloriously, Eden's head popped out. He gulped fresh air and went limp.

"Now is no time to stop," Priscilla said.

"We woke you up before most of the others woke up on their own," George continued, "so you'd have a head start on getting free. Now they are all waking up. You need to get away from them. Now."

Mickey began wrenching Eden's exhausted body free of the stirring flesh. With her head in the open, he could speak. "What happened to everyone?"

"They gassed all of you," Priscilla said.

"It's pitch black. I can't see a thing." Mickey squirmed Eden's hips free.

"We'll direct you," George said. "Just get down to the ground."

Mickey kicked Eden's legs free. Suddenly released, he rolled down the human pile, over heads and knees and shoulders and hips and elbows, until he hit the ground with a jarring thud.

"Get up, Mickey!" Priscilla urged.

George added, "Morlox are coming."

"Can they see me?"

"Of course they can see in the dark," Priscilla said. "They live in the dark."

Mickey grabbed two nearby heads and hoisted himself to Eden's feet. "Now what?"

"Turn around one-hundred and eighty degrees. Now five steps straight ahead," George said, "then a forty-five degree right turn."

Eden(Mickey) did all that.

"Three steps straight ahead," Priscilla said, "then stop. And be very quiet. A Morlox is passing by."

Eden(Mickey) did that, even holding his breath.

"He's gone. Now, seven more steps."

Eden(Mickey) did that. He saw a faint light. "Where's that light coming from?"

"A basement room," George said.

"The room is empty," Priscilla reassured him.

Eden(Mickey) crept toward the light, which grew steadily brighter. "Why is there light if the Morlox don't need light?"

"It's coming from the surface," George said.

"It's one of the access points they use on their raids," Priscilla said. "They muster there so their eyes can adjust to the dim light before going aboveground into full daylight."

Eden(Mickey) limped into an open room. There was a ladder leading to a hole in the ceiling. "I'm supposed to climb that?"

"Yes, quickly," George demanded.

"Before they find you," Priscilla said.

Eden(Mickey) shuffled over to the ladder.

"Now go," George urged. "We'll talk to you later."

Eden(Mickey) panicked. "Where are you going?"

"We have to break off contact," Priscilla said. "You don't realize how difficult it is to reach you through the chip in your head. It takes all we've got."

"It's much easier with your laptop," George continued. "We installed a communication program on it."

"Now go," Priscilla said.

Silence. The voices of George and Priscilla were gone. Eden (Mickey) grabbed the lowest rung. Eden's body ached from the ends of its toenails to the roots of its hair. But then the strands of Eden's hair hurt, too. Everything throbbed with pain. He pulled. Nothing happened. He grabbed the next rung with the other hand, and pulled with both. He felt Eden's toes lift off the ground. He kicked both legs wildly until, finally, one foot was on a rung. He sagged into the ladder to rest.

Eden(Mickey) heard a scuffling noise. Morlox were coming. Adrenaline kicked in, and he scrambled up the ladder. Cautiously extending Eden's head through the hole in the ceiling, he was blinded by the bright sunlight.

Shouts from below, and he felt the ladder shake as a Morlox started up it. Eden(Mickey) crawled up off the ladder through the hole into a bright empty room. Scrambling to Eden's feet, he stumbled across the room out into a hallway, down the hallway, and out an entrance door.

Fresh air washed over Eden(Mickey) as he burst out onto the plaza. It was amazingly empty. "Help me!" Several soldiers rushed up to him, and he collapsed into their arms. "Morlox are after me." Eden(Mickey) pointed back to the building he had emerged from. "Fifth apartment on the left. Down the hole. The people they just captured are only a few meters from the bottom of the ladder."

Soldiers charged into the building Eden(Mickey) had indicated. Leaving him in the care of Albert. Who lowered him to the ground, then backed away. "You are filthy."

Eden(Mickey) inspected Eden's body. Blood, mud, and God knew what else saturated the ripped and torn robe. Other foul slime he did not want to look too closely at covered Eden's arms and legs and face and hair. But there were more important matters. "My laptop?"

"It's at George's apartment," Albert answered. "Can you walk? I'm not strong enough to carry you, and my stomach's not strong enough to touch you."

A vulture swooped down out of the sky. Eden(Mickey) screamed and waved both arms. The vulture flew back up and away.

"It thought you were dead," Albert said. "You smell like you've been dead for a while."

Mickey hauled himself up to Eden's feet. "Help me back to George's."

Albert led the way, five feet in advance.

As Eden(Mickey) limped along behind, he was amazed at the deserted plaza. "Where is everybody?"

"The soldiers cleared the plaza in response to the Morlox raid." Albert glanced back at him. "What did the Morlox do to you down there?"

"The Morlox never got the chance to do anything," Eden(Mickey) said. "But somebody bit my butt."

"I'll take a look at that later," Albert offered. Under Eden(Mickey)'s intense glare, he added, "If you want."

Earth

Edie, still tangled up in the sheets, watched Mickey(Eden) step into undershorts. "Will I see you again?"

Mickey(Eden) poked around inside the front trying to make everything fit right. She looked up at Edie with an idiotic grin. "Until you are sick of me." Then grew serious. "But now I have to get busy." Mickey(Eden) picked up the shirt and looked it over. "I hate putting this rag back on. I could design something so much better." She sighed. "If I had my chip."

"Is that a hobby? Designing clothes?"

Mickey(Eden) slipped the shirt on. "Yes. So is designing rooms." She looked around while buttoning. "I could design you a banquet hall from the palace at Versailles, and fill it with royal courtiers."

"Are you talking virtual reality? With the goggles?"

"VR, sure, you can call it that. But you won't need any goggles." Mickey(Eden) picked up the pants.

"I don't care about any of that, Mickey. Just don't disappear."

She paused with one leg in. "I would never. Willingly."

Edie sat up in bed, holding the sheet to her chin. "What does that mean?"

"If for some reason I got pulled away. Back to where I come from."

"You mean if you got too busy for me?"

"I will be busy, very busy, for a short while. But I won't abandon you." With pants zipped and belt buckled, Mickey(Eden) sat on the edge of the bed with socks. "I don't know what happened to the laptop, but I've got to find it."

Edie sat up in bed, letting the sheet fall down into her lap, and hugged him from behind. "Will you quit about that laptop." She kissed the back of Mickey's neck.

"Damn." Mickey(Eden) turned to look at her. Edie lay back, tossing the sheet aside, seductive and naked. "Damn. Damn." Mickey(Eden) laid down with her as they both tugged at the clothes that had just been put on. "This has to be the last time. Really. I have to go." They worked the pants and undershorts down over Mickey's knees, and Eden kicked them the rest of the way off. "Damn. Damn. Damn."

Edie rolled over onto her stomach. "We haven't tried this way yet."

"One more experiment," Mickey(Eden) said as she climbed onto Edie's back. "Just one more."

Other Earth

Albert and Eden(Mickey) approached the door to George's apartment. "*You* stay out in the hall."

"I'm supposed to keep an eye on you," Albert insisted.

"Not while I'm in the shower." Eden(Mickey) closed the door in his face.

George poked his head out of a sleeping tube in the wall. "What happened to you?"

"I was captured by Morlox." Eden(Mickey) scanned the little room. "Where's my laptop?"

George picked up a remote on a table next to his tube and pushed a button. A shelf slid out of the wall with the laptop on it.

Eden(Mickey) shuffled over to open the laptop. It seemed to be okay. He shut it back down. "I need to take a shower." Eden(Mickey) clapped once and the filthy robes disappeared.

George averted his eyes. "I really wish you wouldn't do that."

Why not, Mickey thought. He didn't care who saw Eden's body. It wasn't his body. "I can't take a shower with my clothes on. Not even virtual clothes."

George's head remained turned away. "I guess you forgot how to do that, too?" With a quiet curse he spoke to the wall. "Stand in the blue circle. Keep your arms at your sides."

Eden(Mickey) stepped inside a small blue circle on the floor. George pushed another button on the remote. A frosted glass tube slid down from the ceiling over Eden(Mickey). It hummed for ten seconds. When the humming ended the tube rose back up into the ceiling. All the grime had disintegrated, and Eden's body was sparkling clean. Eden (Mickey) looked it over, amazed despite his situation, then smiled up at George. "I could sleep for twenty years." He limped across to the empty tube next to George.

George's curiosity got the better of him as he watched his sister's beaten and clawed body scramble up into the tube. "You've got cuts and bruises all over you."

"You should see my butt."

George inspected it as it passed by. "Damn. Do you need rabies shots?"

"I need sleep." Eden(Mickey) settled in under a sheet. "Thanks for helping me, George."

"Of course I'll help you. You're my little sister."

A smile graced Eden's lips as Mickey closed her eyes. "I think you'd help me even if we weren't family. If we were just, say, roommates."

"I don't know about that. You are a real pain in the ass."

"I'm the one with the pain in the ass," were the last words to issue from Eden's mouth before the snoring commenced.

Earth

While dressing, Mickey(Eden) stared down upon Edie fast asleep in bed. How Eden would love to crawl right back in under the sheet and cuddle. Her emotional state wasn't good. Perhaps West Virginia, or Idaho. Coal and potatoes. That was what she felt like. Damn Laurie! She should have slapped her when she had the chance in the diner. Even if it was the wrong Laurie. It would have been *a* Laurie. The right Laurie might have felt it somehow. Actions seemed to reverberate between dimensions.

Eden's separation with Mick had torn her up worse than she imagined. She had been so busy with her work the damage hadn't registered. Now it was caving in on her. Then she had encountered Edie. Herself, in this dimension. The dam of her wounded frustration and rage had collapsed. Edie was so innocent it was like encountering a childhood version of herself.

Was their lovemaking nothing more than masturbation? No, Eden could never accept that. They were two separate individuals. Maybe not totally separate, but they were two individuals. Maybe. Damn, she wished her mind would stop. She understood how people could become alcoholics or drug addicts. Anything, just to shut the thinking down for a while.

The two were entangled in ways Edie could never understand. Would Edie be better off if Eden walked out and never returned? Probably. Would Eden be? Definitely not. She would abandon Edie for a while, she must, in order to complete the Crossover Project. Once she did Edie would understand. Eden would make her understand. Edie would no longer be a cleaning woman. She would join the elite in ruling this conquered world.

Mickey(Eden) turned away from the bed, picked up shoes and socks, and tip-toed from the room.

Other Earth

When Eden(Mickey) woke and looked out the end of the sleeping tube, he saw Albert seated several feet away staring at him. "I thought I told you to wait outside."

"George let me in."

"Where is George?"

"He had to go to work."

Eden(Mickey) crawled naked from the tube. Damn, everything hurt.

"If you'd give me warning I would close my eyes," Albert said as he stared.

Eden(Mickey) hobbled over to open the shelf the laptop was on. "I don't care who sees this body." Eden(Mickey) opened the laptop and perused the files. Glancing up, he found Albert still staring. "If it's upsetting you so badly." Mickey closed Eden's eyes. When he opened them Eden's body was clothed in an old-fashioned grey coat open down to the knees, a grey waistcoat, grey breeches to the knees, and white stockings from the knees down to old-fashioned button-up shoes.

"Why are you wearing men's clothes?" Albert asked. "Such odd ones?"

The reason was Mickey still couldn't bring himself to put on a dress, but he didn't want to tell Albert that. "This is something Gauss would have worn. From the nineteenth century."

"Who is Gauss?"

"He discovered non-Euclidean space, and also contributed to algebra, number theory, statistics, differential geometry, geodesy, and matrix theory. The man was a genius." Eden(Mickey) glanced down at the laptop. "I had him on my laptop before Hypatia. I bet that was Eden's doing. Getting me to swap out Gauss for Hypatia."

"Have you gone totally bonkers?" Albert asked. "I hope so. So I can commit you and go home and get some rest."

"Why don't you stretch out in a tube?" Eden(Mickey) motioned toward the one he had just vacated.

Albert stared longingly at it. "You won't run off?"

Eden(Mickey) pulled a chair up to the shelf the laptop was on. "I've got work to do." He eased down. Damn, that bite hurt.

"Your husband will have my hide if I lose you." When Eden (Mickey) got busy on the laptop and didn't respond, Albert creaked up from his chair and limped over to the tube. "I haven't been this tired for several centuries."

"Just how old are you really, Albert?" Eden(Mickey) asked without looking up.

"Old enough to know better than to trust you, but too old to really care." He kicked his shoes off, clambered into the tube and stretched out.

Eden(Mickey) located an appropriate hologram file on the chip. A sumptuous royal bed chamber appeared. Albert now found himself sunk into a huge canopy bed. "Is that better?"

"Yes. Thank you, Eden." Albert was asleep before his eyes finished closing.

Eden(Mickey) turned back to the laptop, now open upon an ornate writing desk. There was a prominent icon displayed in the middle of the screen labeled "OPEN ME NOW".

"So open it."

Eden(Mickey) glanced up. Lucy stood in the doorway of the sleeping chamber. Lucy? Here? Mickey's mind was too numb for anything but the direct approach. "What are you doing here?"

"I heard about you being grabbed by the Morlox."

"It just happened. Who told you?"

"Mitchell."

Why would Lucy hear such a thing from Mitchell? Mitchell must have told Mick, and Mick told his mother. Lucy was just trying to impress her. There was no reason for Mitchell to give Lucy any such information.

Lucy reclined on a sumptuous daybed. "It wasn't easy getting here. There's a battle going on. I had to pass through checkpoints."

"What kind of battle?"

"The army is going underground after the Morlox. Ralph is determined to make them pay this time for grabbing us off the plaza. The only way I could get through to you was with the pass Mick gave me." She waved a sheet of paper. "I had to see if you were alright."

"I'm fine, grandma," Eden(Mickey) replied with a smile.

Lucy burst into tears. "You've never called me that before." She rushed over to envelop Eden(Mickey) in a sobbing hug.

"Last time I called you that you demanded I not say it in public."

"You have never called me by that name before." Lucy withdrew from the hug and wiped at her tears. "I know our relationship has been rocky."

Warning alarms sounded inside Eden's head. "It has?"

"And that it's gotten worse since you and my son separated."

Red lights started flashing, too. "Your son?"

"Mick."

"Mick is your son?"

"Oh, Eden. What did those horrible Morlox do to you?"

"Made it uncomfortable for me to sit, for one thing." Mickey's mind was reeling, and he had to stall until he could get it back under control. "So why are you so glad for me to call you grandma? Unless…"

Lucy's smile blossomed anew.

"I'M PREGNANT!!"

Lucy's smile faltered at the frightful tone of Eden(Mickey)'s voice. "The baby is okay? The Morlox didn't do anything to harm it?"

Mickey roared into full panic mode. *I'm pregnant. I'm with child. There is another life inside me. Inside my womb. I have a womb? I must, if I'm pregnant. I will give birth to a baby. I've got to get out of here before that happens. I've got to get out of this body before that happens.*

"Eden? Do you need to hook up to your doctor?"

Mickey shot to Eden's feet. "Thank you for coming by to check on me, Lucy. I'm okay. But I've got so much work to do." She motioned to the laptop open with the urgent icon displayed on the screen. "I can't work while you are here. You know that. You are not cleared to see my work." He took Lucy's arm and escorted her toward the door. "I would hate for you to have your mind wiped."

"My son would never wipe his mother's mind." Lucy considered. "I don't think. Anyway, can I say goodbye to my grandchild before I go?"

Eden(Mickey) had no idea what was coming, but nodded yes anyway.

Lucy laid a hand on Eden(Mickey)'s abdomen. "Goodbye, precious."

Oh, god, Mickey moaned with the volume muted. Now he had an image of a baby Gollum inside him. He would never ever touch a pregnant woman's abdomen. Without another word, Eden(Mickey) shoved Lucy out the door and slammed it behind her.

He was pregnant, Mickey raged! Or Eden was. Which meant he was, for the moment. What would happen when they separated? When he finally got back into his own body? Would he carry the baby with him? Back into his male body? Would that be possible? No, it would kill the baby, he was certain. No way could a male body nurture a baby. It would die, and it would probably not be good for the male, either. So it probably wouldn't happen. But would he retain a notion of the baby? A piece of its soul?

Mickey clapped once to have a look at Eden's stomach. It looked normal to Mickey. He wasn't showing. Eden wasn't showing, he quickly corrected. He poked at it. It felt like a normal abdomen. Mickey had no idea what he was supposed to do. Women had long talks with their mothers, saw doctors, read volumes, attended birthing classes, did appropriate exercises, spent hours on online forums. He possessed zilch knowledge about pregnancies. He had never thought he would ever need to possess any. Of course, there was the off-chance he could become a father some day. But if that happened he would go through it in a supporting role with his mate, he would have plenty of time to learn what to do to help her. He never imagined he would ever suffer through a pregnancy himself. With so much else going on! To have it dumped in his lap like this. He certainly didn't want to harm the baby. Eden would never forgive him.

It was at that point the Devil appeared on Eden's shoulder and whispered in her ear. 'This gives you leverage, Mickey. Threaten to hurt the baby if Eden doesn't get you back into *your* body in *your* dimension. It's not like you would really ever actually harm a baby on purpose, just threaten.'

"Get thee behind me, Satan," Eden(Mickey) proclaimed. Mickey would never even *threaten* to hurt a baby. He would care for the life inside this body as best he could while it was in his care. He patted the yet-flat stomach. "Sleep tight, little one. I'll take care of you."

Mickey clothed Eden's body once again with the Gauss outfit then returned to the urgent icon on the open laptop.

Earth

Mitchell, the head of the Physics Department at Northwestern, was sitting at his desk in his office contemplating a pair of little plastic toy giraffes when he realized he wasn't alone. He looked up.

Mickey(Eden) stood before him. "I can't find my laptop."

"And you expect the department to issue you a new one?"

"I expect to find it," Mickey(Eden) said. "Is it here?"

"Not unless you left it here."

"Or you stole it." Before the wrinkled indignation mounting on Mitchell's face could erupt, she pressed on. "My work is on it. You've stolen my work."

The wrinkles erupted. "I have not!"

"Priscilla showed it to you."

"Then take that up with Priscilla."

"I plan to." Mickey(Eden) scanned the room. "Did she leave any of it with you?"

"You mean you didn't back it up?" The wrinkles reformed into a smirk. "You've lost it? All of it? Years of work? You've lost it all?"

"I've got most of it." She tapped Mickey's head. "But bits and pieces have leaked out."

"I assure you there is no leakage here. The little Priscilla showed me she took with her when she left."

"What part did she show you?"

"Pure fantasy. It looked like inter-dimensional field equations. I couldn't follow them."

"Of course not. You could never follow my work. Only Mickey could follow my work." Mickey(Eden) strode from the room.

Mitchell pulled out his phone to make a digital recording. "Mickey Haiku is losing it. He refers to himself in the third person. A sure sign of mental deterioration."

Other Earth

Eden(Mickey) was alone at last. He glanced to Albert snoring in the canopy bed. Nearly alone. Eden(Mickey) clicked on the OPEN ME NOW icon.

George's face appeared. "Hello, Mickey."

"Why didn't you tell me I was pregnant?"

"I wanted to," Priscilla called out from off-screen.

"There are other more urgent matters to contend with," George insisted.

"More urgent than me being pregnant? I don't think so."

Priscilla's face edged into sight on the screen. "Mickey, you can count on me for advice and support throughout your pregnancy."

"Is it a boy or a girl?"

"Just a second." A few moments later, George said, "It's a boy."

"Did you just examine me remotely?"

"No," Priscilla's head once again popped into the screen next to George. "I did. This is why both of us need to be present when we contact you. You were medically examined by a female."

"But I'm a male."

"Your body isn't."

"Male or female doesn't matter," George butted in. "You'll be out of there long before the delivery."

"Now you're talking. How are we going to do that?"

"We have to be in position when Eden opens a portal in your dimension that leads to her dimension."

"When Eden opens a portal in *my* original dimension or in *her* original dimension?"

"In your dimension."

"The dimension I'm in now or the dimension I'm supposed to be in?"

"In your home dimension. The dimension you came from. The dimension you were born in. Is that clear enough?"

"Don't get testy," Eden(Mickey) said. "I'm the one who should get testy. I'm the one with child."

"So now you're going to play the pregnant woman card?" Priscilla asked. "It's not that big a deal. I've had dozens."

"Dozens of babies?" Eden(Mickey) asked in surprise.

"There was a big drive to repopulate our dimension following the

Covid variant D2A surge."

"I don't know that variant."

"D2A stands for Death To All. It was a bad one."

"Never mind," George butted in. "We've got more important matters to discuss."

Eden(Mickey) persisted. "How can you give birth to dozens of children? Isn't your body worn out?"

"We don't deliver babies the way you do in your dimension," Priscilla said. "Popping them out like farts. Eww, so gross."

"Enough!" George demanded. He glared at Priscilla. "I thought we decided it would be less confusing if only one of us spoke with Mickey."

Priscilla withdrew from the screen.

Eden(Mickey)'s insatiable curiosity spiked. "So why are you both here?"

"This is a singular situation. We are dealing with two genders in one body. Each gender needs to be represented by a person of its own gender."

"Why?"

"So no one gets taken advantage of."

"Are you afraid of being accused of sexual abuse by Eden if Priscilla isn't here, too, to look out for Eden's interests?"

"You've got it."

"And George is here," Priscilla said from off-screen, "to make sure I and Eden don't take advantage of you, Mickey."

George glared off-screen. "I thought you weren't talking."

"Sorry."

"So you are both here to make sure neither of you get sued?"

George nodded.

"Are things really that litigious in your dimension?"

"You have no idea," George said. "Now let's get back to the matter at hand."

"Which is?" Eden(Mickey) asked.

"How we are going to stop Eden from destroying your dimension."

"How would she do that?"

"You've seen how crowded her dimension is."

"A good surge of D2A would solve *that* problem," Priscilla called out.

Onscreen, George turned toward Priscilla. "Why don't you retire, unless for some reason we need to examine Eden's body again." George turned back toward Eden(Mickey). "If Eden opens a stable portal between dimensions, people from her dimension will flood into your dimension. With their superior technology and greater numbers, they will overrun you. You will be enslaved."

"If they don't kill you all," Priscilla added from off-screen.

George frowned in her direction. "They won't kill all of you. They need you. You will become the new Morlox."

"Eden couldn't open this portal from her dimension?" Eden (Mickey) asked.

"Not one stable enough," George said. "A portal strong enough for people to pass through has to be opened from the lower dimension."

"She opened one from her dimension big enough to contact me."

"She could accomplish that much."

"Despite our interventions," Priscilla said from off-screen.

Before George could reprimand Priscilla, Eden(Mickey) asked, "What interventions?"

Priscilla's head lunged back onscreen. "We caused her crippling headaches. They would have felled an African elephant. Nevertheless, she persisted."

"I was getting them too!" Eden(Mickey) exclaimed.

"Those weren't as bad as hers. We were just trying to dissuade you, not disable you."

"Are we finished here?" George asked Priscilla.

Priscilla nodded yes and withdrew from the screen.

"So what were all the calculations we were doing?" Eden(Mickey) asked.

"She had to lock down your exact coordinates."

"Like Garmin? Is that all we were doing? Plotting Garmin?"

"It was so much more than satellite navigation. Being in motion is the natural state of things. Consider all the movements you go through every second of your life. From the agitation in the sub-Planck quantum foam up to the expansion of the Universe, and even the attraction of universes from one brane to another in the multiverse. Add in relativistic time effects, which must be considered even when just calculating the aforementioned satellite navigation. Every separate element of your dimension is moving in so many different directions it is incalculable to even your brilliant mind, Mickey."

"Yet Eden calculated it."

"With your help. She couldn't have done it by herself from her end. To transfer her consciousness to you in your dimension, and yours to her in her dimension, she had to know your and her exact positions in every aspect of time and space."

"Even in the quantum realm? What about the Uncertainty Principle?"

"She didn't care how fast any subatomic particles were traveling, so long as she had their positions locked down at the instant of the transfer. They could have possessed infinite speeds, so long as she knew where they were at when she needed to know."

"Is this really the time to discuss quantum theory?" Priscilla butted in from off-screen.

"Why are you so concerned?" Eden(Mickey) asked. "You are obviously far advanced beyond both our dimensions. Why do you care what happens to us?"

"Consider a mountain," George began. "At different elevations different flora and fauna flourish. But each climate zone is affected by others up and down the mountain. An earthquake at the lowest level can shake the entire mountain. A forest fire at the bottom can sweep up to the top of the mountain. On the other hand, a rock slide or an avalanche at the upper elevations can cause destruction in the lower zones. The mountain is one entity, reaching up through many levels. And all these levels, or dimensions, affect each other."

"So you are at a different elevation, a different dimension, on the same mountain we all exist on."

"A higher dimension," Priscilla butted in to emphasize. "Trying to prevent a disaster from below from striking all of us."

George directed a frown off-screen. "Back to the mountain. If the climate changes, flora and fauna move up and down the mountain. If the climate warms, life at the bottom expands to higher elevations. If the climate cools, life at the higher reaches expands to lower elevations."

"Is this so bad?"

"It is for the life already established in these places. Native flora and fauna can be overwhelmed by the intrusive newcomers."

"So we're facing extinction."

"If Eden succeeds in opening a portal between dimensions that physical beings can cross through there will be consequences she hasn't foreseen."

"There always are."

"She believes people from her dimension will be able to pass into your dimension. It would be like stepping into infinity to them, since their world is so tightly rolled up. But not only people from her dimension would pass through. If a portal is opened, all the other dimensions could unfurl into your dimension."

"Sounds bad for us."

"It could be cataclysmic for all dimensions. We don't know. We are still running the numbers."

"So we stop it from happening."

"Exactly. You need to get to her office with your laptop."

"One more question." George appeared annoyed. Nevertheless, Eden(Mickey) persisted. "What happens if Eden fails? If she can't open the portal?"

"That would certainly be good for all the dimensions."

"What about for me?"

"Not so bad. You'll stay here and become a father. Or a mother. Whatever."

"So what's the plan that keeps me from giving birth?" Eden (Mickey) asked.

"Eden will attempt to open a portal from your dimension. Your home dimension. The dimension you were born in. Where she's at now. In your body." George took a deep breath, then continued. "At the moment she does, you've got to be ready to transfer your consciousness back into your body in your dimension while drawing her consciousness back into her body in her dimension."

"How will I do that?"

"You've already got the formulas you and Eden developed on your laptop. We'll upload the latest numbers concerning your and Eden's exact locations in all parameters at the time of transfer. That's why we transported the laptop along with your consciousness when you and Eden opened that weak little portal. She couldn't have moved anything physical through, but we were able to. We also loaded communication software on the laptop so we can video conference like we are doing now. This is much easier than communicating through the chip in Eden's head."

Priscilla shouldered George out from the screen. "I know I'm not supposed to talk, but there is someone lurking outside the building."

"Who?" Eden(Mickey) asked.

George leaned back into the frame. "She'll tell you when we're done talking. We've got a lot of ground to cover and not much time."

"Who is it? Outside George's door?" Eden(Mickey) saw a pained expression on George's digital face. "I can't pay attention to what you say until I know who is waiting to ambush me. It's too distracting. I'll be wondering who it is the whole time…"

"It's Laurie. Now…"

Eden(Mickey) panicked. "What does she want?"

"We don't know."

"You all-powerful beings from a higher dimension don't know?"

"We're not all-powerful. Just more powerful than you and Eden. We've consulted Laurie, but…"

"You've contacted Laurie? And still don't know what she's doing?

That's not very powerful."

"Our Laurie."

"You've got a Laurie?"

"Yes. In our dimension. And she has no idea what your Laurie is after."

"She's not my Laurie. My Laurie is a happily married Army veteran who likes coffee and is interested in physics."

"You are wrong about the happily-married part," Priscilla said from off-screen. "The happily part, not the married part."

George moved over to the side of the screen Priscilla was off-screen from in order to block her access. "Are you sure coffee is all she likes?"

"What does that mean?" Eden(Mickey) asked.

"This Laurie is having an affair with Eden's husband Mick," George said.

"And your Laurie *wants* to have an affair with you, Mickey," Priscilla added from off-screen.

George bristled at the interruption, but gritted his teeth and continued. "All the Lauries are connected. Like everybody else."

This gave Eden(Mickey) pause. "How many versions of us are there? How far up does this go?"

"I don't know. We can't discern any dimensions higher than ours, just like you can't discern our dimension."

"But the numbers suggest there are ten or eleven dimensions," Eden(Mickey) stated.

"Yes. But that doesn't mean we can interact with them. Or that we should."

"Yet you, from a higher dimension, are interacting with me, from several dimensions below you."

"This is an emergency."

"Fine. But I want to know more about Laurie. This Laurie. She is hanging around outside George's door for a reason. I want to know how to deal with her."

George frowned, but relented. "She's the reason Eden left Mick."

Mickey had always thought Laurie attractive. Now he knew why. Apparently, his twin in this world, Eden's ex-husband Mick, thought her *extremely* attractive. Further proof events in one dimension influenced events in the other. Maybe there was a particle that travels between dimensions, Mickey speculated, a boson force carrier that transmits information from one dimension to the other, like a graviton travels between branes. Perhaps Eden had found a way to manipulate this particle so it could carry her consciousness into his dimension and into his body, forcing his consciousness out of his dimension and into her body in her dimension…

"Mickey!"

Eden(Mickey) found George staring at him with an unpleasant intensity.

"Where did you go?"

Eden(Mickey) shook off his reverie. "Nowhere I know of. Which is really true. This is nowhere I ever knew of. And here I am."

"If you start babbling again I'm breaking the connection."

"Fill me in about George. Not you. Or my roommate. I know enough about him. And I don't care about you. My brother George. I mean Eden's brother George. In this dimension." When digital George, glassy-eyed, failed to respond, Eden(Mickey) sloughed on. "He claims to be a car mechanic. I haven't seen a car since I got here."

"Only people living on the eight hundredth floor or above can own cars," George answered.

"Where do they drive them?"

"On the eight hundredth floor and above. There are ramps connecting the floors. They can drive all the way up to the penultimate floor."

"Why not to the ultimate floor?"

"For security reasons. Ralph lives on the top floor. There are bridges connecting all the top floors of all the buildings. So Ralph can drive from building to building."

"Ralph?"

"The Supreme Leader."

"Ralph, an old homeless guy in my dimension, is Supreme Leader in this dimension?"

"Yes. In Eden's dimension he is not homeless. He lives in a beautiful penthouse."

"That's hard to believe."

Priscilla barged back onscreen. "Mickey? Albert is waking up."

Eden(Mickey) looked to see Albert was awake in the canopy bed. "Be careful what you say about what you overheard. Your brain might get wiped."

"That would be a waste of time," Albert said.

"Go back to sleep, Albert." Albert did. Eden(Mickey) turned back toward the laptop. "So how do we proceed?"

"Help Eden carry out her plan," George said. "Only the results won't be what she expects."

"Because you and Priscilla will intervene?"

"Exactly. You need to get to Eden's office and load the files we've placed on your laptop into the system."

"I should trust you two?"

"What other option do you have?" George smiled. "Other than to stay where you are and stock up on diapers."

"Right. I'm on my way." Eden(Mickey) closed the laptop and stood. "As soon as I deal with Laurie."

Earth

"Is that my work?"

Priscilla looked up from the computer on her desk in her office at Northwestern to find Mickey(Eden) standing before her. Scattered across the desk were the printed Photoshop-improved copies of the pictures she had taken of the chalk-smudged remains of the calculations in Mickey and George's apartment. "They mostly seem to be coordinates."

"For a time and place long past. They are irrelevant now."

"Talk to me, Mickey."

"I could tell you without fear of your head being wiped. But there's no time."

By now Priscilla was so accustomed to Mickey's incoherent ramblings she breezed right by this latest one. "What's the rush? You've been struggling with this for years."

"The rush is Mickey. He's no fool. That's why I chose him to start with. He'll figure out what's going on and try to interfere. As intelligent as he is, he might cause some mischief. I've got to move fast." A wistful expression graced Mickey's face. "I've wasted too much time already."

This was unignorable. "Why are you talking like there are two of you?"

"Because there are." Mickey(Eden) turned and hurried away. She stopped at the door. "Have you seen Mickey's laptop?"

Priscilla shook her head no.

"He either hid it or took it with him. Why would he hide it? He didn't know what was happening. I'm sure of that. But he couldn't take it with him, either. I'm sure of that, too. Maybe he tried to take it through and it was destroyed. Then I've got to proceed without it."

"What's on the laptop that's so important?"

"Your doom." Mickey(Eden) dashed out the door.

Priscilla shook her head as she watched him leave. Mickey was getting worse. She should consider an intervention. She looked over the papers scattered across her desk. Except his work was brilliant. He had such a brilliant mind. Why was madness so beautiful?

Other Earth

Eden(Mickey) rushed out of Eden's brother's apartment and down the hall to the entry door. He opened it and looked all around. The plaza was deserted, except for soldiers and some heavy weaponry. He had no time to play games. "Laurie! I know you're out here. What do you want?"

A female soldier emerged from hiding.

"Laurie?"

The female soldier nodded.

"Get in here." Eden(Mickey) waved her toward the entry door. Laurie scurried over in an evasive military fashion, and on inside. She seemed just as fit and attractive as the Laurie in Mickey's dimension. Only this Laurie was an active soldier, whereas his Laurie was a veteran. "What do you want?"

"How did you know I was out here?"

"I'm brilliant. Now what do you want?"

"I was keeping an eye on you."

"Why? Did Mick tell you to?"

"No. Mick doesn't know I'm here."

"Then why?"

"To protect you. The Morlox grabbed you once. They could try again."

This curve was certainly a blind one. Mickey was genuinely puzzled. He had not had a lot of experience with women. His closest approach to one was Priscilla, and that had never gone beyond a hug. In fact, he believed she came around their apartment mostly to see George. So he was intrigued by the fact Mick's lover would be concerned for the safety of his ex-wife. Women sure were interesting, if strictly from a puzzle-solving aspect. "Let me get this straight. You are out here guarding me from attack by Morlox?"

Laurie responded with a solemn nod.

"Why? Were you assigned the duty?"

Laurie shook her head no.

"Please talk to me, Laurie. I don't have a lot of time to waste."

"I know you don't. I respect you so much."

"But not enough to keep you from sleeping with my husband."

Laurie burst out in tears.

"Hey. I didn't know soldiers were allowed to cry. Couldn't you get court-martialed?"

Laurie sniffled back enough sobs to speak. "You can hit me if you want."

"Eden might enjoy hitting you," Eden(Mickey) said, "but frankly, my dear, I don't give a damn." He pumped Eden's fist into the air. "Yes! I've always wanted to say that line, but I never had the opportunity." He beamed at Laurie. "Thank you."

Laurie backed away a step. "You've been under a lot of stress. Mick said so."

Eden(Mickey) calmed. "It might be aftereffects of the gas. The Morlox gassed me. They gassed everybody. So be careful if you go underground. They might try to gas you."

Laurie held up a gas mask clipped to her belt. "We're prepared for that. Only an inbred imbecile would refuse to wear a mask."

"So go kick some Morlox butt."

"I'd feel a lot better knowing you're safe."

Eden(Mickey) studied Laurie. "Aren't there any *unmarried* men interested in you?"

Laurie nodded yes.

"His name is Stan." Eden(Mickey) said this as a statement, not a question.

Laurie's eyes grew large.

"I told you, I'm brilliant. You'd be a lot better off with an unmarried man. Especially since he, too, is a soldier."

Laurie's eyes were on the verge of popping out.

"I appreciate you being honest with me. You seem like a decent person, Laurie. But I've got to go now." Eden(Mickey) hugged Laurie. After Laurie hurried back outside, Mickey slapped the wall with Eden's open palm in joy. "Deal with that, Eden! Whenever you get back! I just made you friends with your husband's lover!"

Earth

Mickey(Eden) sat on the tagged bench in the park, gazing around in wonder at the immense open spaces surrounding her. This wide open world was so distracting. *It will be so good for my people,* Eden marveled. *All this boundless room to spread out in. This is the Promised Land and I'm Moses. I will part the boundaries of the dimensions like Moses parted the Red Sea, and lead my people across into this land of milk and honey. They will be so grateful I might just supplant Ralph. But I don't want to live on the top floor, not since I've seen this Earth. I'll design my own floor here. What amazing vastness and solitude.*

Another pleasant distraction had been encountering her twin in this dimension. Eden wondered if Mickey had met *his* twin yet? Being as it was her ex-husband and they worked together, he probably had. If he'd had the same reaction to Mick as she'd had with Edie they were probably back together. She would rectify that once all this was over. She had no intention of taking her cheating husband back. And she would make quick work of his girlfriend. Laurie would rue the day.

Distractions, distractions. Eden had to get busy. Her world was counting on her. Once the Crossover Project was accomplished she would have time to engage in all her wildest dreams.

A homeless man approached. Mickey(Eden) ignored him until he drew too near to ignore. Until he drew so close she recognized him. No, she exclaimed deep in her soul. It couldn't be. The homeless man stopped before the bench. He was old, filthy, and frail, and stank twice as bad as any Morlox. The few teeth he still had were stained and crooked. His soiled rags were held together only by their stench. And he hadn't shaved, at least with anything sharp, for a long time. When he spoke, his vile breath shoved Mickey(Eden) back. "I could sure use a Big Mac, Haiku."

It was Ralph. The Supreme Leader. In this dimension he was a destitute homeless man. Mickey(Eden)'s reflexes took over, and she stood to attention. "Certainly, sir."

Other Earth

Eden(Mickey) ducked back into George's apartment. "Wake up, Albert." She clapped twice, and the royal bedchamber disappeared.

Albert's ancient eyelids fluttered within the sleeping tube. "Are you ready to go home?"

"No. I've got to get to my office."

Albert moaned.

"Do you have a pass? To get us through the checkpoints?" Seeing Albert was still more asleep than awake, she pressed on. "The plaza is full of soldiers."

"Of course I've got a military pass."

"Then let's go." Eden(Mickey) pulled him out of the tube and onto his feet. She rushed the old man out onto the street.

They were immediately challenged by a soldier. Who smiled. "Hello, Mrs. Hai."

Eden(Mickey) was surprised. "You know who I am?"

"Of course."

"I don't need a pass?"

"Of course not."

Albert brightened. "Can I go back to sleep?"

"No. You're already here you might as well come along."

The soldier activated his radio. "I'll arrange for an escort."

"I'm her escort," Albert insisted.

The soldier sniffed with a disdainful nose. "A military escort. These streets are dangerous. Morlox could pop up anywhere at any time."

"She's just going to her office." Albert pointed to a building across the street. "It's right there."

The soldier turned his back on Albert to arrange for an escort.

"This is why the Morlox are kicking our butts," Albert said to Eden(Mickey). "Soldiers like this."

To Eden(Mickey), the soldier said, "Your escort is on the way." To Albert, he said, "Let me see your pass."

Albert produced it with pride.

The soldier examined it. "This looks counterfeit. I'm confiscating it." He stuffed it in his pocket.

Albert's wrinkles grew indignant. "That is not counterfeit! It was issued by Mitchell, the head of the Crossover Project."

One of the four just-arrived soldiers summoned for escort duty smirked at the old fashioned Gauss outfit Eden(Mickey) was wearing. "The Crossover Project? Is that why she's dressed like that?"

"This is Eden Hai, soldier," his superior with the radio barked. "Treat her with respect or you could find yourself underground mopping up Morlox guts."

Eden(Mickey) turned to Albert. "Just go back to George's and wait for me there."

Realizing he was being dismissed to go sleep some more, Albert voiced no further objections over his military pass being seized. The detail escorted Eden(Mickey) across the street. At the entrance to the building Albert had pointed to they stepped aside to allow her access to the door. The brazen one who had spoken before spoke again. "Here you are, ma'am." He snickered. "Or sir."

Eden(Mickey) chuckled to himself as he walked inside. The fool didn't know how right he was to be uncertain of his gender. He went up to the sprawling directory. The Crossover Project was located on floor 715.

Moments later, Eden(Mickey) exited the elevator and approached the front desk. "I'm Eden Hai."

The receptionist smiled. "Love your outfit."

"I need to get to my office."

"Go right ahead."

"Trouble is, I don't remember where I left it."

The receptionist laughed. "That's a good one, Mrs. Hai."

"I'm serious. I've been having memory issues."

The receptionist grew somber. "I'm so sorry." She leaned forward to whisper. "If they can wipe you then they can wipe anyone." She leaned back and pointed down a hall. "It's ten doors down."

"Thank you." Eden(Mickey) walked away.

Arriving at the tenth door, Eden(Mickey) came face to face with Mick and Mitchell. The first beamed, while the second scowled. "Are you recovered from your ordeal?" Mick asked

"What ordeal?" Mitchell asked.

"She was captured by Morlox."

"Indeed? And how did you escape?"

Eden(Mickey) shrugged. "I found my way up to the surface."

"Indeed? And how did you accomplish that?"

"Is this really necessary, Mitchell?" Mick interceded. "She needs to get to work right away."

"The Morlox capture one of our most prized scientists. Then she escapes, a feat never accomplished before, not even by any of our soldiers. After which a pitched battle breaks out, a battle that at the moment isn't going very well."

"What are you suggesting?" Mick demanded.

"I'm not suggesting anything. I believe I'm stating the case very plainly." Mitchell turned to Eden(Mickey). "What information did you trade for your freedom?"

"That's ridiculous!" Mick objected.

Despite the objection, Mitchell continued to glare at Eden(Mickey).

Mickey's mind went into overdrive. They were going to want to know what this laptop was and why he had it with him, so he might as well strike first with a good lie. Eden(Mickey) waved the laptop before their faces. "I escaped with this."

"What is that?" Mick asked, his curiosity piqued. "It looks ancient."

"It is ancient. But its got a mapping program on it." Both men waited for Eden(Mickey) to continue. "I'm mapping the floors and tunnels of the underground. That's how I escaped. I have good maps through the labyrinth."

Even Mitchell was impressed. "You've got up-to-date maps of the underground?"

"Yes," Eden(Mickey) lied. "And I need to download the program onto my computer so I can disseminate the maps to the military. They are in dire need of them right now. So if you'll excuse me."

"We can't plug any outside devices into our secure system," Mick said.

"It's me, Mick," Eden(Mickey) lied once more. "Your wife. I would never compromise my own work. You know that."

Mick turned to Mitchell. "She's right. She wouldn't."

"Unless she is in cahoots with the Morlox," Mitchell said.

"In danger of repeating myself," Mick yelled, "that's damn ridiculous!"

A tremor passed through the floor beneath their feet. Mitchell looked around, terror-struck. "What was that?"

"It felt like the Morlox just set off an explosive in our basement," Eden(Mickey) said.

Mick was stunned. "They've got weapons that powerful?"

"How many people will die if they start bringing down our 'scrapers?" Eden(Mickey) demanded. He waved the laptop once again. "I've got to do this. Now. The Army is waiting for it."

Mitchell was pale. "If we could feel that seven hundred and fifteen floors in the air, how strong was the blast?"

Mick was only slightly paler. "It doesn't matter. These 'scrapers were built to withstand a direct meteor strike."

"That's never been tested." After drawing a shaky breath, Mitchell continued. "If I authorize this it is to be done under your supervision, Mick. If something goes wrong, it's your hide. Are you willing to accept this?"

"With my wife doing the work?" Mick smiled. "Certainly."

"You're ex-wife."

"A legalistic technicality."

"Then it's on your head. And your mother's." Mitchell turned away.

"What does my mother have to do with it?"

Mitchell walked off without replying.

Mick frowned at his superior's lack of response, then turned his frown on the person he believed to be his ex-wife. "Do you know what he means about my mother?" When Eden(Mickey) shrugged, he took a deep breath. "I've got your back on this, Eden. Even though it might cost me my head." He glanced off in the direction Mitchell had walked. "And my mother's, for some reason."

Can I, Mickey wondered? *To seal the deal. Can I do it?* Eden(Mickey) took a deep, deep breath, and smiled. "Thank you, Mick." He kissed Mick.

Mick jerked back, and looked around to see who was watching. Yet he smiled. "Go do what you need to do."

Eden(Mickey) rushed into Eden's office. *That was so weird.* Mickey had nothing against gays. But he hoped he'd never have to kiss another man for the rest of his life.

Earth

Mickey(Eden) held the door to McDonalds open for Ralph. How could the Supreme Leader have fallen so low in this dimension, Eden wondered? The two were basically the same person. It was distressing. Although it was the twin of the Supreme Leader, Mickey(Eden) still held her breath as Ralph passed by her into the restaurant.

There was a line. Ralph seemed content to wait. Mickey(Eden) on the other hand had to resist an urge to barge to the front. This was the twin of the Supreme Leader! Every person should step aside. She quivered with agitation. "Sir, why don't you take a seat. I'll bring your food to you."

"A Big Mac meal?"

"Of course. Now please sit down. I'd escort you to a table myself, but I'd lose my place in line."

Ralph smiled and shuffled away.

"That old man really stinks."

Mickey(Eden) spun around to find the young man next in line behind her holding his nose. "I will remember you. Although this brain does not possess a chip, I will not forget your face. After the Crossover you will suffer greatly for your insolence."

The young man released his nose and smiled. "The Crossover? Is that like hitching a ride on a comet to a better place?"

"No. The better place is coming here."

"Like Heaven coming down to Earth?"

"It will be no heaven for your kind. You will be sent down to Hellades."

"Is that like a mash up of Hell and Hades? Hellades. I like that."

"I doubt you will enjoy it."

"Mister? Can I take your order?"

Mickey(Eden) didn't react to the cashier until the young man behind him prompted. "He's ready for your order."

Mickey(Eden) turned around to find she was now first in line, and the cashier was referring to her. Eden had a hard time remembering what the gender of this body was. She stepped up and placed an order for a Big Mac meal then dug out Mickey's wallet and produced a five.

The cashier stared. "I need another dollar."

Mickey(Eden) opened the wallet back up. No more bills. "I don't have a dollar."

The cashier offered the five back. "A credit card or debit card will do."

Mickey(Eden) rifled through Mickey's wallet. It was empty. "I don't have any cards."

The cashier stared at Mickey(Eden) in disbelief.

The young man behind Mickey(Eden) stepped up. "I've got you covered." He handed a dollar to the cashier, who then processed the order.

Mickey(Eden) focused now-grateful eyes on the stranger. "Thank you. Perhaps you will not end up in Hellades after all."

"That's a relief," he answered in mock-relief. "I didn't realize you were as destitute as that old guy." He sniffed. "You smell much better."

Mickey(Eden) stepped aside to await the order.

After placing his order, the young man joined her. "Are you two sharing a meal?"

"The food is for the Supreme Leader."

The young man laughed. "Supreme leader of what?"

"You have redeemed yourself. Don't endanger your redemption by mocking." The order came up, and Mickey(Eden) grabbed the tray and went in search of Ralph. She found him seated with an elderly woman. Mickey(Eden) placed the tray before Ralph. "Sir, why are you sitting with this strange woman?"

"Quit kidding around, Mickey," Miriam said. "Who is your friend?"

"I'm Ralph." The old man began unwrapping his food.

Mickey(Eden) peered into Miriam's face. "You have shown kindness to Ralph. After the Crossover you will be rewarded."

"I just asked him to sit with me," Miriam said. "I saw the two of you come in together. By the way, what's the Crossover? Is that something we'll be discussing at Phun With Physics?"

Mickey(Eden) gazed at her with confusion. "I always have fun with physics." He turned to Ralph. "Sir, I have important work I need to do. Is it alright if I leave you for now?"

"Go on," Miriam said. "I'll stay with him."

Mickey(Eden) turned back to Miriam. "You are storing up treasure for after the Crossover."

"I never realized you were so religious, Mickey." Miriam turned to the old man. "Ralph? Would you like a refill?"

"I'll get it." Mickey(Eden) took the cup to the refill station.

The young man from before joined her there. "Do you and the old guy have a place to stay?" He produced a business card. "I live nearby.

You can crash at my place. My address is on the card. It's small, but it's better than a shelter."

Mickey(Eden) studied the card. "You are a freelance designer? Do you design floors? I might contact you after the Crossover."

"I'm not in flooring. My address is on there. Come by if you are ever caught out on the street. That's no way to live."

Mickey(Eden) slipped the card in a pocket then took the refilled cup back to Ralph. "It won't be much longer, sir. Once I complete my work you will take your rightful place on the top floor."

"You physicists," Miriam said. "I never understand a word you say."

Mickey(Eden) strode toward the door. She found the young man with his refilled cup holding it open for her. "You seem like a nice young man," she said, "I am just crazy busy right now. Once all this is over I'll look you up."

"After the Crossover, right?" he followed Mickey(Eden) out. "My phone number is on the card I gave you."

"Your phones won't be any good then."

"So this Crossover will be an Apocalyptic event?"

"It will be for you." Mickey(Eden) strode away.

"What's your name? So we can hook up after the Apocalypse." As Mickey(Eden) continued walking, he yelled after. "I gave you my name! It's on my card!"

Mickey(Eden) stopped to take the business card out and look. Carl Friedrich. "Oh my god." She ran back to the young man standing just outside the entrance to McDonalds and seized him by the arms to pull him close so she could peer into his face. "Now I know why you are being so nice. Why you helped pay for Ralph's meal."

"And why is that?"

"You wouldn't understand." Mickey(Eden) touched Mickey's stomach. "But I'll look you up *before* the Crossover. I've got to make sure nothing happens to you."

"I'm touched."

"So am I." Mickey(Eden) stroked his face. Then hugged him.

Carl Friedrich pushed her back. "I'm not big on hugging. Especially another man."

"I'll contact you before the Crossover. To protect you." Mickey (Eden) ran away.

Leaving a bewildered yet strangely comforted young man standing in front of McDonalds.

Other Earth

When Eden(Mickey) carried the laptop into Eden's office, he stepped inside the main hall of the Royal Society in London. "Wow, Eden," he said, looking all around in awe. "I'm impressed. This looks just like the paintings I've seen." He strode up to a man seated along the wall. Was that Newton? He leaned in for a closer look.

An apple fell from above and struck him on the head. Eden (Mickey) straightened and looked around. *Very funny, Eden.* He picked up the apple. It felt real. He bit into it. The texture seemed right. Then the taste registered. He spit it out. *You need to work on the taste, Eden.* He walked up to the desk at the front of the hall and sat. Setting the apple aside, he opened Hypatia. The OPEN ME NOW icon awaited. He clicked on it.

The image of George and Priscilla's laughing faces appeared onscreen. "That was funny," George said.

"She set up that trap in the hologram," Priscilla said. "Anytime someone gets too close to Newton they get bopped on the head by a falling apple."

"It tasted horrid."

"To you, not to her. That's one of her favorite flavors. Dirty diaper."

"So she didn't do that from my dimension?" Eden(Mickey) asked. "It was pre-arranged to happen?"

"Of course. We can't move living things between dimensions," Priscilla said.

"Let me clarify that," George said. "We probably *could* move living things, but they most likely would no longer be living after the move."

"But that is what Eden is getting ready to do."

"Yes," Priscilla said. "And we have to stop her."

"How can she do this," Mickey asked, "with her being from a dimension beneath yours, while you, being from a higher dimension, can't?"

"By connecting with you," George said.

"The two of you together amount to quite an intellect," Priscilla said.

"How did she do that in the first place? Contact me on her own?"

George nudged Priscilla off-screen. "That was no great feat. Influences pass from higher to lower dimensions all the time. Flashes of brilliance. The 'Eureka!' moments recorded all through your history were merely ideas passed down from a higher dimension."

"So when Archimedes sat down in his bathtub he was contacted by someone from a higher dimension?"

"Yes."

"But he was taking a bath at the time. Don't you people respect our privacy?"

"Do you respect the privacy of the animals *you* study?" Priscilla asked from off-screen.

George continued. "We were growing quite frustrated at the time. We thought he'd never get the notion of displacement."

"You were there? When it happened?"

"Yes."

"But Archimedes lived over two thousand years ago."

"In our dimension time is fluid."

"I have no idea what that means."

Priscilla forced her way back onto the screen. "And we have no time to explain it to you now. You have to get busy."

"Doing what?"

"Get rid of the hologram, for starters."

Eden(Mickey) clapped Eden's hands twice. The London Royal Society hall resolved into a cluttered office of normal dimensions. "This office looks bigger than Eden's brother's entire apartment."

"You are on the seven hundred and fifteenth floor," George said. "People are accorded more space on the upper floors. The more esteemed a person is in Eden's dimension, the more personal space they are allotted."

George butted in. "Now download the program we installed on your laptop into the system."

Eden(Mickey) smiled as he connected the laptop to the desktop before him. "This is so 'Mr. Robot'."

"This will take a while," George warned. "Your laptop is inelegant."

"What can I do in the meantime?"

"Distract your husband," Priscilla said. The screen went blank.

The door opened and Mick entered. He did not look happy. He glanced down at the laptop. "That was some story about mapping the underground. Now what is that thing really?"

Eden(Mickey) lowered his gaze, not sure what to tell him.

"Tell me. Or I'll strip it down to its bits and pixels to find out."

Eden(Mickey) looked back up into Mick's face. "It's from another dimension."

Mick was stunned. "What? How?"

"I don't know how."

Mick stared at him in disbelief.

"That's why it looks so different. It's not from here."

"How did you do it?"

"I'm not sure. I was reaching through. Found the target. I made contact. Several times."

"Who was it?"

"A theoretical physicist. Someone smart enough to be useful."

Mick collapsed into a chair. "Why didn't you tell me?"

"There was no proof. I hadn't made actual *physical* contact. I wanted to announce success. Not an unsubstantiated psychic event. Besides, we haven't been very close lately."

"But you say that thing…"

"Yes. It's his. It came through intact. A physical object passed between dimensions."

"But how?"

Eden(Mickey) leaned back, the devious lobe of Mickey's mind hard at work. "I'll find out. That's why I had to plug it into our system. To duplicate the conditions."

"We could lose our security clearance for plugging an outside computer into our network. Be shut down. Hell, we could both end up in prison. Mitchell is already suspicious of you."

"The risk is worth it if we learn how to pass between dimensions the way that laptop did." Eden(Mickey) walked to the door and closed it. Mickey couldn't believe he was even considering this.

Mick stared coldly at him. "What are you doing now?"

Eden(Mickey) locked the door. Mickey knew he was a woman on the outside. Hell, on the inside, too, the pregnancy proved that. And this man was Eden's husband. There was nothing morally wrong with what he was about to do. "I'm merely analyzing the laptop at this point. The program can run on its own."

"You need to lock the door for this?"

Eden(Mickey) walked back to him. Mickey knew he was going to require some serious therapy after this. "The analysis will take a while." George and Priscilla had said he needed to distract Eden's husband. And the program needed time to run. "The reason I locked the door is for this." Eden(Mickey) clapped once.

Earth

Mickey(Eden) was in a daze as she cut through the park on the way back to the apartment. Carl Friedrich was the name Eden and Mick had chosen for their baby if it turned out to be a boy. Eden had just met the twin of her yet to be born son. She probed Mickey's abdomen. Of course Carl Friedrich wasn't in there. This was Mickey's abdomen in Mickey's dimension. Her unborn son was in her abdomen back in her dimension. Yet it was almost like she could feel him kicking. In Mickey's abdomen here in Mickey's dimension. Although Carl Friedrich wasn't developed enough to kick yet, in her dimension. Yet touching Mickey's abdomen in this dimension felt so reassuring. Could there actually be a trace of Carl Friedrich in Mickey's body?

Mickey(Eden) was so lost in thought she nearly ran into Priscilla, who was standing beside Mickey's tagged bench. She caught Mickey (Eden) to prevent the collision. "It's not safe for you to walk around like this. You could step in front of a bus. Why don't you sit down." Priscilla eased Mickey(Eden) down to the bench, then sat beside her. "I called your name three times."

"You should call me by my real name."

"What is your real name?"

Mickey(Eden) cackled. "You'll know soon enough."

Priscilla let that slide. "Can we talk?"

Mickey(Eden) stood. "I'm very busy."

"I'll walk with you." Priscilla stood and easily kept pace. "What are you trying to accomplish?"

Mickey(Eden) gave her a dark glance. "What do you mean?"

Priscilla produced a sheaf of printed computer papers. "I showed more of your work to Mitchell. He's never seen anything like it. He said it seems to postulate a parity violation between dimensions. And something about a left-spinning superstring and a right-spinning bosonic string forming a heterotic string that loops from dimension to dimension. And something about every particle having a supersymmetric partner in every dimension, that there should be a Smickey, or a Mickino, with different one-half units of spin. He went on about E-eight strings with two hundred and forty-eight rotations spinning in thirty-two directions with four hundred and ninety-six charges. Mitchell totally lost me. But he seemed astounded."

Mickey(Eden) snatched the papers and looked them over. "Quit showing my work around!"

"I'm worried sick about you. If it wasn't for your work being so incredible I'd have you committed. The way you're behaving, I still might. What is going on?"

Mickey(Eden) tossed the papers into the air. "It doesn't matter. No one here can follow my work. Try to commit me if you dare." Mickey (Eden) walked away.

Priscilla scurried about gathering up the scattered papers.

Mickey(Eden) stopped ten paces distant and turned. "Have you seen my laptop?" Mickey(Eden)'s gaze turned malicious. "Or did you steal that, too?" She shook Mickey's head dismissively and walked on. "You are falling out of favor fast, Priscilla. After the Crossover we might wipe you once and for all."

Priscilla stared after Mickey(Eden) with dark concern then resumed gathering papers.

Other Earth

Eden(Mickey) and Mick were sprawled naked across plush cushions alongside an expansive Roman bath. Other nude bathers of both sexes strolled about the pool, or were arranged along with the erotic statuary about the walls. Steam from a hot spring that fed the pool spread throughout the thermae up to the high arched ceiling, blanketing the airy space in moist warmth. Mick's eyes were closed while he gently stroked Eden's breasts.

Eden's eyes were wide. Wide. Open. As Mickey stared at the ceiling. Eden's body was as motionless as one of the statues, but Mickey's mind was racing. *I am going to be so accommodating of any female I might ever yet touch in my life. That was so different than any way I could have possibly imagined. And it was me doing it to me. I see years of counseling in my future. What if I became pregnant? Would I give birth to my own child? Would I be both father and mother to it?*

Mick kissed a nipple. "I've missed you."

That simple kiss took Eden(Mickey)'s breath. Mickey had possessed nipples his entire life, but they sure didn't feel like Eden's. "I've been close at hand," he roused himself to reply.

"But unreachable."

"I'm definitely within reach now." Eden(Mickey) pulled Mick's hand away from Eden's breasts. It was difficult to think while Mick was fooling with them. Mickey wondered how he should play this. Should he try to repair their marriage? Forgive the infidelity? Would that help or hinder Eden? She obviously was having serious problems with her husband, since they were separated. And Mickey had just given her body to him. But that had been a calculated move; simply to buy time. Would it really piss Eden off once she learned what he had allowed to be done to her body? With her ex-husband? Or would she like the idea of getting back together with him? Which would upset Eden more, getting back together with Mick or alienating him further?

Mick's hand eluded Eden(Mickey)'s forestalling grasp and wandered lower. Eden(Mickey) grabbed it before it wandered too low. He looked around, searching for something to draw Mick's attention away from Eden's body. "This Roman bath hologram was a great idea, Mick."

"Yes, we've had wonderful times here." Mick said, without being diverted.

Eden(Mickey) gasped as Mick's hand escaped Eden's and slipped between her legs. "So soon, Mick?"

Mick recoiled with a frown. "You still won't open yourself to me. That's what has caused all our strife. You holding back from your husband."

Do I fight for Eden, Mickey wondered, *or against her. And which way would be against her.* He had to make a quick decision, so he went with the simplest reaction. "Really? You don't think you taking a lover had anything to do with it?"

"We were having problems long before Laurie came into the picture. You know that."

Naturally, Mickey did not know that. He had no idea what their marital life had been like before he crashed it. So he changed the subject. "I met Laurie."

Mick looked doubtful. "When? How?"

"She was worried about me after hostilities broke out with the Morlox. She wanted to stand guard over me."

Mick chuckled. "That sounds like Laurie."

"She's nice. And pretty. And strong. I bet she's a good soldier."

"She is." Mick snuggled up to Eden(Mickey). "But I'd gladly give her up if we could work out our problems and get back together. I'd like to get back together." His hand resumed its probing. "How about you?"

Mickey closed Eden's eyes and gasped, squirming with pleasure. Damn, what Mick was doing felt good. Yet he gritted Eden's teeth and resisted succumbing to it. "Do I want to get back together? I don't know."

"If we did, could you give up Stan?"

Stan? Laurie's husband? From Phun With Physics? Stan was Eden's lover? Mickey wracked his brain for a way to play this to Eden's disadvantage.

Mick misread the emotions playing across Eden(Mickey)'s face. "You won't give him up?"

"I don't know," Eden(Mickey) pleaded, stalling for time.

Mick pulled back. "You won't. I can see it in your face. Even though Stan was just payback for me and Laurie."

"Give me time, Mick. This is a start, isn't it? I've given you my body."

"While hardly touching mine." Mick started to rise from the cushions.

Eden(Mickey) grabbed his arm. "What do you mean?"

"You've always touched me so tenderly, so sensually. Now you won't touch it at all."

No!! No! No. Must I? Do I have to? Eden(Mickey) reached out. This was so wrong. He would never be able to have normal sex as a normal man with a normal woman ever again. Which made him laugh. He'd never had normal sex as a normal man with a normal woman in his life.

Mick was offended by the laugh. "Is this funny?"

"God, no," Eden(Mickey) scrambled to say. "Just uncomfortable. You with Laurie. Me with Stan. And now us." Closing Eden's eyes, with a deep, what could be his last innocent breath, while wishing he was in any dimension other than this one at this time in this place in this body, Mickey touched it. It stirred. Oh god.

Mollified, and really not wanting to fight at the moment, Mick eased back down onto the cushions. "Gently, Eden. You're not shucking corn." An injured tone crept into his voice. "Does Stan like it rough?"

Eden(Mickey) lessened his grip and slowed. "It doesn't matter what Stan likes. I'm with you now."

Why should it matter at all? Mickey had led an incel life. He had no experience with sex, other than to pine after Priscilla. At least this was sex with someone willing, hell wanting, to have sex with him. And, damn his soul, he was enjoying it. He could imagine the real Eden doing this to him. As he was doing to Mick at this moment. In this dimension they were married, so there was no reason not to. No reason not to enjoy doing it. Oh god.

In for a penny in for a pound, or by the looks of it several pounds. Eden(Mickey) rolled over on top of Mick. Mickey had seen people do this in movies on the Internet. He should be able to fake it. Eden (Mickey) reached down to guide Mick in as he settled Eden's hips upon him. "How's this for touching you, Mick?" He smiled at Mick's breathless pleasure as Eden's fingers reached further down between his legs. Mick's eyes rolled up in their sockets. Eden(Mickey) laughed in surprise at his reaction. "Mick, breathe."

Mick at last did. "Ahh, this is the Eden I know and love."

"That's what you think." The retort was lost on Mick, who was ensconced in his sensual delights. Gazing down upon the upturned blissful face, Eden(Mickey) was amazed to see it so filled with such unmasked pleasure. In his dimension his facial muscles had never produced this expression, nothing even close. They had never learned how.

As their lovemaking progressed, Eden(Mickey) was further amazed at how much he enjoyed giving such pleasure to Mick. To his twin. Whether for good or for bad, Mickey thought as he made love to Mick with Eden's body, it looked like Mick and Eden were back together. He then shut down his mind so he could enjoy what was going on with

Eden's body, enjoy the look of pleasure he saw transforming his own face.

Earth

Mickey(Eden) walked into the apartment to find George lounging in the George and Martha easy chair in his undershorts watching a NASCAR race on a tablet. "You watch NASCAR?"

George remained riveted on the race he held in his hand. "Don't get weird again, Mickey."

"My brother watches NASCAR."

George glanced up from the screen. "Since when do you have a brother?"

Oops. She had to remember Mickey didn't have a brother. So many details to keep track of, and no chip to keep track of them with. "We're estranged at the moment." Mickey(Eden) walked into the kitchen and rummaged through drawers. "He's fascinated with cars. He's a car mechanic."

"I don't even own a car. But I'm mechanical. A mechanical engineer."

Of course there would be a connection between the two, she thought. "He would be amazed at the roads here."

"In the city? These roads are no fun. Doesn't he ever get out on the Interstate?"

"What is an Interstate?"

"I hope you're joking." George craned his head away from the race to peer into the kitchen. "What are you looking for?"

"I've lost my laptop."

George returned his attention to the race. "Really? I thought you had it Gorilla Glued to you."

A gorilla? Glued to her? Wouldn't that be dangerous? Not wanting to stoke George's suspicions any further, Eden choked her questions down and continued tearing through the kitchen.

"I thought you looked here already," George called out.

"I'm looking for any notes I might have made."

"You mean on paper? Done with a manual writing instrument? Graphite encased in wood?"

Mickey(Eden) ignored him as she went into Mickey's room to search. Nothing. She dashed into George's room.

"While you're in there would you pick up my clothes?"

"These are clothes I'm walking on?" Mickey(Eden) shot back. "It's not wall to wall carpeting?"

"Whatever happened to the hot girl you met? Eden?"

Mickey(Eden) dashed back out to the living room. "Just what do you know about Eden?"

"Only what you told me. I didn't really expect to meet her. She sounded too good to be real."

"She's real, alright. You'll meet her soon. If I can ever get organized. I just don't like the idea of you thinking she's hot. That's a hell of a way for you to think about her." Mickey(Eden) plopped down into the mouse chair.

"I'm not going to hit on her, Mickey."

Mickey(Eden) glared at him. "You better not. That's sick. It'd be like hitting on your sister." Seeing George wondering at what she had said, she changed the subject. "Maybe we can take a ride on an Interstate sometime."

"Yeah," George forgot about Eden as his enthusiasm blossomed. "I've offered to take you on a road trip before. Are you finally ready to take me up on it? I'll rent a car and we'll tear off across the open countryside. Whenever you have the time. You've been so crazy busy."

"That's nearly over. Are cars expensive to rent? I couldn't even afford a Big Mac meal for Ralph today."

George set the tablet down on the coffee table. "I'll rent it. You know my family has more money than I could ever spend."

"You're rich?"

"My family is. I've told you about my family."

Mickey(Eden) gazed about the apartment. Eden realized she was stirring up George's suspicions and should shut up, but she really wanted to understand Mickey's roommate. He was her brother's twin, after all. "Then why do you live like this?"

"To be with you. You are an amazing person with an amazing mind."

Mickey(Eden) nodded in agreement. This George was in awe of Mickey as much as her brother was in awe of her. "Where would we go on this road trip?"

George shrugged. "Your choice. I've been all over the country, all over Europe and Asia, with my family. You haven't stuck your toe out of Chicago since I've known you."

Mickey(Eden) closed Mickey's eyes and tried to envision open countryside. What an amazing concept. "That sounds wonderful, George. I'd love to do a road trip with you." She opened Mickey's eyes. "As soon as I complete the Crossover. I'll find you and we'll go on that road trip."

George laughed. "You'll find me? Write our address down if you're afraid of forgetting it. With a graphite encased in wood writing device on a thin piece of wood."

Mickey(Eden) stood. "I won't forget where Mickey lives. Where I live, I mean. It's just that it's going to get real crazy real soon. When it does, George, hunker down here and wait it out. As soon as things settle down I'll come for you."

George picked his tablet up and returned his attention to NASCAR. "Are you ready to present your work? Finally?"

"Almost ready, George, almost." Mickey(Eden) headed for the door.

Other Earth

Eden(Mickey) and Mick lounged in each others' arms in the Roman bath. Mick nuzzled Eden's neck. "I am so happy to be back together with you."

Boy, Freud could write volumes, Mickey thought. Mickey untangled Eden's body from Mick's embrace. "The program has run by now."

Mick helped Eden(Mickey) out of the water then followed. "What are our chances?"

"Excellent. That laptop came through undamaged. We should be able to duplicate the event."

"I was asking about the chances for our marriage."

"I don't know. But now is not the time. After the Crossover we'll work on our personal problems." Eden(Mickey) picked up a towel and began drying.

"Our love-making felt different."

"Really?" He handed a towel to Mick.

Mick began drying. "You were so timid. It was like you were cringing at my touch. Not like you at all. You are always so exuberant with sex."

"We've grown apart. It will take time, Mick. We'll talk about it later. I've got to get back to work." He laid the towel aside.

Mick tossed his down, too. "What if something crossed over *with* the laptop."

Eden(Mickey) clapped twice. The Roman bath reverted to Eden's office. "Get dressed. We've more important things to do."

Mick leveled a dark gaze at Eden(Mickey). "Where did we first meet, Eden?"

Eden(Mickey) responded without hesitation. "That coffee shop off-campus. Sorry, I can't remember the name. It was on the corner of McMillan and something."

"High Street." The darkness left his gaze, and he began dressing. "I can't remember the name of the coffee shop, either."

"So can I get back to work?"

"Of course. But if you want to get rid of me you need to put something on." Mick had stopped dressing to ogle Eden's naked body.

Eden(Mickey) activated the Victorian-era Gauss outfit he had been wearing before.

Mick frowned at the selection. "I never did understand your fascination for clothes like that." He finished dressing and left.

As soon as the door closed Eden(Mickey) dashed to Hypatia and clicked on the OPEN ME NOW icon. George and Priscilla appeared on screen. "How did I know where they met?"

"You tapped into Eden's subconscious," Priscilla said. "Her brain *is* physically there inside her skull."

"How? I couldn't do it before."

George turned to Priscilla on screen. "Could someone else have connected with Mickey? And influenced him? From another dimension? One higher than ours? And given him that information?"

Priscilla shook her head no. "More than likely it was an adrenaline surge. At the threat of being discovered. And he was still excited from the lovemaking."

"You watched?" Eden(Mickey) asked.

"I did. George kept his eyes closed."

Eden(Mickey) checked the laptop. "The files have finished loading."

"Can I open my eyes?" George asked.

"Yes, George, I'm decent now."

"I hope so. You two made a lot of noise."

Eden(Mickey) ignored the taunt. "Are we ready?"

"Yes," Priscilla answered. "But Eden isn't."

"It needs to be simultaneous," George said.

There was a knock at the door to the office. "Don't worry," Eden's brother George called out. "It's just me."

Eden(Mickey) closed the laptop. "Come in."

George entered. He looked like he had been hard at work. His hands and coveralls were covered with grease, but his face held only a smirk. "Mick looked real happy coming out of here."

"You don't approve?" Eden(Mickey) asked.

"It's not my business." George closed the door behind him. "We need to talk. I just found out something."

"I'm kind of busy, George,"

"This is too important for you to be too busy."

"Okay. Talk fast."

"Not here." George looked all around.

"Why not?"

"Somewhere secure."

"Where?"

"The garage is secure."

"Where's that?"

George glared at her. "On the eight hundred and seventy-fifth floor. Where it's always been."

Eden(Mickey) stared at him in disbelief.

"You really need to take a long vacation if you keep forgetting this stuff," George spit out with disgust.

"Okay." Eden(Mickey) headed for the door.

"Hold on. You can't go up there dressed like that."

Eden(Mickey) searched the chip. He found some coveralls similar to George's.

"That's better." He smeared grease on Eden's cheeks and forehead. "You'll be my assistant." They walked out of the office to the elevators. As they stepped out on the eight-hundred and seventy-fifth floor they were challenged by armed soldiers. "Really?" George barked.

One soldier stepped forward. "Additional security because of the underground hostilities."

"You think Morlox are ever going to get this high?"

"Just a precaution. That Ralph ordered."

George frowned as he produced his badge. He nodded to Eden (Mickey). "I need help today. They've been abusing their cars a lot lately."

The soldier smiled as he handed the badge back. "I know. They really speed around up here. Reckless as hell."

George led Eden(Mickey) down the hall toward the garage. As they walked under a lane curving down a ramp from the 876th floor a car whizzed by over their heads. It raced down to the end of the hall then on down another ramp to the 874th floor. While Eden(Mickey) remained hunkered down as the roar faded away, George laughed. "They can't crash through these guardrails. You won't get run over."

They walked into a huge garage with several sport cars up on racks. George shook his head. "They really smash up their cars."

Eden(Mickey) looked all around. "This is secure?"

George turned on a switch on his diagnostic console. "It is now. I built this device to interfere with all their surveillance. We're free to talk."

Eden(Mickey) smiled. "I never appreciated the abilities of mechanical engineers."

"I'm a mechanic," George answered. "I don't know where you're getting the engineer from."

"So what's so important?"

George began to speak, but paused when three armed soldiers walked into the garage. "Ma'am, Ralph wants to see you."

George was amazed. "Ralph? Wants to see my sister? Now?"

"Yes." The soldier who spoke raised his rifle and smashed the stock into the diagnostic console.

"What are you doing?!" George yelled.

"I had instructions to disable it." He turned to Eden(Mickey) "Ma'am?"

Eden(Mickey) shrugged. "Lead the way."

The soldier led him out of the garage. Eden(Mickey) looked back. "What about my brother?"

"Don't worry about George. I'll take care of George." Keeping his gaze locked straight ahead, the soldier spoke softly. "You did good, Eden."

This soldier knows Eden, Mickey wailed silently. But Mickey had no idea who the soldier was. "Good at what?"

"Good, good, keep the ruse going."

Eden(Mickey) decided there was nothing to do except admit ignorance. "This isn't strategy. I really don't know what you are talking about."

A crack appeared in the granite façade of the soldier's face. "Did they wipe you?"

"No. At least, not that I remember."

"They wouldn't dare risk it. Your mind is too valuable."

The two reached the road on this floor, and began walking alongside it toward a distant bank of elevators. "Please tell me who you are and what is happening."

"I'm the love of your life. Stan."

Eden(Mickey) jerked around to stare at him. It *was* Stan, Mickey realized. He looked very much like the Stan from his dimension. Mickey had been too distracted to see it before. Now Mickey could feel the attraction. Eden's body certainly remembered Stan, and reacted to his nearness. *My God,* Mickey swore silently, Eden's body was getting all warm and tingly just walking beside him. It sure hadn't reacted this way to her ex-husband. Mickey had a strong urge to hug Stan, to kiss him, to caress him. He needed to think of something dark to distract Eden's libido. "So you are not leading me to my death?"

"I'm not sure what I'm leading you to. All I was told was to bring you to Ralph. But there are rumors."

"Walk slower," Eden(Mickey) said. "I want to hear these rumors."

"Your work is not going to be used the way you think it will be. You think you are opening a gate between dimensions for our people to flood into this wide open frontier and conquer the people living there. Much like Europeans did the Americas. You think you are alleviating our overpopulation. But something more devious is planned."

A car pulled over next to them. "This is much more fun than the elevator. Hop in."

Two armed guards sat in the back. But what amazed Eden(Mickey) was the person sitting in front behind the wheel, the one who had spoken. It was the homeless guy from the alley outside his and George's apartment. Only he was clean-cut and dressed in a well-tailored suit. "Ralph?"

Earth

Upon emerging from the basement apartment, Mickey(Eden) saw a crowd in the alley. She had left Ralph with Miriam in McDonalds. What was the Supreme Leader doing back there? And who were all those other people?

Mickey(Eden) walked down the alley to find out. Drawing near, Eden recognized Mick's assistant Albert was there, along with her lover Stan, Mick's lover Laurie, Mick's mother Lucy, and the old woman she had left Ralph with in McDonalds, or at least this dimension's versions of these people. With all these screaming incongruities clawing at her attention, the one Mickey(Eden) was drawn to first was Ralph. He was clean, and wearing clean clothes. "Sir? Are you okay?"

"We've adopted him," Miriam said. "After he ate another Big Mac meal…"

"And two more refills of Dr. Pepper," Ralph butted in.

"I took him back to my place for a bath. You should have seen that tub after he got out. There is no reason for people to live in such squalor. I've got an extra bedroom, but not a lot of money. So I called up the Phun With Physics gang and told them about Ralph." Miriam looked all around. "As you can see, they all volunteered to pitch in. We're taking Ralph out to buy him some new clothes. While he was in the tub I washed his clothes, but they are rags. Then we're going to the zoo. I want to show Ralph the gibbons. I absolutely adore those little monkeys. They are so cute." Miriam motioned to Ralph's cardboard. "We stopped here on the way so he could pick up his personal belongings."

Mickey(Eden) looked at the piece of cardboard Ralph held. There was an image of Gauss stuck to it.

Noticing what Mickey(Eden) was staring at, Ralph looked around to the others. "That's Carl Friedrich Gauss. The greatest mathematician since antiquity. He never published most of his work. His discovery of the non-Euclidean space was found in his notes after his death." Looking back to Mickey(Eden), he continued. "You took this sticker off your laptop. Replaced it with that sticker of Hypatia."

"Did I give it to you?" Mickey(Eden) asked. "I don't remember."

"You threw it away." Seeing Mickey(Eden) was still yet confused, he went on. "I dug it out of your garbage. I go through your garbage all the time. You've got interesting garbage."

Mickey(Eden) handed the piece of cardboard back to Ralph then turned to Miriam. "So you are taking care of Ralph?" When Miriam smiled and nodded, Mickey(Eden) continued. "It won't be for long. Keep him safe."

"We're all helping out," Laurie said.

Mickey(Eden) lunged at Laurie. "You keep your filthy hands off him!"

Laurie reacted with shock. She was even more shocked when Mickey(Eden) slapped her.

Stan grabbed Mickey and pulled Eden away from Laurie. "Why did you do that?"

Mickey(Eden) hugged Stan and kissed him.

Stan hurled her away. "What the hell, Mickey?!"

Albert stepped up to catch Mickey(Eden). They fell backwards to the pavement, with Albert underneath.

Mickey(Eden) rolled off Albert and looked over his prone body and pained expression. "I'm impressed, Albert. You're trying to be my bodyguard, even here."

Albert opened his eyes. "I don't think I can get up."

"That's okay," Mickey(Eden) said as she rose. "Just lay there and take a nap."

Lucy brushed some dirt off Mickey(Eden)'s clothes. "You are filthy, Mickey."

"I'm okay, Mom."

"I am not your mother."

"I know. You're Mick's mother."

Lucy turned to Stan. "I think you addled him."

"That was nothing," Stan said, his face still fire-engine red. "If he tries to kiss me again I'll knock his head off."

"Why did you slap me?" Laurie asked.

"Because you deserved it," Mickey(Eden) said. "Keep your hands off Mick."

"I've never touched you!" Laurie yelled.

Albert struggled to sit up. "Mickey's been under a lot of stress lately. Cut him some slack."

Mickey(Eden) helped Albert to his feet then turned to Laurie. "I slapped you to send a message to your twin. We experience similar events in different dimensions. Maybe she felt that."

"An inter-dimensional slap," Ralph said.

Mickey(Eden) turned to him. "It seems like some of the Supreme Leader's intelligence has seeped through the dimensions to you, Ralph." She looked around at the alley. "Why didn't you put it to better use?"

"The voices in my head have been a recent development." Ralph handed a wad of paper to Mickey(Eden). "You might can use this."

Mickey(Eden) unwadded the sheets of paper. They were covered with printed-out equations. "These look familiar."

"I dug them out of your garbage," Ralph said.

"It can't be. I never saw Mickey print anything."

"He didn't. You did, Eden. Mickey was asleep. You were working at the blackboard. I came in and told you to print your work out because you might lose access to the laptop."

"You can see me?" Mickey(Eden) asked.

"No. I see Mickey, like everyone else. But I know you're in there."

Miriam placed a comforting arm about Ralph. "I think poor Ralph is worn out."

Ralph collapsed happily into her embrace, resting his head on her bosom while his hand settled upon her rump.

Miriam blushed, but didn't interfere with what he was doing. "We need to get you home. Is that piece of cardboard with that old guy on it all you want from here?"

"That's all I needed," Ralph said. "That and what I just gave Eden."

Stan puffed out his chest and pumped up his shoulders. "What I need is an apology from Mickey."

"For kissing you?" Mickey(Eden) asked, lost in the papers she perused. "I'll never apologize for that, Stan. You are too good in bed."

Stan swung. Albert jumped in front of Mickey(Eden) and ended up flat on his back once again.

"Stan!" Lucy screamed.

"How could you punch such an old man?" Miriam said.

"Not that old," Albert mumbled from the pavement.

Laurie took Stan by the arm. "Let's go, Stan." To the others, "We're done with Phun With Physics. Mickey has clearly lost his mind." The two stomped away up the alley.

Miriam and Lucy helped Albert to his feet and looked him over. "Are you alright, Albert?" Lucy asked.

"He's a tough old coot," Mickey(Eden) said. "Just let him sleep it off."

"You can come back to my place," Lucy said, leading Albert away by the arm. "You shouldn't be left alone after being hit like that."

"It's time we go home too, Ralph," Miriam said. "I've got a lasagna to cook."

As Ralph was led away, Mickey(Eden) finally looked up from the papers. "Do you know what happened to the laptop, Ralph?"

"It crossed over to your dimension."

"Impossible."

"Apparently not."

"How?"

"It had some help."

"Who?"

"Someone above my pay grade."

"You mean from a higher dimension? Higher than mine?"

"I don't know how high." Ralph was led out of the alley by Miriam.

Mickey(Eden) leafed through the printed copy paper. This was exactly what she needed. The calculations she couldn't remember were on these papers. Papers Ralph had told her to print. When had he done that? Apparently when she was far enough through to this dimension to hear him, but not far enough through to remember having heard him. Then Ralph had saved them to give to her. How had he known she would need these? What was going on with the Supreme Leader? Ralph said the information was from a higher dimension. How high? How many dimensions were she and Mickey involved with? How many other players were in this game besides she and Mickey? Someone from higher up was manipulating Ralph. Was anyone manipulating her?

Mickey(Eden) strode down the alley. It didn't matter. Ralph had given her what she needed to initiate the Crossover. She wasn't stopping now. Nothing could stop her now.

Other Earth

Eden's knuckles were as white as piano key ivory. Mickey had never ridden in a car before at such high speed. Ralph was thoroughly enjoying himself. They sped across a floor, slowed very little as they exited the side of the building, rounded a curve in mid-air nearly nine hundred floors above the earth, spending more time grazing the guard rail than not as they curved up to the next floor, then re-entered the building and accelerated across the straight stretch on that floor toward the opposite end. Eden(Mickey) cast a glance to the back seat. Both soldiers sat stoically upright with barf bags deployed in their laps. Just in case.

The car finally skidded up to a barrier on the eight-hundred and ninety-ninth floor. They passed through a checkpoint manned by heavily-armed soldiers, then proceeded on up to the top floor. Once the car stopped, Mickey couldn't loosen Eden's grip on the dashboard; he feared someone would have to pry her fingers off. The soldiers hopped out on either side of the car to offer aid. Ralph brushed the one off as he climbed out under his own power. The other soldier opened Eden (Mickey)'s door and pulled him gently to Eden's feet. Her face was paler than Col. Sanders.

"I love driving!" Ralph exclaimed. "It rattles my gyroscope."

His vision clearing, Eden(Mickey) examined the side of the car. Scrapes and scratches wove about each other like a Rorschach blot. Mickey could see why Eden's brother stayed so busy. The soldier escorted Eden(Mickey) to a nearby bench, then joined the other soldier alongside the abused car.

Only then could Eden(Mickey) look around to assess the situation. The bench was in a lush garden. Ferns and fronds and all manner of exotic greenery abounded. Flowers of every known hue, and some he didn't know, bloomed in ornate pots and hung from intricate trellises. A bed of five large hibiscus flowers with blooms as big as dinner plates caught his eye. Were those human faces in the middle of the blooms? Other exotica drew his attention away from them. Music from stark bright birds flitting all about filled the aromatic air. Statues of stone and marble and steel and glass populated the rain forest growth and imaginative fountains, where crystalline water splashed athletically about. Looking up, he saw slivers of clear blue sky through the dense foliage. He sought out the peculiar flowers once again, but couldn't find them.

"What do you think of the canopy?" Ralph asked. He pointed off into the distance. "All the top floors have a tropical rain forest."

Eden(Mickey) followed Ralph's sweeping arm. There were dozens of other rooftop gardens, with bridges lacing the 'scrapers together. "Who else lives on these top floors?"

"My advisors. They help me maintain control." Ralph frowned at Eden(Mickey). "Could you dress in something more appropriate than greasy coveralls?"

Eden(Mickey) searched the chip and located a revealing summer dress. Not so bad, Mickey judged, now that he had finally donned a dress. He felt as comfortable as he had wearing Lucy's Vegas bathrobe.

Ralph smiled. "Much, much better." He dipped a cloth in a fountain and cleaned the grease from Eden's face.

Eden(Mickey) leaned forward as Ralph scrubbed, knowing the loose top was giving him a good view of Eden's impressive breasts. While he had them he might as well use them.

"Hello, Eden." Mickey opened Eden's eyes to see Miriam standing before him. She was dressed in a provocative summer dress, too, only on her it hung shapelessly.

"One of your advisors?" Eden(Mickey) asked Ralph.

"Personal advisor," Ralph replied, with a pat on Miriam's bottom. "I'm busy now, babe. Why don't you go feed the gibbons."

Miriam walked off into the garden.

"Let's take a walk." Ralph led the way on a different path through the rooftop garden than Miriam had taken. "How well do you know your history?"

Falling into step alongside, Eden(Mickey) evaded the question. "Only what every school child learns."

"When the Rain Plague began, floating cities were constructed on the oceans, but the wild currents and fierce storms destroyed every single one. So humanity retreated to the heights. This plaza is situated in the Himalayas. We built upward into the sky, and downward into the mountains for a firm foundation."

"Where the Morlox live," Eden(Mickey) added.

"Do you know who the Morlox are?" Ralph asked. When Eden (Mickey) didn't reply, Ralph continued. "Immigrants seeking sanctuary. When their lands flooded they sought refuge here. We gave it to them, underground. They labor beneath us to grow our sustenance and manufacture our delights."

"If we saved them why are they attacking us?"

"Successive generations have grown less appreciative. They want to take over the plaza. And they might. We have grown weak, while they have grown strong. We cannot keep them underground much longer."

"If they grow all our food, why don't they simply starve us out?"

"We control their air. We could snuff them out in a matter of days."

"So why don't we? If they are about to overrun us?"

"We depend on their labor. We need to subdue them, not destroy them."

"What if they win?"

"We can cede them ground level. It would take them a long time to fight their way up here." Ralph motioned to the garden, and the other rooftops.

"Couldn't the Morlox eventually reach even these heights?"

"Not before the Crossover. We'll let the Morlox have this miserable little place. While we move into a wide open wilderness."

"That wilderness is already settled. Do you expect to be welcomed with open arms by the natives?"

"We'll subdue them with our superior technology. They will become the new Morlox. Although I foresee no reason to force them to live underground."

They came to a broad fountain with a stone statue of a slight scaly naked little man jetting streams of water from his mouth and penis. Eden(Mickey) noticed several pieces of cardboard and sheets of dirty plastic piled all around it.

Ralph noticed what Eden(Mickey) was looking at. "I don't know where this garbage is coming from. It looks like a homeless camp." He looked back to Eden(Mickey). "I'm sure you've heard rumors."

"I've heard nothing."

"What did your brother tell you?"

"Nothing."

"Maybe he didn't have the chance," Ralph mused.

"Why don't you tell me."

"The top one percent live up here in the canopy." Ralph swept his arm in a dramatic circle. "The rumors are that only we will crossover."

That's what Eden's brother and Stan was trying to warn him about, Mickey realized. The Crossover wasn't to save their people. It was only to save the rulers. "How would you conquer this other dimension with so few people?"

"It would take time," Ralph said. "But it would be a much better situation. We wouldn't war with our new subjects. Why destroy the world we are moving into? With our superior intellect and technology we could infiltrate the highest reaches of their society. In time their world would be ours, without all the strife and destruction of a war."

"What would happen here?"

"Our people would fight it out with the Morlox. Most likely the Morlox would win without us here to direct the fight against them. But that wouldn't be a concern for you."

"I would cross over with you?"

"Of course. You and your brother and your husband and your lover, even your good friend Priscilla. You will be an invaluable asset in our plan to take over this new world. In fact, you'll be one of my top advisors. We will take good care of you, and your family and friends."

"I'll be among the top one percent of the top one percent?"

Ralph smiled a crooked smile. "Do I detect a trace of mockery?"

"What if I refuse to go along with this 'rumored' plan?"

"You've developed the Crossover Project to such an extent we could complete it without you. But we want you with us in our new land." His face crooked more. "If we must we'd drag you along with us, but leave behind everyone you care about. All your loved ones would fall to the Morlox." Ralph extended an open hand. "Do we have a deal?"

Eden(Mickey) shook it. "Of course. I never considered otherwise. I just wanted to hear what was really going on. I'm glad you were finally truthful with me." Was Ralph buying it, Mickey wondered? Ralph thought he was dealing with Eden. He didn't realize the person shaking his hand was from the dimension he thought he was about to conquer. No way was that going to happen. Mickey would die before he let his world be taken over by these maniacs.

Ralph stepped up close. "I'm glad that's settled. It's best to have things out in the open." He slipped the spaghetti straps off Eden's shoulders and pulled the summer dress down to her waist, then stepped back to admire her bare breasts. "Don't you think it's best to get things out in the open?"

"Of course, sir." Eden(Mickey) forced a smile. What did Mickey care? It wasn't *his* body the old fool was drooling over. Eden(Mickey) turned and walked back toward the car.

Ralph's hand settled on Eden's bottom as he stepped up alongside Eden(Mickey). "I need to get you back to your office so you can complete the project." He squeezed for emphasis.

Eden(Mickey) moaned inwardly, but not from the Supreme Leader's groping. There were worse fates to ponder. Such as climbing back into that car for another stomach-wrenching ride.

Earth

Mickey(Eden) walked into Priscilla's empty office at Northwestern with the wad of papers Ralph had provided. Without the laptop she was forced to use another computer. Priscilla's would do. It was time to get to work. Eden would blow open a hole in the barrier between the dimensions. Supreme Leader Ralph had linked her computer in her office in their dimension to the plaza's power grid. With these printed-out computations homeless Ralph had provided she could reach through from Priscilla's computer in Mickey's dimension to access her computer in her dimension. She would blast this dimension so hard the barrier would crumble, and the entire population of her world could pour into this one. Except the Morlox, of course. They would stay behind and rot without their rulers to take care of them.

Mickey(Eden) sat down at Priscilla's desk and dove into her computer. Window after window opened and flashed across the screen, to be covered up by other just-opened windows. Her fingers danced a frantic jig upon the keyboard. Mickey(Eden) soon grew oblivious to the real world while conducting this symphony of mathematics in the digital world.

Sometime later that night Edie, dressed for work, rolled her mop bucket and cleaning cart into the office. She could tell Mickey(Eden) had been there a long time. Coffee cups, Mountain Dew cans, wrappers from vending machine food formed a layer of litter atop the paper sprawl. Edie watched from the doorway for a while before speaking. "Have you been here all day?"

Her voice nearly jerked Eden out of Mickey's skin. She hadn't noticed Eden's entrance. Yanked from the world of numbers yet not quite into the reality of Priscilla's office, Mickey(Eden) looked up and merely stared slack-faced at the intruder.

"Have you eaten?" Edie walked up to Mickey(Eden), looking down at the garbage on the desk. "A meal? Today?"

Eden shook Mickey's head no.

Edie looked at the screen. "What are you doing?"

Eden massaged Mickey's face, whipped up his hair, desperately tried to clear her mind. "Work. What are you doing here?"

"Work."

Mickey(Eden) searched for a clock, couldn't locate one. "What time is it?"

"After three."

Mickey(Eden) searched for a window.

"A.M."

Mickey(Eden) slumped back in Priscilla's chair. "Sometimes I get caught in a time warp."

"I'm sorry I interrupted."

Mickey(Eden) smiled up at her. "It's okay. I need a break." Mickey's stiff bones creaked upright. "I didn't even realize I need to go to the bathroom. I might have peed my pants if you hadn't come by."

"I'll go get you something to eat." Edie glanced disparagingly down at the desk. "Some real food."

"You said you are working."

"I'll take my lunch break now. We'll eat together."

Mickey(Eden) nodded without nodding. She staggered upright.

Edie started for the door. "I'll bring back dinner."

Mickey(Eden) lunged forward and hugged Edie from behind.

Edie broke out of the fumbling embrace. "Stop it. I don't want you to pee on me."

Mickey(Eden) tried for a smile and a witty come-back, but failed miserably. She watched Edie walk away, Mickey's covetous eyes latching onto her tight denim-wrapped bottom as it rolled down the hall. Once Edie disappeared around a corner, Mickey(Eden) heaved a lecherous sigh then went back to the desk and looked down at the computer as if she didn't know what it was. She assaulted Mickey's hair again. "Where was I?" Mickey(Eden) sat to type a few strokes, and a new window opened. Mickey's crossed-eyes leaned into the screen.

Until she crossed Mickey's legs. "Damn. That doesn't do any good." She grabbed his crotch. "Is this how you hold it, Mickey? By squeezing? Shit." Mickey(Eden) jumped up and fled from the room desperately clutching her toy.

Other Earth

Mick ambushed Eden(Mickey) as soon as the elevator doors opened on the seven-hundred and fifteenth floor. After climbing back into Ralph's car, Eden(Mickey) had pulled the summer dress back up into place. The two accompanying soldiers hadn't even blinked at her bare breasts, while Mick seemed upset merely at the disorder of Eden's hair. He attempted to pat it into order. "What did Ralph want?"

"To make me nauseous. The way he drives!"

Mick's tracks froze beneath his feet. "He drove you? In his car?"

"I thought I was going to die." Eden(Mickey) maneuvered around immobile Mick and continued toward Eden's office.

Mick chased after. "Where did he drive you?"

"To the top floor."

This time it was like Mick had become encased in carbonite.

Eden(Mickey) took a half-dozen more steps before realizing he had left Mick behind. He stopped and turned around. "I don't have time for this, Mick. I've got to get back to work."

Mick stumbled forward. "I've never been chauffeured by Ralph. I've never even been in a car, damn it."

"You have not missed out on anything..."

"And I have never been to the top floor! The highest I've ever been is eight-seventy-five! And that was only because your brother works there!!"

Once Mick caught up, Eden(Mickey) took off again. Only now Mick noticed the sexy summer dress. "Why are you dressed like that?"

Only then did Eden(Mickey) remember how Eden's body was clad. "I forgot what I was wearing." He looked around to see if anyone noticed. Every pair of eyes in the office were on the couple. "I suppose this isn't appropriate for the office."

"What *is* it appropriate for?"

"I'll change as soon as I'm in my office." Eden(Mickey) smiled at Mick. "Besides, you don't get to disapprove of what I wear. We're separated."

"What's it like?"

"The top floor?"

"No, the weather. Of course the top floor."

"There's a garden with some weird big flowers. And there's a fountain with a weird statue of a naked little lizard man."

"No orgies going on?" His face congealed into a scowl. "Or is that why you are dressed like that?"

Mickey swept Mick into Eden's office. "If I was dressing for an orgy I'd dress like this." He clapped once.

Despite his best efforts to remain angry, Mick was bedazzled. Recent memories stirred his loins.

"Please close the door, Mick," Eden(Mickey) said. By the time he turned back around from closing the door, Eden(Mickey) was clothed in appropriate office attire. "All those lewd stories are pure fiction. All I saw up there was Ralph, Miriam and two soldiers. I suppose they were his personal guard. I don't know what Miriam is. If she is his concubine, you'd think he'd get a much younger and better looking one."

"Such as you?"

"All we did was walk through the garden and talk."

"Then why were you wearing that dress?"

"Ralph didn't like the greasy coveralls I had on." Before Mick could ask another stupid question, Eden(Mickey) rushed on. "George came by and took me up to his garage. That's why I changed into coveralls." Eden(Mickey) sat at Eden's desk. "Enough. I've got to get to work."

Mick took a deep calming breath. "Is today the day?"

"It could be. If you leave me alone to work."

"What will it be like? Crossing over?"

"I don't know. No one has ever done it before. And no one ever will if you don't leave."

Mick's entire body heaved a sigh. "Alright. Let me know if you need anything."

Eden(Mickey) looked up from the computer to attempt a sexy smile. "I already did." He lowered Eden's head back to the screen as Mick walked out grinning. Before the door closed behind him, the OPEN ME NOW icon popped up on the laptop screen. Eden(Mickey) clicked the icon. George and Priscilla's faces appeared. "Do you know what Ralph is planning?" Eden(Mickey) whispered.

"It doesn't matter what he's planning," George said.

"We're not going to let it happen," Priscilla said.

"Enough of that," Eden(Mickey) insisted. "No more tag team."

"What are you talking about?" George demanded.

"And no more men. I'm sick of dealing with men. Let me talk with Priscilla."

Priscilla, with a smug expression, nudged George off the screen. "You're a man, Mickey."

"I'm so confused I don't know what I am. I just made love to myself. Or my twin. Who looks more like me than me."

"You'll have time to sort all this out later," Priscilla said. "Now we have to focus."

Eden(Mickey) scanned the calculations on the laptop. "You guys have been busy."

"Yes. While you were dallying with your ex-husband and Ralph, we ran all the computations. We're all set on this end."

"What about on Eden's end?"

Priscilla frowned. "There's been a slight delay."

Earth

Mickey(Eden) sat with Edie at a table in an empty break room lined with vending machines. Scattered across the tabletop were the remains of nearly-digestible food. Mickey(Eden) stared into Edie's solemn face as she chewed the final bite of a sandwich she had not tasted. "Can I tell you something without you running away?"

"Does it involve axes and blood and women's body parts?"

"Crazier than that."

Edie stared with apprehension.

"I'm from another dimension."

Edie relaxed. "You don't look different. And I've seen you naked. You're just a physicist."

"The body is from this dimension, but my consciousness isn't."

"So you're possessed."

"Sort of. But not by a demon."

"Then who are you?"

"I am you."

Edie laughed. "I've heard that old Beatles song. Goo goo g'joob."

"Why were you so attracted to me? At first sight?"

"I haven't had time to think about it."

"Take time now."

"I told you I'm not like this."

"I know you're not. Because I'm not."

"Are you trying to get rid of me? You've had your fun and now it's time to get back to work?"

"I'm telling you that you've become involved in an earth-shaking event. I want you to be aware of it."

Edie abruptly stood. "*I've* got to get back to work."

"You listen to hard rock music."

Edie gathered up the garbage. She couldn't resist cleaning, it was her way of life.

"Your favorite color is blue."

Edie carried the garbage to a can.

Mickey(Eden) hopped up to follow. "You like Impressionist paintings." Edie headed for the door. Mickey(Eden) was at her heels. "You enjoy gardening, tomatoes in particular."

Edie stopped in the doorway to frown back at Mickey(Eden). "You saw the cherry tomato plants on my balcony."

Mickey(Eden) spewed on without pause. "You enjoy reading, and your favorites are mysteries and thrillers. You enjoy long walks. You watch little TV, but enjoy documentaries."

"Did you research me?"

"No need to."

"Then what was the name of my first pet?"

"I don't know. But most likely it was a dog. You detest cats."

Edie stared hatefully.

"I don't know the particulars of your history because our life paths are different. Different initial conditions, different choices, different random events. But I know generalities because we share the same likes and dislikes. We share the same core. We are the same."

"So you're a woman trapped in a man's body?"

"For the moment, yes."

"There are doctors who can help you with that." Edie burst out the door.

Mickey(Eden) watched her go. Well, Eden had tried to be honest. But it wasn't to be. She would catch up with Edie after the Crossover. As she had promised others. Now it was time to do the deed. Nearly time. There was one more task to take care of. Mickey(Eden) bolted from the break room.

Other Earth

Mickey stewed at Eden's desk in front of the laptop. "What is she waiting for?"

On screen, Priscilla seemed stumped. "I don't know."

"So what's going on?"

"She's just sitting there staring at the computer."

"She's not working?"

"She's finished, from what I can tell." Priscilla gazed off-screen. "George?"

From off-screen, "So now I'm allowed to speak."

"Just tell me what she's doing!" Eden(Mickey) yelled.

"She made a phone call earlier," George said, "about twenty minutes ago."

"You've got company," Priscilla said. The screen went blank.

The door opened. George walked in, followed by Stan with his gun in hand. Neither looked happy. George was the first to growl. "Why did you come back from the top floor dressed for a cocktail party? Everybody on this floor is talking about it."

Stan followed. "You know there is a reason the words 'cock' and 'tail' are used to describe those kinds of parties."

"Shut the door," Eden(Mickey) commanded.

Stan slammed it. "What was going on with you and Ralph?"

"I was gathering information. Ralph is planning on leaving ninety-nine per cent of the population behind."

"I knew it!" George slapped the desk. "That's what I was trying to tell you in the garage."

"What are you two doing now?" Eden(Mickey) asked.

"I'm supposed to be escorting your brother to jail." Stan holstered his gun. "But screw that. He's family."

"Yeah." George grinned at Stan. "So we came by here instead to see what's going on."

Eden(Mickey) motioned toward the laptop. "The Crossover Program is ready to run."

George approached the desk to look at the screen, which was blank. "Nothing is going on."

"Yet." Eden(Mickey) looked from George to Stan. "You two need to leave. You're interrupting my work."

"We aren't going anywhere, sis," George said.

"We came here to hide out," Stan said. "We'll both be thrown in jail if they catch us."

The door opened and Mick walked in. He froze upon seeing Stan. "What's he doing here?"

"Close the door, Mick," Eden(Mickey) ordered.

When Mick didn't comply, Stan kicked it closed.

Mick backed away from Stan. "What's going on, Eden?"

Mickey threw Eden's arms up in frustration. "I am about to initiate the Crossover, and you men keep barging in here! I need all of you to get out so I can concentrate!"

Mick's eyes grew large. "I want to stay and witness the moment. This is historic. I promise I'll be quiet."

"Yeah, sis," George said. "We want to watch."

Stan patted his sidearm. "You need someone to guard the door. So no one else comes in."

The screen came to life with Priscilla's face. "Your partner should stay off-screen," Eden(Mickey) blurted out before Priscilla could speak. "Another George is here."

George stared at the laptop screen. "Why did you warn Priscilla about me being here?"

"What does Priscilla know about the Crossover Project?" Mick asked. "We've wiped her several times. She shouldn't know much about anything."

Eden(Mickey) glared from one to the other. "I thought you two took a vow of silence."

"Mickey!" Priscilla exclaimed from the screen.

"What?" Mick responded, stooping before the screen.

Eden(Mickey) shoved him away. "She's talking to me." He turned back to the laptop. "What?"

"George said someone just walked into the room where Eden is working," Priscilla said.

"No I didn't," George said.

"You are right here working in this room, Eden," Mick said.

"And no one walked in," Stan said. "I've got the door covered."

"Shut up!" Eden(Mickey) screamed. "All of you!" Back to the screen, "Who is it?"

"We have no idea."

Earth

Mickey(Eden) rose from Priscilla's desk to greet Carl Friedrich. She smiled with joy, while the new arrival had a stern expression. "What's the emergency?"

"I wanted you here for this," Mickey(Eden) said.

"Here for what?" He looked around. "What are you doing here? Did you break into the college?"

Edie walked in.

Seeing her, and how she was dressed, Carl Friedrich assumed the worst. "Are you a janitor?" he directed toward Mickey(Eden).

"*I* am," Edie said. "Do you have a problem with that?"

Carl Friedrich ignored her. "Why are you messing with that computer? You could get arrested."

"He's a physicist," Edie exclaimed. "And a very smart one, too." She glanced at Mickey(Eden) "If a little crazy."

Mickey(Eden) stepped between the two. "Both of you, settle down." She looked to Carl Friedrich. "I wanted you here with me when the Crossover happens. So I know you're safe." She turned to the other. "I'm glad you came back, Edie. I want to keep you safe, too."

"Safe from what?" Carl Friedrich asked. "I was sitting at home watching Legion. They were all singing 'Peace, Love, and Understanding'. You know the episode?" Mickey(Eden) and Edie returned blank stares. "Do you know the song?"

"Of course," Edie replied, "Elvis Costello". The blank stare remained affixed on Mickey(Eden)'s face.

"When I get this wild call from this crazy man I just met this afternoon to rush over to the college, that it was an emergency."

"So why did you come?" Mickey(Eden) asked. Carl Friedrich's face went blank, also. "If I was a crazy man who you'd just met this afternoon, why did you rush over here in the middle of the night?"

With a quiet curse, Carl Friedrich turned away.

"I believe you were compelled to."

He headed for the door.

"Don't leave," Edie said.

Carl Friedrich and Mickey(Eden) both turned their surprised eyes on Edie.

"I want you to be safe, too," Edie said. "I don't know why."

"You two don't even know me," Carl Friedrich said.

"I know," Mickey(Eden) said. "But I'm dying to."

Two sets of eyes turned on Edie. "I have no idea why I'm here," she responded to their stares.

"We are all connected," Mickey(Eden) said, "in ways you could never comprehend." She rushed around to sit before the computer. "But you are about to witness a historic event. I want you both here with me when it happens." She beseeched one then the other. "Will you stay? I promise you will not be disappointed."

At last, Carl Friedrich smiled. "You couldn't get me out of here with a bulldozer, now."

"Every sensible voice in my head is telling me to run," Edie said. "But I haven't been listening to any of them since I met you."

"Good," Mickey(Eden) said. "Now gather around and steel yourselves. We are about to enter The Twilight Moan."

Carl Friedrich and Edie exchanged a questioning glance. "Do you mean The Twilight Zone?" he asked.

"Yeah," Edie seconded.

Mickey(Eden) glanced up. "Yeah? Okay, then. The Twilight Zone. With Rob Sterling?"

"Rod," Carl Friedrich corrected.

"Serling," Edie added.

"Stifle yourselves. You two are spoiling the moment." Mickey (Eden) poised the index finger of her right hand over the Enter key.

Other Earth

Eden(Mickey) sat at Eden's desk with the index finger of her right hand poised above the Enter key of the laptop. Mick stood behind the chair, George and Stan stood on either side, all focused upon Priscilla's image on the screen. "Ready. Ready. Ready," George said in a calm voice off-screen.

"That sounds like me," Eden's brother George blurted.

"Shut up, George!" Eden(Mickey) barked.

"I'm sorry," digital George said in an offended voice that didn't sound apologetic at all.

Priscilla took over. "Wait for it, Mickey, wait."

Mick turned his gaze from the laptop screen to Eden(Mickey). "What am I waiting for?"

"Shut up!!" Eden(Mickey) fumed while holding her breath, not an easy thing to do. George and Stan placed reassuring hands upon Eden's shoulders. Mick knocked Stan's hand off, and replaced it with his own. Eden(Mickey) remained riveted.

"Now!" Priscilla and George exclaimed simultaneously.

Eden(Mickey) pressed enter.

Earth

Mickey(Eden) pressed Enter.

Priscilla ran into the room. "What are you doing in my office, Mickey? On my computer?"

A blizzard of chalk dust filled the air. All four were obscured in the swirling white.

PART THREE
UP, UP, UP...

1.

"Mickey."

George's face hovered before Eden's just-opened eyes. "Who are you?"

"George."

"Which George?"

"The one from your laptop screen."

Mickey shifted Eden's eyes about. Everything was hazy. Or blurry? Was it what he was looking at, or what he was looking at it with, that was messed up? "Where am I?"

"In my dimension."

"Am I alive?"

George smiled. "What do you think?"

"I take nothing for granted anymore."

"People have to take things for granted. For example, when you go to bed at night you take it for granted you will wake up in the morning. If you didn't, you'd be too terrified to ever go to sleep. But people often don't wake up. Many pass away in their sleep. I love that little nursery rhyme we teach our children. 'If I should die before I wake, I pray the Lord my soul to take.' Death should never rhyme."

"Are you ever going to answer my question?"

"You are alive. So far."

Eden(Mickey) could see nothing but a swirling grey fog on all sides. "What happened?"

"I don't know."

Eden's wandering eyes focused once more on George's looming face. "I thought you and Priscilla were in charge."

"We did, too. But something went wrong. We think a higher power intervened."

"From a higher dimension?"

"We assume."

"Did anyone else come through?"

"I don't know."

"Hey, I can move!" Eden(Mickey) exclaimed happily after he learned he was able to punch George in the mouth.

"I noticed," George said from the ground while massaging his bleeding lip. "Why did you move so aggressively?"

"Tell me what happened!"

"I can only tell you what I know. All that I know is you have traveled from Eden's dimension into my dimension."

"From a lower to a higher dimension, same as before." Eden (Mickey) looked Eden's body over with a frown that could have registered eight on the Richter Scale. Her body was clad in the same office attire it had been wearing when he had pressed the enter key back in Eden's office. "Damn. I was so hoping to see my own body again." The frown eased as Mickey's unquenchable curiosity began pondering the ponderables. "It was my body this time. I mean Eden's body. A physical body. That passed through. Not my consciousness into another body, like last time." Mickey flexed Eden's joints and stretched. "Sorry for hitting you. I was getting frustrated."

Eden(Mickey) extended his exploration out beyond the immediate region of the two of them. The billowing grey fog they were shrouded in had no distinguishing characteristics. "Your dimension isn't much to look at."

"That's because you aren't seeing much of it. This is the default setting. Like a New Blank Document just opened in Word. All you see is white, none of the underlying format commands."

"Can you reveal codes?"

George's bloody teeth were revealed in a smile. "Do you think you can handle it?"

"Are you serious? After what I've been through?"

George snapped his fingers.

The greyness swirled away as if down a drain. It was replaced by bright points of light flashing through blackness all around Eden(Mickey) and George, like camera flashes going off during a Super Bowl halftime show. These sudden lights streaked a short distance then faded away. "What are these lights?"

"Subatomic particles. Virtual particles. Popping in and out of existence."

Eden(Mickey) looked around entranced by the bright short-lived dashing jets. "Creation and annihilation, creation and annihilation…" George recited.

"What a waste of time," Eden(Mickey) interjected. "I've heard that one before. How am I seeing them?"

"My dimension is within the quantum foam. Approximately Planck-length."

Eden(Mickey) spun around and around, watching the many lights burst into brilliance then fade away as they flew on brief arcing trajectories through the void. "Virtual particles only exist for picoseconds. These lights are lasting much longer."

"Time is relative. In my dimension it can pass much more slowly than it does in yours. That's why it took us so long to complete the calculations needed to transport you out of Eden's dimension."

"It didn't take that long."

"Twenty-three years and four months." After Eden's lower jaw dropped open, George continued. "This has been my life's work."

An image materialized in the void of Eden plummeting through a blizzard in the mountains, then faded away. "What just happened to Eden?"

"I have no idea."

"Do you get people falling through your dimension often?"

"We didn't use to."

Their environment was rocked as if by an explosion. Eden(Mickey) grabbed George to keep from falling. "What was that?"

"A perturbation. My dimension is very unsettled."

"Like the rapidly bubbling surface of a pot of boiling water."

"Rapidly is a relative term."

Eden(Mickey) stopped revolving. "Okay. I'll accept I'm in the quantum foam. Ant Man did that. Now how do I get back to my own dimension?"

"I don't know how you ended up in mine." When Eden(Mickey) reared back to swing again, George rushed on. "I and Priscilla didn't cause this to happen. Someone else hijacked your inter-dimensional travel and directed you here."

Mickey lowered Eden's balled fist. "Where did Eden end up? She has my body." Another turbulence passed through. Mickey maintained balance this time without assistance as the floor rolled beneath Eden's feet.

George grinned. "You're adapting to my dimension."

"I don't want to adapt to it." Eden(Mickey) relaxed as the ground calmed. "I want to get out of it and back to mine. Now where is my body?"

"It's here, just in a different place. Could be at a different time, too. Space and time are fluid at this level of existence."

"Does that mean you can time travel?"

"Sort of." George pointed behind Eden(Mickey). He saw an image of Eden towering over George as he lay on the ground bleeding from the lip. "That's when you punched me."

"You filmed it. Big deal."

"No need to. The event can pop up at any time, before or after it originally happened." George pointed in another direction. "I couldn't have filmed this."

Eden(Mickey) looked to see an enraged Mickey punching Eden in the face, laying her out at his feet. "When did this happen?"

"In a couple of seconds, I believe," George answered.

"Mickey, you rotten son of a bitch!"

George smiled bigger than ever before. "Uh-oh. Looks like Priscilla has arrived with Eden."

Mickey(Eden) approached from out of the mist that had reappeared with her shouted words, blocking from view the flashing of the emergence and annihilation of matter-antimatter pairs. "You fucked my husband!"

Eden(Mickey) laughed. "With your body."

Mickey(Eden) punched Eden(Mickey), knocking him on Eden's butt, just as Eden(Mickey) had witnessed happen moments earlier. "And what was that bit with Laurie about?" Mickey(Eden) demanded.

Mickey rubbed Eden's sore jaw as he looked up at Mickey(Eden). "I didn't know I could hit that hard."

"That was me. With your fist. Get up."

Eden(Mickey) stayed where he was. "So you can knock me down again?"

"I won't hit you again," Mickey(Eden) said. "I need that body back in good condition."

Priscilla emerged from the fog and walked up alongside George. "Which one hit you?"

"Mickey." When Priscilla continued to stare, George attempted to clarify. "The Mickey inside Eden."

Priscilla nodded. "You're lucky. Looks like the Eden inside Mickey can hit harder."

"Did you have to tell her everything?" Eden(Mickey) yelled up at Priscilla.

"I'll tell you whatever you want to know, Mickey," George said. "Although you made it difficult for me to talk." He touched his still-bleeding lip.

"First off, is anyone else here?" Eden(Mickey) demanded.

"From your dimension, Carl Friedrich, Edie, and Priscilla. One of the other Priscillas. The Teaching Assistant math major." George looked to Mickey(Eden). "From Eden's dimension, her lover Stan, her brother George, and her ex-husband Mick."

Eden(Mickey) stood, keeping a wary eye on Mickey(Eden). "Why all these people?"

"They were close to you and Eden when the Shattering occurred."

"You mean the Crossover?" Mickey(Eden) asked.

"That's what you call it," Priscilla said. "We call it the Shattering. A more appropriate term for what has happened."

"Why does the cleaning woman look so much like Eden?" Eden (Mickey) asked.

"For the same reason you look so much like Eden's ex-husband." George answered.

Images flooded Eden(Mickey)'s mind of Edie embracing Mickey, kissing him, taking off her blouse, running into the living room of her apartment in her underwear, removing her robe to appear naked before him, climbing into bed with him, them making love, again, again, again, in several different positions.

When Eden(Mickey)'s vision cleared, he turned to Mickey(Eden). "Is that like what Priscilla showed you?"

"Of you and Mick. My husband Mick. Ex-husband. A mess I'm going to have a hell of a time untangling. What were you thinking?"

"It looked like you enjoyed making love to yourself," Eden(Mickey) said. "To the cleaning woman. As me."

"How did *you* like it?" Mickey(Eden) asked. "Making love to yourself? To my ex-husband? As me?"

"I almost gagged."

"Really? That's the same reaction I've had lately."

"Who is that man who came here with you?"

"You have to ask?" Getting no response, Mickey(Eden) continued. "He's my son."

Eden(Mickey) looked down at Eden's stomach. "The child I'm carrying?"

"Yes!" Mickey(Eden) yelled, her fury blazing anew. "And you better have taken good care of him!"

"How would I know how to take care of an unborn child?"

"If you don't know, you are going to learn real quick."

"Mickey," George interceded in a calming voice.

"Eden," Priscilla joined in. "We wanted to give you two a chance to get reacquainted, but there are important matters to attend to."

Mickey(Eden) snapped to attention. Eden(Mickey) slouched up alongside her.

"As far as we know," George began, "You eight were the only ones to pass into our dimension."

"Tell us how you plan to get us back to our proper dimensions," Mickey(Eden) said.

"First," Eden(Mickey) said, "something more urgent. Get us back into our proper bodies."

"We can't do that," George admitted.

"Who can?" Eden(Mickey) asked.

"Whoever made *this* happen, I suppose," Priscilla said.

"*Our* plan was to reverse what had happened to start with," George said. "That's what the program we loaded onto your laptop was supposed to do, Mickey. Merely backtrack. You, Mickey, would have passed back into your dimension back into your body. You, Eden, would have done the same. No harm, no foul. Mickey, you wouldn't have fallen for any more tricks Eden might try, while Eden couldn't have accomplished anything on her own. She needs a willing accomplice from a lower dimension."

"By the way, here's your laptop back." Priscilla handed Hypatia to Eden(Mickey).

While an overjoyed Eden(Mickey) looked the laptop over, Mickey (Eden) took over the questioning. "So what happened?"

"Someone from a higher dimension initiated his or her own strategy," Priscilla said.

"It was Ralph," Mickey(Eden) said.

Eden(Mickey) looked up from the laptop. "The Supreme Leader?"

"No," Mickey(Eden) said. "The homeless guy. He's been running things from the start."

"Ralph?" Eden(Mickey) said in disbelief. "The guy living in the alley outside my apartment?"

"Apparently there was a reason he chose your alley to take up residence in," Mickey(Eden) said. "It wasn't a random alley."

"I can't believe Ralph is running the show," Eden(Mickey) said without diverting his attention from Hypatia. "Just the other day I caught him picking through my garbage."

"That brings us back to my question." Seeing Eden(Mickey) was about to object, she rushed on. "Since you can't accomplish what Mickey is asking of you."

Eden(Mickey) turned his attention back to Hypatia. Until a brilliant ball of light the size of a softball whizzed out of the fog and through his chest to exit out his back and disappear into the fog. He screamed. When he realized he could still speak, he did, loudly. "What was that?!"

"A neutrino," George answered calmly. "It happens all the time."

"They hardly ever interact with anything," Priscilla said. "You should be undamaged."

"It interacted with my heart," Eden(Mickey) said. "It's banging away like it's trying to escape my chest." He looked to Mickey(Eden). "I thought I was dead."

"You better not let my body die."

Eden(Mickey) looked to Priscilla. "If this body dies, do I die along with it?"

"Most assuredly."

Mickey(Eden) looked to George. "Then I'd be stuck with his body?"

"Most assuredly."

"Listen to this," Eden(Mickey) said, reading from the laptop. "'The Dynamic Programming Principal', by Samuel N. Cohen. 'Searching forwards for/Control is peering through fog/- do it in reverse'." He indicated the fog all around them. "Appropriate."

"Ignore Mickey," Mickey(Eden) said to George and Priscilla. "He's losing it. So what's the plan?"

George and Priscilla looked at each other with blank faces. "We don't have one," George said.

"We need to work on one," Priscilla said with a sigh. "There goes another twenty-three years." They both walked off into the billowing fog.

Electronica music began playing. A bubble appeared between the remaining two people. It expanded like a balloon. Mickey(Eden) darted around the growing bubble to yank the laptop from Eden(Mickey)'s hands and slap the lid closed, killing the music. The bubble began shrinking.

"What the hell, Eden!"

"I do not intend to die in a strange dimension with that crap ringing in my ears." Eden(Mickey) reached for the laptop, but Mickey (Eden) clutched it ever more tightly. "Didn't you see a bubble was forming?"

"Not the weirdest thing I've seen happen lately."

"Haven't you heard of sonoluminesence?" Seeing the blank expression, she plowed on. "Imagine you run sound waves through a liquid, such as the moisture in this fog, intense enough to create a bubble, a process called cavitation. That was exactly what your electronica music was doing. Since the newly formed bubble was a very low-pressure area in the middle of the higher pressure of the surrounding fog, it would have quickly collapsed."

"Quickly is a relative term here."

"Shut up, runt. If that bubble had burst we'd be dead. The interior of the bubble gets insanely hot. Laboratories have measured the center of a bubble like that at thousands of degrees, with recorded temperatures going as high as twenty thousand degrees Celsius. In comparison, the surface of the sun is only six thousand degrees Celsius.

"The interior is much hotter."

"Shut up, runt. The best way to think of it is as a star in a jar. There would be a blue flash of light in the center of the bubble, normally lasting for just a few trillionths of a second. But time is messed up in this dimension, so who knows how long it could last. This flash of heat and light is sonoluminesence. This isn't just some weird quantum effect, either. It exists in the macro world, too. Ever hear of the mantis shrimp? It hunts by snapping its forelimbs so quickly that it creates cavitation bubbles. The sonoluminesence that follows sends out shock waves that kill its prey. Could sonoluminescent bubbles be made even hotter, to achieve the millions of degrees needed to start a nuclear fusion reaction? Right now, no one really knows what the limitations are."

"So we could have been incinerated in a nuclear event?" Eden (Mickey) asked.

"With a blast of heat many times hotter than the surface of the Sun." Mickey(Eden) handed the laptop back. "No more music while we are in this dimension."

Mickey cradled the laptop to Eden's chest. "When I get back to my dimension I can't wait to let Bicep know their music nearly set off a nuclear explosion."

"If we live that long."

"Do you think we're really in danger here? I just got blasted by a neutrino and it didn't hurt me. Besides, George and Priscilla will figure something out."

"George and Priscilla spent twenty-three years on their first plan, and that didn't work. We need to make our own plan."

"It was *your* plan that got us in this mess."

"Let's check on the others," Mickey(Eden) said.

"You can do that?"

Mickey(Eden) gave a wicked smile. "George didn't teach you how to maneuver through this fluid spacetime?"

Mickey shook Eden's head no.

"Priscilla showed me how. Maybe I'll just leave you here all alone."

"It's your body you'll be abandoning. I might go crazy from loneliness and kill it. Loneliness is a prime cause of suicide, you know."

"Damn." Eden held out Mickey's hand. "Let's go, then."

Eden(Mickey) took the offered hand, and they walked off into the fog. "Where are we going?"

"To find my son."

2.

Carl Friedrich jumped to his feet when Mickey(Eden) and Eden (Mickey) emerged from the fog. "Did we die?!"

Eden(Mickey) laughed. "Do you know why so many people assume they are dead when they find themselves in a weird situation? Because they have no idea what the afterlife looks like. I mean, this could be Heaven *or* Hell."

Mickey(Eden) ignored him and rushed over to hug Carl Friedrich. "Are you okay?"

Carl Friedrich shoved Mickey(Eden) away. "Don't do that!"

Mickey(Eden) held up both arms in surrender. "Okay. Just stay calm." Electronica music began playing. She shot a murderous gaze at Eden(Mickey) and the open laptop. "Really?" A bubble swelled in the midst of the three.

"Sorry. Just wanted to see if it would happen again." Eden(Mickey) cut off the music and closed the laptop. "I *do* experiment once in a while." The bubble subsided.

"What was that?!" Carl Friedrich screamed.

Eden(Mickey) shrugged. "A fiery death."

Mickey(Eden) scowled at him. "You're not helping."

Carl Friedrich screamed again. "Where are we?!"

"In the quantum foam," Eden(Mickey) said. He turned to Mickey(Eden). "Show him."

"He's not ready for that yet," Mickey(Eden) said. "He needs something familiar to reassure him. I've got a McDonalds hologram file on my chip. Activate it."

"Do you think your holograms work in this dimension?"

"You're not standing there naked, are you?"

Eden(Mickey) glowed with realization. "You're right. I've gotten so used to your holograms I accept them as real."

"That's the whole idea, runt."

"Why do you keep calling me that? I'm not *that* short."

"I wasn't referring to your height."

Eden(Mickey) was mortified. "You've seen it!"

"Of course I've seen it. I've *used* it. But I wasn't referring to your manhood, either." Reveling in the baffled expression on her face, Mickey(Eden) said, "The name refers to your intellect. You are a runt compared to me."

"Shut up!" Carl Friedrich demanded. "Tell me what's happened to us or I'll start hitting you two."

Eden(Mickey) smiled. "You wouldn't hit your own mother."

"I'm his mother!" Mickey(Eden) objected.

Mickey patted Eden's stomach. "I'm carrying him."

Carl Friedrich decked Mickey(Eden). He turned to Eden(Mickey). "You're next."

"Okay," Eden(Mickey) said in a calming voice. "Just don't hit me anymore."

"I didn't hit you," Carl Friedrich said.

Mickey(Eden) rose to his feet. "He's referring to his body."

Carl Friedrich drew back his fist at Eden(Mickey).

Mickey(Eden) lunged forward to restrain his arm. "You shouldn't hit a pregnant woman."

That gave him pause. "She's pregnant?"

"Yes," Eden(Mickey) said, coming out of his cower. "With you. So you'd be hitting yourself."

Carl Friedrich was near tears. "Please."

Mickey(Eden) turned toward Eden(Mickey). "Ever locate that McDonalds file?"

Eden(Mickey) closed Eden's eyes. A moment later the three were standing in the middle of an empty McDonalds.

Carl Friedrich ran to the nearest door. It was locked. He kicked it and beat on it with his fists.

"You really thought this would be a good idea?" Eden(Mickey) asked.

"It's a place familiar to him," Mickey(Eden) said. "He'll calm down in a minute."

Carl Friedrich ran to another door and began punching and kicking it.

"He's going to hurt himself," Eden(Mickey) said.

Mickey(Eden) approached Carl Friedrich. "Carl, honey, stop."

Carl Friedrich looked at her as if she were a zombie.

"Settle down, and we'll explain what is going on." When he stopped assaulting the door, Mickey(Eden) took him by the hand and led him to a table.

"I prefer a booth," Carl Friedrich said.

"He's in shock," Eden(Mickey) offered. Eden nodded Mickey's head in agreement as she led Carl Friedrich to a booth.

Mickey(Eden) sat in the booth next to Carl Friedrich, and slipped an arm around his shoulders. "We traveled to a different dimension."

His eyes grew large. "You mean like Stranger Things? The upside-down? Are there monsters?"

"I haven't seen any monsters here." Mickey(Eden) said.

"Any *inhuman* monsters," Eden(Mickey) added, glaring across the table at Mickey(Eden).

"Why did we come here?" Carl Friedrich asked.

"We didn't mean to come here," Mickey(Eden) continued.

"She *meant* to go to our dimension, Carl Friedrich, yours and mine, and destroy it," Eden(Mickey) said. "Talk about monsters."

Carl Friedrich craned his neck to look back at the counter. "Can I have a Happy Meal?"

"You're hungry?" Eden(Mickey) asked.

"Cut him some slack," Mickey(Eden) said. "He's in shock."

"No, that was an honest question," Eden(Mickey) insisted. "Are you hungry?"

"No," Carl Friedrich said. "I just want the toy."

Eden(Mickey) turned to Mickey(Eden). "Are you hungry?"

"Of course not."

"Me neither. And I'm not thirsty. It's been hours since I ate or drank anything. I should be hungry and thirsty. Anybody need to go to the bathroom?" The two heads across from him indicated no.

Eden(Mickey) smiled at Mickey(Eden). "Now listen to what the runt has figured out, Eden. George, or Priscilla, I can't remember which, told me time is fluid in their dimension. That made no sense to me then. But now that I'm experiencing it, it's starting to. Time may not be passing at all for us in this dimension. Or it may be passing so slowly we don't even notice. Or so rapidly weeks whip past us like minutes. It all depends on your frame of reference. George and Priscilla's twenty-three years seemed like only days to us. That's why we aren't hungry or thirsty, or have to relieve ourselves. Very few seconds, perhaps none at all, have passed for us since we got here. We're feeling tired and miserable, sure, but that's from what we went through before traveling here, it's not from anything we've done since we got here." Eden (Mickey) grinned. "Take that, runt!"

"You think they've got chocolate turtle sundaes here?" Carl Friedrich asked, still craning his neck.

Mickey(Eden) mulled it over. "So we will never age in this dimension. Or we'll age very slowly. We would be practically immortal."

"We might not age, but we can certainly die. What if some other particle besides a neutrino had hit me? A highly interactive massive particle like a Higgs boson? I'd be dead meat. And so would your body."

"Why would we be brought here just to die. It doesn't make sense. Someone from a dimension higher than George and Priscilla's sent us into this dimension for a reason."

"Maybe they're not that good," Eden(Mickey) suggested. "They didn't just grab me and you. They grabbed everybody near us at the time, also. So they didn't use a surgeon's scalpel. It's like they're operating with a machete."

"Then we're on our own," Mickey(Eden) said.

"George and Priscilla said they were working on the problem."

"Do you want to depend on those two goofballs?" Mickey(Eden) picked up Hypatia. "Let's see what you've got on this." She opened the laptop and began searching through the files. "You don't know how hard I looked for this thing."

"Can I have some crayons?" Carl Friedrich asked.

"Go get our son some crayons," Mickey(Eden) said, lost in computer files.

"That's sweet," Eden(Mickey) said. "To consider him *our* son." He went off in search of coloring supplies.

Carl Friedrich looked at the laptop screen. "What are you doing, Daddy?"

"I'm not your daddy," Mickey(Eden) replied, distracted. "I'm your mother. You don't really want your Daddy. He's a runt. He went off to look for crayons. Crayon holograms are on my chip. He could just make them appear."

Eden(Mickey) returned empty-handed. "I can't find any."

"Sit down, runt," Mickey(Eden) said. "Everything we need is on your laptop. If I hadn't wasted so much time searching for this we wouldn't be in this situation. I'd have carried out the Crossover much sooner, before you and George and Priscilla had a chance to sabotage it."

Eden(Mickey) sat. "If you'd had the laptop, Ralph and his cronies would have been sitting pretty, while the rest of your world would have been left behind to rot."

"What are you talking about?"

"He was double-crossing you, Eden. Ralph had no intention of bringing all your people into my dimension. Only he and his cohorts would have crossed over, abandoning everyone else to the Morlox."

"That's a lie." Seeing how Eden(Mickey) continued to mock, she went on. "How did you learn this?"

"Ralph told me. After he stripped me half-naked." Seeing the fire rise in Mickey(Eden)'s countenance, he rushed on. "Maybe he did that *after* he told me. I can't remember."

"Who else did you expose my body to?"

"I don't know. It wasn't *my* body, what did I care."

"What all did you do to my body?"

"I didn't do anything to it. But somebody bit you on the butt." As Mickey(Eden) stared at him with growing hatred, he stood. "I'll show you. Carl Friedrich, turn your head."

After Carl Friedrich did, Eden(Mickey) turned around and clapped once.

"My god, that's infected!" Mickey(Eden) touched the sore.

"Oww!" Eden(Mickey) moved out of her reach. "It's sore. It really hurt when Ralph grabbed me there."

"Ralph grabbed my butt?"

"There's more important things to consider than your butt."

"Why doesn't Mommy have any clothes on?" They both looked to see Carl Friedrich had turned back around.

A Wonder Woman outfit appeared on Eden(Mickey).

Carl Friedrich clapped with joy. "Wonder Woman!"

"Really?" Mickey(Eden) remarked.

"*You* designed it," Eden(Mickey) returned.

"For Halloween."

"It'll keep our son happy. Now listen. If you don't believe me about Ralph's plot, ask George. Your brother George. And Stan. They both knew about it."

"I will." Mickey(Eden) stood. "You stay here with Carl Friedrich. I'll go get everybody else."

"You're bringing everyone into this hologram?"

"We have to gather somewhere. Why not here? We all deserve a break today."

"I'm lovin' it!" Carl Friedrich exclaimed.

Mickey(Eden) disappeared into the fog that suddenly swirled into McDonalds.

Eden(Mickey) eased back down into the booth as the fog swirled away, squirming until he found a way to sit that didn't hurt. "Carl Friedrich, huh? She named you after Gauss? That's cool."

Carl Friedrich's face grew stormy. "Where's my happy meal?"

3.

Mickey(Eden) emerged from the fog to find Edie curled into a ball on the white surface of a new blank Word document of a world. Her head shot up with pure venom in her eyes. "What did you do?!"

"Let's wait to talk about it until we get everybody together," Mickey(Eden) said softly, approaching the balled fury with great caution.

"How many is everybody?"

"There are eight of us." Mickey(Eden) reached out a hand.

Edie pulled herself to her feet with the offered assistance. "Where are we going?"

"McDonalds."

~ * ~

Mickey(Eden) emerged from the fog to find Priscilla pacing in a circle. She ran up and seized Mickey(Eden) with both hands. "Where are we?"

"In another dimension."

"Can we get back?"

"Let's wait and talk about it when we're all together."

"Who else is here?"

"Mickey." Mickey(Eden) dismissed her confused look. "And others." She led her into the fog. "I'll show you."

~ * ~

Mickey(Eden) emerged from the fog to find her brother George stretched out asleep on the ground. "Really?"

George opened his eyes. "Hi, Mick."

"It's not Mick. Certainly not the slime ball Mick you know." Eden shook Mickey's head. "How can you sleep?"

George stretched. "I figured somebody'd be by eventually. How's the Crossover going? Did Ralph pull it off?"

"So Mickey was telling the truth."

"Why do you keep referring to yourself in the third person?"

"Ralph was planning to double-cross me?"

George stared, rubbing his chin.

Mickey(Eden) sighed. "To double-cross your sister, then?"

"Yes, just like me and Stan told her. Is she okay?"

"She's around. Get up."

George climbed to his feet. "Where are we going?"

"McDonalds."

~ * ~

Mickey(Eden) emerged from the fog to find Mick reciting multiplication tables. Seeing himself approach, he didn't complete the 22's. "Are you the me from the lower dimension?"

"Sort of."

"How can it be 'sort of'? You look just like me."

"We're not in the lower dimension. We're in a higher dimension."

"We went the wrong direction!"

"I'll answer all your questions when we're all together."

"How many people crossed-over?"

"Eight."

"Is that all?! Damn, so Ralph's plan worked."

"It didn't work. He's not one of the eight." Mickey(Eden) reluctantly took his hand. "One more thing, Mick. Just because you slept with my body doesn't mean we're back together."

Mick tried to pull his hand free, but failed. "I never slept with you! I've never slept with *any* man! I'm not…"

And they were gone.

~ * ~

Mickey(Eden) emerged from the fog to find Stan standing erect with feet planted wide, shoulders squared and chest out, hands clasped behind his back. He appeared ready for anything.

"I'm sorry for getting you into this, Stan," Mickey(Eden) said.

"*You* didn't get me into anything."

Mickey(Eden) smiled. "But I'm glad you're here. I can't think of anyone I'd rather have protecting me."

"Why would I protect you?"

Eden extended Mickey's hand. "Come with me and I'll tell you why."

"Where are we going?"

"To where everyone else is."

Stan grasped the outstretched hand. "Is Eden okay?"

"Mostly."

~ * ~

When Mickey(Eden) and Stan stepped out of the fog into McDonalds, Eden(Mickey) was flat on the floor at Carl Friedrich's feet, bleeding profusely. Mick and George were holding Carl Friedrich back, and Edie and Priscilla were standing next to each other watching from a safe distance.

Stan charged forward and pummeled Carl Friedrich to the floor. He jumped onto his chest and continued whaling away on him.

George and Mick seized Stan. They were unable to pull him off Carl Friedrich, but at least they prevented Stan from raining down any more blows.

Edie and Priscilla rushed to Eden(Mickey) with handfuls of napkins and tried to staunch the bleeding.

"What happened, Mickey?!" Mickey(Eden) demanded.

"Carl Friedrich snapped out of it," Eden(Mickey) said, "and started hitting again."

Mickey(Eden) climbed up onto a table. "Freeze! Everybody! Just stop it!"

Everyone froze, and lifted their heads toward her.

"I'm sure you all have a lot of questions." Mickey(Eden) glared down at Eden(Mickey). "Which it looks like Mickey has done a lousy job answering." She looked around at everyone else. "So please don't hit me or my son anymore." She directed her ire at Eden(Mickey) again. "I am holding you accountable for the damage done to my body. Whatever wounds I sustain I will have them done to your body twice as bad." Looking around again, she smiled. "I'm sure I could get several volunteers to beat me senseless." Mickey(Eden) looked around at the likely volunteers. "Let me give a quick rundown of what has transpired, without interruption, then I'll take your questions."

A ball of light the size of a bowling ball blasted through a window into McDonalds, spewing broken glass everywhere. It sped across the room then shattered an opposite window on its way out. Six of them either froze, or screamed, or did both. "That was no neutrino," Mickey (Eden) calmly noted. "That particle interacted with the windows. It must have been a Higgs boson."

"No way was that one-twenty-five GeV," Mickey(Eden) disagreed, just as calm. "It wasn't massive enough. It could have been a W boson. Positive or negative."

"Or maybe a Z boson," Eden(Mickey) speculated.

Carl Friedrich kicked a chair leg and sent the chair clattering across the floor. "There the nerds go again! Who cares which it was. I'd guess whatever it was could kill us. Tell us what's going on!"

People slowly eased back into motion. Stan knocked Mick's hands off, then George helped Stan up off Carl Friedrich. No one offered to help Carl Friedrich up, so he remained sprawled on the floor. Edie stood to face Mickey(Eden), while Priscilla remained crouched on the floor attending to the injuries of Eden(Mickey), who was still prone on the floor next to Carl Friedrich.

Mickey(Eden) resumed. "I reached from a higher dimension into a lower one to contact Mickey with the intent of opening a portal between the dimensions." Seeing unenlightened faces all around, she started over. "Let's try it this way. *Eden* reached from a higher dimension into a lower one to contact Mickey with the intent of opening a portal between the dimensions. Eden's dimension is crushingly overcrowded, while Mickey's dimension is vastly under-populated. But people from a dimension higher than Eden's contacted Mickey and helped him thwart her plans. But someone from an even higher dimension than theirs carried out their own strategy and directed the eight of us into this dimension, the one where the two who assisted Mickey exist."

Mickey(Eden) took a deep breath as she looked around. She saw puzzled faces, but no indignant ones. So far, so good. "Now comes the confusing part. When Eden in her dimension first contacted Mickey in his dimension, at first all she could manage were a few words and a crude hologram of herself. As Eden strengthened the connection between the two dimensions, she refined her hologram and exerted more influence over Mickey, who was proving to be a gullible easily-manipulated imbecile. The two of them managed to open a portal between the two dimensions, but it was so weak it allowed only the consciousness of each to crossover, Eden's into Mickey's body and Mickey's into Eden's body. So this is really Eden inside Mickey's body speaking to you, while it is really Mickey inside Eden's body that is bleeding on the floor." She focused on the bleeding body below her. "I'm keeping track of the blood missing from my body, Mickey. You will replace each and every drop."

Before anyone could react to Mickey(Eden)'s speech, the floor of McDonalds bubbled up, knocking everyone off their feet. Mickey(Eden) was flung from the table to the floor. Eden(Mickey), who was already on the floor, smiled at her. "My, that was a big one."

"A big what?!" Carl Friedrich screamed.

"Perturbation," Eden(Mickey) said.

"Are we in California?" Edie asked. "Was that an earthquake?"

"We're in the quantum foam," Eden(Mickey) said. "But we should be okay. So long as bubbles don't form. If one does then we'll need to keep very quiet. And no singing."

Mickey(Eden) sat up. "So you are going to scare them worse than ever?"

"They need to know what's going on."

Everyone began struggling to their feet. "What were you saying?" Stan asked.

"That I am really Eden." Mickey(Eden) pointed at Eden(Mickey). "And that is really Mickey."

"That makes sense," George agreed. "I thought my sister was losing her mind. But it was only Mickey." He glanced to his brother-in-law. "Not you. Imbecile Mickey."

"I'm not an imbecile!" Mickey roared, springing to Eden's feet. He slashed the air pointing at Mickey(Eden). "That's just *her* version of the story!"

"Are we going to do the George and Priscilla thing?" Mickey(Eden) asked Eden(Mickey).

George and Priscilla looked at each other and shrugged.

"Only one of us should talk," Mickey(Eden) said. "It will be a lot less confusing."

"By all means," Mick said with a grimace. "Don't make it any more confusing."

"And please don't hit Mickey anymore," Mickey(Eden) said. "I don't want any more damage done to my body."

Stan walked over next to Eden(Mickey). "I'll guard your body."

"What about me?" Mick said as he approached Eden(Mickey)'s other side.

Stan confronted him. "I've got her body. You can have that thing." He pointed to Mickey(Eden).

"I don't think so," Edie said, walking over to stand before Mickey(Eden).

"So what's the plan?" Stan asked, the good soldier awaiting orders.

"Eden doesn't have one," Eden(Mickey) said. "But I do. I was busy while Eden was gathering everybody together." He scowled at Carl Friedrich. "Before I was beaten bloody." Eden(Mickey) walked to the table where Hypatia was open. "Using the program George and Priscilla installed, I've plotted a course out of this dimension."

Mickey(Eden) rushed over to look. "Where to?"

"I'm not sure."

Mickey(Eden) pushed Eden(Mickey) back. "You're bleeding on the keys."

George pressed some new napkins to Eden(Mickey)'s bleeding nose. "Here you go, sis."

Mickey(Eden)frowned at George. "That's not your sister."

George appeared befuddled. "But it's your nose that's bleeding, isn't it?"

Mickey(Eden) turned to Eden(Mickey). "Did Carl Friedrich hit you in the stomach?"

"No, I covered up. I protected our son."

"Thank you." Mickey(Eden) turned back to the laptop. "Why don't you go check on our son while I go over these numbers?"

"What if he starts hitting me again?"

"He won't hit you," Stan said. "I'll see to that." He escorted Eden(Mickey) to Carl Friedrich, who was still on the floor.

Carl Friedrich covered up, thinking Stan was back to hit him some more.

"Do you still want a happy meal?" Eden(Mickey) asked.

"No," he growled. "I want some answers. Why do you keep calling me your son?"

Mickey touched Eden's stomach. "I'm pregnant with your twin from Eden's dimension. This fetus inside me and you are nearly identical. That's why she thinks of you as her son. But her son is really in here." Mickey patted Eden's as yet unshowing abdomen.

Carl Friedrich sat up. "This is a nightmare."

"I thought so, too, at first," Eden(Mickey) said. "But it's all too real."

"I'm not doubting it's real," Carl Friedrich said, 'but it's still a nightmare."

Stan hauled Carl Friedrich to his feet. "Nightmare or not, we deal with it."

"So this is really Mickey I'm speaking to?" Priscilla had walked up behind them.

"Yes."

"Prove it."

"You know that time at your grandparents' house when you took a shower while I was there? You asked for a robe after you finished, and I gave you that little pink thing to put on. You had more appropriate robes in your closet, but I wanted to see you in that one."

Priscilla smiled. "I know what's hanging in my closet. I wanted you to see me in that one, too." Her smile fell into a frown. "I wanted Mickey to see me in it."

Eden(Mickey)'s face lit up. "Really? I never realized. I thought you came around the apartment to see George."

"What about George?" George asked, stepping up beside Priscilla.

"I thought Priscilla was sweet on you," Eden(Mickey) said.

"No way," Priscilla frowned, looking George over. "Go clean your nails."

"I'm a car mechanic!" George swore. "My hands get greasy!" He walked away in a huff.

Having overheard the exchange, Edie commiserated with George. "I'm a janitor. We work for a living. These intellectual snobs look down on people who do an honest day's work."

George looked Edie over. "You're pretty, but you look way too much like my sister." He abandoned her.

Since Stan had left Mickey(Eden)'s side, Mick approached. "So you are really Eden? My wife Eden."

"Ex-wife, Mick," Mickey(Eden) said without diverting any attention from Hypatia. "Get lost."

"That isn't how you treated me last time we were together. In the Roman bath."

Mickey(Eden)'s head jerked up. "He used *that* holo? The one from our wedding night? The one we go to every wedding anniversary?" When Mick smiled and nodded his head yes, she raged on. "How did he know about it? Did you suggest it?" Mick stopped smiling and nodding. "You did! You scumbag!"

"I thought it was you!"

"You should have known it wasn't me. I wouldn't touch your slimy body."

"I wasn't sure how you'd react," Eden(Mickey) said, smiling. He and Stan, Carl Friedrich, George, Priscilla, and Edie had all been attracted to the loud voices. "Looks like I played it right."

"*This* is who you made love to, Mick," Mickey(Eden) said, indicating Eden(Mickey). "It wasn't me."

"Who was *I* making love to?" Edie demanded.

"His body," Mickey(Eden) jabbed the chest she now possessed with an index finger. "My soul," she said, jabbing the side of the head she now possessed.

"You *are* a monster," Priscilla said to Mickey(Eden). "If you caused all this."

Mickey(Eden) smiled back. "I had some help."

"I'm surprised you admit it," Eden(Mickey) said. He nodded at the laptop. "What do you think?"

"It should take us out of here," Mickey(Eden) replied.

"Take us where?" Edie asked.

"We don't know," Eden(Mickey) said. "But anywhere is better than here."

Priscilla hugged herself. "You got that right. If big balls of light can smash through windows here."

"Don't you need a power source?" Mick asked. "Last time you were plugged into our power grid."

"The laptop is connected to a power source," Mickey(Eden) said.

"I just don't know from where."

"Maybe George and Priscilla connected Hypatia to a power source in this dimension," Eden(Mickey) suggested.

"Why do you keep blaming me and Priscilla for stuff?" George asked.

"Okay," Mickey(Eden) said. "We're ready. Everybody gather in close."

All eight scrunched in tight.

"Hold onto each other," Eden(Mickey) said.

He took Mickey(Eden)'s free hand, Priscilla took hers, George took hers, Stan took his, Carl Friedrich took his, Mick took his, Edie took his and laid her free hand on Mickey(Eden)'s shoulder.

Mickey(Eden) pressed the enter key.

4.

Eden(Mickey) and Mickey(Eden) stood atop a bluff overlooking an ocean. Thin patchy grass twisted up out from gravelly arid soil. The gentle surf lapped against red, green, and brown algae-coated rocks on the shore below. The air was clear, bright blue with high thin insubstantial clouds. The sun blazed away, but didn't provide much warmth. A slight breeze stirred the cool air across an inanimate landscape upon which not a single creature could be spied. Mickey(Eden) gazed all about the wide open wilderness in stunned wonder. Concerned with her dazed silence, Eden(Mickey) asked, "Are you okay?"

Without taking her eyes off the horizon, she spoke in awed reverence. "Is this what open countryside looks like?"

"Yeah. Much better than that sardine can of a world you live in."

"I've never seen anything so beautiful. This is what I wanted for my people. A world like this."

"That was never going to happen. Ralph had other plans."

"He was only one man. And not that bright. I could have outwitted him."

"Maybe. You are a very manipulative person." Eden(Mickey) glanced at the laptop Mickey(Eden) held, which was still open. "You should close that. You'll drain the battery."

Mickey(Eden) wrenched her adoration from the vast vistas all around to the laptop she held. "The battery should have gone dead long ago. I don't know where it's drawing power from." Despite saying that, she closed the laptop.

"Do you think the others are still alive? Wherever they are?"

Mickey(Eden) returned her attention to the immeasurable kilometers of hilly dry tundra grassland, calm water and empty skies. "If they're still in that last dimension they should be okay. They shouldn't die from dehydration for years."

Eden(Mickey) joined in searching all around. "George and Priscilla might show up to help them."

"I doubt it. The two of them may be from a higher dimension, but they're dumber than us."

Mickey lowered Eden's gaze to scan their more immediate vicinity. "Have you been bitten?"

Mickey(Eden) laughed. "Is my butt hurting you?"

"No. I mean insect bites. Have you noticed any insects?"

Mickey(Eden) searched for insects, and didn't find any. "Not a one."

"Birds? Shouldn't there at least be seagulls?"

Mickey(Eden) scanned the skies, but saw only pale blue streaked with whispy white clouds. "What elevation do you think we're at?"

Eden(Mickey) looked down to the ocean. "Near sea level."

"Are you short of breath? Like we are high up in the Rockies?"

Eden(Mickey) took several deep breaths. "Your right. It's hard to breathe."

"Let's exert ourselves and see what happens." Mickey(Eden) started down toward the shore. "I wish you'd get out of that stupid Wonder Woman costume."

Eden(Mickey) followed. "It is kind of chilly. What do you suggest?"

Mickey(Eden) halted to face him and spread Mickey's arms. "Something more appropriate to our surroundings."

Mickey closed Eden's eyes and searched the holo files. He found a dress similar to the dress Julie Andrews wore in the opening scene of 'The Sound of Music'. Since donning the summer dress in the Supreme Leader's rooftop garden, the notion of wearing a dress no longer bothered him. "How's this?"

Mickey(Eden) smiled. "Much better."

"Would *you* like something appropriate?" Eden(Mickey) asked. "You look rather like Ralph. When was the last time you changed clothes?"

"Are you referring to your Ralph? The old man in the alley?"

"Yes. Your Ralph is a disgusting old lech."

"You didn't!"

"No, I just let him squeeze you a little."

"I hate you, Mickey."

"Are we going to fight? Is that how we exert ourselves?"

"No. I don't want to hit my own body anymore. I thought we'd explore our surroundings."

"Do you want fresh clothes or not?"

"Can I trust you not to dress me in something ridiculous?"

"I promise."

"If you try anything funny I'll punch myself in the balls."

Eden(Mickey) grinned. "You have no idea how much that hurts."

"Of course I don't. But it could damage you. You might want to have children at some point." Mickey(Eden) began undressing.

"I'm carrying a child right now."

"*My* child."

"*Our* child."

"For the moment." Mickey(Eden) stepped out of the undershorts and tossed them aside.

Eden(Mickey) frowned as he stared at his naked body. "I really look that bad?"

"Worse. I designed a hiking outfit for Mick that should fit."

Eden(Mickey)'s frown evolved into a rollicking laugh.

"Come on, Mickey. I don't want to stand here naked all day."

Eden(Mickey) pointed. "My dick is getting hard."

Mickey(Eden) looked. It was.

"You're getting excited staring at yourself. That's twisted."

"Put some damn clothes on me!"

"No." Eden(Mickey) clapped once. "Take a good look."

Naked Mickey(Eden) stared at Eden's suddenly naked body. "I'm not getting turned on looking at myself. You look like Edie."

"Who?"

"The cleaning woman. At the college." Mickey(Eden) covered Mickey's privates with both hands. "She's beautiful."

"Of course you think she's beautiful. She looks just like you. So stuck on yourself." Eden(Mickey) had a hard time containing his mirth. "I can see you really, really like her."

"Yes. And you do, too. Your body does. That's who it's responding to. Edie, not me."

"So you got to know her pretty well?"

"Intimately."

"Is she a nice person?"

"Of course. Why?"

"I'll only sleep with a woman if she's nice."

"She's much nicer than you. She wouldn't make me stand out in the open countryside naked."

"What does it matter? Nobody's here to see us."

"We don't *know* that."

Eden(Mickey) nodded then closed Eden's eyes. The hiking outfit appeared on Mickey's body and 'The Sound Of Music' dress reappeared on Eden's body. "Better?"

"Much." Mickey(Eden) continued down the bluff.

Eden(Mickey) followed. "I'm getting used to wearing a dress. Should that be something to worry about?"

"Only if you continue wearing dresses after you get back into your own body."

"Do you think that will ever happen?"

"It better, or we both might commit suicide."

"Would it be suicide if you killed my body, or if I killed yours?"

"If a body kills itself, that's suicide."

"Yeah, but…" Eden(Mickey) fell silent.

"But what?" When Eden(Mickey) didn't answer, Mickey(Eden) stopped to look back.

Eden(Mickey) was doubled over gasping for air. "You're right. It's hard. To breathe."

Only then did Mickey(Eden) realize she, too, was panting. "We aren't high up, so the oxygen content in the air in this dimension must be lower than what we are used to."

"Are we going to suffocate?" Eden(Mickey) was panicking from not being able to catch his breath.

"No, Mickey, calm down. We just have to take it slower." Mickey(Eden) sat on a rock and pulled Eden(Mickey) down beside her. "Take slow deep breaths. That's it. Relax. We're going to survive this. If we keep our heads and work together."

Eden(Mickey) collapsed into Mickey's arms. "You've put me through so much."

Mickey(Eden) hugged Eden(Mickey). "I know. I'm sorry. We'll both get back where we belong. I promise."

Eden(Mickey) sobbed into Mickey's shoulder. "I don't know what's wrong with me. I'm not usually like this. I can't remember the last time I cried."

"Was it the last time you were pregnant?"

Mickey raised Eden's sniffling face from Mickey's damp shoulder. "Is that what this is?"

"I've read up on pregnancy," Mickey(Eden) replied. "Pregnant women get emotional. You'll start having bad mornings soon, also."

Eden(Mickey) pulled away from her. "I really hate you."

Mickey(Eden) laughed. "That's the way a pregnant woman often feels about the person responsible for her condition. Except I didn't get you pregnant."

"Yes you did! By forcing me into your pregnant body."

"Okay, but I didn't impregnate you."

"My twin from your dimension did. Unless it was Stan?"

"It wasn't Stan. The baby is definitely Mick's."

"So I'm staring at a twin of the man who impregnated me."

"Mick didn't impregnate you. He impregnated me."

"But I'm the one with the baby in my belly."

"It's *my* baby in *my* belly."

"So I'm just a surrogate mother?"

"Yes. That's a healthy way of thinking about it. And we both want a good outcome for this baby."

"Will I get to see the baby? After it's born? I'm getting kind of attached to it."

"I doubt it. If we both make it back home we'll be in different dimensions." By that time their breathing had returned to normal. "Okay, now?"

Eden(Mickey) nodded yes. They both stood and continued descending. Soon they were crunching across the stony beach. "I'm thirsty," Eden(Mickey) said.

"Me too. So time passes in this dimension at the pace we are accustomed to."

Eden(Mickey) looked out at the ocean. "You think we can drink the water?"

"We can't drink salt water."

"How do we know it's salt water in this dimension."

"I'll try it first. If you drink it and it's bad, it might hurt the baby." Mickey(Eden) kneeled at the waters' edge.

"Don't drink that."

Both their heads jerked about searching for the source of the high squeaky voice. They saw a slight scaly naked little man about a half-meter tall standing atop a rock looking at them.

"I think I just marked the baby," Eden(Mickey) said.

"That's an old wives' tale," Mickey(Eden) said. "You can't mark a baby."

The little guy hopped sprightly off the rock and approached a pool of trapped water. He spit into the pool several times then turned back to the pair. "You'll be able to drink that water in a bit."

"What did you put in it?" Mickey(Eden) asked. "What's in your spit?"

He shrugged. "It makes the water good."

Mickey(Eden) turned to Eden(Mickey). "He has desalination spit."

"Are you hungry?" the little guy asked.

"I'm starving," Eden(Mickey) said. Looking to Mickey(Eden), he hurried on to say, "I know, I know, I'm pregnant."

The little guy scraped some green algae off a rock and stuck it in his mouth. "Try this."

"Me first," Mickey(Eden) insisted.

"That's rude," the little guy said.

"You don't understand. I'm testing it. To see if it's safe for the baby." She nibbled, considered, gobbled. "It's good."

Eden(Mickey) scraped off a bit and chewed. Then gagged, spitting it out. "Stinky socks!" Mickey(Eden) and the little guy stared. "It tastes just like that chip your brother gave me." He continued to spit, trying to get the taste out of Eden's mouth.

Mickey(Eden) shrugged as she scraped off more to eat.

Eden(Mickey) watched with disbelieving eyes. "Your brother *said* you like stinky socks."

"The water should be good now," the little guy said.

Eden scooped some water into Mickey's mouth, swallowed.

"What's *that* taste like?" Eden(Mickey) asked. "Armpit lick?"

"It tastes like water," Mickey(Eden) said.

Mickey stooped to scoop some water into Eden's mouth, then spit it back out.

"Does the water also taste bad to you?" the little guy asked.

"No," Eden(Mickey) replied. "I'm just trying to get the taste of stinky socks out of my mouth." He scooped down several handfuls.

While he drank, Mickey(Eden) conversed with their host. "Have you seen any others like us wandering around lost?"

"No. Just you two."

"My name is Eden, by the way." She motioned toward Eden (Mickey), who was still scooping up water. "Her name is Mickey."

"My name is Belos."

"Do you live nearby?"

"In the ocean."

"You're amphibious?"

Belos nodded his head.

His curiosity piqued, Eden(Mickey) scrambled over to join the conversation. "This looks like ancient Earth. Far back in deep time, maybe a billion years or more ago."

"It's not," Belos affirmed.

"Then where are we?" Mickey(Eden) asked.

"Earth. It's just not ancient times."

"Then when is it?" Eden(Mickey) asked.

Belos shrugged. "We've lost track."

"What happened, then?" Mickey(Eden) asked. "To the Earth? In your dimension?"

"We have legends of the Fall. The land became unlivable. The oceans nearly so. The Gods changed us, the few select, the worthy, to live in the sea, on the ocean floor near the vents, so humanity wouldn't become extinct. Now the Earth is healing. So we are coming back onto the land."

Eden(Mickey) turned to Mickey(Eden). "They were bioengineered to live in the sea. Now they are evolving to come back onto the land. Life is following the same path as before." He looked to the land. "That's why the air is so thin. There are no trees to produce oxygen."

He looked down to the rocks. "And probably not much algae."

"There once were trees and there will be trees, the stories say," Belos said.

"Why is he so small?" Mickey(Eden) asked.

"We are not small," Belos insisted. "Nothing in the ocean is bigger than us."

"Most of marine life must have died out, too," Eden(Mickey) said. Turning back to Belos, he asked, "Are there no predators?"

"WE are the predators," Belos insisted.

"His size makes sense," Mickey(Eden) said. "A smaller size would require less nutrients. Life in the oceans might have been taken down close to zero."

Eden(Mickey) stared at a nearby rock coated in algae. "Life is coming back to the land."

"And so will we," Belos said. "The prophecies proclaim."

"Mammals returned to the oceans before," Mickey(Eden) said. "Whales, porpoise, seals, manatees. I don't see why it couldn't happen again. It happened naturally before. This time it got a jump-start from bioengineers." She scraped some algae off a nearby rock and ate. "We've got food." When Eden(Mickey) frowned, she hurried on to say, "You'd get used to the taste of stinky socks. Water, air. No predators bigger than us. We could live here if we had to."

Eden(Mickey) glared. "We won't have to." He sat on a rock and opened Hypatia.

"What about the others?"

"Maybe the program can track them down." Eden(Mickey) got busy on the laptop.

"I must go back to the ocean," Belos said. "I am drying out."

"Thank you," Mickey(Eden) said. She indicated the pool. "For giving us good water."

Belos pointed to a larger pool. "Too big for me to spit in, but I could pee into it."

"No, thanks, this pool should do. We hope to leave soon."

"I will come back to check on you. Goodbye, Eden and Mickey."

Eden(Mickey) watched Belos walk into the ocean and disappear beneath the surface. "Ralph had a statue that looked like Belos in his penthouse garden. It spit and peed water."

"That's curious." Mickey(Eden) squatted down beside Eden (Mickey). "But we have other curiosities to consider. Did you find the others?"

Eden(Mickey) glanced up from the laptop screen. "They're not in this dimension. I don't know where they are."

"Let's hope Ralph, your Ralph, is taking care of them."

"Do you really think a homeless man is behind all this?"

Mickey(Eden) shrugged as she stood. "Can you get us out of here?"

"Yes. But do we want to? Here, as you pointed out, we have air, food, water, no predators larger than us, and a friend who will help. The next dimension might not be as hospitable."

"Do you want to stay here and raise a family?"

"ONE child," Eden(Mickey) insisted. "You are not impregnating me again."

"I could, without impregnating you, at least for a while." Mickey (Eden) grinned. "Pregnant women can't get pregnant while they are pregnant. And nursing mothers hardly ever get pregnant."

Eden(Mickey) stared aghast down at Eden's breasts. "You expect me to nurse the baby?"

"If the baby is born before we get back to our own dimensions what else is it going to eat?" They both stared at Eden's breasts. "You'll be lactating soon."

Eden(Mickey)'s mortification grew. "They're going to fill up with milk?"

"That's nature's way, Mickey."

"It's not nature's way for a man." Eden(Mickey) looked back up into Mickey(Eden)'s face. "And you are not laying a hand on me even if you can't get me pregnant."

"Are you sure? I've read hormones in pregnant women spike really high."

"Keep it up and I'll take off and leave you here."

Mickey(Eden) smiled. "You're not about to leave your body behind."

Eden(Mickey) sighed. "I guess we're stuck with each other."

Mickey(Eden) took her own hand. "Face it, Mickey. The three of us are just one big happy family."

"Who is happy?" Eden(Mickey) snarled, pressing the enter key.

5.

Eden(Mickey) and Mickey(Eden) appeared in a deep dark forest. Shadows danced across writhing roots through the tortured limbs of twisted trees. The air was full of furry cries, predators lurking at the edge of sight and sound, with an occasional pair of glowing eyes, and whispered growls. The miasmatic stench of swamp decay hung limply about like a mildewed death shroud. The scant bits of night sky to be seen through the smothering leaves was a ponderous black, over-laden with clouds that appeared as solid as the mucky slop the two were mired in. A sense of dread was as palpable as the shadows shifting all about them.

"Damn, Eden, where'd you take us?" Eden(Mickey) asked. A flash of much-too-close lightning revealed a large dark shape several meters distant.

"What was that?" Mickey(Eden) exclaimed.

"I have no idea." Eden(Mickey) closed the laptop and passed it off. "How do I do this?"

"Do what?"

Eden(Mickey) squatted and pulled up his dress. "Go in the woods."

"Are you serious? Go behind a tree."

"Behind these trees? In this dark? No way."

"Then squat lower. If you don't want to…"

"Shit. This is a lot easier for men."

"A lot of things are physically easier for men. It's the intellectual activities they have problems with."

Eden(Mickey) raised up and straightened his dress.

"Can we go see what that big thing is now?" Mickey(Eden) asked.

"Just a minute. I have to find some new socks and shoes."

"You need to squat lower."

"Now's a good time to tell me this."

Mickey(Eden) took a deep breath. "I know. Allowances need to be made."

"For pregnant physicists. I've heard something like that before."

"Edie kept saying that. Except for the pregnant part." Mickey (Eden) passed the laptop back. "Can we go now?"

"Don't get snippy. You said you'd help me with your pregnancy."

"The fetus exerts pressure on an expectant mother's bladder, which makes her urinate more often."

"Yeah, so quit snipping at me."

"Pregnant women get more irritable, too."

"A pregnant man gets extremely irritable."

"Okay," Mickey(Eden) said. "I'll watch it. Now let's go see what this big thing is." She and Eden(Mickey) tiptoed through the dark foreboding shapes crowding in on them. They held their breath with both hands and tried not to slop too loudly through the mud sucking at their feet. Weeds and tall grasses clutched at their hesitant legs. Until, bang! "I found it," Mickey(Eden) whispered loudly, standing before the thing she had walked into.

"What is it?"

Mickey(Eden) stroked it with timid fingers. "It's solid. Flat. Feels like metal. The surface is rough, like it could be rusted."

Eden(Mickey) opened the laptop and activated the flashlight app.

"Damn, Mickey," Mickey(Eden) cried out. "You blinded me."

"Mickey! Is that you?" a woman shouted from out of the night.

"We're over here!" another female voice called out.

Eden(Mickey) swung the laptop light about the ground trying to locate the voices. "I can't see you," he called out.

"No kidding," Mickey(Eden) said. "You're blind. You're a physicist and you don't understand how pupils work?"

"Follow my voice." This voice was male.

Mickey(Eden) shuffled toward the voices. Until she crashed to the ground. "Found them."

Eden(Mickey) swung the laptop light about trying to locate everybody.

"Cut that light off," a female voice ordered. "You'll blind all of us."

Eden(Mickey) did, then tripped and landed on something soft.

"Ow." The other female voice exclaimed.

"Who am I laying on?" Eden(Mickey) asked.

"Edie."

"Who else is here?" Mickey(Eden) asked.

"Priscilla."

"Carl."

"We're tied up," Edie said.

"Who tied you up?" Mickey(Eden) asked.

"Untie us and we'll tell you," Priscilla said.

Eden(Mickey) got busy with Edie, while Mickey(Eden) got busy with Priscilla.

"Don't forget about me," Carl Friedrich said.

Finished with Priscilla, Mickey(Eden) moved on to him. "I got you, honey."

"Don't call me honey."

"Come on, Eden," Edie complained.

Eden(Mickey) fumbled with the ropes. "I'm not any good with knots."

"I bet Mickey couldn't even unfasten his own bra," Mickey(Eden) quipped.

"Let me do it." Priscilla barged in to finish untying Edie.

Eden(Mickey) relinquished the task. "Who tied you up?"

"A monster," Priscilla said. "He was huge and dressed in long black robes, like a priest."

"His skin is pale white, like a ghost," Edie added.

"He's really strong," Carl Friedrich said.

"But he didn't hurt you?" Eden(Mickey) said.

"Not yet," Priscilla answered. "We didn't fit."

"Fit where?" Mickey(Eden) asked.

"In there," Edie pointed at the large metal object Mickey(Eden) had walked into. "There's a little swinging door on top. He tried to jam us through it, but none of us would fit."

"What is that thing?" Eden(Mickey) asked.

"Can we talk while we're walking?" Carl Friedrich said. "I want to put some distance between that thing and me." The three previously-tied up people stood.

"It looks like a large yellow collection box of some sort," Priscilla said.

"With a monster inside," Edie added.

"We could hear it growling," Carl Friedrich said.

"The big guy was trying to feed us to it," Priscilla said.

The five waded through the clammy dark away from the large yellow box. "You wouldn't fit, so he tied you up and took off?" Mickey(Eden) asked.

"He said he was going after an axe," Edie said. "To chop us up, so we'd fit through the swinging door."

"He was going to shove us through the door one piece at a time," Priscilla said.

Carl Friedrich tripped and fell face-first into muck. Mickey(Eden) raced to his side. "Are you okay, baby?"

"Stop that," Carl Friedrich complained, spitting out muck.

"I didn't call you honey."

"I am not your son. I'm as old as you are." Despite his complaints, he allowed Mickey(Eden) to pull him to his feet.

Once she'd hauled him up, Mickey(Eden) turned to Eden(Mickey). "Get us out of here."

"I need some light. I can't do anything in the dark."

"What happened to that light you had?" Priscilla asked.

"Everyone bitched about me using it."

"Just give us some warning," Edie said.

Eden(Mickey) squatted down in the muck beside Carl Friedrich with the laptop.

"Again?" Mickey(Eden) exclaimed. "Already?"

"No! I'm plotting a course out of here." Eden(Mickey) turned on the light.

Everyone looked away. When Carl Friedrich did he saw a pair of eyes glowing in the dark. "What's that?"

Mickey(Eden) looked. "Probably just a raccoon."

"Awfully big raccoon," Priscilla said.

"I found what Carl Friedrich tripped over." Edie held up a half-meter tall white wooden cross.

There's four other ones just like it stuck in the ground. I saw them when Eden…he…she…whoever cut the flashlight app on." The small white cross in her hand ignited. With a scream of fright and pain, she flung the burning wood down.

Carl Friedrich scrambled to his feet. "What the hell!"

Priscilla pointed to the other four small wooden crosses. "They're all on fire."

"Is the KKK here?" Carl Friedrich asked.

Mickey(Eden) stomped on the cross Edie had held, trying to put out the flames. "The Klan's crosses are a lot bigger. These crosses look like ones you'd find at a roadside memorial where someone died in a car accident." Despite the stomping, the fire would not go out. "Keep working, Mickey. Don't let this distract you."

A low growling laugh echoed from out of the dark.

"How about that?" Eden(Mickey) asked. "Can I let that distract me?"

The other four gathered in a protective circle around Eden(Mickey).

A tall pale figure in long black robes appeared in the light of the burning crosses holding a large ax. In a bone-chilling booming voice, he proclaimed, "I see two more intruders have foolishly ventured into the Spirit Realm."

"He's back!" Carl Friedrich yelled.

"Everybody get in close," Eden(Mickey) said. "As close as you can."

The other four sat on Eden(Mickey). "Haven't you got the coordinates out of here yet?" Mickey(Eden) asked.

"Not yet. But I jiggered the Hide Holding hologram file around." The five, plus the laptop, disappeared. "I expanded its range a little."

The tall ghoul with the ax froze, puzzlement on his pale face.

"It's working," Mickey(Eden) whispered. "He can't see us."

"Ow," Edie whispered. "Priscilla. You're crushing me."

"Be quiet," Mickey(Eden) croaked.

"Ow," Edie repeated. "Your bony butt hurts." She shoved Priscilla.

Priscilla tumbled off the huddling gang into the muck. Right at the ghoul's feet. He raised the ax. Priscilla cowered.

"Close your eyes!" Eden(Mickey) ordered. He activated the laptop light and aimed it at the ghoul's eyes, and also turned on Bicep and blasted electronica music at full volume.

The ghoul jumped back, dropping the axe to cover his ears. Priscilla scrambled back on top of the other four and out of sight.

"It's too late for that," Mickey(Eden) said. "He knows where we're at now."

Eden(Mickey) laughed. "Yeah, but I immobilized him."

"What is that crap?" Carl Friedrich asked.

"You shouldn't call it crap," Eden(Mickey) said. "It saved your life. That thing covered his ears, not his eyes."

Priscilla writhed over the top of the other four. "Am I safe? Can he see me now?"

"I'm sorry, Priscilla," Edie apologized.

A huge Native American warrior in deerskin pants, with elaborate ink designs covering his bare upper torso, emerged from the trees.

"Mickey!" Priscilla yelled. "There's another one!"

Splayed across Eden(Mickey), with the other three piled atop her, Mickey(Eden) grunted. "Get us out of here, Mickey."

Eden(Mickey) pressed the Enter key.

6.

Eden(Mickey) found himself sitting in the middle of a city street twenty lanes wide. Vehicles whizzed by in a blur, whipping Eden's hair about in their jet stream. Although unnicked, he was terrified of moving. He huddled up into as small of a ball he could draw Eden's body into, and trembled.

A vehicle halted beside Eden(Mickey). "Destination?" a male voice with a southern twang inquired.

Mickey unballed Eden's head to see who was asking. A small go-cart idled without a driver. On the dash was a video screen with the face of Elvis Pressley. Just like in that game on Mick's computer, Mickey marveled. The different dimensions must have been seeping into each other even back then.

The face of Elvis on the dashboard cleared its throat. "Ma'am?"

"How about my own dimension?"

"Recalculating," Elvis said in an irritable tone.

"Somewhere safe, then."

"Climb in, darling."

Eden(Mickey)'s skirts were whipped about by wheeled-contraptions rocketing past as he quivered upright while clinging to the car, anticipating any second to be smeared into the pavement. "I should change clothes before I get in. That was terrifying, and my bladder isn't as strong as it should be."

"You wanna know something—on you, wet is my favorite color."

"I really don't think you'd like this shade of wet." The Sound of Music dress was replaced by a NASCAR racing jumpsuit, which Eden had designed for her brother. "This is dry and doesn't stink. And it's appropriate." Eden(Mickey) climbed in.

"Buckle up, darling."

Eden(Mickey) obeyed, and they sped off with Elvis singing 'Rock-A-Hula Baby'. "Do you have any Bicep?"

"What's that, darling?" The go-cart topped a hundred, then a hundred-twenty, maneuvering deftly through traffic and slipping by other vehicles traveling just as fast without collision, or even squealing tires. Despite near miss after near miss, no horns blared.

Eden(Mickey) white-knuckled the seat. "Do you have to go so fast?"

"You think this is fast?"

"No! I don't! You don't have to show me fast!"

The go-cart pulled off the road into a covered parking slot. "I don't have time to shift into fast. We're here."

Mickey unclenched Eden's eyes and looked around. "Where are we?"

"You asked for a safe place. Safest place I know. A police station."

A covered walkway led from the parking slot to the blank side of an office building. Eden(Mickey) wobbled out of the vehicle. "What do I owe you?"

"Nothing, darling. Just follow that dream wherever that dream may lead." The go-cart zoomed away.

Eden(Mickey) looked up and down the street. The traffic was horrendous. Vehicles of all sizes, from Segway-like conveyances carrying packages up to semis pulling triple trailers, hurtled past and around each other miraculously without even scraping. She saw no drivers. No pedestrians, either. The wide sidewalks were jammed with carts rolling up and down them. Some were the size of shoeboxes, others as big as refrigerators, all on wheels. They moved much more slowly than the vehicles on the street, but dodged each other in the same fashion.

"Do you need help, lady?"

Startled, Eden(Mickey) spun around to see a large screen displaying a life-size image of John Wayne in full cowboy regalia had rolled up behind her. "Have you seen anyone else like me recently?" he asked.

"No, ma'am."

"How about asking around?"

"No other pilgrims have been outside today."

"How about beyond the city?"

"No, pardner."

"You checked that quickly?"

"That wasn't quick. Do you want to see quick?"

"No, I'm good. Can you tell me where I am?"

"I see you have a chip in your head. I'll drop data in."

Mickey held Eden's head with both hands as he scowled up at John Wayne from the sidewalk. "Is Wile E. Coyote here? With his ACME hammer?"

On the screen, John Wayne pulled out a six-shooter and fired. Eden(Mickey) started to scream, but was flooded with immense relief so suddenly he had no chance to. John Wayne holstered his gun.

"What did you shoot me with?"

"The gun was just theatrics, ma'am. I buffered the areas of your brain that were causing you distress."

"Thank you." Mickey closed Eden's eyes as he sat up to peruse the new data on Eden's chip. "People do not venture outside in the daytime because exposure to sunlight is lethal. The cover above the walkway provides shielding."

"Correct," John Wayne responded.

"Robots run society during the day. People come out to play at night."

"Correct."

"I am the only person to arrive today from another dimension."

"Correct." The screen with the image of John Wayne rolled away into a niche in the wall of the police building, with the screen facing out. He tipped his hat, "Be seeing you, pardner."

Eden(Mickey) approached the solid front of the building. As he neared, an opening appeared, like the new data just uploaded to the chip informed him it would. He walked through into a small lobby and approached a screen mounted in a kiosk with the image of the mathematician Bernhard Riemann on it. "I need to speak to Ralph," Eden (Mickey) stated.

Riemann's fuzzy-bearded bespectacled face morphed into Ralph's. "Hello, Eden."

"I hope I didn't wake you."

"Elvis already did. He said he picked up a hysterical woman in the middle of the street."

"It seems I was the only one to make it into this dimension. Any idea what happened to the others?"

"No. But I know where your laptop is."

Only then did Eden(Mickey) realize he didn't have it. He had been so terrified sitting in the middle of one-hundred mile an hour traffic he'd forgotten about it. "Is it alright? I need it to get out of here."

"I've got it. Elvis brought it to me. You left it in the taxi."

"Can I have it back?"

"Of course. Come and get it."

"Where is it?"

"At my domicile. Elvis is waiting outside to bring you to me."

"Couldn't he have just given it back to me?"

"I want to talk with you, Eden. It's not every day someone pops in from another dimension."

"Okay. I'm on my way." Eden(Mickey) started to turn away from the screen, then turned back. "Could you ask Elvis not to drive so fast?" But the screen had already reverted to Riemann's calm stare.

Elvis was waiting at the parking slot where he had dropped Eden(Mickey) off. "Any requests?"

"Yes," Eden(Mickey) answered as he climbed in. "Drive slower."

"I meant songs?"

"You don't know that one? It was recorded by the rock group I Wanna Live."

"I have to go the speed limit. If I go slower it fouls up the traffic pattern." The go-cart whipped into traffic and accelerated. He began singing 'Suspicious Minds'.

"Appropriate," Eden(Mickey) said. "I feel like I'm caught in a trap and I can't get out." The city bled by in a blur. For miles. Tens of miles. "How big is this city?"

Elvis stopped singing to respond. "Didn't John Wayne do a data dump onto your chip?"

"It felt like some kind of a dump." Eden(Mickey) scanned the chip. The city spanned nearly the entire North American continent. The Atlantic and Pacific bordered it east and west. In the south there was a wall across the south side of what had been the Panama Canal, which had been enlarged so much as to completely separate the continents of North and South America. In the north it fizzled out into what remained of the Arctic. The city was appropriately named North America. He was shocked upon checking the population: one-hundred. "One hundred people. That's hard to believe."

"The city runs on its own," Elvis said. "People are superfluous."

"I'm surprised you bother with people, then."

"We enjoy our pets."

"You consider people pets?"

"North America would crash and burn if left to people. We feed them, groom them, take them for walks." Elvis pulled into a covered parking slot alongside the road. "We're here."

Eden(Mickey) climbed out onto the sidewalk, and the go-cart zipped away. He stood before a lush rain forest garden. It reminded him of the garden on the top floor of the 'scraper supreme leader Ralph had driven him up to, only much grander. Water from a fountain hidden deep in the trees shot twenty meters up into the air above the tropical foliage.

Eden(Mickey) followed a gravel path that wound through the dense jungle. Gibbons and spider monkeys swung through the branches. Chimpanzees and gorillas prowled about on the ground. Lemurs and tarsiers scurried through the underbrush. Eden(Mickey) came to a large pool in which Ralph lounged. "Join me." He snapped his fingers.

The NASCAR jumpsuit disappeared. Mickey tried to find a hologram to put on Eden's naked body, but access to the chip was blocked.

"I'm jamming your chip," Ralph said.

"Where's my laptop?"

"The gibbons took it." When Eden(Mickey) searched the trees, he continued. "They'll bring it back. Unless you throw a hissy fit and refuse to join me. I might let them keep it then."

As Eden(Mickey) waded into the pool, he dredged up the old argument— 'what did he care, it wasn't his body'. Only it was starting to feel more and more like it *was* his body. He eased down into the pool across from Ralph to conceal Eden's nakedness in the water. A gorilla sat down at the edge of the pool and stared at him. "Aren't they dangerous?"

"They've been trained. They're like pets."

"The robots think you are their pets."

"We let them think that. Have you had anything to eat?"

Eden(Mickey) couldn't remember the last bite he had taken. Had it been that horrid algae in Belos' dimension? "Several worlds ago."

A covered serving dish bobbed to the surface and floated across to Eden(Mickey). He lifted the lid to find an assortment of fruit and a glass of water. He selected a banana. "It won't taste like stinky socks, will it?"

"They are delicious."

Ralph was right. While Eden(Mickey) devoured bananas and orange sections and pineapple slices and bunches of grapes, washed down with sparkling ice cold water, Ralph busied himself with a virtual computer that appeared in the air before him just above the pool.

When Mickey could not force another cherry between Eden's lips, he replaced the lid on the serving dish and it floated away. "Taking care of business?" he asked Ralph.

"More of an amusement. North America and Australia just leveled Southeast Asia." When Eden(Mickey) appeared appalled, he continued. "War games. Not real. I formed an alliance with Australia to attack Southeast Asia. The ultimate target is China. Tonight was merely a strike at an ally to weaken China. We've concluded hostilities successfully for the night. Now it's time to play." The virtual computer faded away, and he spread his arms wide. When Eden(Mickey) just stared, he said, "Do you want your laptop back?"

Eden(Mickey) tried to put him off. "I'm pregnant."

"I know."

"My butt's infected."

"I can take care of that for you."

"Really?"

Ralph lowered his arms to reach for a tray that wheeled out of the trees across the ground and floated across the pool to him. "Let me see."

Eden(Mickey) swam across the pool to the side Ralph was on. Reaching shallow water, he walked up to him and turned around. The bite was livid red and swollen.

Ralph dipped his fingers into a split coconut filled with a thick white goo. He slathered it across the sore. "All better now."

Eden(Mickey) turned and smiled down at him. "That was fast. It doesn't hurt at all."

Ralph raised his arm to indicate he sit beside him. When he hesitated, Ralph said, "The lotion is waterproof."

Eden(Mickey) didn't know what else to do. He had to get his laptop back. He dropped down into the muddy bottom of the pool beside Ralph. Settling into the squishy bottom didn't hurt at all. "Thank you."

Ralph slipped an arm around Eden's shoulders. "It's not often I receive guests in my garden." His hand slid down to grasp a breast.

Eden(Mickey) relaxed into his embrace, determined to ignore his groping. "It's hard to believe there are only ninety-nine other people in all of North America."

"It's all there on your chip."

"Which I can no longer access since you jammed it."

Ralph began toying with a nipple. Eden(Mickey) tried to put him off. "I'm pregnant, and those are really tender."

Ralph released the breast with an irritated sigh. "We maintain a population of one-hundred. When one of us dies, a child is conceived in the lab to replace him or her. Fifty men, fifty women. A perfect balance."

"What do you do?"

"Amuse ourselves. I'm the military leader of North America, so I conduct war games. The Commercial leader devises economic trade wars. The Cyber leader undertakes cyber-attacks. And so on. Each of us has a specific sphere of influence we compete against the other cities in."

"It's all just games? Nothing is actually going on?"

"Of course." Ralph's rejected hand snaked down into Eden's lap and slipped between her legs.

Mickey gritted Eden's teeth. "The robots would never allow it."

Ralph sat up straight, withdrawing his wandering hand. "What do you mean?"

"The Artificial Intelligence that runs the world would never allow you to do any real physical damage to the planet."

"We can do whatever we wish," Ralph insisted.

"You can do whatever the AI allows."

The virtual computer re-appeared before them. "I can order whatever act of war I choose."

Eden(Mickey) pointed at the map. "If China is your real target, then strike at China."

"Done." Ralph launched missiles from submarines submerged all across the South Pacific.

"Look." Eden(Mickey) saw a barrage of missiles launched from the China mainland toward North America and Australia. "A counterstrike."

"No problem," Ralph said. "I have enough missiles on the mainland to take them out."

"What about Australia?"

"I'll let China nuke Australia. One less power to worry about, and China depletes its stock of nuclear missiles doing it." Chinese missiles struck all over Australia. The entire continent went red. The missiles hurtling toward North America crossed over Hawaii.

"Why didn't China hit Hawaii?"

"I ceded Hawaii to China long ago. It was indefensible." Ralph began pressing buttons. "Now to take out their incoming missiles." On the virtual computer screen a barrage twice as large as the approaching Chinese missiles left the continent and flew out over the Pacific to intercept.

The Chinese missiles veered. The North American missiles continued past, then began dropping into the ocean. Ralph cursed. "Damn. The Chinese have developed some new evasion capabilities, and they jammed my missiles." The Chinese missiles straightened their erratic trajectories and continued toward the west coast.

A tremendous explosion erupted nearby. Eden(Mickey) jumped up. "You said this was a game!"

"It is. No people will get hurt. We never target each other's human populations."

"But that was a real missile!"

"So what? The robots will repair the damage." Ralph busied himself with the virtual computer. "I've got to develop some new evasive capabilities for *my* missiles."

"Can you unjam my chip? I'd like to get dressed since there is a war going on."

"Sure. The mood's kind of spoiled now, anyway. I'll find you something nice." Ralph snapped his fingers.

Eden's body was clad in a clinging black strapless club dress so short it showed off matching panties. Eden(Mickey) looked it over.

"Really, Ralph?"

"Don't bother me now. I'm busy." He waved Eden(Mickey) away.

"What about my laptop?"

"Miriam!"

A gibbon swung down out of the trees with the laptop.

Eden(Mickey) was intrigued. "Why did you name it Miriam?"

"She took care of Ralph in your dimension, so I'm taking care of her here."

Intrigued morphed to horrified. "That's really Miriam?"

"Yes. And that gorilla who has been watching over you this whole time is your boyfriend Stan. Now leave me alone. I'm kind of busy here. Check your chip. It's not jammed anymore."

When Eden(Mickey) checked the chip he learned that millions of human psyches had been downloaded into computers. Since only one hundred were implanted into embryos conceived in the lab at any one time, many others had been downloaded into primate minds. Miriam's psyche had been downloaded into this gibbon, while Stan's had been downloaded into this gorilla.

Eden(Mickey) waded out of the pool to confront the gorilla. "I'm sorry, Stan." Taking the laptop from the gibbon, he said, "I'm so sorry, Miriam."

Miriam peed on him. As Eden(Mickey) scrambled backwards, the gibbon flung poop. The gorilla smacked the gibbon, knocking it flat on its back.

Eden(Mickey) kicked off the four-inch heels and started to flee. He froze when a menacing three meter tall robot rolled toward him. It rolled past without notice on toward Ralph. While Eden(Mickey) watched, the virtual computer faded away and the pool drained, leaving naked Ralph stuck in the mud. As the robot approached, he began to whimper. "No, Gort, no."

"Bad Ralph!" Gort barked. "Go sit on your paper!"

Without a word, Ralph crawled on all fours up from the bottom of the pool to some newspaper spread out on the ground nearby.

"Stay!"

Ralph hunkered down and quivered.

Eden(Mickey) ran out of the garden clutching Hypatia.

To find Elvis waiting at the curb. "Where to, miss?"

"Is Ralph really your pet?"

"Yeah. I think he's going back to obedience school."

"Are you really Elvis?"

Elvis laughed. "No, darling. I'm an impersonator who worked in Vegas. How am I doing?"

"I couldn't tell you. I never listened much to Elvis. Do you know two musician robots called Bicep?"

"Yes, ma'am. But they're in a different city. Western Europe."

Eden(Mickey) climbed into the go-cart.

Elvis groaned. "Why do you stink whenever I pick you up?"

"I told you what happened before. This time a gibbon peed on me and threw poop on me." Eden(Mickey) looked herself over for scat. "Can you drive me to another dimension?"

"I can if you program the route in your laptop."

While 'Are You Lonesome Tonight' began playing, Eden (Mickey) opened the laptop and got busy.

7.

Eden opened Mickey's eyes to find herself sunk into the most comfortable bed she had ever stretched out on. Much better than in that dark horrid forest where they had all been piled on top of each other in that horrid muck. Now, this bliss. Maybe that fool Mickey had done something right for a change.

Mickey(Eden) didn't realize she was naked until she sat up. Eden had no idea what could have happened to the hiking outfit. The hologram should have sustained itself while traveling between dimensions. It had before. Had something happened to her chip? Mickey better not let anything happen to it.

Yet Mickey(Eden) felt comfortable without clothes. It was warm and humid, a tropical clime. The aromatic scent of a spring garden filled the air—lilac, honeysuckle, magnolia, and other varieties of blooms she couldn't place. She was outside surrounded by lush brilliant flowers and livid greenery of innumerable shades.

"Hello, Mickey."

Mickey(Eden) looked to see a dinner-plate size hibiscus bloom facing her. In its center was a human face. Lucy's. "That's startling."

"Not as startling as you showing up naked. Would you like something to wear?"

Eden tried to cover Mickey's nakedness. "Sorry about that."

"Don't worry about it. Let me be a grandmother. Grandmothers have seen too much to be prudish about such things."

Lucy was her mother-in-law, Eden thought, not her grandmother. Lucy hadn't been told about her imminent grandchild yet. Unless Mickey had blabbed. But this was a different Lucy in a different dimension, not Eden's mother-in-law. It was so confusing meeting familiar people in such unfamiliar places. How much more unfamiliar could it get – a huge flower with Lucy's face on it speaking to her. How was she even doing that without moving her lips? But the flower wasn't too discerning. The Lucy flower saw Mickey and didn't realize it was actually dealing with Eden.

"Here." A large leaf extended out of the greenery offering a scrap of green. "It's so warm here you don't need much."

Mickey(Eden) crawled out of the bed, which once off it she saw was a large thick leaf, and looked the garment over. It was smaller than a Speedo. She stepped into it and pulled it up, poking around in front to get comfortable. Mickey's penis was fun, but it sure got in the way.

"Better?"

"A little." Mickey(Eden) stopped rearranging things and looked back at Lucy. "How are you speaking? Your lips don't seem to move."

"My thoughts are traveling into your brain through your nose. The olfactory tract carries the information to the olfactory cortex, which is part of the limbic system, which is tied in with your emotions. From there the information is sent to the auditory cortex, where they are translated into words you can understand."

"My nose is my ears?"

"Your nose is your nose. You're just smelling the scents of my thoughts."

"A form of telepathy?"

"It's much more. You can also detect pitch, and localize sounds in space, and identify who is producing the words."

"So you don't have a tongue, vocal chords, or larynx?"

"Correct. Our expressive faces are merely an evolutionary advance that helps us attract pollinators."

A talking flower with a fake face that looked like her mother-in-law. Mickey(Eden) had to get out of this whacky dimension as quickly as possible. She looked around. "Is anybody else like me here?"

"No."

"I don't just mean here," Mickey(Eden) tried to explain. "I mean in your dimension."

"No."

"How can you be sure?"

"Our roots are intertwined."

"Like the aspens? How far are you connected?"

"Across the entire planet," Lucy said. "We are essentially one organism." She shook her petals. "Enough of this. It's time for refreshments. I put the order in. It will be here directly. While we're waiting, let's go for a walk." Leaves parted, presenting a limb.

Which didn't appear wide or substantial enough to support Mickey (Eden). "I'm to walk on that?"

"Yes."

"How high up are we?"

"A hundred meters or so."

Mickey's body seemed awfully ungainly for Eden to attempt something like that. She tried to decline. "My balance isn't that good. I might fall."

"My leaves would catch you." Large leaves rose up on both sides, forming a railing of sorts.

Mickey(Eden) stepped out onto the limb, holding onto leaves on both sides. She steadily became steadier. Once away from the trunk, she felt brave enough to look down. She couldn't see the ground, only a mass of tree limbs and thick green foliage. Looking around on all sides, she saw the tree she had arrived on, and many others it was thickly entangled with. Looking up, she saw a tiny patch of open sky far above thinning branches. "This is one organism? Amazing."

Another large hibiscus flower emerged from out of the greenery, and Lucy's face reappeared. "You seem more comfortable."

"I am." Mickey(Eden) let go with both hands. "Except it's hot and steamy. I'm not used to the jungle." She was used to the cold clime of the mountaintop, while Mickey's body was used to the cold temperatures of Chicago.

A large leaf beside her began fanning. "How is that?" Lucy asked.

Mickey(Eden) faced the fanning leaf and sighed. "Wonderful." But her mind was far from wonderful. How could she think about Chicago or the weather while in this mess? Was her attention starting to meander like Mickey's? Was her mind and his starting to merge? That was a scary thought. She did not want to start thinking and behaving like that imbecile. Eden had to do something totally un-Mickey like in order to cling to her own personality. She noticed a thick vine hanging next to the limb she was on. "Can I be Tarzan? Your leaves would catch me, wouldn't they? If I fell?"

"Of course. See that tree at two o'clock? Swing over there. Your coffee and cookies will be waiting for you."

Mickey(Eden) grasped the thick vine. The protective leaf railing parted, and she jumped off the limb. She couldn't resist howling like Tarzan as she swung through the air. It was exhilarating. Arriving at the designated tree, she landed on a thick limb and let go of the vine. She lost her balance and started to fall backwards, but leaves came up from behind to steady her. Mickey(Eden) grabbed the trunk with both hands and hugged.

Lucy's face appeared on a nearby hibiscus bloom. "How was it?"

Mickey(Eden) was too surprised by Lucy's abrupt appearance to answer her question. Instead, she asked one of her own. "How do you do that? Go from one flower to another?"

"I told you we are one organism, interconnected through our root system. We can travel at the speed of thought from one node to another." A large leaf extended out bearing green coffee in a cup fashioned from bark, and several green cookies. "If you let go of the tree I'll serve refreshments."

Mickey(Eden) released the trunk and settled down on the thick limb she had landed on. "The coffee is green."

"It's the chlorophyll. It gets into everything."

"It looks gross."

"It tastes good," Lucy assured. "Chlorophyll is tasteless."

Mickey(Eden) sipped. Lucy was right. She studied the green cookies. "White chocolate macadamia," Lucy cooed. "Your favorite."

That might be Mickey's favorite, Eden thought, but her favorite was raspberry chocolate chunk. Her mother-in-law would know that, but not this Lucy. People weren't identical across different dimensions, merely close approximations of each other. Mickey(Eden) nibbled. The white chocolate macadamia was delicious, even colored green. So she gobbled. This was much tastier than Belos' algae, the last food she had consumed.

Four other large hibiscus flowers emerged from the leaves, with a human face in the center of each dinner plate size bloom: Albert, Miriam, Laurie, and Stan. "Fun With Fysics is now in session," Lucy proclaimed.

Mickey(Eden) nearly choked. Eden had no idea how Mickey ran the meetings. "Let's do something different," she stuttered. "Since I'm a visitor to your dimension, why don't you five run the meeting and teach me all about your world?"

"Wonderful idea," Lucy proclaimed. She looked around. "Who wants to go first?"

"Certainly not you," Miriam said with a sniff. "You've had Mickey to yourself long enough."

Albert extended his bloom above the others. "Lucy and Miriam act like they rule this world. Maybe someone else would like to speak."

Lucy extended her bloom to block Albert. "We do rule, Albert."

"This, and other worlds." Miriam smiled her appreciation to Lucy then turned her bloom back toward Mickey(Eden). "Most animals never got a foothold on land in our dimension. We allowed a few that proved useful, such as flying insects and birds that help with pollination. We permitted no others."

"How did you prevent them from moving onto land?" Mickey (Eden) asked.

"The first to venture out of the water were small," Miriam continued. "Easy to strangle with root and vine."

"We allowed no animals a chance to evolve to a larger size," Laurie said.

"Plant life here seems much more mobile than in my dimension," Mickey(Eden) said.

Lucy laughed. "And more intelligent. Didn't you feel that vine you swung on wrap around you? It wouldn't have let you fall."

"I didn't notice," Mickey(Eden) admitted. "I was too scared."

"That's enough, Lucy," Albert scolded. "Let us talk, too." The flower with Lucy's face turned away.

"That's your best side, dear," Miriam said.

"Lucy told me you are all connected through your root systems," Mickey(Eden) said. "That you are all part of a single world-spanning organism."

"That's right," Albert said.

"How do you span the oceans?"

"We've restored the land bridge between the northern continents with seaweed," Stan spoke up before Albert could reply.

"Also, we're connected to great masses of seaweed in the oceans that gather immense amounts of sunlight for photosynthesis," Laurie added.

"A dimension where fauna never developed," Mickey(Eden) marveled.

"Except for some birds and flying insects," Miriam prompted.

"That's why we have developed such beautiful faces," Laurie said. "The competition for their attention is intense."

"And our aromas," Stan added. "We've developed some extremely pleasing aromas to attract the pollinators."

"And to communicate our feelings ," Lucy said. "The limbic system that carries sounds also processes our emotions."

"That's how you talk to each other?" Mickey(Eden) asked.

"No, we communicate with each other much more directly through the root system we all share."

"Always so technical, Lucy," Laurie complained. "Always so involved with numbers. Let Mickey just enjoy us." All five lined their blooms up in a row before Mickey(Eden). "Which of us do you think smells most enticing?"

Mickey(Eden) set her coffee down and stood to smell each. Their scents were overwhelming. "How can I choose? You all smell wonderful."

"We can tell," Lucy said with a giggle.

"Are you happy to see us, Mickey?" Miriam asked, "or is that a stamen in your pocket?"

Mickey(Eden) glanced down to see the little green leaf bulging out in front. Damn, Eden swore silently. Mickey's thing was out of control. And it was becoming aroused by flowers? Eden was shocked back to awareness when Laurie rubbed her face up against the bulge. She jumped back and lost her balance. Mickey(Eden) was caught before falling. Glancing down, she saw she was sitting on Albert's smiling face.

Mickey(Eden) also noticed Mickey's legs were a pale green. She scrambled back up onto the limb she'd been standing on, struggling for balance. The five flowers encircled her to prevent her from falling, or from escaping.

Eden saw Mickey's entire body was a pale green. "Why am I turning green?"

"It's the chlorophyll," Lucy said.

"It gets into everything," Miriam said.

"Might as well get used to it," Albert said.

"Before long you'll be as green as everyone else," Laurie said.

"We can help it along," Stan said. All five flowers rubbed their faces all over Mickey's body from head to toe and front to back.

Mickey(Eden) lurched away from them, but couldn't move. She looked to see vines had wrapped around Mickey's feet, securing them to the limb she stood on. She pulled with all her might, but his feet wouldn't budge. She bent over to pull the vines away, but as soon as she pried one off two more attached themselves. Both feet were lashed tightly.

"Might as well relax and enjoy it," Lucy said.

"Your feet will grow their own roots soon," Miriam said.

"You'll be tied into our root system," Albert said.

"You'll become a part of us," Laurie said.

"Until we release you to pollinate," Stan said.

Green tendrils and thin vines swarmed across Mickey's trapped body, seeking out every recess and ingress. Mickey(Eden) screamed! Until green growth filled Mickey's mouth.

8.

Mickey whiplashed onto Eden's butt and slid several meters, clutching Hypatia to Eden's chest. Had Elvis shot him into another dimension at a hundred miles an hour? No way. That would have broken Eden's neck. But he must have been going pretty fast. Now Eden's butt ached again, after Ralph had just gotten it to stop hurting.

Eden(Mickey) looked around. He had landed on a metal floor in a large long dimly-lit room stacked with crates. He was in a cargo hold of some kind. Standing with Hypatia in one hand, with the other he tugged the hem of the short black dress Ralph had put on him as far down as it would go, which was barely below Eden's hips. This dress was ridiculous, but Mickey could access no other holograms to replace it with. Ralph had somehow damaged the chip when he jammed it. Eden was going to kill him. But he had more immediate concerns, such as where the hell was he now? The chilly air was stale, but breathable. He could sense no movement, yet this structure was too streamline to be a warehouse. It was designed as part of a vehicle, he was sure of it, albeit a large one.

Mickey set off to explore this new dimension, rubbing Eden's once-again sore butt with her free hand as he limped about. Many of the crates were busted open. Looking into one, he found metal pieces scattered all about inside it. Whatever had been in there had been torn apart. Had this vehicle the cargo hold was inside of been in a wreck? The room itself looked undamaged. Instead, it looked like someone had broken into the crates and deliberately smashed up whatever was inside.

Eden(Mickey) arrived at a hatch door that was ajar. Shouldn't a hatch be secured at all times? Maybe there had been a fight. That would explain the smashed crates. He could be walking into the middle of a war. Perhaps he should just escape this dimension. But then Mickey (Eden) or the others might be here, too. He had to find out.

Mickey snuck Eden's head through the hatch, expecting to get it shot off. But the narrow hall was empty. He stepped through and looked around. No one in sight. He walked down the empty passageway. Like the cargo hold, it, too, was dimly-lit and chilly. Rounding a corner, he found Eden's brother George sprawled on the floor. He ran up and shook him.

George's bleary eyes opened and tried to focus. "Sis?"

"Mickey Haiku. Are you okay?"

"Don't know." He went into spasms.

Eden(Mickey) held him down. "The answer to my question is no. Don't try to move."

"Have to find the others." The spasms subsided as he stopped trying to move.

"Who else is here?"

"Stan and Mick. Not you, the other Mick. My brother-in-law."

"Are they in the same shape as you?"

"If they're alive. I was hit with a stun gun."

"Who shot you?"

"Noah."

"Noah who?"

"Noah! He thinks this is the ark!"

Eden(Mickey) looked around. "We're inside an ark?"

"We're inside a space ship." George moved without thrashing. "I think I can get up now."

Eden(Mickey) rose and helped George to his feet. He trembled, but remained upright by leaning heavily on Eden(Mickey). "Where's the rest of the crew?"

"Noah stunned them like he did me."

"Why?"

"He's crazy as a bedbug. He thinks he is Noah and this is the ark." George shuffled his feet. "I think I can walk now."

The two shuffled down the hall. "Any idea where to find Stan and Mick?"

"No idea."

"I would have thought Stan would put up a good fight, with him being a soldier."

"Stan was the first one Noah stunned. Before we knew what was going on. Noah stunned Mick next. I got away. For a while."

"At least he isn't killing people."

"He is killing people." George lurched to the right at the intersection. "This way. Now be quiet. We're getting close to the bridge."

"Why is he killing people?" Eden(Mickey) whispered.

"He thinks they are doves. He's shooting them out into space."

"Why?"

"He's sending them out to search for dry land."

"That's insane."

"No shit. After I got away, I hid out in the cargo hold with a member of the crew. He told me what's going on. This space ship *is* an ark. The Earth was destroyed, or was about to be destroyed—he was babbling—so this space ship was loaded up with ten thousand people, seeds, and equipment they would need to start a colony on a hospitable exoplanet. Nearly everyone was put into suspended animation, leaving only a skeleton crew awake to man the ship. These support crews rotate in and out of suspension to do tours of duty. When Noah's tube was opened it was discovered it had malfunctioned. He'd been awake for years trapped in his tube. The tube had sustained him just as it would have had he been asleep, but held in isolation for so long he had gone bat-shit crazy. Claimed to be Noah, and said the ark had been infiltrated by evil animals. They put him in sick bay, but he got loose and got hold of a gun. Then he started stunning people and shooting them out into space."

"How many of the crew is left?"

"None. I was the last person he hunted down." George smiled. "But he doesn't know you've arrived from another dimension. Where have you been?"

"Spending quality time with Elvis. Where have you three been?"

"McDonalds."

"You've not been anywhere else?"

"No. Have you?"

"I was with Eden. Your sister Eden. Actually, this is her body. I'm just borrowing it."

"I got that part. What happened to her?"

"I don't know. We got separated."

George tugged on Eden(Mickey)'s arm. "The bridge is just around the corner and through a hatch." They crept forward, and Eden(Mickey) peeked around the corner. He saw a pile of bodies, with Stan on top. Beyond them the hatch was open, but Noah wasn't in sight.

Eden(Mickey) and George crawled up to the pile and grabbed Stan by the arms. When they pulled him off the other bodies, he stirred like he was waking up. Eden(Mickey) clamped a hand over his mouth and let George do most of the pulling. They drug his limp body around the corner out of sight of the bridge and started shaking and slapping him.

When Stan realized it was George and Eden(Mickey), with Eden's hand over his mouth, who had him, Stan knew to be quiet. He remained quiet as his waking body spasmed, and listened to them fill him in on what was going on.

Once Stan's trembling subsided, they could turn to other matters. "We've got to find Mick before Noah stuffs him into a discharge tube and shoots him out into space," George said.

Stan attempted to rise, but Eden(Mickey) prevented it. "Sit still. We'll go get him. If we're not too late."

"No." Stan struggled to his feet. He swayed, but remained upright.

"I've trained for combat."

"You just recovered from a stun blast," George objected. "You're in no condition to fight."

"How many fights have you been in?" Stan looked from one to the other.

"Do food fights count?" Eden(Mickey) asked.

"I've been in plenty of fights," George answered. "With my sister." He glanced at Eden(Mickey). "I won a couple of them."

"Right. Here's the plan. I'll charge straight for him. You two swing out on either side of me. He'll shoot at me first since I'll be coming straight for him. That means when I draw his fire, you two have to take him out. That's why we need to spread out and not give him one easy target to shoot at. Got it?"

"I've got a better plan," Eden(Mickey) said. "One that doesn't involve you getting stunned again."

"I'm all ears," Stan said.

Eden(Mickey) opened the laptop. "I'll draw him out here then you two grab him." He led the way to just outside the bridge. "Don't attack until I give the signal. I'll get him good and crazy first." He turned on the microphone and held the open laptop up to the open doorway with the volume maxed out. "Noah!!" boomed into the bridge. "This is God. You messed up!"

"How, Lord?" came the plea from the bridge.

"I told you three-hundred cubits long. You built the ark two-hundred cubits long."

"No! I measured!"

"You measured wrong! Get out here and measure again!" Eden(Mickey) stepped back from the door and nodded at George and Stan. "Get ready."

Stan smiled at George. "I've got this."

Noah stepped through the hatch with a tape measure in hand. Stan clobbered him. Noah went down like a sack of sin.

Eden(Mickey) squatted down beside Noah. "Look who it is."

"Mitchell," George said. "The head of the Crossover Project."

"The head of the Physics Department," Eden(Mickey) said.

"I'll watch whichever Mitchell this crazy guy is," Stan said. "You two go see if Mick is still with us."

Eden(Mickey) and George ran onto the bridge. They found Mick sprawled out in the middle of the floor, lined up to be the next to search for dry land. The two revived him. While Mick spasmed, Eden(Mickey) stood. "He'll be confused enough when he comes to. I shouldn't be the first person he sees. He'll think his wife has saved him."

George stared at him. "It's easy to forget you're not really Eden."

"I don't have any difficulty with it." Eden(Mickey) joined Stan outside the hatch. "Noah's not woke up yet?" He smiled. "You really walloped him."

Stan showed off the gun he'd taken from Mitchell. "He started to wake up, so I stunned him. Is Mick okay?"

"Yeah, he's coming around." Eden(Mickey) looked around. "Think we can save the human race?"

"How's that?"

"When we entered this dimension we landed on this space ship instead of on Earth. That probably means there is no one still alive on Earth. All that remains of the human race in this dimension could be on this space ship."

"We need to bring someone out of homeostasis who knows what's going on." Stan stood. "I'll find something to restrain Noah with."

"I doubt Mitchell, or Noah, damaged the ship if he really believes this is the ark. But he did wreck a lot of the equipment they'll need to start a new colony. I just hope he didn't do anything to the seeds."

"Or to the people in suspended animation," Stan added. He left in search of restraints.

Eden(Mickey) walked back around the corner to retrieve Hypatia. When he opened the laptop, the OPEN ME NOW icon popped up on the screen. He clicked on it.

George and Priscilla's worried faces appeared. Both spoke at once. "Eden is in trouble."

9.

Eden(Mickey) arrived so suddenly on the limb Mickey(Eden) was rooted to he lost his balance and fell. Before he could catch his breath to emit a second scream, a large leaf caught him. The laptop, which he had let go of to grab at everything rushing past as he plummeted, continued downward. A dish plate-sized hibiscus bloom with Albert's face in the middle stretched out before him. "Hello, Eden."

Eden(Mickey) was too breathless to respond. Also, Mickey wasn't in the habit of conversing with flowers, even ones that resembled someone he knew. Considering the dimensions he had passed through recently, this wasn't beyond the Pale. In fact, the Pale could be a dimension of its own. It would make sense, since beyond the Pale could mean moving beyond another dimension, which certainly would not be inconceivable considering how many dimensions he had recently moved through.

Another large leaf holding the laptop it had caught stretched out to Eden(Mickey)'s level, accompanied by another large hibiscus bloom, this one with Stan's face in its center. "Isn't she talking?"

"Not yet," Albert said. "She may be in shock."

"A shot of chlorophyll might fix her up," Stan said.

That snapped Eden(Mickey) out of it. "No need for that," he said to both of them. "Thank you for saving my life," he said to Albert. He snatched the laptop. "Thank you for saving my laptop," he said to Stan.

Three more large hibiscus blooms appeared amid the foliage. "Your daughter has much better manners than you," Miriam said to Lucy.

Damn, Mickey swore silently. *Flower versions of the Phun With Physics coffee klatch. Not too discerning versions. They didn't realize which Eden they had encountered. They believe I'm Edie, the Eden from the dimension their Phun With Physics twins inhabit, which is my dimension, and not the dimension this body is really from, which is the next highest dimension above mine, which is...*

"Poke her," Miriam suggested. "See if she'll talk again."

"I can talk," Eden(Mickey) blurted. "I just get lost in thought sometime." He sat up in the leaf that had caught him. "Have either of you seen a young man recently?"

"Mickey," Lucy said. "He just arrived."

"Can you take me to him?"

Albert, upon which Eden(Mickey) sat, and the other four flowers stretched upward to the limb he had arrived upon. Mickey(Eden) was so green and blended in so well with the surroundings he hadn't seen her when he had first arrived. Eden(Mickey) stared with horror. "What have you done to my body!?"

"Mmmpppfff."

Eden(Mickey) realized Mickey(Eden) couldn't talk properly because of the vines puffing out both cheeks and spewing out between the lips. "Why am I green?"

"You're not green," Miriam said. "Mickey is."

"What is that?" Albert asked, nodding toward the laptop.

They didn't know what a laptop was, Mickey wondered. "I'll show you." He opened Hypatia and turned the screen toward them. "You can play games on it."

"I love games," Laurie said.

"Except the 'he loves me, he loves me not' game," Stan said.

Lucy leaned in close. "What kind of games do you have?"

"Number games," Eden(Mickey) said, opening the inter-dimensional travel program.

"I like numbers," Lucy said.

"I'm good with numbers," Albert said.

"Single-digit ones," Miriam sniped.

Mickey noted once again how personalities carried over from dimension to dimension as his fingers flew across the keyboard setting up the inter-dimensional travel program.

"I don't understand these numbers," Lucy said.

Eden(Mickey) realized Lucy was getting suspicious. How did he know this? He studied the flower, but couldn't see suspicion in her bloom. Eden(Mickey) realized he was smelling it. Lucy was giving off a scent that registered as suspicion. Amazing. A society that communicated olfactorily. How complex...

"Mmmpppfff!"

Eden(Mickey) glanced up to find Mickey(Eden) glaring at him. He looked away. It was unsettling to see himself so green. But had Eden realized he was getting distracted by his surroundings and losing focus on what he was doing? Could she read him that well? It was amazing how close they had grown. But maybe it shouldn't seem so amazing, considering each possessed the others' body...

"MMMPPPFFF!!"

Eden(Mickey) looked up to find Mickey(Eden) had grown an even darker shade of green. He doubled down on setting up the program.

"How much longer, Eden," Lucy asked, reeking of suspicion, "before we can play?"

"I almost have the game set up."

"This is boring." Laurie said. "Let's play another game." A dozen tendrils from the stem of her flower slipped inside the low top of Eden(Mickey)'s strapless black dress.

"Yes, I like this game better," Stan said, as a dozen tendrils from his stem slipped up the high hem of the little black dress and inside the matching black panties.

Eden(Mickey) caught his breath as they stroked sensitive places. *Nearly done. Can't stop now. Focus. Focus. Foc…*

"I don't like that game," Lucy insisted. "I want to play the number game." A tendril of hers reached for the Enter key.

…us. Focus. Fo. Eden(Mickey) slashed out a hand to grab Mickey (Eden)'s hand just as Lucy pressed the enter key.

Eden(Mickey), Mickey(Eden), and the Laurie and Stan flowers appeared on the floor in the bridge of the space ship. Their sudden appearance elicited screams from George, Mick, and Stan as they all leaped back away from the unheralded new arrivals. Eden(Mickey) collapsed onto Eden's back, writhing in pleasure, as the Laurie flower and the Stan flower continued to probe and caress sensitive places.

Stan was the first to recover. He aimed a stun gun at the Stan flower, but faltered upon recognizing his own face staring back at him from the large hibiscus bloom. Before he could regain enough nerve to pull the trigger, the two giant flowers faded away. Unnerved nearly as badly as if he had shot himself, Stan swung the stun gun around at forest green Mickey(Eden).

"MMMPPPFFF!!!" Eden said as she shook Mickey's head in an emphatic no.

"That's Mickey," George exclaimed. "Eden, I mean. Don't shoot her. Him. Whoever."

Eden(Mickey) released a long satisfied sigh. "I'll never look at a garden plant in the same way again."

"What were those things?!" Mick demanded.

"Stan and Laurie from another dimension," Eden(Mickey) said. "They must have come along with us because they were tangled up with me."

"I am *that* thing," Stan said with a shaky voice. "In another dimension?"

Eden(Mickey) shrugged as he tugged the panties into place.

"So where did they go?" Mick asked.

Eden(Mickey) shrugged as he pulled the hem of the short dress down.

Stan's shaky arm finally lowered the stun gun. "What happened to

Mickey?"

Eden(Mickey) pulled the top of the dress back into place. "Untangle those vines tying her up and she'll tell you."

George began pulling the vines from Mickey(Eden)'s mouth. "Don't bite me."

Once Mickey's mouth was partly cleared, Eden spit out the rest. "That was Hell!"

Mick freed Mickey's body from the rest of the vines. "Nice Speedo."

Stan dropped down beside Eden(Mickey). "Are you okay?"

"Give me a chance to catch my breath and I will be." Eden(Mickey) looked around until he located the laptop on the floor next to him. He laid a reassuring hand on it. "I tricked them into thinking we were going to play a game."

"Are you bragging." Spit. "About out." Spit. "Witting flowers?" Spit, spit.

The fading passion banished by anger, Eden(Mickey) glared at Mickey(Eden). "I saved your life!"

"You saved your body." Spit. "You could care less about my life." Spit. Spit.

"Why is my body green?"

George and Mickey helped Mickey(Eden) upright. "It's just chlorophyll. It should wear off."

"What were those things?" George asked.

"They were from a dimension dominated by flora. Not a good place for animals. Unless you're willing to help pollinate."

Eden(Mickey), aided by Stan, struggled upright. "There's a weed coming out of my left ear."

Mickey(Eden) swiped at it. "Can I have some decent clothes? Or do you enjoy seeing your body parade around in this little green scrap?"

"I can't. When Ralph jammed your chip he damaged it somehow. I can't access the hologram files. We're stuck with what we're wearing."

"*You're* stuck," Mickey(Eden) objected. "This leafy thing is real. It can be replaced." Mickey(Eden) tried to tug the tiny garment into a better position, but it was hopeless. "Where did you meet Ralph?"

"In the last dimension I was in." Eden(Mickey) laughed. "You should have seen him. When I left he was being made to sit on his paper. He was being punished for starting a war with China." The other four stared. "You had to have been there."

George took Mickey(Eden) by the arm. "There are thousands of people on this space ship. We can find something better for you to wear." The two went off in search of clothes.

"How about you?" Stan asked Eden(Mickey). "Want to find something else to wear?"

Mickey tugged on the black material in a futile attempt to get it to cover more of Eden's body. "I can't. I'm stuck with this hologram until Eden's chip starts working again." He gave up on trying to make the little black dress decent. "Have you revived any of the crew?"

"No. We wanted to wait for you to get back."

"Did Mitchell ever wake up?"

"Yeah," Mick said.

Mick and Stan led Eden(Mickey) to a corner of the bridge where Mitchell was trussed. "What all did you wreck?"

"It doesn't matter," Mitchell replied in dismay. "I built the ark wrong."

"You really think you built this space ship by yourself?" Eden (Mickey) asked.

"My family helped."

"That wasn't the voice of God you heard," Eden(Mickey) pressed on. "It was me."

Mitchell glared at him. "Satan."

Eden(Mickey) turned away from Mitchell. "He's useless. He probably doesn't know what all he has done. Let's wake up someone who can find out."

Mickey(Eden), clad in a baggy jumpsuit, and George caught up with the other three en route to the hibernation tubes. "What are you doing?"

"We're going to wake up the captain, or whatever high-ranking officer we can find." Eden(Mickey) smiled. "Glad to get some real clothes?"

Mickey(Eden) smiled right back. "You should see what a nice shade of forest green you've turned down there."

"Will you two stop it," Stan ordered. "We've got to see if we can save this mission." When they both fell silent, George and Mick shrugged at each other behind their backs, puzzled that both of them would heed Stan.

The five found the huge open expanse of the ship where the suspended bodies were housed. They worked their way through the tubes, relying on Stan to recognize any markings that related to rank. At last, Stan stopped before a tube. "This person isn't the captain, but she's high up."

Eden(Mickey) began to study the controls on the tube, but was nudged aside by Mickey(Eden). "Out of the way, runt."

When Stan looked to Eden(Mickey) to see if he was alright with this, he shrugged. "Eden is smarter than me. No argument about that."

A few minutes later the tube opened. A young naked female was revealed, with tubes and wires attached all over her body. Eden(Mickey) nudged Mickey(Eden) out of the way. "A female should do this."

"You're not really a female," Mickey(Eden) replied.

"We'll both do it then," Eden(Mickey) said.

Mickey(Eden) shrugged. "The arrangement George and Priscilla have makes better sense now." Both started disconnecting the wires and tubes. Once the woman was free, Eden(Mickey) draped a sheet across her.

A few minutes later the young woman opened her eyes. She looked back and forth from Eden(Mickey) to Mickey(Eden).

"There's a problem," Eden(Mickey) said.

"We need you to wake up and assess the damage," Mickey(Eden) said.

She sat up. "The awake team?"

"They were all shot out into space," Eden(Mickey) said.

"Dead?"

"Of course dead," Mickey(Eden) said.

"Be patient with her," Eden(Mickey) said. "She's still waking up."

"Who are you?"

"There are five of us," Mickey(Eden) said. "We came from a different dimension."

"How?"

"We have no idea," Eden(Mickey) said. "Are you ready to get up?"

The woman nodded. She tossed aside the sheet without concern for her nakedness as Eden(Mickey) and Mickey(Eden) helped her out of the tube to her feet. She looked around as they held onto her while she struggled for balance. "You said five?"

"We sent the other three men back to the bridge," Mickey(Eden) said. "Thought you'd appreciate the privacy."

"Can we get you some clothes?" Eden(Mickey) asked. When she nodded yes, Eden(Mickey) said, "Lead the way."

She shuffled, with the other two on either side holding an arm for support, toward a locker at the foot of the tube. "What's your name?" Mickey(Eden) asked.

"Carla."

Mickey(Eden) stiffened.

Noticing, Carla asked, "What's the matter?"

"Nothing," Mickey(Eden) insisted.

"Let's get you dressed," Eden(Mickey) added while staring at Eden(Mickey), intrigued by her reaction to the name.

In the locker they pulled out a jumpsuit similar to what Mickey

(Eden) had found, only the shoulders were plastered with bars. "What's your rank?" Eden(Mickey) asked.

Carla, with their assistance, began dressing. "Second in command."

"What happened to the Earth?" Mickey(Eden) asked.

"A gamma ray burst of total disruption event level was detected in our spiral arm of the Milky Way. Earth was directly in its path. We were sent to scout out promising exoplanets beyond the range of the burst."

"The Earth has been destroyed?" Eden(Mickey) asked.

"It hadn't been before we left, but it probably has been by now. There was no avoiding it. There was no way to shield against such destructive power rushing toward the planet."

"Where are you headed?" Mickey(Eden) asked.

"First stop is Proxima Centauri." She shrugged. "You can let go of me now. I'm steady." The two released Carla with reluctance. She stretched, flexed, writhed. "My mind is clearer now. Tell me what's gone wrong."

Mickey(Eden) took up the tale. "A madman killed the other members of the awake team and tried to sabotage the mission. We stopped him, but he wrecked a lot of equipment in the cargo bay. We don't know what else he might have done. That's why we woke you. Your tube was the highest ranking officer we could locate."

"I can check all the ships systems for damage from the bridge." The three began a slow walk, but instead of heading for the hall Carla directed them to a nearby station where a mobile chair was docked. "People are weak when first awakened, so transport is provided for them." She disconnected the charging cable, undocked the chair, then climbed on. "I'll meet you at the bridge." Carla raced ahead.

The two followed on foot. "Our daughter?" Eden(Mickey) asked.

"*My* daughter," Mickey(Eden) insisted. "With a name like Carla. Awfully close to Carl."

"She does look like me." Eden(Mickey) glanced at Mickey(Eden). "I mean you." He looked away. "Of course she reached a high rank on such an important mission. Looks like she inherited our high intelligence."

"She didn't inherit anything from you," Mickey(Eden) said.

"If she was inside me for a while, she might have," Eden(Mickey) said. Since Mickey(Eden) didn't offer any more arguments, he changed the subject. "Why did you design such an indecent dress as this? You said you don't like to show off your body."

"I designed it to wear in private on special occasions to please my husband. Back when I wanted to please him."

Eden(Mickey) let it go. "Are you recovered from your ordeal in the last dimension?"

"Are you?" When Eden(Mickey) appeared baffled, Mickey(Eden) continued. "You sure were enjoying yourself with those two flowers."

"I suffered that to rescue you!"

"Sure didn't look like you were suffering. Now I know what to get you for your birthday, Mickey. A hibiscus."

"The only thing I want from you is my body back. The right color."

Mickey(Eden) held up an arm and pulled the sleeve back. "It's fading."

Eden(Mickey) grabbed the arm and pulled it up close to see. "How can you tell in this light?" Mickey started to release it, then pulled it up to Eden's nose. "You smell funny."

"Don't be ridiculous." Mickey(Eden) slung Eden(Mickey)'s arm free.

"You can't hide your smell, Eden. I was in the plant dimension long enough to smell all kinds of stuff there. You smell like you like me. For rescuing you. For carrying your child. It might even smell like— dare I say it—love?"

"Whatever you are smelling is coming from *your* body."

"That *you* are in."

"Don't act any dumber than you are!" Mickey(Eden) stormed ahead.

Eden(Mickey) called out, "That's it, Eden, get far enough away I can't smell your love for me!"

When Eden(Mickey) arrived back on the bridge he found Stan conferring with Carla, while Mickey(Eden) stood several meters back glaring at them, and George and Mick standing even further back watching all three. Eden(Mickey) joined George and Mick. "Where's the crazy guy?"

"Out searching for dry land," George answered.

Mick laughed. "Carla launched him out into space. She is ruthless."

Eden(Mickey) walked toward Mickey(Eden), but as he neared he stopped to sniff. "I smell jealousy," he said softly. "Are you jealous of Stan for being with Carla? Really?"

Mickey(Eden) raised a fist. "I'm going to break that nose. I don't care if it is mine."

Eden(Mickey) stepped back. "What's going on with you?"

Mickey(Eden) lowered the fist. "Apparently I have children all through the dimensions. I encounter one, and she'd rather take up with Stan than me, her mother."

"You don't look like her mother. She's more likely to take up with me."

"Another reason for me to hit you."

"Eden, they're both military. That's why she and Stan are comfortable in each other's company."

Mickey(Eden) studied Eden(Mickey). "Maybe you aren't such a runt."

Eden(Mickey) joined Stan and Carla. "Will the ship make it to your intended destination?"

"Yes," Carla answered. "The mad man did no real damage to the ship itself. The equipment he damaged can be repaired. We certainly have enough time to work on it before it is needed."

"What's your plan?" Eden(Mickey) asked.

"I'll rouse a maintenance team to check all the tubes to insure no others have malfunctioned, then repair the damage done to the equipment in the cargo hold. I'll also awaken the next scheduled awake team and inform them what has happened, then have them put me back under. After that, the maintenance team will go back under once the repairs are completed, and we'll resume our normal schedule of awakenings."

Mickey(Eden) wedged herself between Carla and Stan, forcing both to take a step back. "I'd like to hear about your life on Earth, Carla. About your family, your youth, your school and military training. All about you."

Carla glanced from Mickey(Eden) to Stan. "I really don't have time."

"We don't, either," Eden(Mickey) said. "We have to move on."

"What's the rush?" Mickey(Eden) barked.

"I assume this long strange trip we're on is leading somewhere," Eden(Mickey) said. "We need to get there."

Carla turned back to the systems check she was engaged in.

Stan whispered into Mickey(Eden)'s ear. "Carla is lacking in social skills. Probably the only reason she's not captain."

"Of course she's lacking in social skills," Eden(Mickey) said. "Look who her mother is."

Mickey(Eden) reached back to deliver a roundhouse, but Stan restrained her.

Eden(Mickey) left them to sit at an empty station and open Hypatia. George and Mick joined him. "Where we off to now?" George asked.

"I don't know." The screen was blank—no OPEN ME NOW icon. "George and Priscilla have abandoned us again."

"Where are the other three?" Mick asked.

Eden(Mickey) began setting up the program. "Last time I saw them this ghoul was chasing them with an ax." Eden(Mickey) glanced up to see Mickey(Eden), Stan and Carla at the control console. "Hey, Stan!"

Stan joined the other three. "What do you need, Mickey?"

"I feel safer with you beside me. You said you were going to protect Eden's body." He smiled at Stan. "In the previous dimension I was in you were watching over me as a gorilla."

"Of course I'll protect you, as a human or a gorilla." Stan looked at the other two men, who both took a step back. "Are George and Mick bothering you?"

"Not at the moment." Eden(Mickey) took a long time setting up the program. George and Mick grew bored, and withdrew to nose around the bridge.

Which drew a rebuke from Carla. "Don't touch anything!" When Eden(Mickey) glanced back, he saw Carla and Mickey(Eden) deep in conversation.

After delaying as long as he could in order to give Mickey(Eden) time to spend with her daughter, Eden(Mickey) sat back and stretched. "We're ready!" George, Mick, and Mickey(Eden) joined him and Stan at the laptop. Eden(Mickey) smiled up at Mickey(Eden). "Did you get to spend enough quality time with your daughter?"

"No," Mickey(Eden) replied. "But thank you for the time I got."

"Good luck!" Carla called out.

The five all waved to her, then clasped hands in a tight circle around Hypatia. Eden(Mickey) pressed the enter key.

10.

Eight spastic bodies raised a tsunami in warm flat water. Mickey panicked, kicking Eden's legs wildly while holding Hypatia above her head to keep it dry. Stan calmly took the laptop from him. "Stand up."

Mickey stopped kicking and set Eden's feet on solid ground. The water came up to her chest. No longer fearful of drowning or ruining the laptop, he looked around. All eight were present. Eden(Mickey) hugged Priscilla. "I'm glad you're okay." He gazed upon Edie and Carl Friedrich. "You two, as well."

Mickey(Eden) waded over to hug Carl Friedrich, but he pushed her away. "Don't do that."

Mickey(Eden) backed off with a scowl. "All my children are such brats."

Priscilla laughed. "I'm sorry, but the thought of Mickey having children is too weird."

"Why is that?" Mickey(Eden) replied with a sharp edge. "Do you think no woman would be attracted to a man as intelligent as Mickey?" Priscilla started to object, but Mickey(Eden) wouldn't let her. "The Priscilla in my dimension is not such a condescending snob." Mickey(Eden) waded away.

A remorseful Priscilla turned to Eden(Mickey). "I didn't mean anything by it, Mickey."

"Don't worry about it," Eden(Mickey) said. But Mickey did. Eden had just taken up for him. He couldn't smell any emotions coming off her any more. The effects from being rooted in the flora dimension must have worn off. But that sounded like she cared what Priscilla thought about him. Scary. He covered his unease with bluster. "Your green is fading."

Mickey(Eden) looked up at the blazing sun. "Just when I need it."

Eden(Mickey) also looked up, his mind engaging. "Do you think chlorophyll would act as a sunscreen?"

"Have you ever seen a sunburned plant? Most of them are out in the sun all the time."

"Will you two nerds shut up," Carl Friedrich cut in before it got any weirder. "No one cares about yours or any plants' suntans."

George's cry of "Shark!" made everyone forget about tans. They jerked back away from the fin speeding toward them.

Except Stan. He passed the laptop back to Mickey(Eden) then

jumped forward with fists balled, ready to rumble. Instead, he laughed. "That's not a shark. It's a dolphin." The fin rose out of the water as the dolphin surfaced. Stan petted it, and it butted him playfully.

Edie waded up to Mickey(Eden). "Where are we?"

Eden(Mickey) looked all around. "The sun is hot. The water is warm and calm. Nothing to see except deep blue water." Her gaze locked onto a small island a hundred meters distant. "And a white sandy beach." She looked back to Edie. "I'd say the south Pacific, or Caribbean."

"Let's talk about it on the beach," Mick said. They were all staring at the island. "There really might be sharks out here."

"Wait." Stan shielded his eyes from the blazing sun to squint across the dazzling water. "There are people on the beach."

"Do any of them have axes?" Carl Friedrich asked.

"Not that I can see," Stan answered, "But we'll soon find out."

Mickey(Eden) stepped up alongside Stan to squint toward the island, also. "Yeah, they've seen us."

George shaded his eyes and squinted, too. "A bunch of them are wading out to us."

"I count ten," Stan said. "Everyone form up behind me. We'll wade in and meet them halfway."

Mickey(Eden) lunged forward. "Wait. If it comes to a fight we don't have a chance. There's a lot more than ten on the beach. Let's just stay here and see what they want." She scowled at Stan. "And try to not act so belligerent."

Eden(Mickey) stepped up to the other side of Stan, while everyone else gathered behind. Eight of the approaching ten halted in knee-deep water, while the other two continued out.

The advancing two halted in waist-deep water. The well-tanned young man and young woman in swim suits bore a strong resemblance to Stan and Laurie. Mickey(Eden) looked to see how Stan reacted to encountering yet another twin from yet another dimension.

Surprisingly well, with a grin. "Who are you, brother?" Stan asked.

"Stanley, and this is Lori," the man said. "And I'm not your brother."

"What part of the infected world have you come from?" Lori asked.

"We come from a different dimension," Mickey(Eden) said. "And I'm sure we're infected with something. Everybody is."

"We carry the Pris Virus," Stanley said.

Priscilla's interest ticked up. "The what?"

"The one true virus that protects us," Lori added.

"Let's talk about this on the beach," Stan said.

Stanley blocked Stan's path. "Let's not."

Eden(Mickey) handed the laptop to George. "Hold onto this. In case I get knocked on my butt." He stepped between Stan and Stanley. "It would be more comfortable on the beach."

"We've already sacrificed ourselves," Lori said, "to keep you from infecting everybody else. We won't let you come any closer."

"If you try to infect our world, others will sacrifice themselves to stop you." Stanley pointed to the eight men gathered in knee-deep water.

"How have you sacrificed yourselves?" Mickey(Eden) asked.

"After you leave we will swim out until we are exhausted, then drown," Lori said.

Stanley continued. "We will not return to spread your diseases to our people."

Stan nodded approval. "Spoken like truly heroic soldiers."

"I want to hear more about this Pris Virus," Priscilla said.

"You'll learn about her soon enough," Lori said.

Stanley revealed sparkling teeth in a grim smile. "She is already becoming acquainted with all of you."

"We've been infected that quickly?" Mickey(Eden) asked.

Lori's stoicism broke. "Don't worry, it will be painless. You'll simply lose consciousness, collapse, and drown."

"Hello, Mickey."

The voice in Eden's head sounded like Priscilla. "Is this the virus?"

Mickey(Eden) grabbed Eden(Mickey) by the arm. "What's going on, Mickey?"

"Leave him alone!" Stanley advanced on Mickey(Eden). Stan grabbed him.

"Don't fight!" Lori said. She pointed back to the gang of eight men in knee-deep water. "These men will come to our aid. They are too many for you to fight. But you would infect them with your diseases. All you would accomplish would be the needless death of others."

"She's right," Eden(Mickey) said to the others. "Don't start fighting. I'm okay." He closed Eden's eyes and focused his attention on the voice in her head. "Who am I talking with?"

"Pris," Lori answered.

"Why do you call it Pris?" Priscilla demanded to know.

Eden(Mickey) waved his arms. "Will everybody shut up so I can talk to the virus!"

"That sounds too weird even coming from you, Mickey," Edie said.

Eden(Mickey) ignored her and all the others. "Why do you want to kill us?"

"The diseases you carry could infect all remaining healthy people on Earth," the Pris Virus answered.

"You have no defenses against our germs?"

"Not anymore. The Final Pandemic nearly wiped humanity out."

Eden(Mickey) looked toward the beach. "Is this all that survives?"

"No. There are other islands scattered throughout the South Pacific that were isolated enough to escape infection. And there are a few straggling survivors of the Final Pandemic that happen upon us."

"Do you kill these survivors? Before they can infect the others?"

"I wasn't designed to kill people. I was designed to kill the virus that brought on the Final Pandemic. When it first struck, a team of scientists retreated to a remote island to fashion me. By the time they released me most of humanity had already died. I was only able to spread throughout the South Pacific."

"Stanley and Lori claim you will kill us. But you say you aren't lethal to humans."

"Stanley and Lori don't fully understand me."

"I sure don't understand you. You are an intelligent virus?"

An image of Priscilla in a nightgown imprinted with the image of the Disney Little Mermaid Ariel shimmered into focus before Eden(Mickey). It was one of the nightgowns Mickey had seen hanging in Priscilla's closet back in her grandparents' house in Evanston. "Is anyone else seeing this?"

The other seven looked around at each other. "Seeing what?" Mickey(Eden) asked.

"Pris has appeared to him," Lori explained.

"Really? What does an intelligent virus look like?" Priscilla asked.

"Like you," Stanley said. He turned to Lori. "How is this possible?"

"Never mind," Eden(Mickey) said. "I just wanted to know if anyone else could see her."

"No," Lori said. "She has appeared only to you this time." She looked around to the others. "She appears to us sometimes, to guide us."

"She has never appeared to an outsider before," Stanley said.

"I'm honored. Now everybody shut up so I can talk with her." Eden(Mickey) turned his attention back to the Pris Virus. "I'm sorry. You were saying?"

"I was crafted using stem cells donated by a woman named Priscilla. She looked much like one of you." The Pris Virus pointed toward Priscilla.

When Eden(Mickey) turned to see who the Pris Virus pointed at, Priscilla noticed his stare. "What is she saying about me, Mickey?"

"That the Priscilla in this dimension donated the stem cells the virus was crafted from."

The Pris Virus continued. "My complexity was so enhanced by the scientists that as more and more copies of me spread I attained awareness. I have evolved far beyond what the biologists designed."

"Can't you just kill the dangerous germs we carry without killing us?"

"I have never encountered the germs you carry. I was designed to kill a specific virus, and its variants. I can accomplish nothing against the diseases you harbor."

"But you can still kill us."

"I can cause your death. If I rendered you unconscious, the cause of your death would be drowning."

"What if I tell you we are not survivors of the Final Pandemic. That we have come here from another dimension."

"Even if that is true, you are still carrying diseases that will harm us."

"What if we go no further? What if we agree to leave, without infecting any others than these two?"

"Where would you go?"

"To another dimension. Where our diseases won't harm anyone."

"Go." The image of Ariel-clad Priscilla dissolved from before him. Eden(Mickey) looked to Stanley and Lori. "We can go."

"We know," Lori said. "Pris just told us."

"Come with us," Eden(Mickey) said. "If you stay here, you have to die. Come with us and live."

"You'll kill us anyway. Your germs will."

"You don't know that for sure," Eden(Mickey) said. "There's no going back for you. You can't take the chance of returning to your people and infecting them. I get that. But you don't *know* that we have fatally infected you. So come with us." Eden(Mickey) turned to George. "Open Hypatia." When he hesitated, Eden(Mickey) rushed on. "Hurry. Before the Pris Virus changes her mind."

Priscilla snatched the laptop from his hands. "If George won't, I will." She opened it and held it out so Eden(Mickey) could use it. "Just get us out of here. Knowing I am a virus in this dimension is too creepy."

Eden(Mickey) began setting up the inter-dimensional travel program.

Mickey(Eden) took Lori and Stanley by their hands. "You're with us."

Stan clapped his twin on the back. "What have you got to lose, brother? Other than drowning."

Mick slipped an arm around Lori's waist. "We're going to have to get better acquainted, beautiful." When Stanley glared at him, Mick moved his hand higher up her back. "Sorry. But she looks just like someone I know." He glanced at Mickey(Eden). "Used to know. Once knew. But have forgotten about. Nearly forgotten." He turned back to Lori, looking her up and down with hungry eyes. "Anyway, come with us, please."

"Mickey, my arms are getting tired," Priscilla complained.

"Almost ready." Eden's fingers flew across the keyboard. "While you're waiting…" Bicep blared electronica out over the ocean. The dolphin that had butted Stan earlier swam up and bowled Eden(Mickey) over.

Stan wrestled the dolphin away from Eden(Mickey). "I don't think he likes your music."

Eden(Mickey) struggled to his feet then waded back to Priscilla to turn the music off. "Is that better?"

"Yes!" everyone but the dolphin yelled. He could only yip for joy.

Eden(Mickey) resumed setting up the program.

"You people are crazy," Lori said.

"But we're still breathing," Mickey(Eden) said.

"So far," Carl Friedrich chimed in.

"Where are you taking us?" Stanley asked.

"I have no idea." Mickey(Eden) poised a finger above the enter key. "You all know the drill. Everyone gather round tight and hold onto each other."

Mickey(Eden), Lori, Stanley, Priscilla, Carl Friedrich, Edie, George, Mick, and Stan huddled around Eden(Mickey). He activated the program.

11.

Cold gusting wind knocked Eden(Mickey) about snow-covered rocks while slicing through the sopping clinging little black dress that left much of Eden's wet tropical sun-baked skin exposed.

Mickey(Eden) caught her before her body toppled over the edge of an icy precipice. He hugged her close. "We've got to protect the baby." Their soaked clothes were already crusting with ice. "Find us some dry winter clothes."

"I can't." Eden's bare legs folded under the onslaught of the frigid howling wind.

Mickey(Eden) tried to support him, but instead they both tumbled into a snow bank. He rolled over on top of Eden(Mickey), still trying to protect the unborn child.

"Your chip still isn't working," Eden(Mickey) managed to say between clacking teeth, shivering so hard Eden's skeleton was in danger of coming apart at the joints. "Where are the others?"

"Forget the others." Mickey(Eden) was frantic. "Where's your laptop?"

"Priscilla had it. She was holding it while I set up the program." Eden(Mickey) dug around in the snow searching for the laptop. "We'll die if it's not here. There's no way to move on from this dimension without it. We'll freeze to death."

Mickey(Eden) clutched Eden(Mickey) to her. "If we do the baby will be the last to go."

"Quit calling it the baby. His name is Carl Friedrich."

"Or Carla." Mickey(Eden) wrapped Mickey's legs tightly around Eden's bare legs, trying to shield the exposed skin from the wind.

Eden(Mickey) snuggled into Mickey(Eden)'s embrace. "You don't know? If it's a boy or girl?"

"I didn't want to know. I know so much it's hard to be surprised. I wanted this to be a surprise. As intelligent as I am there is little left in the world that surprises me..."

"Listen!" Mickey raised Eden's head to cock a frozen ear.

"What do you hear?"

"Bicep."

"Can't be. You're hallucinating."

"The laptop is here somewhere. It's playing Bicep. Get up." Eden (Mickey) fought to free Eden's nearly frozen body from Mickey's clutches. "Let me go!"

It was difficult for Eden to relax Mickey's stiff limbs and numb hands.

Eden(Mickey) broke free, staggered up and stumbled away, leaning into the fierce blinding gale in the direction of the music. "This way!"

Mickey(Eden) crawled upright, also. Eden(Mickey) was fading away into the white, her footsteps already filling in by the time he lurched after.

Eden(Mickey) pulled on the music like a lifeline. It grew louder. The rhythms blasted through the gale-force wind, echoed off the frozen rocks and surged into burning ears.

Rounding a bare rock outcropping, Eden(Mickey) saw a cave opening ahead. Within it a bonfire blazed and music roared. He glanced back to make sure Mickey(Eden) was coming then staggered forward. The wind eased as he approached a sheltering crag. He stumbled a few more steps through the blaring electronica into the entrance and collapsed into miraculous warmth.

Two human forms in tight body suits and ski toboggans that concealed their faces emerged from deeper in the cave. "You've got to get those wet clothes off," a female voice told him. "We've got dry clothes for you."

Mickey(Eden) staggered out of the blizzard into the cave and collapsed before the blazing fire. "You, too," the other person said with a male voice. "Take those wet clothes off."

"I can't take mine off." Eden(Mickey) said with a whimper. "The chip has been damaged."

"Yes you can," the female said. "I fixed the chip. It's working now."

Eden's hands missed their first attempt at clapping since her body was shivering so badly. The second attempt was closer. The third try succeeded, and Eden's body was naked. While the female toweled it with a thick furry animal hide, Eden(Mickey) asked, "When did you repair the chip?"

"The last time we met."

Before Eden(Mickey) could delve further into the matter, Mickey (Eden) asked, "Is Priscilla here?

The woman toweling off Eden(Mickey) paused to remove her ski mask. It was Priscilla, the one from the Planck-length dimension. "Yes."

"Do you have my laptop?" Eden(Mickey) asked.

"Of course." She pointed to the rock the laptop was open on. "Where do you think the music is coming from?"

Eden(Mickey) looked all around the cave. "Are the others here?"

"No. Just me and George." At that the man helping Mickey(Eden) peel off the icy jumpsuit removed his ski mask to reveal himself as George, the one from the same dimension as this Priscilla.

"It's the goofy George and Priscilla," Eden(Mickey) moaned. Before either could object to being called goofy, he asked, "How did you get the laptop? From Priscilla? The other Priscilla? The one I left standing in the ocean?"

This Priscilla pointed to Mickey(Eden). "Eden gave it to me."

"When did I give it to you?" Mickey(Eden) asked.

George laughed. "When is a slippery question."

Dry, Eden(Mickey) rushed over to inspect the laptop.

"And you call me goofy?" Priscilla followed with an armful of clothes. "Put some clothes on."

"Yeah, Mickey," Mickey(Eden) yelled. "I know you don't care who sees me naked, but don't make me come down with pneumonia." She looked back to George, to find him leering at her naked body. "Do you mind? You look like my brother. It's creepy seeing you ogle me. I mean my body. My brother's sister's naked body. Stop it."

"I'm not your brother." Despite the protestation, George averted his attention.

Mickey(Eden) yanked the towel from George's hands to finish drying off. Turning back to Eden(Mickey), he yelled, "Turn that shit off and put something on!"

Suddenly, silence. Eden(Mickey) closed the laptop then dressed in the clothes Priscilla offered, which was an outfit identical to what she and George wore—a thin two-piece elastic body suit, boots, gloves, and ski mask toboggan. "This is awfully flimsy."

Priscilla helped him tug everything into place. "The insulating factor of this material is remarkable."

In a few minutes both of them were dry and clad in outfits that covered them from shoulders to toes. "Have you seen the others?" Mickey(Eden) asked.

George and Priscilla both shook their heads no.

"Then how did you get my laptop?" Eden(Mickey) demanded.

Priscilla looked to Mickey(Eden). "I told you. Eden gave it to us."

George took up the tale. "You said when we got here we were to build a blazing fire and blast Bicep."

Mickey(Eden) was lost. "I don't remember saying that."

"You must not have said it yet." Eden(Mickey) turned to the other two. "So now what?"

Priscilla appeared mystified. "You don't remember that, either? You told us to escort you to the throne room."

George looked around in awe. "That was the first time I'd ever been this high up on the mountain."

"What mountain are we on?" Mickey(Eden) asked.

"Remember our discussion about the mountain?" Priscilla asked Eden(Mickey). "We are at the peak of the mountain now."

"You mean we've reached the highest dimension?" Eden(Mickey) asked.

"Yes," George said.

"Isn't it amazing?" Priscilla asked.

"It's Arctic," Mickey(Eden) complained.

"Actually, it's Himalayan," George corrected.

"On a clear day you can see Chomolungma from here," Priscilla said.

"Is that supposed to mean something?" Mickey(Eden) asked.

"It's the Tibetan name for Mt. Everest, runt." Eden(Mickey) turned to George and Priscilla. "Let's go see that throne room we told you to take us to."

"First." Priscilla pulled up Eden(Mickey)'s top and pressed an ear to Eden's bare stomach. A moment later she pulled the top back down and straightened with a smile. "The baby is fine."

Mickey(Eden) picked up both of their ski mask toboggans. "Good. Let's get going."

Mickey(Eden) picked up Hypatia, and they followed George and Priscilla deeper into the cave away from the roaring fire and the blasting wind at the entrance. Before the firelight faded away they reached a heavy metal door set in rock. It was illuminated by wall sconces burning on either side. "This is as far as we go," George said.

"What are you two going to do?" Mickey(Eden) asked.

Priscilla waved. "Return to our own dimension." The two walked away deeper into the cave.

Eden(Mickey) and Mickey(Eden) stared at each other. "I guess this is it," Eden(Mickey) said. "We're in the uppermost dimension. We finally get to meet the wizard behind the curtain."

"I sure hope so," Mickey(Eden) responded. She reached for the large iron handle.

"Wait," Eden(Mickey) said. "I hear something."

Four people approached from out of the shadows. George and Priscilla walked into the torchlight with two others.

"I thought you were going back to your own dimension," Eden(Mickey) said.

"We are," George answered, as the foursome halted.

"But you just left," Mickey(Eden) said.

"That hasn't happened yet," Priscilla said.

"But you two were just here," Eden(Mickey) insisted.

"Maybe for you we were just here," George said. "But not for us."

"Then how are we here already?" Mickey(Eden) asked. "You two just saved our lives."

The two shrugged then turned away.

Mickey(Eden) yelled after them. "When you come back be sure to build a big fire. And be sure to blast Bicep on my laptop so I can hear it and find the cave."

George looked back. "We don't have your laptop."

"You will after I give it to you."

"Why don't you give it to me now?"

"Then you would just have to give it back to me again. We'd be trapped in an infinite loop."

"You'll also need to escort us to the throne room," Mickey(Eden) said.

George turned back away shaking his head, but Priscilla turned around suddenly and hurried back. "I almost forgot to do something." She smacked Eden(Mickey) up side of the head.

Eden(Mickey) glared up at her from the ground. "What was that for?"

"I had to jar the chip to get it working again." She joined George, and the two disappeared into the gloom of the cavern.

Which left the two they had escorted standing there. The male and female were clad in the same kind of body suits and ski mask toboggans.

"Take your masks off," Mickey(Eden) barked. "So we can see who you are."

Both masks came off, to reveal the faces of the islanders Lori and Stanley. "We had the masks on for a reason," Stanley said.

"Our noses are still cold," Lori said. "We went from the balmy South Pacific to this frozen place."

"With only wet swim suits on," Stanley emphasized. "I thought we were dead."

"We've never even ever *seen* snow before," Lori said, with a shiver in her voice.

"Snow is so cold." Stanley hugged himself.

Eden(Mickey) stood, rubbing the reddened side of his face. "Even now?" It was surprising how a mental problem could distract him from a physical problem, even pain. "Our suits keep us at a comfortable warmth."

"My skin's warm," Stanley explained, "but my marrow is frozen."

"Complain, complain," Mickey(Eden) chided. "You two would have died if not for us."

"We nearly *died* because of you," Lori differed.

"Is everyone ready to see who the master of the universe is?" Eden(Mickey) butted in. She pulled open the door, and the four walked through.

They entered a large sparsely furnished room. There was a stone fireplace in which logs crackled and spat sparks. Amid smoky shadows a stone floor and bare stone walls could be seen. In one wall there was a metal door like the one they had entered through, flanked by two small windows.

Eden(Mickey) crossed over to look out one of the windows. All he could see in the swirling snow was a small balcony. He groaned. The scene outside the window was just like the backdrop of the vision he had seen of Eden falling through a snow storm in the mountains. Was this where it happens? And was it really Eden he saw falling to her death? Or was it him inside Eden's body that he saw falling? He glanced back to Mickey(Eden). Should he warn her?

Mickey(Eden) noticed the concerned look. "What?"

Eden(Mickey) decided to say nothing. If it happened here then it would be he who died, although it was Eden's body that would perish. Eden and his body would live on. So he was the one who had to be wary, not Eden. "Nothing."

Eden(Mickey) turned away from the window. Against another wall were two elaborately-carved bejeweled lushly-cushioned highly-polished wooden chairs. Two tapestries hung on the wall behind these thrones. On one were numbers of many different sizes and whimsical designs, while on the other was the image of a monkey.

In the middle of the room was a long wooden table with an array of wooden chairs. Before two of the chairs were rustic place settings. In the wooden bowls were a stew, on the stone plates hunks of bread and cheese, and clay goblets held a drink. A small candle sputtered before the two settings.

Stanley and Lori rushed over to the fireplace to warm themselves.

Eden(Mickey) had other imperatives. He hurried to the table. "We're starved."

Mickey(Eden) placed a restraining hand on his shoulder. "We're not alone." She directed his attention to a shadowy corner.

The giant hibiscus flowers with the faces of Stan and Laurie faced them. They were in large pots, and a root from each had grown out to connect with the other. "Is Eden here?" the Stan plant asked.

"We were interrupted," the Laurie plant said.

Eden(Mickey) stared at the two plants with naked yearning. Yet he sagged with a sigh. "Maybe later." He bolted for the table.

Lori stared at the two giant flowers in surprise. "Why do these strange creatures look like us?"

"We're sisters," the plant Laurie said, stretching a dozen tendrils out toward islander Lori.

"Leave them alone."

Everyone turned toward the voice. George stood in the open doorway leading back to the cave with Priscilla at his side. Laurie's tendrils withdrew from Lori. "You two were told to remain quiet."

The plant Stanley pointed a tendril at Mickey(Eden). "He spoke first."

Priscilla turned to Mickey(Eden). "Sorry about this. They weren't supposed to accompany the two of you to the dimension the spaceship was in." She motioned toward Eden(Mickey). "But they were both making love to Mickey at the time the inter-dimensional travel program was activated. Since they were so intimately entwined with Eden's body they traveled with it. But they couldn't remain in the space ship, that would have caused an even bigger disruption in the Shattering. So while the program was still running they were snatched from the spaceship to here, where they would cause the least problems."

"Until you two can figure out what to do with them," George finished.

"Us two?" Mickey(Eden) was surprised. She glanced at Eden (Mickey). "It's up to us what happens to these two?" A malicious grin graced Mickey's face as it gazed upon the pair of giant potted flowers.

"It's always been up to you two," Priscilla said.

George turned his attention to islanders Stanley and Lori by the fire. "What are they doing here?"

"You brought them," Eden(Mickey) said, his attention torn between what was going on with George and Priscilla and the food on the table. He knew the stew must be getting cold.

"Ahh." George grinned. "Was that before or after we brought the pair of hungry lions here?" Seeing the baffled stares grow worried, he continued. "The ones from Mitchell's ark."

"That's enough," Priscilla said. "Stop teasing. You are confusing them."

"I'm just getting him back for punching me."

"I never punched you." Eden(Mickey) said. "Yet. That must mean I get to sometime in the future." He grinned. "I'm looking forward to that."

George was perplexed. "Are you sure that hasn't happened yet." He felt his lower lip. "My lip's swollen."

"It may have happened for you already," Eden(Mickey) said, "but not for me. I guess that means you get punched twice."

George pondered, then darted forward. "Let me see your knuckles."

Priscilla grabbed him. "He's messing with you, George. Because you were messing with him about the lions. He already punched you, when he first arrived in our dimension. We need to go. We've told them too much already." She scowled at Eden(Mickey). "The spaceship wasn't that kind of ark. There are no lions here." George glowered at Eden(Mickey) as Priscilla pulled him out through the door leading to the cave.

Mickey(Eden) turned to Eden(Mickey). "Did you really punch George?"

"Yes," he said as he sat at the table. "It was the most fun I've had since all this started." He glanced at the two plants. "Nearly the most fun."

"The fluid space-time of their dimension would be too confusing for me," Mickey(Eden) said.

"Are you certain time is so linear for us?"

Mickey(Eden) pinpointed her hateful snarl on the two plants. She wasn't about to get sidetracked into a discussion with Mickey about time. She had revenge on her mind. "Eat before it gets cold."

Eden(Mickey) would not be deterred, either. "Do you think the increase of entropy really forces the arrow of time to go only one way? Haven't you ever done things you have no memories of doing? Maybe you *had* done them but were presently at a time before you did them. Or haven't you ever walked into a place you'd never been before that seemed familiar to you? Maybe you had been there but were presently at a time prior to that. And déjà vu, what do you think that's all about if not kinks in your timeline?"

Mickey(Eden) was too single-minded at the moment to consider time paradoxes. She turned back on the plants with a vengeance. "So we get to decide what happens to you two. This is going to be the most fun *I've* had since this whole thing began."

The Stan and Laurie plants shrank down into their pots as far as they could. "We didn't mean you any harm," Stan said.

"We were only trying to take care of you," Laurie said.

Islanders Stanley and Lori abandoned the fire to step between the two plants and an advancing Mickey(Eden). "You will not harm our brother and sister." In appreciation, the Laurie plant curled her tendrils around Stanley, while the Stan plant curled his tendrils around Lori.

"Like hell I won't," Mickey(Eden) said. "They rooted me to a tree and stuffed my body full of vines!"

"You mean my body," Eden(Mickey) mumbled with a mouthful of

food.

"I was the one who suffered through it." Mickey(Eden) sniffed. A vile smile slid across Mickey's lips as she glared at the plants. "Is that fear I smell?" She sniffed again. "Or is it terror?"

"They are kind of fun," Eden(Mickey) said, smiling at the two plants. "I've got some unfinished business with them myself."

The Laurie plant reached out one tentative tendril toward Eden(Mickey).

Mickey(Eden) slapped the tendril down. "Don't think this is over." She joined Eden(Mickey) at the table. "No stinky socks?" Getting the answer by the way he was devouring the fare, she looked over her shoulder. The Stan and Laurie plants had embraced islanders Stanley and Lori with their tendrils. "That's disgusting."

Gobbling, Eden(Mickey) looked to see what was going on. "When I finish eating I think I'll join them."

Mickey(Eden) turned hateful eyes on him. "Not with *my* body."

A door that had been concealed by the tapestries opened behind the thrones, yet no one entered. A loudly muffled argument could be heard. "Are George and Priscilla back again?" Eden(Mickey) speculated. "Or have they just gotten here?"

"I don't know when it is, but who else quarrels like those two?"

The hushed sharp voices quieted. Miriam emerged from behind the tapestries holding the hand of the gibbon walking at her side. Next came Lucy in a gown emblazoned with numbers of all shapes and sizes and creative calligraphies. "Welcome to the highest dimension," Miriam bid.

Lucy smiled, stepping out from behind her. "I see Eden and Mickey have already partaken of our hospitality."

"It was getting cold." Eden(Mickey) slurped. "Just keep that gibbon away from me. It peed and threw poop on me last time."

"That wasn't Ralph, Mickey," Miriam said, glancing down to the gibbon. "That was me."

"So don't do it now, for sure," Eden(Mickey) said. "That would really be disgusting."

Mickey(Eden) stared at the gibbon. "That's the Supreme Leader?"

Eden(Mickey) stared at the gibbon. "It could be the homeless guy from my alley."

"This isn't the Ralph either of you know," Miriam answered. "I just named him Ralph. I thought the name fitting considering how Ralph has treated me in other dimensions."

Islander Lori opened her arms wide. "He's so cute."

Miriam released the gibbon's hand, and it scurried over to Lori.

When she stooped to pick him up, the gibbon grabbed a breast. Lori squealed and slapped the squeezing hand away. The gibbon ran back to Miriam's side.

"Sure acts like Ralph," Eden(Mickey) said between slurps.

Lucy and Miriam took their seats on the thrones, each before the appropriate banner. The gibbon climbed up into Miriam's lap, while Lucy fingered the numbers carved into the arms of her throne. "Hello, Stanley and Lori. You two are as unexpected as your floral twins were."

Everyone turned to look at the two potted plants in the corner wrapped all around the two islanders. "Did George and Priscilla bring the plants, too?" Eden(Mickey) asked.

"No," Lucy answered. "They just popped in one day. Out of the blue. We have no idea where they came from."

"I do," Mickey(Eden) said. "They come from this horrible jungle dimension."

"Our whole world isn't jungle," the Stan plant protested. "You visited the equatorial zone. At other latitudes there are forests and plains and prairies and steppes and tundra and deserts, and even mountains like this. Like the old tale of the seven blind men and the elephant..."

Looking up from an empty bowl and a bare plate, Eden(Mickey) cut him off. He'd heard that old story too many times. "Why are we here?"

"Because you two shattered the barriers between dimensions," Miriam said.

"We directed you here, from lower dimensions up through higher ones," Lucy said. "Patching and shoring up the barriers as you went. It was all part of my plan."

"*Your* plan?" Miriam sniffed. "You mean *Mitchell's* plan. *Your* plan had more holes in it than second-hand underwear."

"At least I came up with a plan." Lucy looked down her sharp nose at the monkey. "You're too busy fussing over that stupid monkey..."

Mickey(Eden) butted in. "I don't recall fixing anything." She looked to Eden(Mickey) "Do you?"

"Are you going to finish that?" Eden(Mickey) asked, indicating the untouched food on the table before Mickey(Eden). She shoved it all over to him, and he resumed eating.

"Your passing through the dimensions wove all the barriers between them back together," Lucy said.

"Like a needle pulling thread through a ripped piece of fabric." Miriam pantomimed sewing.

"All that's left for you two to do is tie off your sewing." Lucy pantomimed tying off sewing. "You need to do that from Mickey's dimension, where the whole thing began."

"Does that mean we can go back home now?" Mickey(Eden) asked.

"Back to Mickey's dimension," Miriam said. "But why are you so anxious to go back? You were so anxious to leave your dimension in the first place."

"From here you have a glorious opportunity," Lucy said. "From this uppermost dimension you can influence events all down the mountain."

Eden(Mickey) looked up from licking Mickey(Eden)'s bowl. "How do you know this is the uppermost dimension?"

Lucy smiled with indulgence. "We're at the top of the mountain."

"So? There could be dimensions above the mountain. In the clouds. Have you never considered Heaven?"

Miriam also produced a smile. "There is no Heaven."

"How can you be sure?" Eden(Mickey) set aside the licked-clean bowl. "*We* can't perceive dimensions higher than *ours*. So if there was one higher than this." He swept both arms about. "How would you know?"

"There are eleven dimensions," Lucy stated. "This is the eleventh. You are wasting our time on fruitless speculation and naval gazing."

"Oh, Mickey knows the contours of his naval very well," Mickey(Eden) said.

"Enough," Miriam commanded. "We have many important things to discuss."

Eden(Mickey) cast his gaze up to the ceiling. "How about a sign?"

A cold blast of air swept down the chimney and extinguished the fire, propelling smoke and ashes all through the room. Mickey(Eden), Lucy and Miriam jumped up to escape the billowing mess, while Eden(Mickey) covered up the remaining food in an attempt to preserve it. The gibbon squealed and ran about. The islander couple erupted in coughing. The two plants looked at each other and, unbothered since they didn't inhale any of the ashes, merely shrugged.

"That was just the wind!" Lucy exclaimed, backing away from the fireplace.

Eden(Mickey) picked errant ashes out of the food. "Great timing, for *just* wind."

"Are you saying you *knew* the wind was going to blow out the fire?" Miriam asked.

"I was hoping *something* would happen," Eden(Mickey) said. "I just didn't know what. That's how signs work. You ask for one, then rue what it turns out to be."

Mickey(Eden) continued to brush ashes off her bodysuit. "Did it have to be so messy?"

"To get everyone's attention?" Eden(Mickey) stopped bothering with the ashes on the food. "To show that someone higher up is paying attention to us? Yes."

"There is no one higher than us," Miriam insisted. "We are at the peak. We are the crown of creation."

"And you've got no place to go," Eden(Mickey) added in a sing-song voice. He turned to Mickey(Eden). "Did you know the lyrics from that Jefferson Airplane song from the sixties, 'Crown of Creation', came practically word for word from a science fiction novel written in the nineteen-fifties by John Wyndham?"

Mickey(Eden), accustomed to the odd tangents Mickey's mind went off on, ignored him and remained focused on Miriam. "How can you be so sure?"

The Laurie plant squealed from the corner. The gibbon was grop-ing a petal.

"Ralph!" Eden(Mickey) yelled. "Knock it off!" He looked back to Miriam. "Are you positive that isn't really Ralph?"

Miriam appeared mystified. "I just named him Ralph."

Eden(Mickey) smiled. "That proves my point. A being from a higher dimension suggested you name the gibbon Ralph because it really is Ralph. Their commands come down to us in lower dimensions as irresistible urges or flashes of insight out of the blue."

"What about us?" islander Stanley asked. His and Lori's coughing had eased.

Miriam was too involved considering who the monkey at her side really was, so Lucy answered him. "We can return you to your dimension. Or you can remain here."

"It's so cold here," Lori said.

"You'll get used to it," Lucy said. Seeing their doubtful expressions, she continued, "Even if you don't, isn't the cold preferable to drowning?"

Lori and Stanley looked at each other, neither confirming it was.

"We're ready to go back," Mickey(Eden) said.

Miriam focused a critical eye on them. "Why are you so eager to go back? Imagine the power you can exert throughout the world from here."

"You would be like gods," Lucy said.

"Like us," Miriam added.

Eden(Mickey) glanced up at the ceiling. "I think the real gods are above you."

"Was it you two who intervened and screwed up George and

Priscilla's plans?" Mickey(Eden) asked.

"Nothing got screwed up," Lucy said. "Their plans were part of our plans. They did exactly what we wanted them to do."

Lucy turned to the two islanders. "Have you decided?"

"We'll stay," Lori said. Stanley nodded in glum agreement.

Miriam noticed Eden(Mickey) had opened his laptop and begun setting up the trans-dimensional navigation program. "Don't bother."

"The program only moves you one dimension at a time. In only one direction." Lucy said. "Up."

"You two need to go all the way down," Miriam said, "and go up from there."

"All the way down?" Mickey(Eden) blanched. "Into a dimension lower than Mickey's?"

"There is only one dimension lower than Mickey's." Lucy said.

"Follow us," Miriam said. The two walked to the door leading out to the balcony.

Eden(Mickey) closed the laptop, and he and Mickey(Eden) joined them. When Lori and Stanley started to follow, Lucy raised a hand. "Not you two. Wait for us here."

"While you're waiting." Miriam pointed to a broom in the corner. "Clean up all these ashes."

"So Lori and Stanley are going to be your slaves?" Mickey(Eden) asked.

"Servants, not slaves," Miriam said.

"What did you expect?" Lucy asked. "They certainly aren't our equals." Both older women pulled their shawls tight. "You need to put your toboggans on and pull your ski masks down over your faces."

While Eden(Mickey) and Mickey(Eden) did this, Miriam opened the door to the balcony. A gust of wind swirled snow into the room. Even though not dressed for the weather, the frigid white blast didn't seem to effect either of the elderly women. Miriam and Lucy stepped out onto the balcony.

The other two followed, hunkering down in the icy howl. Eden (Mickey) walked across the small balcony to the railing and peered over. There was nothing to see other than a whirling dervish of snow. He had a bad feeling about this. It looked just like the snow he'd had the vision of Eden plummeting through. "Why are we out here?"

"To jump," Miriam said.

Eden(Mickey) drew back flat against the door, as far away as he could get from the edge of the balcony. "No way."

"It's the only way," Lucy said, taking Eden(Mickey) by the arm and urging him forward. "You will plunge all the way down to the lowest dimension."

"Will we survive?" Mickey(Eden) asked.

"We haven't killed you yet."

"There's always a first, and last, time," Eden(Mickey) said.

Miriam extended an arm out over the railing. "Feel that?"

Eden held Mickey's arm out. There was a strong updraft.

"That will keep you from falling too fast." Miriam pulled her arm back. "You won't die."

Eden(Mickey) seized the railing with both hands. "What about the baby?"

Since Miriam was distracted trying to pry Eden's fingers from around the railing, Lucy took over persuading. "You have met your grown child in other dimensions. So it must survive the plunge."

"Come on, runt," Mickey(Eden) offered a hand. "Let's do this together. As a family."

"I've never even set foot on a roller coaster," Eden(Mickey) protested.

"Then you are in for the ride of your life." Mickey(Eden) clasped Eden's hand.

Eden(Mickey) allowed her to pull him over the railing. Standing on the edge, he looked down. He could see nothing but a blizzard of white.

When Eden's knees buckled, Mickey(Eden) grabbed Eden(Mickey). "Maybe I should hang onto this." Mickey(Eden) took the laptop. "It's safer with me. You're liable to pass out and drop it."

Eden's eyes were still locked onto the tumultuous white depths. "I wish I hadn't eaten so much."

"I warned you the morning sickness would start soon," Mickey (Eden) said.

"How am I to know when it's morning, the way we're bouncing around from one dimension to another," Eden(Mickey) replied.

"That will soon be over," Lucy said.

"A pregnancy only lasts nine months," Miriam added.

"We'll be back in our own bodies by then, right?" Eden(Mickey) asked.

Lucy shrugged. "You can't expect us to solve every problem." She and Lucy withdrew back inside and locked the door. They smiled out at them, one from each window on either side of the door.

Mickey(Eden) peered down into the abyss. "Now would be a good time for one of your signs."

The updraft doubled in force. It nearly knocked both of them over the railing and back onto the balcony. Mickey(Eden) smiled, then let go of the railing and stepped off. The powerful updraft flipped her to horizontal, and she hovered face-up in mid-air before the balcony. "Look, Mickey. You were right. Someone in a dimension higher than this *is* taking care of us." Mickey(Eden) pointed to the windows. "Look at them."

Eden(Mickey) looked back to find Miriam and Lucy both gazing upward in surprise as if trying to peer into a higher dimension.

Mickey(Eden) returned her gaze to Eden(Mickey). "Let go, Mickey."

Eden(Mickey) released the railing finger by finger. The updraft lifted him up off the edge of the balcony and flipped Eden's body to horizontal, face-down. The two floated side by side, bobbing up and down. "Is this what climbing the first hill of a roller coaster is like?"

Before Mickey(Eden) could answer, the updraft died. They plummeted.

12.

Eden(Mickey) smacked down onto something soft. His first thought was to feel Eden's abdomen, as if he could tell if the baby had been injured. His second thought was to roll over so he didn't throw up all over himself. Once the heaving subsided, he tried to determine what he had landed on. It was so dimly lit wherever he was at he couldn't see what it was. He probed the softness until he also felt some hardness. Hard bones. Soft flesh. He had landed on a pile of people.

Was he back underground? With the Morlox? On another heap of gassed captives? Eden(Mickey) scrambled off the bodies. Eden's hands and knees immediately scraped hard ground. This was a much smaller heap, in which he hadn't been entombed. By that time Eden's eyes were adjusting to the faint flickering light. It wasn't pitch black, like in the Morlox underground. Careful to avoid the vomit, he felt around until he determined there were only three bodies.

"What happened?"

Eden(Mickey) couldn't tell where the panicked male voice came from, but he assumed it was from one of the bodies he had landed on. "Who is this?"

"Carl Friedrich. Who is this?"

"Mickey. In Eden's body. Are you okay?"

"No. I hurt like hell. Something just slammed into me. What's going on?"

A female voice called out. "Eden?"

"No, Mickey. Who is this?" Eden(Mickey) asked.

"Priscilla. What's going on?"

"I don't know," Eden(Mickey) said. "But I'm sorry about throwing up on you. There was this fall like a bottomless roller coaster, and I've got morning sickness."

"You didn't throw up on me," Priscilla said.

"I threw up on somebody. Carl Friedrich?"

"I don't feel anything gross on me."

"Somebody else is here," Eden(Mickey) said.

"It's me. Edie. I feel clean, too. But I hurt, too, like Carl Friedrich said."

"Yeah," Priscilla said. "Me, too. How did we all get hurt?"

"I landed on you. And I know I threw up on someone." Eden (Mickey) leaned in close to the pile of bodies. He located a face and squinted, trying to see in the dim light. It was Priscilla. "I found you, Priscilla."

Priscilla screamed.

Eden(Mickey) lurched back. "What's wrong?"

"I just saw myself. Laying on the ground. With vomit on my face."

"Sorry." Eden(Mickey) wiped at the sickness, trying to clean Priscilla's face.

"Is there a twin of me in this dimension?"

Before Eden(Mickey) could consider this possibility, there was a loud thump! And a grunt. Then a moan. "Who else is here?" he called out.

"Just me," Mickey(Eden) replied. "How'd you get so far ahead of me?"

"Because you're such a lightweight."

"Mass doesn't determine how fast you fall," Mickey(Eden) said. "Galileo proved that centuries ago."

"That was a joke, runt. Did you land on some people?"

"I landed on something soft. People?" After a moment, she added, "Yeah, people."

"There should be three of them."

"Any idea who they are?"

"Mick, George, and Stan. They should start waking up in a minute."

"What's going on, Eden?" Carl Friedrich demanded from the dark. "Mickey here doesn't have a clue."

Mickey(Eden) failed to answer.

"I'm so relieved you survived the fall, Eden," Eden(Mickey) said. "I had a vision of you falling through a blizzard in the mountains. I assumed you were falling to your death."

"And you didn't warn me about this vision?"

"I thought it was me I was seeing. Your body with me in it. That was falling."

Anger rose in Mickey(Eden)'s voice. "You better not let my body die, Mickey!"

Stan interrupted the argument. "Why are you laying on top of me, Eden?"

Mickey(Eden) smiled down at him. "I thought you liked having me on top."

"Not when you look like Mickey."

"I'm so glad you're okay, Stan, I could kiss you, but you probably wouldn't appreciate a kiss from Mickey. Anyone else able to speak yet?"

"Yeah," Mick replied. "Is the baby okay, Mickey?"

There was no reply from Eden(Mickey).

"Mickey is too mad at me to talk to me, Eden," Mick told Mickey(Eden).

"This Mickey, me, is the Mickey who is mad at you." Mickey(Eden) turned toward Eden(Mickey). "Mick wants to know if the baby is okay? I'd like to know your thoughts on that too, dear."

"I didn't hear Mick ask anything." Eden(Mickey) answered.

"Mickey didn't hear you, Mick."

"HOW IS THE BABY!!!" Mick asked. Silence.

"You didn't hear that?" Mickey(Eden) asked in disbelief.

"I only hear you," Eden(Mickey) said. He laughed. "I know what's going on. Who's the runt now, Eden?"

"You've been here longer than me," Mickey(Eden) protested. "You've had longer to think about it."

"Me and you are the only ones talking," Eden(Mickey) said.

"You're wrong. I've been talking with Stan and Mick. If George is here, he hasn't woke up yet. My brother can sleep through anything."

"The three of them, and the three I landed on, are still out cold," Eden(Mickey) said. "At least their bodies are."

"No, we're not." Protestations came from Priscilla, Carl Friedrich, and Edie.

"Did you just hear Priscilla, Carl Friedrich, and Eden all claim they are awake?" Eden(Mickey) asked.

"No," Mickey(Eden) replied.

"That's because their voices are only in my head," Eden(Mickey) said.

"You mean Stan, Mick, and George are in here with me? In *your* body?"

"Seems that way," Eden(Mickey) said. "That's why I can't hear Stan and Mick talking, or George snoring. Those voices are only in your head. In *my* head, I mean. That you are also in."

George awoke with a snort. "What's up?"

"I've got three men in here with me." Mickey(Eden) answered. "And I don't want to hear any dirty jokes about a foursome. You are one of the three men, George, so don't gross me out."

"Actually, there are two men and two women in *your* body," Eden(Mickey) said. "There are three men and one woman in *my* body."

"Does that mean we're dead?" Priscilla asked.

"Good question," Eden(Mickey) replied. "I'll check." He inspected the three bodies he had landed on, doing his best to avoid the mess he had made on them. They all were breathing, and had good heartbeats. "All three of mine are alive. Check yours, Eden."

Mickey(Eden) did. "Yeah, they're all alive. Must be in some kind of coma." She looked the laptop over. "Your laptop seems intact." She crawled across to the other pile of bodies and handed it to Eden(Mickey).

When Eden(Mickey) opened the inter-dimensional travel program, Carl Friedrich yelled, "Wait a minute! If you two go on to another dimension, will you leave us behind in this one?"

Eden(Mickey) looked up to Mickey(Eden). "Carl Friedrich has a good question."

"I don't give a damn if you think it's a good question," Carl Friedrich fumed. "Just give me a good answer."

"Give us a minute," Eden(Mickey) told Mickey(Eden). He closed Eden's eyes so he could concentrate on the conversation inside Eden's head. "You are with me now. In this head. So how could I leave you behind?"

"This is really weird for me," Edie said. "I can see my body when you look at it. but I'm here, inside you, seeing it myself through your eyes."

Eden(Mickey) laughed. "Now you know what I've been dealing with. I'm often staring at my own body through Eden's eyes."

"This isn't funny, Mickey," Priscilla objected. "I'd like to get back into my body at some point."

Eden(Mickey) stopped laughing. "Okay. See if any of you can move my right hand. Eden's right hand. *This* right hand."

"I can't!" Edie cried out.

"Calm down," Eden(Mickey) said. "That's a good thing. We wouldn't want four people animating one body. It would be chaos."

"So you are still in control of Eden's body, Mickey?" Priscilla asked.

"And we're just along for the ride?" Carl Friedrich asked with a snarl.

"Seems that way," Eden(Mickey) said. He opened Eden's eyes, to find Mickey(Eden) had his closed. "I'm done."

"Shut up," Mickey(Eden) snapped. "We're still talking."

While waiting, Eden(Mickey) started setting up the program on the laptop.

"Where are we going now?" Priscilla asked.

"Home, I hope," Eden(Mickey) said. "Lucy and Miriam said we were falling to the lowest dimension, and that it was only one dimension below ours. If I tally up all the dimensions I've visited, this makes the eleventh. So this should be our last inter-dimensional jump. "

"I hate you when you babble like that!" Carl Friedrich yelled.

"Quit yelling," Eden(Mickey) replied. "You're giving me a headache."

"And you threw up on me," Carl Friedrich said.

"A pregnant woman gets sick," Eden(Mickey) said. "I couldn't help it."

"Maybe I can't help giving you a headache!" Carl Friedrich said.

"If you keep yelling I'll drown you out with Bicep."

"No!" Edie begged.

"Be quiet, Carl Friedrich," Priscilla demanded.

"What was that about Bicep?" Mickey(Eden) asked. "You were muttering to yourself."

Eden(Mickey) looked to see his eyes were open. "I was muttering to Carl Friedrich." There was silence inside Eden's head. "Good. He's so mad at me he's not talking."

"You never answered Mick's question," Mickey(Eden) said.

"I didn't hear Mick's question," Eden(Mickey) replied.

"How is the baby?" Eden's hand slipped up Eden(Mickey)'s top to probe her own abdomen.

"Can you tell anything?"

Eden withdrew Mickey's hand and pulled the top back down. "No. Get us out of here."

"What about us?" Mick asked.

"As long as we're in physical contact with all of your bodies, we should be okay," Mickey(Eden) replied.

"We got left behind before," Priscilla pointed out.

"And we were holding onto each other then," Edie added.

"But this time you are all in our heads," Mickey(Eden) said. "So you should all go along wherever our heads go."

"So what happens when we get back?" George asked. "Will we still be stuck in your heads?"

"I don't know," Mickey(Eden) said. "Maybe what's happened here is a feature of this low dimension. Perhaps the energy level is so low here it can't support eight individuals. So your consciousness' were forced into us while your bodies went into a coma. If that's the case, then when we move on up to the next highest dimension, Mickey's dimension, which has a higher energy level, we should separate out back into eight individuals."

"This situation reminds me of a Bose-Einstein condensate. The way things congeal into a single glob at absolute zero, then separate back to the original individual things once the temperature rises sufficiently." Eden(Mickey) wiped Eden's brow. "Without the absolute zero part." Seeing the puzzled look on his face, he replied, "You were talking out loud."

"Let's keep doing that," Mickey(Eden) said. "That way maybe we can follow the conversations going on in each other's heads if we can hear at least one side of them." She started to rise, but collapsed back. "I feel really weak. See if you can get up."

Eden(Mickey) attempted, failed. "I can't. And I feel really sick."

Shrieks of "No!" from Priscilla, Carl Friedrich, and Edie echoed inside Eden's head.

"Maybe we should sit still and see what we can learn from here."

"It's really hot," Mickey(Eden) said.

"That could be these suits," Eden(Mickey) said. "Their insulating factor is high."

Mickey(Eden) peeled her shirt off. "No, it's not these clothes. It really is hot."

Eden(Mickey) pulled his shirt off, too. "You're right. It's stifling."

"Look down," Carl Friedrich suggested.

Eden(Mickey) looked down.

"You've got nice tits."

Mickey jerked Eden's eyes back up. "You shouldn't talk about your mother like that."

"I am not your son!"

"All three of my guys are upset with you for flashing my tits," Mickey(Eden) growled. "I'm not too happy about it, either."

"You could look away." Eden(Mickey) raised Eden's arms to slip the top back on.

"Nah," Mickey(Eden) said. "I'm actually kind of enjoying the sight. They look just like Edie's."

Eden(Mickey) pulled the shirt on. "There's something twisted about that, but I'm too tired to figure out what." He sniffed. "Something stinks."

"All that puke you spit up on us," Edie said.

"I smell it, too." Mickey(Eden) said. "Rotten eggs?"

"Sulphur." Eden(Mickey) said. "You think this is Hellades?"

"Are we in Hell?" Edie asked.

"Please don't leave us behind in Hell," Priscilla pleaded.

Carl Friedrich scoffed. "There is no Hell."

"Maybe leave him behind," Edie suggested.

"Will everyone please be quiet," Eden(Mickey) begged.

"Yes, please," Mickey(Eden) said. "Mickey and I are trying to learn what's going on here and we can't think straight with all this jabbering in our heads." There was silence inside both heads.

"I'm feeling pretty bad," Eden(Mickey) said. "If I pass out we might never get out of here."

"You're right, we shouldn't linger," Mickey(Eden) agreed. "Besides, we don't know what being here in this low energy is doing to the baby. It might cause a birth defect."

Hearing that, Eden(Mickey) got to work in a panic setting up the inter-dimensional travel program on Hypatia. Until he heard a soft moan. He looked around, but could see nothing in the dim haze. "Did you hear that?"

"Yes," Eden, Carl Friedrich, and Priscilla all answered.

"I told you three to be quiet."

"I heard it," Mickey(Eden) said. "It's getting louder. Hurry up."

"Okay," Eden(Mickey) said. "I'll concentrate on this. You watch out for whatever is moaning." He resumed setting up the program.

Mickey(Eden) grabbed George and drug him across to the other pile of bodies. "If we're going to travel up to the next dimension we all need to be together."

"Please don't let Mickey vomit on me," George said.

Mickey(Eden) pulled him up onto the pile of Priscilla, Carl Friedrich, and Eden. "If he does, when we get out of here and you're still in a coma I'll clean you up." She drug Stan over next, and piled him on.

"Mickey," Priscilla spoke up, "I just saw it out of the corner of your eye. George's hand is on my butt."

"I thought you liked George," Eden(Mickey) said, distracted with the laptop.

"Not this George. Eden's brother. I like our George. Your roommate."

"So it's okay for my roommate to have his hand on your butt?"

"No!"

Eden(Mickey) paused working to slap George's hand away. "How's that?"

"Thank you, Mickey."

Mickey(Eden) pulled Mick's body up onto the pile. "I considered leaving this body behind."

"If you did you might get stuck with him in your head," Eden (Mickey) replied.

"Then he's coming for sure," Mickey(Eden) said. "Did you find out what the moaning is?"

"I hear it all around us."

"It's getting louder."

"They must be getting closer."

"Who?"

"Damned souls, probably."

Eden(Mickey) looked up in shocked disbelief. "You think this is really Hell?"

"Hellades. Yes. Let's get out of here before the guy with the horns and pitchfork shows up." By this point the moaning had grown to a steady rumble.

"I'm ready," Eden(Mickey) said. The two of them stretched out across the six prone bodies, then grabbed each other's hand. Mickey (Eden) held onto the laptop with her free hand, while Eden(Mickey)'s index finger on his free hand hovered above the enter key.

Mickey(Eden), Eden(Mickey)'s grim face mere inches away, said, "If you get sick again please don't throw up in my face. Remember, it will really be your face you're throwing up on."

Eden(Mickey) smiled back. "Yeah, but you'll be the one to experience it."

A large ball of fire blazed into existence a meter away. As the flames ebbed, a human form began to materialize.

"It's the Devil!" Mickey(Eden) screamed. "Go!"

Eden(Mickey) stared into the flames. The way they danced, the way the hue shifted from yellow to orange to red to blue, the figures that took shape within, small human forms screaming in agony, torturing each other, pleasuring each other. A face began to take shape within the flames. A bright visage of flickering evil.

Mickey(Eden), who never saw the entrancing face of fire since Mickey's head was turned away toward Eden's mesmerized face, released the laptop to jam Eden's index finger down onto the enter key. Just as the pile of bodies was engulfed in flames.

PART FOUR
NEARING (NEARLY) NORMAL

1.

Eden(Mickey) threw up.

Once the heaves subsided, he saw he was on the floor and Mickey (Eden) was kneeling at his side stroking her own hair. "All done?"

Eden(Mickey) peered up into his own weary yet excited eyes. "Where are we?"

"Home. At least your home."

Eden(Mickey) saw they were in the basement apartment. The sight of the blackboards and the two easy chairs was comforting. "Back to where it all began." He kissed Hypatia. She had gotten them back home. Heaving a sigh, only then did he notice the other six bodies strewn across the floor. "Are they alive?"

"Don't know yet. When I woke up you were tossing." Mickey(Eden) struggled upright.

"Any of them screaming in your head?" Eden(Mickey) asked. "Mine are quiet."

Mickey(Eden) paused to consider. "Mine, too. I hope it stays that way."

"Yes. Having you in my body is bad enough. I don't want another three people tromping around in there." Eden(Mickey) watched Mickey (Eden) stagger over to Stan. *Interesting first choice,* he thought.

Mickey(Eden) dropped down to Stan's side and shook him. "Stan. Wake up."

His eyelids cracked. "Where are we?"

"Mickey and George's apartment. We made it to Mickey's dimension. Are you okay?"

Stan sat up. "Yeah." He looked around at the others. "How about everybody else?"

"Will you check on them? I've got to take care of Mickey. He's sick. Again."

Stan turned his dazed gaze to Eden(Mickey). "He's pregnant. Pregnant people get sick. Fact of life."

Mickey(Eden) drew back, offended. "I don't know if it is or not. I've not experienced it much myself yet. Maybe if *I* was in control of my body it wouldn't be getting so sick. A lot of it is willpower. I've got a strong will. Maybe *I* could keep my breakfast in my stomach."

"Are you jealous of yourself?" Stan staggered to his feet. "Don't do this to me, Eden." He staggered away toward Priscilla.

Mickey(Eden) rose and kicked the George and Martha chair. "Is there a mop in this *dump*, Mickey?"

"Bathroom closet," Eden(Mickey) said. He tried to stand.

Mickey(Eden) headed for the bathroom. "Sit still. I don't want you falling and harming my baby."

Eden(Mickey) settled back down to the floor. "So it's back to being *your* baby."

"It always has been my baby. You're just a babysitter." Mickey (Eden) cursed upon entering the bathroom. Two men sharing one bathroom. Disgusting. She located the mop and bucket. While filling the bucket in the tub, she stared at the shower head. She wanted a shower so bad. And to get out of this hot bodysuit she had sweated in so much while in Hellades. Maybe Mickey could find a nice dress for his body. She laughed, imagining Mickey's body in a dress, and his reaction to seeing it.

When Mickey(Eden) rolled the filled bucket into the living room, she saw Priscilla on her feet, Edie sitting up, and Stan rousing George. Eden(Mickey) was on hands and knees waking up Carl Friedrich. Mick was still out cold. "Is my ex-husband dead?"

"Probably not," Stan answered. "We just haven't got to him yet."

Priscilla stooped down to him. "I'll see."

Mickey(Eden) glowered at Eden(Mickey). "I thought I told you to sit still."

"I wanted to check on our son," Eden(Mickey) replied, then hastily corrected. "Your son."

Mickey(Eden) talked while mopping. "As soon as everyone is awake, we need to figure out what we're going to do."

Edie turned to her. "We're back, right?" She turned to Eden (Mickey). "Back where we're supposed to be?"

"You four might be back home," Mickey(Eden) answered, "but four of us aren't."

Eden(Mickey) gazed all around. "This looks like my dimension. But it could be a different one. One that looks like ours."

"How do we find out?" Priscilla asked.

Carl Friedrich sprang to his feet. "I'll let you know."

"What are you doing?" Mickey(Eden) asked.

"Getting away from all you crazy people." Carl Friedrich headed for the door.

"If you leave here," Mickey(Eden) said, "you might not be able to get back. If this isn't really your dimension."

"She's right, Carl Friedrich," Eden(Mickey) said, rising from the floor.

Carl Friedrich crossed to the door. "You can't stop me from leaving."

Stan leaped forward. "I bet I can." He placed a heavy hand on the front door to keep Carl Friedrich from opening it.

Eden(Mickey) looked around at everyone, including Mick, who was just opening his eyes under prodding by Priscilla. "Let's talk this over before we do anything rash."

Mickey(Eden) wrung the mop out. "For one thing, me and Mickey are still stuck in the wrong bodies."

With a curse, Carl Friedrich walked away from the door. Stan leaned against it to keep anyone else from leaving.

Eden(Mickey) collapsed into the mouse chair. "Do pregnant women always feel so lousy?" He pointed toward the kitchen. "There should be food and drink. If anyone is hungry. I'm not, for a change. I just threw up my appetite." He pointed toward a closed door. "Don't go in there."

Mickey(Eden) rolled the bucket back to the bathroom. "Is your roommate asleep in there?"

Eden(Mickey) brightened, looking to Eden's brother. "Yes! Change of plans. George? Go in and wake up George. It'll scare the shit out of him."

Instead, Eden's brother headed for the kitchen in search of food.

"When can we go home?" Priscilla asked. "I've got puke all over me."

"You can take a shower here," Eden(Mickey) offered.

Priscilla looked herself over in disgust. "And put these filthy clothes back on?"

"I'll find something for you to wear," Eden(Mickey) said.

"And put *your* filthy clothes on?" Priscilla asked with just as much revulsion.

"He's talking about a hologram," Mickey(Eden) said.

"Just go on and take a shower," Eden(Mickey) said. "Let me know when you're done and I'll dress you."

"I'll let you know when I'm done," Priscilla said. "I don't know about the you dressing me part." She walked into the bathroom and closed the door.

George walked out of the kitchen with a bag of chips and a beer, and a sour expression. He read the bag. "Salt. And vinegar. Yech." He looked to Eden(Mickey). "And you complain about stinky socks?"

Mickey(Eden) looked to Carl Friedrich and Edie. "You two can shower next since you're both wearing puke, too."

Mick laughed. "Eden is just a bag of barf."

"I'm pregnant," Eden(Mickey) said.

"With *your* baby," Mickey(Eden) added. She looked to Eden (Mickey). "That's not a good thing, is it? Us finishing each other's sentences."

The closed door opened and George emerged bleary-eyed in his undershorts. "What's the racket about?"

"We've got company, George," Eden(Mickey) said. "You might want to put some pants on."

George froze and looked around. Until his eyes latched onto the other George. "What the hell?"

"Such a slob," Eden's brother said. "Go put some pants on."

George locked eyes with Mickey(Eden). "What is this, Mickey?"

"I'm not Mickey," Mickey(Eden) said.

"Go put some pants on and I'll explain it to you," Eden(Mickey) said. George ducked back into his bedroom.

Carl Friedrich banged on the bathroom door. "Don't use up all the hot water! I've got puke on me, too!"

Mickey(Eden) picked up Hypatia and brought the laptop to Eden(Mickey). "Can you send us back to our dimension?"

Eden(Mickey) opened it. "Do you want to go back? In my body?"

"No. But George, Stan, and Mick can go back."

"What if the Morlox have overrun your world? Do you want to send them back into that?"

"So what do we do?" Mickey(Eden) asked.

Eden(Mickey) stood. "First I need to plug this in. We've lost whatever power source we had. The battery is almost dead."

As Eden(Mickey) walked toward his bedroom with the laptop, George emerged, with pants on, from his. "Are you Eden?" he asked.

"No. But this is what Eden looks like. Not bad, huh?" Eden(Mickey) led George over to Eden's brother. "This is your twin from another dimension. His name is also George." Turning to Eden's brother, he said, "This is my roommate, from my dimension."

"Mickey," roommate George whined, "who is this really?"

Eden(Mickey) looked to Eden's brother. "Explain it to him. I've got other things to do." He walked into his bedroom to locate the charging cord.

Mickey(Eden) followed him in. She scowled all around the tight room. "What a dump."

Eden(Mickey) smiled at her. "You like that movie, too?"

Mickey(Eden) surveyed the disarray. "The movie that quote's from? On the chair?"

"Yes. Who's Afraid of Virginia Woolf? In that movie Martha,

Elizabeth Taylor, quotes Bette Davis from another movie. 'What a dump'."

"What's the other movie?" There was a sharp edge of challenge to Mickey(Eden)'s question.

"I don't know. Some Bette Davis movie."

" 'Beyond The Forest'," Mickey(Eden) answered with satisfaction. "The Bette Davis movie was 'Beyond The Forest'. Where she said, 'what a dump'."

Eden(Mickey) plugged in the laptop and sat on the bed to search through the files. "Never heard of it."

"Of course not, runt." Mickey(Eden) sat beside him. "What are you doing?"

"Our betters on the mountaintop said they loaded stuff onto the laptop for us."

"Lucy and Miriam aren't our betters," Mickey(Eden) said.

"They believe they are. Just like you believe you are my better."

"You two should shut the door."

They both looked up at Edie standing in the open doorway. "We're just talking," Eden(Mickey) said.

"I'm not being unfaithful to you," Mickey(Eden) said.

"I'm too messed up to care about that," Edie said. "Priscilla's yelling that she's done and needs some clothes."

"That's your call." Mickey(Eden) took the laptop.

Eden(Mickey) rose with a groan and limped out. Stan still guarded the front door. The Georges were at the kitchen table deep in conversation over chips and beer. Carl Friedrich was slumped into the George and Martha chair with his eyes closed. Mick joined Eden(Mickey) at the closed bathroom door. "Did I really make love to a man?"

"No. You made love to your wife's body."

"With a man inside it."

"It was still her body, so technically it wasn't infidelity, or homosexual." He turned his attention to the door. "Priscilla, are you dry?"

"Yes."

Eden(Mickey) closed Eden's eyes. "How's that?"

A moment of silence from the other side of the door. Then, "Is it real?"

"It looks real and it feels real. No one can see through it. It won't disappear unless I make it disappear."

"You wouldn't do that?"

"You're my friend, Priscilla. I would never embarrass you like that."

"I would trust you, Mickey, only you don't look like Mickey." The bathroom door opened. Priscilla was clad in Cinderella's gown.

"I'm next!" Edie bound across the room from Mickey's bedroom to the bathroom.

"I'm sorry I don't have clean towels for everyone," Eden(Mickey) said.

"I don't care. I just want to get this filth off me." Edie slipped past Priscilla. "Will you dress me, too, in something clean?" She snickered, glancing at Priscilla. "Just not as a Disney princess."

"Sure," Eden(Mickey) said. "And don't blame Priscilla. It's her grandmother's fault."

Edie shut the door. Priscilla spun around, admiring the Cinderella gown.

"By the way, Priscilla," Eden(Mickey) interrupted her spin. "Did I take the laptop from you while we were in the ocean? Last thing I remember from that dimension you were holding it while I set up the program."

"You and Eden disappeared. Then George and Priscilla appeared. Some other George and Priscilla. They grabbed the islander Stanley and Lori, and all four of them disappeared. Then you came back. I guess it was really Eden, in your body. In Mickey's body. Darn it, it gets so confusing. Whoever it really was that looked like you took the laptop from me then disappeared with it."

Mickey shook Eden's head. "I don't remember doing that. Eden says she doesn't remember doing that, either. So what happened next?"

"I woke up inside your head in Hellades."

Before Eden(Mickey) could delve any deeper into the mystery, Mickey(Eden) emerged from Mickey's bedroom with a stunned expression. "The inter-dimensional travel program is gone."

"How are we going to get home?!" Mick yelled.

Mickey(Eden) shrugged. "I don't know."

"Let me see." Eden(Mickey) took the laptop. "There's a new file."

Mickey(Eden) stared at the screen. "There is? Where?"

Ignoring her, Eden(Mickey) opened the file. After scanning it, he looked up with a scowl. "You won't believe what Lucy and Miriam expect us to do."

"I could care less what they want us to do," Mickey(Eden) wailed. "How are the four of us getting home?"

2.

Edie requested clean jeans and a plain tee shirt after her shower. Eden(Mickey) and Mickey(Eden) caught each other looking Edie over when she emerged clean and refreshed from her shower. Both averted each other's eyes from the form they were both attracted to. Meanwhile, while Stan was distracted searching for a deck of cards, Carl Friedrich slipped out the door. He had been slouched down in the George and Martha chair feigning sleep, biding his time for an opportunity to make a break.

Eden(Mickey) accepted his roommate George's longstanding offer to go on a road trip in order to carry out the tasks Lucy and Miriam had assigned on the laptop. Of course, Mickey(Eden) was going, too. Priscilla agreed to go along to help with the driving, since neither Eden (Mickey) nor Mickey(Eden) could drive. Stan, Mick, and Eden's brother George agreed to lay low in the apartment until the travelers returned. Edie volunteered to look out for the three. Mickey's roommate George left her a debit card to use. He also made arrangements to rent a car for the road trip. The benefits of belonging to a wealthy family.

Before departing, the four dropped in on Ralph. They discovered him and Miriam in the alley huddled beneath his cardboard and plastic. She appeared happy, even though nearly as soiled as her companion. "I thought Phun With Physics took him in off the street?" Mickey(Eden) asked her.

"*I* took him in," Miriam said. "But he insisted on coming back here. Said he had to keep an eye on Haiku." She peered deeper into the pile of plastic they were ensconced in. "It isn't so bad under here. There's a lot more room than you'd think."

Mickey(Eden) stooped down to peer into Ralph's face. "What dimension are you from?"

"I like the Fifth Dimension," Ralph answered. "You know, 'up, up and away'."

"Don't be cagey," Mickey(Eden) said. "You aren't who you appear to be."

Ralph turned to Miriam. "You saw me in the tub, Miriam. Who do I appear to be?"

Miriam blushed ten shades of red. "He needed a new bar of soap."

Eden(Mickey) interrupted. "He's just a homeless guy. Been living in this alley since me and George moved into our apartment."

"Yeah," George corroborated.

Mickey(Eden) wasn't buying it. "Keep an eye on the apartment, Ralph. Three visitors from my dimension are in there."

Ralph focused a surprisingly bright gaze on Mickey(Eden). "Axiom of choice, Well-ordering principle, and…what's Zorm's Lemma?" Mickey(Eden) appeared baffled. "Haven't a clue, have you? Didn't think you were really Mickey."

Eden(Mickey) stepped up with a smile. "That was mathematical haiku by Jason Callahan. Here's one by Christina Caroll. 'There's not enough room/in seventeen syllables/to contain infin-'."

"Glad to see you made it back, Haiku."

Mickey cupped Eden's breasts with both her hands. "Things are still messed up."

Mickey(Eden) slapped her own hands away from her breasts. "Leave my tits alone."

"I've got some to play with, too." Ralph fondled Miriam. She turned ten deeper shades of red, but didn't try to stop him. "But Eden's are a lot bigger."

"They're getting even bigger." Eden(Mickey) frowned at Mickey (Eden). "They're filling with milk."

"It's called lactating," Mickey(Eden) replied with a snarl.

"Actually, lactating refers to them secreting milk." Priscilla glanced down at her own small breasts. "I've read."

Ralph released Miriam. "By the way, the baby is healthy."

Mickey(Eden) nudged Eden(Mickey) out of the way get in Ralph's face. "Who *are* you?"

"Just what you see. Only once in a while a lady from above speaks to me."

"Lucy or Miriam?"

"I'm right here, Mickey," Miriam said.

Ralph shrugged. "Just some dame."

"How long has this been going on?" Mickey(Eden) asked.

"It goes on all the time," Ralph answered. "And not just to me. To a lot of people. Most aren't aware they are being contacted by someone from a higher dimension."

"Can we go now?" George asked.

"Go on and get the car," Eden(Mickey) said. "Pick us up at the coffee shop."

"I'm with you." Priscilla followed George out of the alley.

That settled that, Eden(Mickey) thought as he watched the couple walk away. Priscilla was with George. He turned back to Ralph. "Is there anything you can tell us?"

"Grasshopper, not to understand a man's purpose does not make him confused."

Miriam cackled. "Grasshopper! I love it. Mickey, you have a new name."

"I gave him a new name, too," Mickey(Eden) said. "Runt."

Eden(Mickey) rose in a huff. "I see there's nothing else to be gained here." He turned to go.

Mickey(Eden) straightened to leave, too. "You seem to know what's going on, Ralph. So tell me how are the four of us getting back to our dimension?"

"Come see me when you finish your tasks."

Eden(Mickey) walked away up the alley, and Mickey(Eden) hurried after. "You move fast for a grasshopper."

"Did you see Ralph groping Miriam? That's the way he keeps groping me. Ralph is the same old lech in every dimension."

The two cut through the park en route to the coffee shop. Mickey(Eden) plopped down on the Planck bench. "We did a lot of good work here."

Eden(Mickey) sat down beside her. "You deceived me."

"I've given you a fantastic adventure." Mickey(Eden) took her own hand. "And helped you fulfill a lifetime dream."

"My dream was to contact other dimensions, not to become a woman." Mickey pulled his own hand up onto Eden's abdomen. "And you've given me more than just an adventure."

Mickey(Eden) slipped her hand inside his shirt to prod a breast. "These *are* filling up. We need to find you a maternity bra. They need the support."

"Let go of me." Eden(Mickey) glanced around to see who was watching as he forced his hand out of the shirt.

"They're my breasts," Mickey(Eden) snarled. "I was just assessing how full of milk they are."

"Why didn't you design one?"

"I was always going to. But I got so busy with the Crossover Project, then so angry with Mick when I found out about Laurie. I never got around to it."

"Will you stick around to help with the rest of the pregnancy? Help with the delivery? Help raise our child?"

Eden slipped Mickey's hand free of her own hand's restraining grasp to settle on Eden's stomach. "I *want* to stay with my child, but I don't know if we *can* stay together. I and Stan and Mick and George have to get back to our own dimension somehow."

"Even like this?" Mickey spread Eden's arms, indicating the two of them.

"I've gotten used to being like this," Mickey(Eden) leaned in to kiss her own lips.

Eden(Mickey) jerked back and pushed Mickey(Eden) away. "What are you doing?"

"It's my body. Why shouldn't I kiss it?"

"Not while I'm in it. This is too weird."

Mickey(Eden) leaned further back. "Making love to my ex-husband wasn't too weird for you."

"Mick only looks like me. This Mickey, you, really is me."

Mickey(Eden) took a deep, deep breath. "You're right, Mickey. We need to stay focused." She stood.

"Was it me you were kissing?" His tone turned accusatory. "Or was it Edie?"

Mickey(Eden) pulled him up from the bench while gazing into her own eyes. "You sure look like Edie."

"You kissed me because I look like Edie. You are in love with Edie because she looks like you. Which means she looks like me. So you are in love with me. Because I *am* you. So you are actually in love with yourself."

"You think too much."

"Yeah, it's a curse. I just wish you'd leave me out of it. Maybe I should just lay down with a good book while you go at it with your body."

"No need to get mean about it. I'll leave you alone."

Exiting the park, they crossed the street and entered the coffee shop. Eden(Mickey) searched for a table by the window so they could watch for George and Priscilla. "This is the first place I saw you, Eden." Eden(Mickey) pointed out the window to the sidewalk across the street in front of the park where he had glimpsed her standing in a downpour. "You were only a smudge in the rain."

Mickey's name was called out. They both looked to see Lucy, seated with Albert, waving at them. When they drew near, Lucy's face clouded. "Edie? Where have you been? I couldn't reach you."

"We've been off exploring," Mickey(Eden) said, covering for the person Lucy thought was her daughter. They sat with her and Albert.

"I was afraid the Morlox had grabbed you again," Albert declared.

They both froze. "The what?" Eden(Mickey) managed to utter.

"What are Morlox?" Lucy asked Albert. He merely shrugged.

"Albert has taken to speaking in tongues," Eden(Mickey) said. "Just like Ralph."

Lucy focused on Eden(Mickey). "Did you quit your job?"

"No, Mom," Eden(Mickey) stuttered out.

"The baby is okay," Albert declared. "Nothing you have been through has harmed it."

"What baby?" Lucy asked Albert. After he once again shrugged his ignorance, she turned to Eden(Mickey). "Are you pregnant?" She turned to Mickey(Eden). "Are you the father, Mickey?"

"No!" they both blurted.

"We're just friends," Mickey(Eden) added.

"Close friends," Eden(Mickey) added.

"We met at the college."

"Where she works," Mickey(Eden) stammered on.

"He means where I work." Eden(Mickey) nervously shifted from foot to foot.

Lucy's face, turning from one to the other, was a mass of confusion. "Then who is the father?"

"Mick," Mickey(Eden) said.

"Not me. Another Mickey. Mick. Like Mick Jagger."

Lucy finally focused on Eden(Mickey). "How far along are you?" The two stared at each other. Lucy grew even more concerned. "Haven't you seen a doctor yet?"

"Have I?" Eden(Mickey) asked Mickey(Eden).

"Of course you have." Mickey(Eden) turned back to Lucy. "We were going to tell you. We just haven't yet."

"Why would *you* tell me?" Lucy asked.

"He's helping me with the pregnancy," Eden(Mickey) said. "Isn't the father helping you?"

"The father is a rat," Mickey(Eden) said.

Lucy reached across the table to clasp Eden(Mickey)'s hands. "I'll help you, Edie, any way I can. After all, it's my grandchild."

"No it's not," Albert declared.

"You are not helping!" Eden(Mickey) yelled, pulling Eden's hands free. "Whoever you are."

Albert looked around at the other three. "I was an eighty-nine year old man last time I looked in the mirror."

Lucy scowled at him. "You are losing your mind, Albert."

A horn blared. They all four looked out. George had pulled up in front of the coffee shop in a rental car, with Priscilla seated in back. Mickey(Eden) was grateful for the interruption. "That's our ride." She stood and yanked Eden(Mickey) up.

"Where are you going?" Lucy asked.

"On a road trip," Eden(Mickey) said. "I'll come see you when we get back."

"It's been interesting talking to you, " Mickey(Eden) said to Albert. "Whoever you really are. Keep in touch. Through Albert or Ralph or whoever."

Albert stared dumbly as Eden(Mickey) drug Mickey(Eden) across the coffee shop. "We've got to let Edie know she's pregnant."

Eden(Mickey) was aghast. "She is? Is it mine? I mean yours? With my body? And my genes?"

Mickey(Eden) led the way outside. "Of course not, runt. But we've got to cover for Albert, or whoever it was, blurting out about you, I mean me, us, being pregnant. *Edie* is not pregnant."

Eden(Mickey) jerked free. "Thank god! We've got enough children all over the place."

When they reached the car, George opened the front passenger door. "Mickey should sit up front with me and give directions." Eden(Mickey) climbed in front with the laptop.

"By all means, grasshopper should." Mickey(Eden) joined Priscilla in back.

George looked from one to the other. "I won't ask what that's about."

"Damn Ralph. And Albert," Mickey(Eden) fumed. "Miriam and Lucy are interfering."

"Or someone higher," Eden(Mickey) said. "Whoever it is, is keeping track of us. Maybe they'll help when we need it."

Mickey(Eden) slapped George lightly on the back of the head. "Don't drive like you usually do. This isn't a NASCAR race."

George looked at her in the rearview mirror. "I hardly ever drive."

Eden(Mickey) smiled back at Mickey(Eden). "This isn't your brother, runt. Keep your Georges straight."

"Where are we headed?" Priscilla asked.

"Fermilab," Eden(Mickey) said.

George pulled out from the curb. "Not much of a road trip. Google says it's about eighty kilometers."

Eden(Mickey) studied the laptop screen. "I've got a feeling this is just the beginning."

"Why do you say that?" Priscilla asked.

Eden(Mickey) held up the laptop screen for her to see. "The last line on the message I got read, 'This is just the beginning'."

"What are we supposed to do at Fermilab?" Mickey(Eden) asked.

"There's a file for me to deliver to Jack Truby."

"Who is Jack Truby?" George asked.

"No idea."

"How are you going to get the file to him?" Priscilla asked.

"No idea."

"You'll probably let him squeeze some part of my body," Mickey (Eden) said. "That's your usual strategy."

Eden(Mickey) beamed back at her. "It's worked so far."

Mickey(Eden) slumped back into the seat. "If I ever figure out a way to kill you without killing myself or my baby, Mickey, you're dead."

3.

Before setting out for Fermilab, George drove by Priscilla's grandparents' house so Priscilla could put on some real clothes. Eden(Mickey) remained out in the hall while Priscilla went into her room and closed the door. "You know I've seen you naked twice, Priscilla."

"You have not."

"Actually, it was your twin in Eden's dimension, but she looks just like you."

"You are not watching me change clothes, Mickey. Just get rid of this Disney dress."

Mickey closed Eden's eyes.

"That's not funny, Mickey." The bedroom door flew open. Priscilla stood before him in the flimsy pink robe. "Take this off me and don't put anything else on me. *After* I close this door."

Eden(Mickey) smiled. "I just wanted to see you in it one more time."

Priscilla smiled, her fierceness dissolving. "Okay." She pirouetted, giving Eden(Mickey) a three-hundred and sixty degree view. "But no more digital clothes." She closed the door.

Eden(Mickey) shook his head when the door opened to reveal Priscilla in baggy jeans and a Woody and Jessie tee shirt. "How many Disney shirts do you own?"

"They're presents from my grandmother." They emerged from the house to join George and Mickey(Eden) in the rental car.

It didn't take long to drive from Evanston to Fermilab. "That's impressive," George remarked as he admired Wilson Hall. Two cement arches separated by a central section of glass curved upward toward each other to tower sixteen floors above three long narrow reflecting pools. It was easily by far the tallest structure on Fermilab's campus.

"It was designed after the gothic cathedral in Beauvais, France," Eden(Mickey) said.

Priscilla craned her neck out the window to look up. "Looks more like the Atari logo."

Eden(Mickey) exited the front of the car. "That sculpture in the reflecting pool is a hyperbolic obelisk. If anyone is interested."

"No one is, runt." Mickey(Eden) leaned back into the back seat. "Are you sure you're the one to do this? Alone?"

"Yes," Eden(Mickey) responded. "You're liable to blurt out something about the Morlox or nine-hundred story buildings."

"Just what are we doing?" Priscilla asked.

"Delivering information." Eden(Mickey) opened her door.

"How? Walk up to the information desk and ask for Jack Truby?"

"Either that, or walk into the lobby and clap my hands once." Eden(Mickey) walked away from Mickey(Eden)'s muttered profanities.

Upon entering the cavernous atrium lined with international flags and thronged with visitors wandering amongst floral gardens and verdant greenery, Eden(Mickey) doubted anyone would even notice if he clapped once. He stopped to look straight up. A scrap of sky could be seen through a small glass ceiling spanning the rectangular space where the pair of cement arches nearly converged sixteen floors above. He walked up to the information desk. "I need to speak with Jack Truby."

The young woman smiled up at him. "Mr. Truby is not available without an appointment."

"Can I make an appointment?"

"Don't worry about seeing him, Mickey," the woman said. "Just give the flash drive to me and I'll see that he gets it."

Eden(Mickey) handed it to her. He walked out to the car and climbed back in front. "Couldn't get in to see him?" Mickey(Eden) asked with a smirk.

"I gave it to the woman at the information desk," Eden(Mickey) said.

"YOU WHAT?!"

"She knew me. She said she'd give it to him."

Realization dawned on Mickey(Eden), if not the other two. "Was it like Ralph and Albert?"

"Yeah. Let's go get some breakfast."

"First tell us what's going on," Priscilla demanded.

"Miriam and Lucy, or someone from a dimension much higher than us, have loaded files onto Hypatia with information needed to finish repairing the damage we've caused. Apparently repairs need to be done not only from within each dimension, but also from without. Only this first file was available, which I loaded onto a flash drive. Instructions on the laptop state the next file will be unlocked once this one has been delivered."

"What is Jack Truby going to do with these files?" Priscilla asked.

"Devise a Theory of Everything that ties gravity in with the electroweak force and the strong force, I think. It was either that or a list of the particles and forces that make up dark matter and dark energy. I had a hard time making sense out of it."

"You would have a hard time making sense out of e equals mc squared," Mickey(Eden) said. "You should have let me handle the flash drive."

Eden(Mickey) turned to George. "Let's find an IHOP."

A flash of light in the periphery of Eden(Mickey)'s vision caused him to hop back out of the car. Across the parking lot he saw the George and Priscilla from the subatomic dimension watching them. Brilliant arcs of light flashed all around them. One would appear out of nowhere, streak a short distance, then flame out and disappear, time and time again. Until a bowling-ball sized particle blasted through Priscilla, shredding her torso in a burst of blood and gore.. George screamed, kneeling amid the pulpy remains of her mangled body. The image faded.

"What's wrong?" George asked.

Eden(Mickey) turned his mournful stare to Priscilla. Her body was still intact. It hadn't been destroyed by a massive subatomic particle. That had happened to the Priscilla from the dimension in the quantum foam. *Had* it happened there? Or was it *going* to happen? Time was slippery in their dimension. So maybe she hadn't perished so horribly. Eden(Mickey) certainly hoped not. How had he seen that, anyway? Had the walls between dimensions become so weak he could see into their dimension from his own? Or could the events from one dimension spill into other dimensions now? Could a massive W boson slice out of their dimension into his, and kill his Priscilla, sometime in the future? Had the boundaries between the dimensions become that onion-skin thin?

Mickey(Eden) joined Eden(Mickey) outside the car. "I thought you wanted breakfast."

"Did you see anything weird happen in the parking lot?" Eden (Mickey) pointed to where he had seen the vision.

"No."

"I just saw into another dimension. Or something from another dimension passed into this dimension and did something terrible. Or will sometime in the future."

"What did you see?"

Eden(Mickey) leaned in close to whisper. "Priscilla get wiped out by a giant W boson." They both cast dark looks at Priscilla. She stared back at them anxiously. "It probably wasn't her," he continued to whisper. "It most likely was the Priscilla from the dimension we traveled to first."

As the whispering and furtive glances continued, Priscilla grew ever more apprehensive. "What did you see, Mickey? Did you see something bad happen to me?"

"Mickey is just seeing things," Mickey(Eden) said, attempting to calm Priscilla while glaring at Eden(Mickey).

Eden(Mickey) took the cue. "Eden's right. I'm seeing crazy stuff."

Priscilla wasn't appeased. "What did you see happen to me, Mickey?"

George attempted to placate a distraught Priscilla. "Mickey's exhausted. It was nothing, I'm sure. Let's go eat."

Later, Mickey(Eden), George, and a still-prickly Priscilla watched in awe as Eden(Mickey) finished off a country fried steak and eggs combo with a heap of hash browns and two pancakes on the side. Wiping Eden's mouth, he looked up. "What?"

"No one said anything, little mother," Mickey(Eden) said.

"I'm going to be sick." Priscilla smiled. "I'll throw up on *you*, Mickey, for a change."

Mickey(Eden) scooted back. "Just be sure to target the right Mickey."

"Do you know yet what the next destination is?" George asked.

Mickey(Eden), who had possession of the laptop while Mickey gorged her body, opened it up. The only thing on the monitor was the photo Priscilla had taken of Mickey in front of his blackboard, which was displayed on the splash screen. "How do you access it?"

"Click on the Biggest Blunder."

Mickey(Eden) studied the screen. "There are blunders all over the blackboard. Which one is the biggest?"

"You're kidding. You don't see the cosmological constant?" Seeing Mickey(Eden)'s bewildered expression, he took the laptop from her. The equation for Einstein's cosmological constant, labeled the biggest blunder, was in the middle of the screen. He pointed. "The biggest blunder. It's right there."

The other three heads leaned in to look. "I don't see it, Mickey," George said.

"Just that picture I took," Priscilla said.

Mickey(Eden) grew irate. "What's going on, Mickey?"

Eden(Mickey) smiled all around. "I guess the higher powers will only communicate with me." Relishing the moment, he waxed on. "You know, Einstein never really said the cosmological constant was his biggest blunder. People think it was George Gamow who came up with that." Getting no response, he went on. "It wasn't a blunder anyway. Einstein was just way ahead of his time. His 'blunder' was actually describing dark energy, decades before anyone else ever imagined the stuff." Receiving only impatient glares, he sighed and clicked on the cosmological constant icon. Google Maps opened, with a destination plotted to San Diego.

George studied the map. "That's over three thousand, three-hundred and fifty kilometers."

"We can switch out drivers and go all night," Eden(Mickey) said.

"I've never driven," Mickey(Eden) said.

"Mickey never has, either," George said. "He must be talking about me and you, Priscilla."

"Mathematicians have more important things to do than drive," Eden(Mickey) said.

"I'll warn you right now," Mickey(Eden) said, "we'll be making a lot of stops."

"Have you got a small bladder, too?" Priscilla asked.

"No. Mickey has a crowded bladder."

"We can pick up some Depends," George said, "or an empty mayonnaise jar." And they were off.

4.

Priscilla nudged Eden(Mickey) awake. It was daylight. They had arrived in San Diego in the middle of the night and pulled into a rest area. George had been driving when Eden(Mickey) had fallen asleep, but now Priscilla was sitting behind the wheel. Eden(Mickey) hopped out and rushed to the bathroom.

Returning to the car, Eden(Mickey) saw George asleep sprawled across the back seat with his head in Mickey's lap. Mickey(Eden) didn't seem to mind being forced up against the door by George. She was staring down into George's lax face with affection. When Eden(Mickey) climbed back in front, Mickey(Eden) smiled up at him. "He doesn't snore."

"I know," Eden(Mickey) replied. "I've lived with him for years. I've slept over with your brother, too. He rattles the walls." He checked the time. "The lab should be open by now. Wake George up."

"I hate to," Mickey(Eden) said. "He drove most of the night."

"I'm awake," George growled. He sat up, with aid from Mickey (Eden). "You okay, Priscilla?"

"No. Can we switch?" She and George traded places, and George drove from the rest area into the parking lot of the Scripps Institution of Oceanography at UC San Diego in La Jolla.

"Let me do it this time," Mickey(Eden) insisted.

"Go for it." Eden(Mickey) handed the flash drive to her.

"What's on it?" Priscilla asked.

"Information on how to genetically modify a person to make them amphibian," Eden(Mickey) informed.

"I missed that dimension," Priscilla said.

"I missed all of them," George said with a mouth-wrenching yawn.

"It was my favorite one," Mickey(Eden) said. "Wide open country-side with no one in sight but us and Belos. It was Heaven."

Mickey(Eden) walked in through the front door up to the reception desk. "Can you deliver something for me to Hank Flores?"

The receptionist appeared doubtful. "What do you have?" Mickey (Eden) produced the flash drive. The receptionist reacted as if she were being offered a human finger. "You're not even allowed to bring that into the building." The receptionist reached for the phone. "I'm calling security."

"Never mind. I'm gone." Mickey(Eden) hurried away out the front door.

As Mickey(Eden) climbed into the backseat, Eden(Mickey) asked, "What happened?"

"She threatened to call security," Mickey(Eden) said.

"Threatened, hell," George said. A security guard strode briskly toward their car.

"Give it to me." Eden(Mickey) snatched the flash drive.

The security guard arrived at the driver side. "What are you people doing here?" he demanded of George.

Before George could blurt out something incriminating, Eden (Mickey) leaned across the front seat to look out the lowered window up at the man. "I need to deliver something to Hank Flores."

The security guard smiled. "It took you long enough to get here, Mickey."

"We stopped to get some sleep." He handed the flash drive out the window to him. "Be sure to get that to Mr. Flores."

"I'll deliver it personally as soon as he comes in this morning." The security guard slipped it into his pocket. "There's a public beach a couple of miles from here." He pointed off in the direction. "I suggest you see it. You'll find it interesting." He looked around at the other three. "You've come half-way across the continent, might as well stick your toes in the Pacific Ocean while you're here." He walked away toward the building.

"How did you do that?" Mickey(Eden) demanded. "He was ready to arrest me."

"I didn't do anything." Eden(Mickey) leaned back into his seat. "Whoever is helping us is apparently tuned in only to me."

"So you're our Neo," George said.

"Just keep Hugo away from me." Eden(Mickey) shrugged. "Let's go find that beach."

"That sounds wonderful to me," Priscilla said as George backed out of the parking space and headed across the lot for the entrance. "I'd love to stretch out on the sand for a while."

"It sounds like a waste of time to me," Mickey(Eden) said.

"It's not a waste of time," Eden(Mickey) insisted. "If the person from a higher dimension who is helping us took the trouble to tell us about this beach, we should check it out." He looked back to Mickey (Eden). "You're just sour because you don't get to be Keanu Reeves."

When George pulled into the lot at La Jolla Shores Park, Priscilla asked, "Can we relax on the beach for a while?" It was a beautiful sunny day, and being mid-day mid-week not crowded.

"Sure." Eden(Mickey) slouched down out of sight in the front seat.

"Who wants a swim suit?" The other three slouched down, also.

Eden(Mickey) changed his and Mickey(Eden)'s holograms right away, but had to wait for Priscilla and George to take off their real clothes. Eden(Mickey) glanced into the back seat to find Priscilla squirming out of her jeans.

"Mickey! Stop watching me get undressed."

"Sorry." Eden(Mickey) turned back around.

"Anybody want to watch me?" George asked as he pulled his pants off.

"What's the big deal?" Eden(Mickey) quipped. "You never wear pants anyway. You go around in your underwear all the time."

"Yeah, no big deal, I've seen my brother take his clothes off before." Mickey(Eden) focused her attention on Priscilla, who was down to her underwear. "It's more fun watching Priscilla."

Priscilla reached around to unfasten her bra. "I know that's not really you, Mickey, watching me undress. I know it's really another woman and should be no big deal, but it looks like Mickey watching and it's bothering me." She had loosened her bra, but hesitated at taking it off.

George glanced from Mickey(Eden) to Eden(Mickey). "You two give Priscilla a break. Quit watching her." Mickey(Eden) looked out the window.

Eden(Mickey) turned toward George. "How about you?"

George was watching Priscilla slip her loose bra down her arms. "Oh. Right." He turned around to look out the front windshield.

After George and Priscilla were both clad in hologram swim suits, all four got out of the car and walked across the beach toward the ocean. George and Priscilla waded into the surf, while Eden(Mickey) walked up the beach. Mickey(Eden) followed. "You're not getting wet?"

"We're here for a reason." Eden(Mickey) pulled at the one-piece Eden's body had on. "Rather conservative."

"I prefer showing off my mind to showing off my body."

"Not anymore."

"Spherical bastard." They walked a while in silence. "Tell me what you are looking for, Mickey, and I'll help."

"You didn't see Priscilla get mangled by that massive boson, so I doubt you'll see anything else."

"You really believe you are the chosen one?"

"*You* chose me, Eden."

A few more steps were taken in silence, then Mickey(Eden) said, "You were the most intelligent being I could reach."

"The most intelligent being you could manipulate," Eden(Mickey) clarified.

"Let's at least get our feet wet." Mickey(Eden) walked into the water.

"Your world is nothing but water, and a few mountain tops sticking up out of it. I wouldn't have thought water such a novelty for you."

"In my dimension it's so cold, not enjoyable at all. This is very pleasant." She waded out deeper. "I'm going for a swim. I'll catch up with you later."

Eden(Mickey) watched her swim out a ways. This was a strange sight for him to see. Mickey didn't know how to swim, yet his body was stroking smoothly through the rough surf.

Eventually, Eden(Mickey) continued his trek. Mickey had seen an event take place in another dimension. Or an event from another dimension had crossed over to take place in this dimension. The barriers between the dimensions had been damaged by his and Eden's initial crossing. The damage required additional repairs to keep the dimensions from bleeding into one another. The means to do this was on his laptop. It was up to him, since he seemed to be the only one interacting with this being from a higher dimension, to carry out these repairs. This higher being had directed him to this beach. So there must be something for him there.

Eden(Mickey) saw it. Several large rocks the waves were crashing over. In the bright sunlight wet colors glistened, green and brown and orange. Could it be the algae from Belos' world? He waded out to the rocks. It looked like the algae from that dimension. He scraped off some and tasted it. Stinky socks! Just like in Belos' dimension. He spat it out.

"What did you find?" Mickey(Eden) had swum up unnoticed.

"Stinky socks. From Belos' world."

Mickey(Eden) scraped some off and chewed. She made a face, spitting it back out. "It doesn't taste like stinky socks."

"This is just ordinary algae to you?" Eden(Mickey) speculated. "So not only can you not see the intrusion of the other dimensions into ours, you can't taste them, either. You can't sense the other dimensions whatsoever."

"And you can," Mickey(Eden) replied. "That, or you're hallucinating."

"Let's go back. I'd like to catch a short nap in the sand before we hit the road again." The two waded in and walked back up the beach the way they had come.

Until a flashing police light caught Eden(Mickey)'s attention. "That looks to be near where we parked." Hearing a siren, he saw another flashing light, an ambulance screaming toward them up the highway.

"Hurry, Mickey." Mickey(Eden) ran across the beach toward the rental car. Eden(Mickey) followed at a more leisurely pace. The only time Mickey Haiku had ever run in his adult life had been to impress Priscilla.

By the time Eden(Mickey) reached the rental car, a crowd had gathered around it. Medics from the ambulance were examining a body prone on the pavement beside the car. George was with a police officer, who was looking over a sheaf of papers. Priscilla and Mickey(Eden) stood side by side watching. Eden(Mickey) joined the two. "What happened?"

Mickey(Eden) glared at him. "You left the laptop in plain view."

"The car was locked."

"He tried to unlock it." Mickey(Eden) motioned toward the unconscious young man the medics were attending to.

"He tried to break in and steal it, Mickey," Priscilla said.

"So what happened to him?" Eden(Mickey) asked.

"I'd say your friends from a higher dimension didn't want him to have it," Mickey(Eden) said.

George joined them. "The cop thought I had some exotic illegal anti-theft equipment on the car. I told him it was a rental, and showed him the papers. He contacted the rental car company, and they assured him none of their vehicles have anything like that installed on them. So he told me we can go. And to keep our valuables out of sight from now on."

"What happened to him?" Eden(Mickey) motioned to the motionless body.

"The medic says he shows signs of severe electrical shock," George said.

"From what?" Priscilla asked.

"You know what," Mickey(Eden) said.

"If a laptop battery had discharged that kind of energy it would have burned up the laptop," George said. "Look at it." He pointed in through the car window. "It's undamaged."

"Maybe Hypatia was only a conduit of that energy," Eden(Mickey) said.

"What energy?" George demanded. "From where?"

"A higher dimension."

"If we're allowed to go, then let's go," Priscilla urged.

George checked with the police officer. He moved the crowd out of the way. George climbed behind the wheel, and they drove off. He glared at Eden(Mickey) sitting next to him. "We'll lock it up in the trunk next time we stop."

"Like hell we will." Mickey clutched Hypatia to Eden's chest. "I'm not letting go of it until we finish this road trip."

"Don't hold it so close to my breasts," Mickey(Eden) said. "With power like that it might cause cancer."

George focused his glare on the laptop. "Keep it away from me. I saw what it did to that guy."

"Aren't you afraid of it, Mickey?" Priscilla asked. "I don't want to touch it. Not after what I saw happened to that young man."

"They won't hurt me."

"You hope," Mickey(Eden) said. "You know, most prophets don't come to a good end."

George glanced into the rearview mirror at the chaos receding behind them. "Where are we going now, Neo?"

"I'll let you know." Eden(Mickey) got busy with the laptop. A few minutes later he said, "Shadytown."

Priscilla leaned over the seat to look at the screen. "Where is that?"

"Ohio. Just north of Cincinnati."

George pounded the wheel. "You're kidding me! We're driving back halfway across the continent?"

Eden(Mickey) studied Google Maps. "More like three-fourths."

"Why do we have to zig-zag like this?" Priscilla asked.

"Seems that whatever we're doing has to be done in the order in which we visited the dimensions."

"We're already worn out," George said. "I can't drive another two days non-stop."

Eden(Mickey) nodded toward the screen. "Thirty-two hours. Google says."

"We need to stop and get some sleep somewhere," Priscilla said.

"And we can't make it too hard on the baby," Mickey(Eden) said. She turned to George. "Can you spring for a room?"

"We'll get several."

5.

George exited I-40 in Oklahoma City before getting on I-44 for Tulsa. The four crawled out of the car into the motel lobby. Sometime during the drive from San Diego, Eden(Mickey) had changed everyone out of their swim suits. "Can we make do with two rooms?" George asked.

"Sure," Eden(Mickey) answered. "How are we doing this? Do we separate by gender? Priscilla, do you want to share a room with a female body or with an actual female?"

"I don't want to share a room with either of you weirdoes," Priscilla said.

"Don't over think this, Mickey," George added.

"We're too tired to do anything but sleep anyway," Priscilla said. "Right, George?"

After a noncommittal grunt George opened a door, and he and Priscilla disappeared into a room.

Mickey(Eden) led Eden(Mickey) into a room across the hall. He collapsed on the bed while she checked out the bathroom. "If I get a shower will you find me some new clothes in the morning?"

"Yes. I'll even find you some pajamas for tonight."

"Good luck with that. I never designed any pajamas."

Eden(Mickey) sighed, then clapped Eden's hands once. They were both naked in an instant. "Don't wake me up when you come to bed."

"Aren't you getting a shower?"

"In the morning. Or afternoon. Whenever I wake up." After a moment, when Mickey realized no water was running, he opened Eden's eyes to find Mickey(Eden) still in the bathroom doorway looking her own body over. "Stop it. I'm not Edie." Eden(Mickey) tussled with the covers to get under them.

"This is the first time we've slept together."

"Hardly," Eden(Mickey) said. "I've slept with my own body every night of my life. Until recently."

After another fourteen hours of driving the following day, George cruised through a quiet suburban neighborhood in Shadytown. He was inhaling coffee. Priscilla was stretched out in the back seat with her sleeping head in Mickey(Eden)'s lap, who was lolled back, also sound asleep.

Only Eden(Mickey), seated up front next to George, was fully awake. "We're getting close." George turned down a side street. "There's the address," Eden(Mickey) said. "That house. Pull over."

George pulled to the side of the road in front of a small bi-level with a bicycle in the front yard. Eden(Mickey) climbed out with a sign, a nail, and a hammer. On the sign was a sketch of the large yellow box they had seen that night in the spooky woods dimension. He affixed the sign to a wooden telephone pole just above a notice for a missing dog.

By the time Eden(Mickey) got back into the front seat, Priscilla had risen from Mickey(Eden)'s lap in the back seat, and they were both gazing about in stunned silence trying to get their bearings. "What is this going to do?" George asked.

"I posted it in front of Sean's house. He'll see it and be alerted to the coming danger." He fastened his seatbelt. "Let's go."

George pulled out, but slammed on the brakes, jerking everyone forward.

"What was that for?" Mickey(Eden) growled from the back seat.

"A cat ran out in front of me."

Eden(Mickey) watched the cat stroll away. "It's a good thing you didn't squish her. That was a black cat."

Priscilla completed an impressive yawn. "Since when did you turn superstitious, Mickey?"

"I'm not. But Sean is going to need Maeve's help."

Mickey(Eden) looked from George to Priscilla. "I'm sure this makes sense to someone."

"What now?" Priscilla asked. "Drive to Honolulu?"

"I don't know," Eden(Mickey) opened Hypatia. "Instructions for what we need to do next haven't been unlocked yet. Stop for gas."

George sighed. "The tank is nearly full."

"So is mine."

George pulled into the first gas station he came to. Eden(Mickey) hopped out and, after ordering everyone to keep a close watch on the laptop, limped into the bathroom. He glanced in the mirror while running water in the sink, and nearly screamed. The reflection of an entrancing young woman with coal black hair stared back at him. She seemed as surprised to see Eden's face as Mickey was to see her. "Who are you?" the face in the mirror asked.

"Mickey Haiku. Who are you?"

"Seraphina. Why are you possessing this female?"

"To repair the damage to the barriers separating the dimensions."

Seraphina smiled. "The walls have become very thin. Evil spirits are slipping into this dimension to come to Robar's aid and save his ancient tree. Soon we will own this dimension."

The mirror cracked. Seraphina's surprised expression shattered into dozens of fragments. Eden(Mickey) picked up the piece that contained Seraphina's left eye. Bloodshot and cloudy, with wrinkles and sagging bags, it no longer appeared young. "I don't think so." Eden(Mickey) tossed the mirror sliver into the toilet and flushed.

When Eden(Mickey) walked out of the bathroom, he saw George was cleaning the windshield, while Mickey(Eden) and Priscilla were out of the car stretching. "What now?" George asked.

Eden(Mickey) opened up the laptop sitting in the front seat. "There's a campground not too far from here where I'm supposed to deliver a message to someone. We can rest up there."

"We don't have any camping equipment," Priscilla pointed out.

George climbed back in behind the wheel. "We'll go car camping."

It was dark by the time George pulled into the campground at Cedar Bog. He secured a site from the campground host. After parking the car, George stretched out in the front seat and Priscilla stretched out in back. Mickey(Eden) tagged along behind Eden(Mickey). "Heading for the bathroom?"

"Of course. Then into the bog."

"Why?"

"We're here for a reason, Eden. Even if you can't sense the reason."

Once Eden(Mickey) finished in the bathroom, they found the trail-head leading into the bog. They traversed the boardwalk deep into the dark dank gloom in silence. Until Mickey(Eden) saw something in the shadows, something big and monstrous. She jerked to a halt, looking all around in a frantic rush.

Eden(Mickey) was surprised. "You saw something?"

"Something really big," Mickey(Eden) said. "I just got a glimpse of it. It's gone now."

"It was a wooly mammoth."

They both jerked around at the voice in the dark. An old woman stood in the muck several meters away from the boardwalk. "Can you see her?" Eden(Mickey) asked.

"Of course," Mickey(Eden) answered. "It's an old woman."

The old woman ignored her and focused on Eden(Mickey). "Why are you here?"

"To warn you the barriers between dimensions have grown weak, and evil spirits are entering your dimension."

The old woman cackled. "That means good spirits can come through, too."

"If there are such things."

"There are. Thank you for your warning. I'll pass it on."

"To Sean?"

The old woman frowned. "How do you know my grandson?"

"Someone from a higher dimension told me about him. Why are there wooly mammoths in this bog?"

"Time is unsettled here."

"Do you know George and Priscilla? Time is unsettled in their dimension, too."

The old woman faded away into the gloom.

"Who was that?" Mickey(Eden) asked.

Eden(Mickey) shrugged. "Someone familiar with wooly mammoths."

"Aren't wooly mammoths extinct in your dimension?"

"They are."

"Then how did I see one?" Mickey(Eden) smiled. "Can I see things from other dimensions now?"

"That wasn't from another dimension. It was from another time. George and Priscilla's dimension must be affecting mine now. At least here in this bog. We've got to end this before we get dinosaurs strolling down Michigan Avenue." The two walked back along the boardwalk the way they had come.

When they got back to their site, George and Priscilla were already asleep in the car. "You can have the picnic table," Mickey(Eden) said.

Eden(Mickey) climbed up onto it. "Where are you going to sleep?"

"I'll take the roof." Mickey(Eden) climbed up onto the trunk, then on up to the roof. As Eden stretched out, a heavy cloak appeared on Mickey's body. Snuggling into it, she looked to the picnic table and saw Eden(Mickey) burrowed deep into an identical cloak. "Thanks, Mickey." But as Eden(Mickey) closed her eyes, Mickey(Eden) just couldn't resist. "Did you see that sign by the entrance to the boardwalk?"

"No. What did it say?"

"Some warning about rattlesnakes."

Eden's eyes popped back open. "That's not funny."

"Good night, runt." Eden closed Mickey's eyes with a smile. Until the cloak wrapped up around her disappeared. She opened Mickey's eyes to find Eden(Mickey), still wrapped up in a cloak, glaring at her. "Give it back."

"What was that about rattlesnakes?"

"Massasauga rattlesnakes live in the bog. I was reading about them while you were in the bathroom."

"If a rattlesnake bites me, the baby gets poisoned, too."

"I know. I'm sorry I said anything about it. It's not going to happen. If you had half a brain you'd know snakes are not nocturnal."

"It's *your* brain I have."

"I wish you'd learn how to use it. Look, you know I wouldn't take a chance with my baby. Now give me my cover back."

Mickey closed Eden's eyes, and the cloak reappeared on Mickey (Eden). They both settled down to sleep. Still, Mickey(Eden) snickered when she peeked to find Eden(Mickey) wide-eyed and searching the ground all around the picnic table.

6.

At the creak of dawn—it wasn't bright enough yet to be considered the crack—Mickey(Eden) roused Eden(Mickey) from atop the picnic table. No other campers were stirring in the quiet, no breakfast fires yet lit the gloom. She presented the laptop to him. "I couldn't find any information about our next destination."

"Of course not." Eden(Mickey) moaned as he reached for it.

"What's the matter?"

"My back aches from sleeping on this picnic table."

Mickey(Eden) set the laptop down. "Roll over." Eden(Mickey) tried, failed. Eden rolled her own body over onto its stomach then slipped Mickey's hands under the heavy cloak to give a back rub.

"Aaahhh. That's wonderful."

Mickey(Eden) rubbed in contented silence for several minutes. She seemed to get as much pleasure out of giving it as Eden(Mickey) got receiving it.

"Come on, you two!" George called out from the car. He was helping Priscilla crawl out of the back seat. "I want to know where we have to go next."

Mickey(Eden) smacked Eden's butt. "Get up. I'm curious, too." Helping Eden(Mickey) up off the table, she expected to be rebuked for the smack, but one never came.

Priscilla managed a semi-smile. "You two seem to be getting along better."

Mickey(Eden) grew defensive. "It's *my* back I'm taking care of."

Eden(Mickey) sat up at the picnic table and opened the laptop. "Did either of you see any rattlesnakes last night?"

"Rattlesnakes? In Ohio?" Priscilla sounded skeptical.

Mickey(Eden) shrugged. "There are signs in the campground warning about massasauga rattlesnakes."

"I don't care how many rattlesnakes are here," George said. "Just don't tell me we have to drive back to the west coast."

The cosmological constant equation was displayed in the middle of the screen. Eden(Mickey) smiled at Mickey(Eden) "Still can't see the equation?"

The smoke coming out of Mickey's ears was nearly visible. "Just read it."

Eden(Mickey) laughed as he clicked on the greatest blunder icon.

"This is a short trip. Northwestern University."

"You mean we're going back to Evanston?" Priscilla nearly screamed. "Back where we started?"

"We can drop you off," Eden(Mickey) offered. "If you've had enough."

Priscilla considered, briefly. "No. George needs someone to help with the driving. You two are useless."

"We can rest up at the apartment," Eden(Mickey) suggested.

"Sure," Mickey(Eden) replied. "It'll give us a chance to check on the others to see how they're doing."

The apartment was empty when the four travelers entered. "Wonder where everybody is?" George asked.

Mickey(Eden) seethed. "They were supposed to lay low."

"I'm sure they're okay," Eden(Mickey) said. "Edie is looking after them."

"Don't talk so loud, you guys," Priscilla said. "You'll wake me up."

George smiled. "You can have my bed."

Priscilla took his hand. "You can have it, too. After last night neither of us are passing up a chance to sleep on a mattress." She led George into his room and shut the door.

"My bed is big enough, too," Eden(Mickey) offered. "Go ahead. I'll be right there." Mickey(Eden) didn't budge. "What now?"

"I don't want to sleep in my clothes."

Eden(Mickey) clapped once, and they were both naked. Mickey (Eden) closed the bedroom door, while Eden(Mickey) went on into the bathroom.

Returning from the bathroom, Eden(Mickey) found Mickey(Eden) already under the covers. She grinned up at him. "Even when *you* are exhausted *I* still look really appealing. Is it like that with all men? No matter what is going on with the woman you can still get horny?"

"I'm too exhausted to try to untangle all that. Move over." Eden(Mickey) climbed in with Mickey(Eden).

"Can we at least cuddle?" Mickey(Eden) asked, curling up to him from behind.

"Cuddle up to your body all you want," Eden(Mickey) replied. "But your body is going to sleep." Within a minute Eden's body was snoring. Within two minutes Mickey's body was, too.

~ * ~

Electronica music emanated from Hypatia. Like cold fusion, high intensity cooking at so low a temperature. Belfast bubbled up soul like Atlanta once did. Cool, cool spice skimmed across the surface like a perfectly-thrown stone skipping off into infinity. Electricity woven into a God's eye for the ear. Rip van Twinkle could dance to these killer slo-mo breaks, melancholy melodies and distant wails.

Bicep shimmered into existence amid the waves of audio. "Mickey," Matt said.

"That's beautiful, guys. Don't stop," Eden(Mickey) urged. "We can talk later. Keep the trance going,"

"Eden," Andy said.

The music began to fade. "No one understands you," Eden (Mickey) lamented.

"We're big in five dimensions," Matt said.

"U2 only made it in three," Andy said.

"Elvis knows you," Eden(Mickey) said. "Go cart Elvis," he clarified.

"He knows our robots," Matt said.

"Bicep impersonators," Andy said.

"Robot Bicep impersonators?" Eden(Mickey) asked. "In Vegas?"

"They play Red Rock Lanes," Matt said. "It's off the Strip."

"You can spare and strike to our music," Andy said.

"Can you quit talking and start the music up again?" Eden(Mickey) asked.

"No," Matt said. "You need to pay attention."

"We're here to tell you everyone needs to return to their own rightful dimension to restore order in all the dimensions," Andy said.

"How can we do that? The inter-dimensional travel program has been deleted."

"A way will be provided," Matt said.

"Now you need to wake up," Andy said.

"Mickey, wake up."

Mickey opened Eden's eyes. Mickey(Eden) was sitting up next to him in bed. "Bicep's not here. We're not in Vegas. Or Red Rock Lanes, whatever that is. We're in Evanston."

Mickey knuckled Eden's eyeballs. "I never noticed that bump on the inside of my right thigh."

Mickey(Eden) glanced at it. "It's sore. You need to have it checked out when you get a chance."

"Great. With everything else going on, now I have to worry about a tumor."

"Don't be a hypochondriac."

"Passing through all these dimensions like we've been doing is bound to be hard on our bodies. It could cause cancer."

"It's most likely an infected pimple. Can I have some clothes?"

"Give me a minute." Eden(Mickey) yawned, stretched. "How are the others this morning?"

"Gone. George drove Priscilla to her Grandparents' house."

Eden(Mickey) sat up in bed. "How about the other others?"

"They're back. Edie took them to the lakefront yesterday. She's been showing them all over Chicago. They can't believe how wide open this dimension is."

"I was afraid of that. Do they want to stay?"

"Stan doesn't. I don't think Mick will, either. But George, my brother George, seems to be getting attached to Edie. Despite her looking like me. Or maybe because of that." Mickey(Eden) frowned. "My brother might have incestuous tendencies."

"Inter-dimensional romance gets complicated."

"You think *their* romance is complicated?"

"Are you still seriously attached to Edie?"

"Oh. That. That was purely physical. I've moved on."

"To me." Eden(Mickey) spoke the two words as if a death sentence.

"How can I not be attracted to you? You are so beautiful."

Eden(Mickey) tried to choke back a laugh, failed. "So you are attracted to me for the same reason you were attracted to Edie. You look at me and see you."

"I look at Edie and see someone who *looks* like me. I look at you and actually *see* me."

"So all you need to be happy is a mirror."

"It's not just that. The stuff we've gone through together. You rescued me from the giant flowers."

"I rescued my body from the giant flowers."

"A body that I was in. You rescued both of us."

Eden(Mickey) sagged down into the bed. "This is so twisted."

"Yes it is. And you'll never in your life meet anyone else who can twist you up like I do. Talk about two people made for each other. We are two people made *of* each other. We could never be happy with anyone else."

"What about Stan?"

"Stan's a lovely guy, but he's no Mickey Haiku."

Mickey spread Eden's arms wide. "Look at me, Eden. I'm no Mickey Haiku."

"Sure you are. It's just that Mickey Haiku has gotten a lot more interesting."

Mickey dropped Eden's arms and sighed. "What do you want to wear?"

"Something warm. We spent so much time in the south where it was steaming, and now we're back here in the north where it's cold."

"You don't have temperate zones in your dimension?"

"In the mountains it's always cold." Jeans and a sweatshirt and woolen socks appeared on both of them. Mickey(Eden) stood. "We're dressing alike?"

"I'm too tired to search for another holo." Eden(Mickey) stood. "Matt and Andy were trying to tell me something." Receiving a blank stare, he explained further. "Bicep. The duo that plays the music I like."

"In your dreams?"

"It wasn't a dream. I don't know what it was. But I need to listen to more of their music to see if I can find any hidden messages."

"Have you got headphones?" Mickey(Eden) asked. Eden(Mickey) glared. "Just to keep the peace."

The two emerged from Mickey's room. Mick, Eden's brother George, and Stan were sprawled around the living room, and Edie was in the kitchen cooking breakfast. "Look at the Bobbsey Twins," Mick said.

"The Bobbsey Twins were brother and sister," George said. "You two don't act like brother and sister."

"Neither do you and Edie," Mickey(Eden) said.

George glared at the body his sister was inhabiting. "We are not brother and sister."

Edie emerged from the kitchen. "Can everyone stop arguing long enough to eat?"

"Oh, hell, yeah." Eden(Mickey) bee-lined into the kitchen, and Edie dished up a plate for him. "I hope you four weren't too conspicuous out and about yesterday."

"Just a local showing three tourists around town. They loved it. They are amazed at the open spaces."

"How's Eden's brother doing?"

"He loves it here."

"You know he has to go back to his own dimension."

"If he does maybe I'll go with him."

"You can't."

"Are you going to stop us?"

"I didn't make the rules, Edie. Everyone needs to end up in the right place in order to restore integrity to the separate dimensions."

Edie stormed out of the kitchen. "Come on, George. We'll get breakfast at my place." She opened the front door and impatiently waited. George shrugged at his sister then followed Edie out the door.

When Eden(Mickey) emerged from the kitchen with a piled-high plate, Mickey(Eden) said, "You handled that smoothly."

Eden(Mickey) continued to the mouse chair. "Get out of my

chair." Mick sprang up, casting an anxious glance at Stan.

"You can have my chair," Stan offered Eden(Mickey) as he stood.

"I don't want your chair." Eden(Mickey) sat down to eat. "I want my chair."

Mick started for the George and Martha chair Stan had just vacated.

Mickey(Eden) beat him to it. "I'll take it, Stan."

Mick looked askance at Mickey(Eden), until he remembered it was really Eden he faced. He backed off to let his ex-wife have the chair.

"Go get something to eat," Mickey(Eden) told Mick. Turning to Stan, she said, "Before it gets cold." The two went into the kitchen. Glaring at Eden(Mickey) while sinking into the Martha and George chair, Mickey(Eden) said, "At least Edie finished fixing breakfast before you ran her off."

"Am I the only one worried about this mess?" Eden(Mickey) said between shovelings.

"I thought we were taking a day off to rest."

"Rest. Really? I didn't get much rest last night."

"It's a small bed! And you planted my butt right in the middle of it!"

"You were aroused all night long."

"Exactly. So do you think *I* slept soundly?"

Standing in the kitchen doorway, Stan grinned at Mick. "I wish those two would get it over with and just make love already."

"Shit." Eden(Mickey) slung his half-empty plate down onto the coffee table and jumped up. "You can have the chair back, Mick." He snatched up Hypatia and stormed into Mickey's room. "I've got to figure out what Bicep was trying to tell me." He glared back at Mickey (Eden). "And I don't have any headphones." He slammed the door. A moment later electronica blasted out from Mickey's bedroom.

Mickey(Eden) turned to a baffled Mick and Stan and shrugged. "Pregnant women."

7.

After Eden(Mickey) gave up on finding any hidden messages in Bicep's music, Mickey(Eden) led the way to Carl Friedrich's apartment. Approaching the door, Eden(Mickey) asked, "He works out of his home?"

Mickey(Eden) shrugged as she rang the doorbell. "This is the address on his card."

"Go away!"

"Come on, Carl Friedrich," Mickey(Eden) said. "We've got to talk to you."

"I've got a gun."

"You'd shoot your own mother?" Eden(Mickey) asked.

"In a heartbeat."

"We're not going to hurt you," Mickey(Eden) said. "I promise I won't even hug you."

"What about that big goon?"

"Stan?" Mickey(Eden) asked. "He won't hug you, either. He's not here."

"You two are alone?"

"I swear."

The door opened. Carl Friedrich stood before them holding a gun.

"I thought you were bluffing," Eden(Mickey) said.

"I live in Chicago. Of course I own a gun. What do you want?"

"Can we come in?" Mickey(Eden) asked.

Carl Friedrich stepped back, but didn't lower the gun. After the two entered, he closed and locked his door.

Eden(Mickey) moved through the small room. It was crammed with a standing desk and drafting table and whiteboards. "I never cared for whiteboards," he said. "Blackboards are classic."

Carl Friedrich set his gun down. "Have you two saved the world yet?"

"We're concerned with saving you right now," Mickey(Eden) said.

"I need saving?"

"The boundaries between the dimensions have weakened," Eden (Mickey) said. "We're worried what that might do to you."

"Remember the exploding McDonalds?" Mickey(Eden) asked. "The spooky forest with all the evil spirits? The ocean with the deadly Pris Virus? Hellades? These were all dimensions you visited. What if a gap between this dimension and one of those opened up and sucked you back in?"

"How?" Carl Friedrich sat down next to his gun.

"Consider a bowling alley," Mickey(Eden) said. "When the lanes are brand new it's merely a flat surface having no effect on the balls at all. But over time many balls travel across them towards the head pin. These heavy balls traveling nearly identical paths eventually wear slight grooves into the wood lanes, making it easier for a ball to follow one of these grooves to the head pin. We have worn grooves into the substance of the dimensions with our travels. Any one of us could slip into one of these grooves and follow it into a dimension we previously visited."

Carl Friedrich sagged into his chair. "So I'm doomed."

"Not doomed, in danger." Mickey(Eden) hugged him. "We just want you to be aware of the danger. Check in with us if anything weird happens." Carl Friedrich was so bummed out he didn't object to the hug.

Or to Eden(Mickey) when he wandered into his kitchen. "What have you got to eat?"

Later that day the two went to Mitchell's office at Northwestern. He was seated at his desk hugging himself, and his breath was labored. "What's wrong with you?" Eden(Mickey) asked.

Ignoring her, he focused on Mickey(Eden). "I hope you and Priscilla have a good excuse for disappearing."

"Really, Mitchell," Eden(Mickey) pressed. "You look terrible."

Shivering, Mitchell turned toward him. "Do I know you?"

"We're researching a project together," Mickey(Eden) replied.

"Your trans-dimensional project?" Mitchell stood and walked around his desk to confront Mickey(Eden). "You can actually follow E-Eight strings through two hundred and forty-eight rotations into other dimensions?"

Eden(Mickey) approached Mitchell's desk to examine the model on it. Noah's Ark, with several pairs of animals waiting to board. He picked up a monkey to look it over.

Mitchell noticed. "It's a gift for my grandson."

Eden(Mickey) set the little plastic monkey down. "Never knew you were interested in Bible stories."

"You look familiar." Mitchell leaned over to look closer. "I've seen you in the building."

Mickey(Eden) stepped between the two. "So we're okay to continue working on our project. You won't cut Mickey's, I mean my, funding off?"

Mitchell looked from one to the other, finally focusing on Mickey

(Eden). "Not at the moment. Your equations show unreasonable effectiveness." He stepped back around his desk, hugging himself. Noticing the two glance at each other with concern, Mitchell said, "Lately, I can't get warm. And I can't seem to catch my breath. The pressure in my head makes it feel like it's going to explode. Must be sinuses." He shrugged. "If you ever do manage to travel between dimensions and discover one without pollen, be sure to take me with you."

Mickey(Eden) smiled. "Of course. We might even send you out to look for dry land. It was an olive leaf, wasn't it, the dove brought back?"

Eden(Mickey) yanked her away from the desk. "We'll keep you informed of our progress, Mitchell, promise." Going out the door, he whispered to Mickey(Eden), "He's freezing and can't hardly breathe."

"He was shot into space."

"In a different dimension."

"He could be slipping down one of those bowling alley grooves we warned Carl Friedrich about."

"But Mitchell never traveled to any other dimension."

Eden(Mickey) towed her companion down the hall. "So it's getting worse than we thought. Faster than we thought. We can't waste any more time. We need to finish this."

"Of course," Mickey(Eden) agreed. "After we make one more stop."

Later that day, Lucy smiled upon opening the door of her condo to find Mickey(Eden) in the hall. "What a pleasant surprise." She beckoned him to enter.

"I can't stay," Mickey(Eden) said. "I'm trying to locate Miriam and don't know where she lives."

Lucy huffed. "What do you want to see *her* about?"

"Actually, I'm looking for Ralph. He's not in his alley, and he was with Miriam last time I saw him."

"Ralph has disappeared. Miriam doesn't know where he is, either."

"Thanks for letting me know." Mickey(Eden) started to leave.

"How is Edie?" Lucy asked. "She won't answer my calls."

"Edie is busy with a new boyfriend."

"Who is he? This other Mickey?"

"Albert had it wrong. His name is George. He was also wrong about Edie being pregnant. Her test was a false positive." Mickey(Eden) hurried away before Lucy could probe any further.

In the first floor lobby, Mickey(Eden) found Eden(Mickey) dozing in a chair. She sat beside him. "Wake up, sleepyhead."

Mickey cracked Eden's eyelids. "You kept me awake all night poking me in the butt."

"Sorry. I can't control that thing."

The eyelids cranked open half-way. "Does Lucy know where Ralph is?"

"No. He's disappeared. We'll have to go on without seeing him."

"Is Lucy worried about her daughter?"

"I told her Edie was busy with a new boyfriend."

"That she can't keep," Eden(Mickey) insisted.

"We don't know that for sure yet."

"I do. Matt and Andy told me so."

"In a dream." Mickey(Eden) yawned. "I didn't get much chance to dream myself. Does that thing ever keep you awake all night?"

"No. So don't mess it up. I want it back in good working condition."

"It works too good, that's the problem." Mickey(Eden) stood.

"There's a solution to that problem." Seeing he had pricked her interest, Eden(Mickey) continued. "I'm right-handed."

Mickey(Eden)'s face lit up. "You'll have to show me how."

Eden(Mickey) sputtered in disgust. "Me? Jerk myself off with your hand? While you watch? Through my eyes?"

The happy expression on Mickey's face collapsed. "Forget it."

"I'll try my best to. What's next?"

"Northwestern University. We'll give George and Priscilla a break this time. We can take the el."

8.

Eden(Mickey) and Mickey(Eden) walked across the Northwestern University campus. On the wide lawn before the building housing the Institute for Experiential Robotics a sharp breeze startled Eden(Mickey) so badly he dropped Hypatia.

Mickey(Eden) snatched the laptop before it hit the ground. "That was close."

"It sure was." Eden(Mickey) looked all around.

"*I'm* talking about the laptop. What are *you* talking about?"

"Didn't you feel that gust of wind?"

"No." While Mickey(Eden) stared with concern, another gust of wind battered her companion. "But I just saw my hair go crazy. What's going on?"

"I think vehicles traveling a hundred miles an hour are whizzing by me." Something unseen whizzed past so massive and fast and close Eden(Mickey) was spun completely around. When he stopped spinning he was standing in the middle of the twenty-lane highway he had previously found himself in the middle of. Vehicles of all shapes and sizes hurtled by within fractions of a centimeter. Mickey hunkered down into as little of a space he could compress Eden's body into.

"You again."

Eden(Mickey) peeked to see Elvis had stopped beside him.

"Get in, darling."

Eden(Mickey) toppled into the go-cart, and they rocketed away.

"You don't smell too bad today."

"How did this happen?"

'Kentucky Rain' began playing. "I don't know, but you better hurry up with these repairs. I just drove into the cargo hold of a space ship."

"How did you get back?"

"Another portal opened up and I drove back here where I belong. Just in time. This mad woman was chasing after me, said she was going to send me out to look for dry land. Whatever that meant."

"That was Carla. Eden's daughter."

"Your daughter?"

"No, Eden's daughter." Eden(Mickey) ignored the weird look Elvis gave him from the dash monitor. "Can you get me back to my own dimension?"

"Sure. The co-ordinates from the last time are still in my memory."

"Good thing it was you who stopped for me."

"Darling, every vehicle on the roads of North America is driven by me. We all share the same memory bank."

"Oh. So nobody *but* Elvis was going to pick me up."

"I told you I'm not really Elvis. I'm an impersonator. My real name is Aaron. Now hold on."

"Just not so..."

"...fast!" Eden(Mickey) skidded on the seat of his pants for three meters across the green at Northwestern he had disappeared from.

Mickey(Eden) ran across the lawn to him. "Are you okay?"

"I landed on my butt. Damn, it hurts again."

Mickey(Eden) helped him up. "That's actually *my* butt, but never mind. Where did you go?"

"Into another dimension. The one where an Elvis impersonator is a go-cart."

"He drives a go-cart?"

"No. He *is* a go-cart." Mickey limped about, testing out Eden's legs. "Nothing's broken." He gingerly rubbed her butt. "It's getting worse. I physically passed into and out of another dimension. Elvis, I mean Aaron, told me he did, too. We've got to quit messing around and finish this."

Eden(Mickey) limped into the Center for Robotics and Biosystems, where he delivered to an engineering professor the plans for a quantum computer with DNA data storage and silicon spin qbit wafers powerful enough to host an AI that could run a program that could completely automate the entire world.

After, they walked to Priscilla's grandparents' house, several blocks off-campus. Mickey(Eden) was impressed. "Priscilla is well off in this dimension."

"Her grandparents are well off. She's a T A."

"That's a rude thing to say about her. Besides, her T and A aren't that hot."

"T A stands for teachers assistant, runt."

Priscilla answered their ring. She noticed Eden(Mickey)'s grimace. "Are you okay, Mickey?"

"My butt's sore. Again."

"You should have seen it," Mickey(Eden) said. "Mickey slid on the grass ten yards for a first down on my butt."

George stepped up behind Priscilla. While she was fully dressed, as usual he was only wearing undershorts. "Want me to take a look at it?"

"You don't need to see my butt," Mickey(Eden) snarled.

"You don't need to see her butt," Priscilla said. "I mean his butt.

Anybody's butt." She smiled. "But mine."

George backed away raising both hands. "Sorry. Just offering to help."

Eden(Mickey) entered. "I see you've made yourself at home here, George."

Mickey(Eden) entered right behind with a disapproving scowl at his lack of pants. "My brother is not such a slob."

"Quit picking on George," Priscilla said, closing the door. "He just woke up."

"Of course he did," Mickey(Eden) said.

"Then you should be rested up and ready to hit the road again," Eden(Mickey) said.

"Already?" Priscilla whined. "Mitchell has been screaming for me. I'm way behind. And I'm so tired I can't even think straight this morning."

"Is your mind foggy?" Mickey(Eden) asked. "Are you having a hard time remembering things?"

Priscilla looked at her with dazed eyes. "Exactly."

Mickey(Eden) turned to Eden(Mickey). "The Priscilla in my dimension must have gotten wiped again."

"*This* Priscilla has worse problems." Eden(Mickey) focused a concerned gaze on her. "Have you had a bad stomach ache lately?"

Priscilla scowled at one then the other. "What is going on with my body?"

"Your twins in other dimensions are having a difficult time," Eden(Mickey) answered. "The sooner we get these repairs done, the sooner our twins will stop affecting us. We just saw Mitchell, and you're good with him. So stay here and see if you can clear your head. This next trip is a short one. The Chicago Botanical Garden."

"Couldn't you have taken the el?" George protested.

"I want to swing by the apartment to check on everybody there, too."

"Easy walking distance from an el station," George insisted.

"Nothing is easy walking for me. I bet my butt is blacker than it is blue." Eden(Mickey) started to unfasten the jeans.

"No you don't!" Mickey(Eden) grabbed her own hands. "Don't go showing off my butt to everybody."

George smiled at Eden(Mickey). "You can show me later." He went off in search of pants.

9.

George parked the rental car in the Botanical Garden lot. Watching Eden(Mickey) ease out and limp forward, he said, "Too bad I can't park in a handicap space."

"I can't believe someone working here can be of any use to the flora dimension," Mickey(Eden) said.

"The file just unlocked on Hypatia claims a brilliant young botanist works here," Eden(Mickey) said.

Mickey(Eden) took her own arm to help Eden(Mickey) walk. "Is he really brilliant, or does he become considered brilliant because of the information you're about to give him?"

Eden(Mickey) gratefully leaned on her. "I'm sure the work he does with what we give him will make his career."

They came upon the young intern at work at the science center. "Excuse me," Eden(Mickey) said. "I have something important to give you." He offered a flash drive. "There is information on here about splicing human genes into hibiscus flowers."

"Thank you, Mickey." The young man thoughtlessly stuck the flash drive in his lab coat pocket then returned to work.

"That was easy," George said as Eden(Mickey) rejoined the other two.

"We're getting a lot of help," he replied.

En route back to the parking lot, they passed through a garden bursting with vibrant blooming plants. And the Albert plant. "Mickey!"

They all turned toward the huge hibiscus flower with the dinner plate-sized bloom that held Albert's face. George freaked. "What the hell is that!"

Eden(Mickey) was surprised. "You can see it?"

"Of course we can see it," Mickey(Eden) said. "It's Albert. He's worked for my ex-husband's family forever."

"These rifts are getting worse," Eden(Mickey) said. "Until now I was the only one who could see this shit."

Mickey(Eden) leaned in close to sniff Albert. "You're terrified."

"I'm scared chlorophyll-less," Albert answered. "Where am I?"

Mickey(Eden) smiled with malice. "Want to play a game, Albert? How about 'she loves me, she loves me not'?"

"No!" Albert ducked back to hide amid the other flowers.

"We can't torture him," Eden(Mickey) said.

"Why not? He tortured me."

Eden(Mickey) pulled her back. "Hold onto her, George." After passing Mickey(Eden) off, he plunged into the blooms looking for Albert, but couldn't find him. "He's gone."

"Yeah, right," George said, releasing Mickey(Eden). "He's rooted in the ground. Or can these plants walk?"

"You wouldn't believe what these plants can do," Mickey(Eden) said.

Eden(Mickey) kept rifling through the flowers. "He must have slipped back into his dimension."

"Miss? Did you lose something?"

All three spun to find a security guard had walked up behind them. "No," Eden(Mickey) stuttered. "I just love these flowers."

"Then why don't you not damage them so they will survive for other people to enjoy?"

George grabbed Eden(Mickey). "She gets carried away."

Mickey(Eden) grabbed him, also, and the two tried to hurry Eden (Mickey) as he hobbled off. "We have got to finish fixing this," Mickey (Eden) said. "This is so bad. Believe me, you do not want those plants taking root in your dimension."

George drove to his and Mickey's apartment. The trio entered to find Mick and Stan playing cards in the kitchen. For no apparent reason, Mick slapped a stack of cards in the middle of the table.

"That looks frightening," Mickey(Eden) said.

"Let's kibitz later." Eden(Mickey) bolted for the bathroom.

George joined the two men in the kitchen. "What are you playing?"

"Egyptian Rat Screw," Mick said.

"Never heard of it." George shrugged. "I'm not a big card player."

Stan slapped the pile in the middle. "Then you were never in the military. There's a lot of time to kill in the barracks."

Mickey(Eden) joined them at the table just as Mick and Stan slapped hands together on the middle pile. "Maybe you two just like holding hands. You have been spending a lot of time together."

Eden(Mickey) returned from the bathroom. "Have you two been comparing notes on Eden?"

Stan glanced at him. "You've got such a high opinion of yourself."

Mickey(Eden) waved. "Stan, I'm over here."

"I don't care where you are, Eden," Mick joined in. "You're not the center of our universe."

George leaned in to slap the pile. When Stan and Mick both glared up at him, George shrugged. "You guys missed a slap."

"We're not playing marriages," Stan said.

Mick looked at Mickey(Eden), then Eden(Mickey). "We left that one out on purpose."

George withdrew his hand from the king and queen. "Oh. Sorry."

"I thought you've never played Egyptian Rat Screw," Stan said.

"I catch on quick."

"Want us to deal you in next game?" Mick asked.

George caught the other two giving him dire looks. He turned back to the table. "I can't. We've got to go. Here." He pulled out his wallet and dropped a wad of twenties on the table. "If you guys need anything while we're gone. There's not a lot of food in the apartment. Or if you want to see a movie, or go out for drinks, or a ballgame."

Stan smiled up at him. "Thanks, George."

"We might be gone for several days, and you guys don't have any money, at least none that's good in Chicago."

"You don't have any good-looking sisters, do you, George?" Mick asked.

Mickey(Eden) slapped Mick on the back of the head, only somewhat playfully. "It's the other George who has the good-looking sister."

Eden(Mickey) walked out of the kitchen. "Wish us luck."

Mick and Stan resumed Egyptian Rat Screw without wishing anything.

"You sure do throw money around," Mickey(Eden) said to George as they followed Eden(Mickey).

"This is the adventure of a lifetime for me. Every rich kid does the Europe tour. How many have done the dimension tour? This is fantastic."

Eden(Mickey) walked outside. "So we swing by to pick up Priscilla and hit the road again."

"Where to this time?" Mickey(Eden) asked.

10.

It was late morning when Priscilla pulled off Highway 101 into the parking lot of the NASA Ames Research Center gift shop in Mountain View outside San Francisco. George had driven most of the non-stop thirty-three hour trip. At present he was stretched out across the back seat with his head in Mickey(Eden)'s lap. Eden(Mickey), seated up front with Priscilla, looked back to see Mickey(Eden) running his fingers through George's hair. "You're making me look gay."

"I can't help it. He looks so much like my brother."

"I don't think so," Priscilla said, nodding toward George. "*His* nails are clean."

"I wonder how many Georges there are?" Eden(Mickey) said.

"And how many Priscillas?" Priscilla said.

"The George and Priscilla who pop up on my laptop screen seem to be a couple."

"They sure bicker like a couple," Mickey(Eden) said.

"Like you two?" Priscilla asked.

They looked at each other with surprise. "We're not a couple," Eden(Mickey) said.

"Really?" Priscilla said. "Me and George figured you two were sleeping together."

"We *have* slept together," Mickey(Eden) said. "But me sleeping with my own body and Eden sleeping with her own body hardly constitutes sleeping together. In the usual sense of the term."

Priscilla smiled. "If ever there was a couple made in heaven."

"Made in Hell more like it," Eden(Mickey) said.

"It's Mickey's fault they haven't done anything," George said, rousing to their voices. "He's scared of women."

"I am not!" Eden(Mickey) leaned over the front seat to get in George's face. "Look at me. I *am* a woman. How can I be scared of them?"

George raised up from Mickey(Eden)'s lap. "You *were* scared of them. I have no idea how you feel about them now that you've turned so weird." He rubbed his eyes. "I kept waiting for you to make a move on Priscilla."

"Yeah," Priscilla agreed from behind the wheel. "Me, too."

Eden(Mickey) retreated back against the front passenger door. "Priscilla is a good friend."

"So how do you feel about Eden?" George asked.

Eden(Mickey) pierced Mickey(Eden) with his laser gaze. "She's the rat who tricked me into helping her wreck worlds."

Mickey(Eden) started crying. "I can't do this anymore."

"Okay," Priscilla said. "Time out."

George took sobbing Mickey(Eden) in his arms and glared at Eden (Mickey). "I bet Oppenheimer didn't catch this much grief for developing the atomic bomb."

"Actually," Priscilla said, "he did."

Eden(Mickey) turned back around to Priscilla. "Let's just finish this."

Mickey(Eden) drew away from George. "Sorry about that."

"I thought the pregnant woman was supposed to be the emotional one," Eden(Mickey) accused.

"Leave her alone, Mickey," George said.

"Yeah, Mickey," Priscilla chimed in. "Other women can get emotional, too." She nodded toward the back seat. "That is a woman in your body. Don't be such a jerk to her."

Inside the gift shop, Eden(Mickey) gave a flash drive to a guide waiting for his tour group to gather. He assured Mickey he would get it to the appropriate engineer working at Ames. When Eden(Mickey) returned to the car he saw George and Priscilla had changed places. After he climbed into the front next to George, they all three demanded to know what was on the flash drive. Eden(Mickey) told them it was plans for a better suspended animation pod. "That's what caused all the trouble in the first place. Mitchell's pod going bad. Apparently, quite a few of them malfunctioned. I gave Ames designs for a much improved pod. The spaceship should complete its journey without Noah taking over the ship."

George rubbed his weary forehead. "Where to next?"

Eden(Mickey) opened Hypatia and got busy.

George looked from Mickey(Eden) to Priscilla. "Are we okay to keep going? Or do we need to stop for some sleep."

Priscilla yawned and stretched. "We just drove to the west coast. Again. I need a bed."

"That depends on how far it is," Mickey(Eden) added.

Eden(Mickey) looked up from the laptop. "Atlanta."

"Atlanta?!" Priscilla whined. "How far is that?"

Eden(Mickey) consulted Google Maps. "Thirty-eight hours."

George pulled out his phone. "I'll find us a motel." Before he got far into his search a bird landed on the hood.

Eden(Mickey) studied it with apprehension. "George, a dove just landed on the car."

George glanced up from his phone. "Is that an olive leaf in its mouth?"

"You're seeing this? That's not good." Eden(Mickey) looked to Priscilla. "Can you see it, too?"

"Of course. Why wouldn't I see it?"

A body hurtled down out of the sky and crashed into the next parking space. All four screamed! "My God!" Priscilla screamed loudest. "That's Mitchell!"

"Are you sure?" George asked.

"You think I wouldn't know my own boss?!" She hopped out of the car.

"I'm sure he's dead, Priscilla," Mickey(Eden) said.

The frozen body slipped on through the pavement into the ground out of sight.

"And back in the dimension he belongs," Eden(Mickey) said. "Get in the car, Priscilla, before another frozen body comes crashing down on your head."

Priscilla hopped back in.

"We need to get out of here before a falling body wrecks our car," Mickey(Eden) said.

George peeled out of the parking lot. "Let me see the route." Eden(Mickey) held up the laptop so George could see the screen. On Google Maps the route from San Francisco to Atlanta was displayed. "How far is Albuquerque?"

"Sixteen and a half hours," Eden(Mickey) replied.

"I just woke up. I can drive us that far." George glanced at the screen again. "How far from there to Oklahoma City?"

"Eight hours."

"Can you take us that far, Priscilla?"

"Yes. If bodies are falling out of the sky. We've got to keep going."

"How far from there to Atlanta?" George asked Eden(Mickey).

"Thirteen hours."

"I can do that after an eight-hour break."

Eden patted Mickey's lap. "I've got your pillow right here."

George frowned back at her. "I'd prefer a softer lap."

"You're not getting mine," Eden(Mickey) said.

Priscilla glared at Eden(Mickey). "You are getting your driver's license when we get back to Chicago."

11.

George had been driving in the dark for hours by the time he exited the circle freeway that looped Atlanta. He and his three passengers looked more dead than alive. They pulled into the nearly-empty lot at the CDC. "They're closed. Nothing we can do tonight. We either sleep in the car or we find rooms."

"I need a room, George," Priscilla said. "I need a bed."

George turned to the others. "How about you two?"

Mickey(Eden) shrugged. "No problem with us sharing a room. We share everything else."

A short while later the four stood in the hall outside their adjoining motel rooms. George unlocked one of the doors. "Me and Priscilla are going to the pool. A swim will feel great after being in the car for three days."

"They might even have a hot tub," Priscilla added. "That would be marvelous."

"Do you need suits?" Eden(Mickey) asked.

"No," Priscilla said. "We packed real ones this time." They went into their room to change.

Mickey(Eden) followed Eden(Mickey) into their room. "Do you want to go to the pool?" she asked.

Eden(Mickey) sagged into a chair. "No. All I want to do is take a shower and sleep for twelve hours. If you want to go I'll find a swim suit for you."

"I think I will. If you are just going to sleep. I'm too wound up. I can still see Mitchell's body hitting the pavement three feet away from me." Once she was garbed in swimming trunks, Mickey(Eden) grabbed a room card and left.

~ * ~

"Damn." The clock radio showed eleven forty-five. "Didn't even make it to midnight." Eden(Mickey) climbed out of bed in the dark. *Eden did a good job getting in bed quietly,* Mickey thought as he plodded to the bathroom. On the way back he saw Mickey(Eden) hadn't made it to bed. The three of them must be partying in the other room. But what if they weren't? A dead body had just fallen out of deep space from a different dimension and then disappeared into the pavement right next to them. Anything could happen. "Damn, damn."

Eden(Mickey) conjured up the same outfit as the night before. He listened at George and Priscilla's door. No party going on in there. No answer to repeated knocks, either. The pool closed at ten, so they couldn't still be there. There was a small lounge. Eden(Mickey) tromped down to it. Why was this place open, he wondered upon entering? It was a morgue. The three were not in the lobby, either. He stepped outside the main entrance. The rental car was still parked in the same space in the lot, so they hadn't driven anywhere. The gym would be closed. Where were they?

Eden(Mickey) decided to try the pool anyway, since that was where they had been headed. Maybe they had talked someone into keeping it open after hours. Rounding the corner, he saw the pool was dark. He cupped hands to the glass. No one was in there.

"Can I help you?"

Eden(Mickey) turned to find a young housekeeper with a well-stocked cleaning cart. "Could you let me into the pool? I lost something and I might have left it in there."

"Sure thing, Mickey." The woman unlocked the door then pushed her cart away.

Now Mickey knew something was going on. He was getting help from higher up. Eden(Mickey) walked around the pool looking for any sign of them. He certainly wasn't expecting what he saw. A dolphin surfaced in the middle of the pool then dove back below the water and disappeared. A rift between dimensions had opened in the middle of the swimming pool. Eden(Mickey) hurried around to the shallow end and waded out to waist-deep water.

The next instant Eden(Mickey) was waist-deep in the placid ocean off the tropical island in the dimension all eight of them had visited. The dolphin surfaced next to him, yipping away. He petted its slick head as he studied the island. It was night and the beach was deserted. Eden(Mickey) waded in, calling out everyone's names.

All three ran out of the trees onto the moonlit beach. "Thank God you're here!" Mickey(Eden) ran out into the ocean to hug him.

Eden(Mickey) returned the hug. Surprisingly, he was just as glad to see Eden. Not only his body, but Eden. "Is everyone okay?"

Mickey(Eden) escorted him onto the beach. "Yes, we're okay. Just scared shitless."

"No one was on the beach when we arrived this time," Priscilla said." We were lucky it was the middle of the night."

"We've been hiding in case anyone showed up," George said.

Priscilla hugged herself. "Hiding and freezing."

Eden(Mickey) looked out to sea. Light from the hotel pool shown out of the rift and sparkled on the dark water. "Why didn't you just walk back to the hotel?"

"That's not funny," George said.

"It wasn't meant to be." Eden(Mickey) pointed to the light. "The rift is right there."

All three looked to where he pointed. "I don't see anything," Mickey(Eden) said.

Eden(Mickey) examined the three baffled faces. "You can't see that light? Coming from the hotel?" All three shook their heads no. He took Mickey(Eden)'s hand. "Hold hands and I'll walk you through it." They did as instructed, Mickey(Eden) nearly crushing her own hand as they waded out toward the light.

Eden(Mickey) led the other three single file back into his dimension. They splashed past him to flee up out of the pool. He exited in a more leisurely manner. George glanced at the clock on the wall. "It's nearly one."

Priscilla gushed in relief. "We were there for hours. We thought for sure you'd sleep through till noon, and even then it would take you a while to figure out what had happened. And there was no guarantee you could do anything about it. We knew if the beach bums we saw before returned to the beach in the morning they would kill us."

Mickey(Eden) smiled at Eden(Mickey). "I knew Mickey would come for us."

"For my body, you mean."

"Of course." She hugged Eden(Mickey) "But for me, too."

The four walked the deserted halls to their rooms. As soon as their door closed, Eden(Mickey) clapped once. Water dripped off their naked bodies onto the carpet. Mickey(Eden) fetched two towels from the bathroom, and they dried off.

Eden(Mickey) caught Mickey(Eden) staring at her own body while they toweled off. "Worried about your butt?" He turned around. "The latest bruises are fading. It should be alright as long as I don't ride with Elvis again."

Mickey(Eden) took her own body by the shoulders and turned it back around. "That wasn't what I was looking at. Your stomach looks puffy. You're starting to show." She kneeled and kissed her own bare abdomen. "I appreciate you taking such good care of my baby."

"Hey," Eden(Mickey) said. "I'm still wet."

Mickey(Eden) raised up and backed off, and they both finished drying.

Eden(Mickey) climbed into bed and rolled away. Mickey(Eden) climbed in and cuddled up from behind. "I was so scared, Mickey. I didn't think we were getting out of that one. I thought I'd never get to see my baby."

Eden(Mickey) remained stiff as a board. "I'm not going to abandon you, Eden. You've got my body."

"Is that all you care about, Mickey? Getting your body back?"

"And getting this baby out of me." The board warped a little as Eden(Mickey) relaxed a bit. "Without delivering it."

Mickey(Eden) tightened her warm embrace. "You may *have* to give birth to the baby. We don't know how long we'll be stuck in each other's body."

The board stiffened up again. "That can't happen."

Mickey(Eden) pulled her own body even closer. "Why not? My body is designed to give birth. You won't have any problems." She kissed the back of her own neck. "You won't be doing this on your own. I'll be with you all the way."

"Unless you get stuck in some weird dimension."

"If I do you'll come get me. Just like tonight. And like you did with the flower people." She sighed with contentment. Until Mickey shifted Eden's hips about. Mickey(Eden) scooted back. "Am I hurting your... my...*our* sore butt?"

"No. You're poking me again."

"Sorry. I told you I don't know how to control this thing."

"I do." Eden(Mickey) rolled over to face himself. He stared solemnly into his own eyes. Until he closed Eden's eyes. "Mickey sex ed one-oh-one. He likes for his balls to be touched." He cupped his own balls with Eden's soft fingers.

Mickey(Eden) gasped. "Yes. I can see why. Or feel why." After thirty seconds without breathing, she asked, "Why did you close your eyes?"

"I don't want to watch myself doing this. I don't want to watch how I react to this being done to me. I might can go through with this as long as I don't witness it."

"Eden sex ed one-oh-one. She likes parts of her body other than the obvious parts to be touched." Mickey(Eden) stroked her own shoulders and sides and back.

Mutual well-educated caressing coaxed both bodies to attention. Until Mickey withdrew Eden's hand. "Not too much touching. For a man that can cause disaster."

Mickey(Eden) laughed. "It wouldn't be a disaster. We've got all night."

"Half the night. It's well after midnight." Mickey rolled over onto Eden's back. "Is this a good position? I don't know what works best for you."

"What did Mick like?"

"He didn't like. He said I was tentative and withholding."

Mickey(Eden) burst out with a loud guffaw. "No shit. First time making love as a woman? I *bet* you were tentative and withholding."

"First time making love at all."

"Really?"

Eden(Mickey) nodded yes.

"So your first was with my lousy ex-husband." Mickey(Eden) rolled over on top of her own body.

"This is no better. Eden, in my body, is making love to herself, with me inside."

"Shut up, Mickey. Don't overthink this like you do everything else. Just go with it."

They did.

12.

The next morning at breakfast the other three watched in awe as Eden(Mickey) devoured mass quantities of eggs, muffins, bacon, waffles, sausages, bagels, fruit, and doughnuts. Priscilla smiled. "You really worked up an appetite last night."

Eden(Mickey) looked up with a mouthful of biscuits and gravy, but decided to keep eating rather than reply.

"You've got a glow about you this morning," George commented.

This time Eden(Mickey) stopped eating and glared at Mickey (Eden). "What did you tell them?"

"Eden didn't say anything," Priscilla said. "You are just acting so guilty."

"Mickey has nothing to feel guilty about," Mickey(Eden) said. "Let him eat."

Eden(Mickey) resumed shoveling. While the other three smiled at him.

After breakfast they drove to the CDC. "What have you got for them?" Mickey(Eden) asked.

"The design for a vaccine that will take down the virus that causes the final pandemic, so a self-aware virus never evolves."

Once that was delivered, they all gathered around Hypatia to learn their next destination. "Pike's Peak," Eden(Mickey) announced.

"Colorado," George moaned. "Another day's drive."

"Actually, Google Maps says it's twenty-two hours," Eden(Mickey) said.

"What are we going to Pike's Peak for?" Priscilla asked.

Eden(Mickey) closed the laptop. "We'll find out by the time we get there."

Two-thousand, two-hundred and seventy-nine kilometers later, Eden(Mickey) forced George to drive slowly up the twisting route to the top of Pike's Peak. "I'd hate to ride along with Ralph driving this," Eden(Mickey) said. "He'd send us hurtling over the edge."

"Some view," Priscilla noted from the back seat.

"How high are we?" Mickey(Eden) asked.

Eden(Mickey) consulted Hypatia. "It's four thousand, three hundred and two meters at the top."

"I can sure tell the difference in the air," George said.

"Yeah," Eden(Mickey) agreed. "It's cold and there's not much oxygen."

"It feels like we're back in Belos' dimension," Mickey(Eden) said.

George pulled into the parking lot. "At least it's a weekday. There's a couple spaces left." He backed into a tight spot.

Onto the edge of a rocky snow and ice covered crag. The other cars were gone, the parking lot was gone, the visitor center was gone. A blizzard swirled around the car, obscuring the world.

"You parked in another dimension!" Eden(Mickey) screamed.

George shifted into forward.

"No! Look!" There was nothing but air in front of them. "The rift has closed. If you pull forward you'll drive right off the top of the mountain."

George turned to him in a panic. "What do I do?"

"Put on the emergency brake, for one thing," Priscilla yelled.

George shifted into park, cut off the engine, and put on the emergency brake, yet still kept his foot jammed down on the brake pedal. "Now what?"

"Check your rental agreement," Eden(Mickey) said. "See if driving into another dimension is covered."

"You're joking?" Priscilla squealed. "Now? I'm about to wet my pants."

"Don't do that. It's liable to freeze."

"Another joke?" Mickey(Eden) said. "You sure are calm about this."

"I've been through too much crap lately to get upset over something as trivial as this."

George gripped the wheel with both hands. "Trivial? You feel that? The car's rocking. The wind is hurricane force."

"Nah," Eden(Mickey) replied, "I'd say more like tropical depression force."

"Knock it off." Mickey(Eden) smacked the back of her own head, not playfully at all. "Do you think we're close to that cave?"

"Do you think I know?" Eden(Mickey) said. "Look around. What do you see? Snow and rocks. Does any of it look familiar, Eden? No, it's just snow and rocks."

"How much gas do we have?" Priscilla asked.

George checked. "Three-quarter tank. Where are you wanting to drive to?"

Priscilla hugged herself. "Nowhere. Start the car and run the heater. It's getting cold fast."

"Wait a minute." Mickey closed Eden's eyes. Winter coats appeared on all four. "Is that better, Priscilla?"

"Yes." Priscilla cuddled up with her new coat. "Thank you, Mickey."

"Everybody keeps thanking Mickey for their clothes," Mickey (Eden) snarled. "It's *my* chip. I designed the clothes."

George ignored the whining. "We still need to run the heater."

"Hold on," Eden(Mickey) said. He started to open the door.

"You're going out there?" George asked. "Are you crazy?"

"Do you want to die of carbon monoxide poisoning? You backed into snow. I want to make sure the exhaust pipe is clear." Eden(Mickey) pushed open the front passenger door against the fierce wind, then hung onto it as he clambered out into the snow. He shoved it back closed with help from George pulling from inside. Holding onto the car, Eden(Mickey) edged around to the back, where he knelt to clear snow away from the exhaust pipe.

When Eden(Mickey) rose and turned back around, the Pris Virus stood before him, wearing the same Ariel nightgown from Priscilla's closet as before. Scrambling back away from this sudden unexpected appearance, Eden's feet slipped and he tumbled into the snow.

"I'll lead you to the cave." The Pris Virus walked away from the car along a narrow icy ridge.

Eden(Mickey) pulled himself up and flung the front passenger door open. "Let's go. She's leading us to the cave."

George cleared the windshield with the wipers. "Who is?"

"You can't see her?" All three shook their heads no. "Then get out and follow me. Hurry. I don't want to lose sight of her." Eden(Mickey) slipped and slid after the Pris Virus. He heard the others get out and slam their doors. Not wanting to risk losing sight of their guide in the snowstorm, he didn't look back to see if they were following.

The cave entrance soon came into view. Eden(Mickey) stumbled in after the Pris Virus. The other three stumbled out of the snow into the cave, also. "Is she still here?" Mickey(Eden) asked.

"Who?" Priscilla asked.

"Your twin," Eden(Mickey) answered. "The virus from the dimension we went swimming in last night. Now be quiet. All of you. So I can find out what's going on." He turned toward the Pris Virus. "Thank you for saving us."

"I brought you here for a reason. Things have changed here since you went to Hellades. Lucy and Miriam have been deposed."

"Really?" Eden(Mickey) chuckled. "That's not so bad. I didn't like that version of them anyway. Way too arrogant."

"Their usurpers are worse. Remember you brought Stanley and Lori with you?"

"Yes. And the plant versions of Stan and Laurie showed up, too."

"That's what ruined my plans."

"How?"

"I did not like the way Lucy and Miriam were treating my Stanley and Lori. As servants. They were assigned the most menial demeaning work in this dimension. It was degrading to watch my people treated that way."

"You were watching? From a lower dimension?"

"No, from this dimension. Stanley and Lori carried me here inside their bodies. So I infected Lucy and Miriam."

"You killed them?"

"No. I told you I wasn't designed to kill people. But I can affect vital organs. So I afflicted their most vital organ. Their brains. Now Miriam and Lucy are much less intelligent than Stanley and Lori. Now it's Lucy and Miriam doing all the worst jobs, while Stanley and Lori rule."

"And through them, you. Isn't that what you wanted?"

"It was. Until the flowers interfered. Lucy and Miriam had kept them under control. They had been potted and stuck in a dark corner. But now they have corrupted their twins. The Laurie plant enticed Stanley with her scent, and the Stan plant did the same with Lori."

"Their scents, yes," Eden(Mickey) said, remembering. "They give off such powerful scents."

"So now all Stanley and Lori want to do is dally with the plants."

"Why don't you mess with their brains? Like you did with Lucy and Miriam?"

"I wasn't designed to infect plant life."

"What do you want us to do about them?"

"You and your friends need to get rid of the plants. If you do, I'll help you drive back to Pike's Peak."

"You'll reopen the rift? You can do that?"

"While the barriers between dimensions are so weak I can. Once you pitch the plants off the balcony into Hellades, I'll reopen the rift enough for you to leave."

"Won't Stanley and Lori be upset with us doing that?"

"Once they're out from under the influence of the plants they'll get over it." The Pris Virus motioned toward the iron door. "They are in the throne room."

"All four of them?"

"Yes. They have become inseparable." The Pris Virus began to fade away, then came back into focus. "One more thing. A short while ago I hurt really bad. In my midsection. Like I'd been hit in the stomach with a baseball bat. Any idea what that was?"

"Not really," Eden(Mickey) lied. "Are you okay?"

Suspicion oozed from her eyes. "I think you do know. Remember, I have infected your body, too. Yours and Eden's bodies. I can strike at any time."

"Don't damage my mind," Eden(Mickey) pleaded. "I need it to do these repairs."

"I'm watching you, Mickey. From inside Eden's body." The Pris Virus faded away.

Eden(Mickey) turned back to the other three. "You didn't hear any of that?"

"No," Mickey(Eden) said. "What does she want us to do?"

"Toss the plants into Hell."

"She wants us to kill them?" George asked.

"I'm good with that," Mickey(Eden) said.

"I'm not. What did they do?" Priscilla asked.

"Doesn't matter," Mickey(Eden) said. "They are monsters."

"We fell to Hell and it didn't kill us," Eden(Mickey) said.

"You had something soft to land on," Priscilla said. "I'm still sore from that. "I've been on Tylenol Three since we got out of Hell."

"If we do this, the Pris Virus will help us drive back to Pike's Peak." He gazed back and forth between the two wavering faces. "We'll be saving Stanley and Lori. And it won't necessarily kill the plants."

"They're monsters," Mickey(Eden) broke in. "You two should have seen what they did to me."

"To *my* body," Eden(Mickey) added.

Finally, George and Priscilla closed their eyes and nodded yes.

Eden(Mickey) turned toward the iron door. "Me and Eden will grab the Stan plant. George and Priscilla will get the Laurie plant. We toss them both off the balcony." He swung open the door.

None of them were prepared for what they encountered in the throne room. Stanley sat in Lucy's throne with the Laurie plant entangled all about him. Her bloom nestled on his shoulder while tendrils swarmed across his body and inside his clothes, stroking every conceivable sensitive place. Lori sat on Miriam's throne with the Stan plant engaged with her body in the same fashion. All four faces smiled at them when they entered. Stanley spoke first. "Hello, travelers."

Priscilla whispered into Eden(Mickey)'s ear. "What are we supposed to do now?"

George found Mickey(Eden)'s ear. "We can't throw the plants off the balcony without throwing Stanley and Lori off with them."

"I'll take care of Stanley and Lori." The words of the Pris Virus echoed in Eden(Mickey)'s head. "Just get them out onto the balcony."

"Looks like you've fared well here," Eden(Mickey) said. "Much better than drowning."

"Thank you for bringing us here," Lori said.

Eden(Mickey) coughed. "Do you mind if we step out onto the balcony to talk? You two must be used to the flowers' aromas, but they are stifling to us. Out in the fresh air would be much better." Mickey (Eden) followed Eden(Mickey)'s lead and coughed. The other two joined in a moment later.

Stanley and Lori looked to each other. The Stan plant and Lori looked to each other. The Laurie plant and Stanley looked to each other. The two plants looked to each other. At last, all four heads nodded yes. Stanley and Lori stood. When they did, the plants remained attached to them. The four led the others out the door onto the balcony. As they walked ahead, the flowers turned their blooms back to keep an eye on the four behind. There would be no sneaking up on them.

The cold wind out on the balcony was slashing. Stanley and Lori shivered. "We're not staying out here long. We have never gotten used to this cold." The Stan and Laurie plants seemed to wither in the cold blast. Hailing from the tropics in their dimension, they weren't used to this intense cold, either. There was a sudden gust howling out of nowhere. It was so strong the plants ducked their blooms to avoid it. Stanley and Lori, staggered by the frigid blast, grabbed the balcony railing to keep from falling. Despite this, they both slumped to the floor, motionless.

"I knocked my people out," Eden(Mickey) heard the Pris Virus say inside his head. "Go."

Eden(Mickey) lunged forward. "They're not used to this cold!" he yelled to the plants. "It's too much for them. We've got to get them back inside." The plants nodded their agreement. Mickey(Eden) followed his lead to Stanley, while George and Priscilla went to Lori. Instead of lifting Stanley up, the two grabbed the plant Laurie and yanked her away from his unconscious form. The plant was so numb from the cold it didn't resist. George and Priscilla followed their lead and did the same with the plant Stan. The four of them pitched the two plants off the balcony.

The plants, realizing at last what was going on, recovered quickly. They both wrapped tendrils around the railing to break their fall. While George and Priscilla backed away, Eden(Mickey) and Mickey(Eden) both grabbed the tendrils and tried to pull them loose. Before they could, the plants stretched other tendrils out to ensnare the two. They were pulled off the balcony, also, to dangle above the chasm along with the plants.

A strong updraft welled up from below and held the four level with the balcony. There was a loud snap, then another, from above. Two large icicles plunged toward them and sliced through the tendrils that were holding Eden(Mickey) and Mickey(Eden). Both of the plants bellowed in pain, and with the sudden agony released their holds on the railing. At that point the updraft abruptly failed, and all four plummeted out of sight into the icy mist below.

George and Priscilla rushed up to the railing and leaned over to see what had happened to the falling bodies. All they could see was the swirling snow they had plunged into.

Until the powerful updraft returned, forcing the two back from the railing. Eden(Mickey), Mickey(Eden), the Stan plant, and the Laurie plant all emerged from the mist. The four rocketed back up past the balcony, on up to disappear into the clouds.

13.

"How are you doing?"

Mickey opened Eden's eyes to find his body looming over him. "I don't know." Looking around, he saw Eden's body was stretched out on a small narrow bed. They were in a brightly-lit cell of a room with metallic walls and floor. The cool air smelled stale, but with no stench of sulphur. "This doesn't look like Hellades."

"It's not. We're in the dimension above the mountaintop."

"I knew it!" Eden(Mickey) sat up, ecstatic. "I knew there was a higher dimension than that. Lucy and Miriam aren't smart enough to have planned all we've been through." He realized they were wearing lightweight jumpsuits. "How'd we change clothes? If I was asleep?"

"My chip was overrode. These are real clothes we have on."

"How did you override the chip?"

"I didn't."

"I did."

Eden(Mickey) looked to see a middle-age woman standing in the open doorway.

"You threw up all over yourself," Mickey(Eden) said. "And me. On the way up here. I think we were half-way down to Hellades when Carla yanked us all the way back up here."

"Carla?" Eden(Mickey) studied the woman. She did seem older than who he had supposed her to be, the officer they had awakened on board the space ark. "That's not Carla?"

"Carla was her mother."

"That's your granddaughter? She's older than us."

Mickey(Eden) merely shrugged.

"Where are we?"

"In orbit above Earth," Carla answered. "Want to see?"

Eden(Mickey) nodded as Mickey(Eden) helped him to Eden's feet. "Did you clean me up?" he asked her.

"Yeah. I couldn't stand seeing that puke all over me." Mickey(Eden) led him out.

Eden(Mickey)'s foggy brain cleared sufficiently for him to go into a panic. "Why are we in orbit above Earth? Why aren't we in interstellar space?" He turned frantic eyes upon Carla. "Why did we come back to Earth? Isn't it going to be destroyed?"

Carla attempted to calm him. "This isn't the star ship you were on before. That was a different dimension, the one Eden tells me you met my mother in." They entered the lounge, where Carla presented an expansive view of the Earth in space. "Of course it's not really glass. A piece of glass that big would be impractical in space. There are cameras on the hull outside…"

Mickey(Eden) smiled. "She sounds just like you, Mickey, the way your mind wanders."

Eden(Mickey) walked over to gaze down upon Earth. "Be quiet, both of you, and let me enjoy the view." He eventually turned his gaze elsewhere, to other parts of the extensive station. "A lot more impressive than the ISS."

"That's because Space X built half of this." Carla pointed to some elaborate architecture in the image projected from outside. "That's the Musk wing." She turned back to Eden(Mickey). "That's where the flowers are. Elon was so delighted with Stan and Laurie he offered to keep them until I figure out what to do with them."

Eden(Mickey) snickered. "I thought he was smarter than that."

"His namesake was. This generation of Musk?" Carla made a dismissive motion with her hand. "People have always imagined the human race striking off for a new home planet once the Earth became unlivable. But do you realize how rare planets like ours are? First, one would have to be located. Then the human race and all it needed to survive would have to be transported across vast interstellar distances to get there. Besides, humans have spent millions of years adapting their bodies to this environment, and adapting the environment to our requirements. For better *and* worse, we have been terra forming Earth for millions of years. Much easier to remain here on this planet that our bodies are entangled with and clean up the mess we made. The planet itself is pretty durable. After the human race was reduced to a few hundred million, genetic samples were taken of the survivors and stored safely off-planet in several locations, such as here and on the moon and on Mars and in the asteroid belt. We certainly didn't want to put all our eggs in one basket, so to speak. While from this station the restorative terra forming is carried out. The brightest scientists and their descendants have labored for generations performing this work…"

"That included us, Mickey," Mickey(Eden) interrupted. "Our twins." She motioned toward Carla. "And descendants." She smiled so big her lips were about to burst. "Do you know who this is?"

Eden(Mickey) glanced away from Earth to Carla. "Carla. Your granddaughter. You already told me."

"Yeah, but do you know who she is?"

"Sounds like I must be missing something, so go ahead and

enlighten me."

"She's a twin of *our* granddaughter," Mickey(Eden) said.

Eden(Mickey) glanced down to her abdomen. "You said Mick is the father."

"Of Carl Friedrich." Mickey(Eden) hugged Carla. "This is a twin of the daughter of the baby we made in Atlanta." Carla shrugged her off. Mickey(Eden) frowned at her. "Why is it none of my children, and grandchildren, like to be hugged?"

"But I'm pregnant. Pregnant women can't get pregnant. Again. While they're still pregnant. The first time."

"You did. Or my body did. My body is so screwed up with you inside it got pregnant. Again. While you were already pregnant."

Being Mickey, his curiosity was stoked. "How's this going to work? Will the babies be born at different times?"

"No," Mickey(Eden) answered. "Same time. She will just be several months premature."

"Will she be okay?"

Mickey(Eden) laughed as she motioned to Carla. "Her mother was. And this Carla looks pretty healthy to me."

"So I'm carrying *two* babies, and one of them is mine. You can have Carl Friedrich."

"You can't play favorites with your children," Mickey(Eden) admonished. "That's not being a good parent."

"I don't have to play favorites. Only one of them is mine." Eden(Mickey) looked away from admiring Carla back to Mickey(Eden). "How did you find out? That Carla is my daughter. Our daughter."

"When I was talking with the Carla on the bridge of the space ship in the other dimension."

Eden(Mickey) thought back. On Mitchell's ark he had stalled while setting up the inter-dimensional travel program so the mother and daughter could have some time together. While he delayed, Mickey(Eden) and Carla had conversed by themselves on the bridge for quite a while.

"Carla was describing what it was like being in suspended animation, and then she told me about a nightmare she'd had while in her tube. About being captured and ravished by giant plants. And what had made the nightmare even more horrible was it had happened to her while she was a man. She had dreamed about what had really happened to me. So we started comparing notes."

Could that be where nightmares come from, Mickey wondered? Experiences of our twins, or people we are related to, like our children and grandchildren, in other dimensions? That would explain why dreams seemed so real, if they happened for real in a different dimension. And it would also feel familiar, since it happened to a blood relative. Could DNA possess memories of what went before? And could these memories pass between dimensions? How many generations would this genetic memory go back? To our primate ancestors? In the robot world dimension Stan's and Miriam's consciousness had been downloaded into primates? How interconnected could life be? Through how many dimensions?

"Earth to Mickey."

Mickey snapped out of his reverie. "Sorry. How did you find out Carla…" He patted Eden's stomach. "…this Carla is my daughter?"

"She checked the computer records after you left," Carla said. "You and Eden really are her parents. My grandparents, in this dimension. Remember the first time you were on the mountaintop you asked for a sign?"

"That was you?"

"I couldn't refuse my grandfather."

"Unless," Eden(Mickey) said, "someone in a dimension higher yet has been manipulating you."

Mickey(Eden) rushed over to slap a hand over her own mouth. "Don't ask for a sign!"

Carla frowned at that notion. "It's possible. But not likely."

Mickey pulled his hand off Eden's mouth and pointed down to Earth. "At least you're not as arrogant as Lucy and Miriam down there on the mountain top, denying it could even be possible. I must have raised your mother right."

"Just like a man," Mickey(Eden) said. "Taking credit for nothing of his doing."

Eden(Mickey) patted Eden's stomach again. "I've been taking good care of this baby. Or babies, since there are two of them in there."

Mickey(Eden) turned back to Carla. "So are we done?"

"As far as I'm concerned. The plans of Supreme Ruler Ralph were thwarted by Planck world George and Priscilla. Their plans were overruled by Miriam and Lucy from the mountaintop, who were usurped by the Pris Virus. But I trumped them all. I'm the one who has been directing your cleanup of all the damage you did to the dimensions. Just like I am directing the cleanup of the planet."

"There is still one little detail," Eden(Mickey) said.

"Are you worried about the plants?" Carla asked with a tease in her voice. "They are Elon's problem now."

"I don't think it's the flowers Mickey is concerned about," Mickey (Eden) said, also with a tease in her voice.

"Can we have our own bodies back now?" Eden(Mickey) pleaded.

Carla turned on heel. "Follow me."

Mickey(Eden) smiled as they followed. "You're not going to like this."

Eden(Mickey) bit Eden's tongue until they arrived at a cavernous chamber in the center of which was a large piece of equipment that looked like a carnival ride. Two long metal arms extended from a central hub, and on the end of each arm was a small padded cage just big enough for an adult to sit in. "What is it?"

"A centrifuge." Carla walked over to the controls. "We've got to separate souls from bodies so they can go back where they belong."

Eden(Mickey) paled. "How fast does it go?"

"Don't worry about it," Carla said. "You'll quickly pass out."

"Is it safe for the babies?"

"Of course. I wouldn't let any harm come to my grandparents' twins."

Mickey(Eden) smiled. "You've been dying to get your body back. Now's your chance."

Surprisingly, tears streamed from Eden's eyes. "I enjoyed our night in Atlanta. We'll never get to do that again."

"Yes we will."

"But I won't be you. I'll be me. It won't be the same. I have never had sex with a woman. *As* a woman, yes, but not *with* a woman. I'm an incel."

Mickey(Eden) hugged him. "I don't think that label applies to you anymore. Besides, it will be me you make love to. You've been me long enough not to be scared of me, haven't you?"

"I'm terrified of you." Eden(Mickey) glanced to find Carla had busied herself at the controls and was trying her best not to listen. "Besides, we have to go back to our own dimensions. I'll never see you."

Mickey(Eden) sighed. "I know. Maybe we can have some time together before we go our separate ways."

"But you're pregnant. I mean I'm pregnant. This body is pregnant. You'll have to go back to have the baby. Both babies. So that's another thing. I'll never get to see Carla. My baby. Or Carl Friedrich. As a baby." Eden(Mickey) rubbed Eden's abdomen. "I've got *two* babies in there and I'll never get to see either of them."

"You'll get to spend time with Carl Friedrich as an adult. And there is a version of Carla somewhere in your dimension."

"The centrifuge is ready whenever you are," Carla called out.

"Ready?" Mickey(Eden) asked.

Eden(Mickey) nodded yes. He hugged Mickey(Eden) as if to

merge their bodies. Finally, Eden(Mickey) pulled back, with tears streaming. "It's this pregnancy. It makes women emotional. You said."

Mickey(Eden) escorted him to the centrifuge. "Yes, it does." Arriving at one cage, she relinquished Eden(Mickey) to Carla.

"Relax. It won't hurt." Carla strapped Eden(Mickey) in.

He tried to get comfortable in the cage. "Do you enjoy electronica?"

"What?"

"Give it a try. And read some mathematical haiku." Eden(Mickey) adopted his recitation voice. "All throughout nature/The Fibonacci Sequence/Spiraling outward." Back to a normal voice, he continued, "That was 'Fibonacci', by Benjamin Gaines."

Carla stepped back with a smile. "I'll read some, Granddad."

Mickey(Eden) stepped up for one last loving look. "See you on the other side." She walked away with Carla to be strapped into the other cage.

Eden(Mickey) watched them cross the huge room. *I'll pass out,* Mickey thought, *and wake up in my own body. I'll have my little buddy back between my legs. I've wanted this ever since I first woke up in Eden's body. So why am I crying?* He glanced down at Eden's stomach. *I like the idea of carrying life inside me. Not so much the giving birth part, I'm glad I'm missing that, I've seen too many movies where the woman screams and kicks all about, that doesn't look like fun at all. But the idea of nurturing another human being within my body. Walking around with another little life tucked inside me. That's an incredible feeling.*

"Ready?!"

Eden(Mickey) looked to see Mickey(Eden) was strapped into the other cage and Carla was at the control console. Eden(Mickey) gave a thumb up. He watched Carla manipulate the controls. The metal arms began to move, slowly, smoothly, steadily gaining speed. Mickey closed Eden's eyes. When he opened them he would be looking through his own eyes. The centrifuge arm was getting faster, with each revolution swinging more rapidly. He hoped he didn't make too much of a mess this time.

Part Five
Mickey and Eden

1.

The first thing Mickey did upon regaining consciousness was feel for his balls. Yes! The second thing was to touch his abdomen. No! The baby was gone. He had felt something before, he didn't know what, it was too early to feel the baby moving, but he had felt something inside Eden's belly. Now it was gone from his belly. He sighed. With relief or regret? He would never again be pregnant. Relief, without a doubt.

The third thing he did was look around. He was still on the space station orbiting Earth, in a room similar to the last one he had awoken in. Only he was naked this time. He saw a jumpsuit laid out for him. Maybe he could find something better to wear. He closed his eyes to search the hologram files. He could not find any clothes. That, he at last realized, was because there was no chip in his head holding the files. The chip was in Eden's head. So jumpsuit it was.

Mickey sat up. So far, so good; no queasiness. Then he remembered he wasn't pregnant anymore. He was amazed at the pang of sadness that thought brought him. But it was only a pang. He gave an obligatory sigh for what he had lost, then tossed the sheet aside. It was his body he saw. His male body. Everything back where it belonged. Yeah!

Mickey carefully rose to his feet. Again, no seasick feeling while standing on dry land. That was good. Maybe he could eat Mexican again. Also, no urgent desire to locate a bathroom. *I'll miss you, Carl Friedrich and Carla, but then I won't.* Now all that was left to do was get back to Chicago.

Mickey put on the jumpsuit then walked out of the room and down the hall to the bridge. Even walking felt different, with a different distribution of weight. He had trouble maintaining his balance, and stumbled several times. Yet by the time he arrived at the bridge he was walking normally. He found Carla in the captain's chair staring at a monitor. "I'm back," Mickey announced. Her eyes never left the screen. "Where's Eden?"

"She hasn't come around yet."

He joined Carla. "What's going on?"

"I'm working on a problem in one of the dimensions."

Mickey looked at the monitor. "That looks like Belos' dimension. What's the problem?"

"There are no predators larger than Belos in the ocean. Which means there is no impetus for his people to move onto the land. They are happy and content in the ocean."

"Why not leave them in the ocean?"

"There are continents of dry land for them to move onto. Humans need to reclaim that realm."

"If that's the case, make the oceans uncomfortable for them."

"A meteor strike? That would make it uncomfortable, but it could prove disastrous. Look what it did to the dinosaurs."

"How about great whites?"

Carla turned her eyes from the monitor to Mickey. "You mean sharks?"

"Yes. Not a harmless variety like nurse sharks, but Jaws-caliber sharks. Great whites. Maybe they would chase Belos and his people out of the water up onto dry land."

Carla mulled over his suggestion. "It would take time for them to evolve." She was soon lost in thought.

"I won't bother you anymore if you tell me where Eden is."

Carla waved off in a vague direction. "There's food in the galley if you are hungry."

"I'm not. Isn't that wonderful?" Mickey bounded off in the vague direction indicated.

He located the room Eden was in by following her moans. "Good morning," he said in as chipper a voice as he could muster.

Eden rolled over away from him.

"Now you know what I saved you from."

"It was a month," Eden growled.

"That's one-ninth of your pregnancy I saved you from."

Eden rolled back over and gave him a wretched attempt at sarcasm. "That was great, Mickey, you came up with that fraction so quickly, I didn't realize you were so good with numbers. Now why don't you make yourself useful and find me a bucket."

"I have no idea where a bucket is. Why don't I help you into the bathroom instead?"

Eden nodded then threw back the covers. She was naked. When she saw Mickey looking her over, she moaned. "Don't even think about it."

What a difference it was to look at Eden through his own eyes. Instead of looking at her body with her eyes, from the perspective of being in her body. With his eyes he saw her already-ample breasts were swelling even larger with milk. Her hips were swelling wondrously also. Her shapely legs…

"Mickey! Stop it!"

Mickey snapped out of his trance. He helped her to her feet and escorted her into the bathroom.

Eden closed the door in his face. "I have reclaimed my body, Mickey. You no longer need to be so involved with it."

"Eden, there is no depth of your body I'm not familiar with." When the retching began, Mickey backed away from the door. "Not that I want to be that familiar with it anymore."

When several minutes later the bathroom door opened, Eden was pale and weak-kneed. Mickey escorted her back to bed. He helped her to sit on the edge, then went back to the bathroom to wet a wash cloth and grab a towel. When Eden looked up questioningly at his return, he said, "You've got stuff on you." She reached for the wash cloth, but Mickey batted her weak hand away. "I've got it." He washed her. "You helped me through *my* pregnancy. I'm not going to forget that."

"A month, and you think you know what pregnancy is like. Want to switch back for the delivery?"

"No, thank you. I'm glad to have my buddy back."

Eden snorted. "You can have it. That thing is a pain in the ass."

"It sure was. You kept poking your sore butt with it."

Eden's sour mood lightened at the memory. "I did more than that with it."

"I know. Edie sure was taken with you."

"I wasn't thinking about her. I was thinking about us. In Atlanta."

"Oh, what a night." He took the wash cloth and towel back into the bathroom. Returning, he found Eden reclined on the bed with the covers turned back. "Really, Eden? You were just sick."

"I'm not as weak as you. I recover quickly." She patted the bed. "I'm dying to find out what it's like making love to you in a normal way."

Mickey became a statue.

Eden was honestly puzzled. "What's wrong?" Then she figured it out. "You're kidding. I've lived inside that body. And now you are too shy for me to see it? That's hilarious."

"Close your eyes."

"No way. Strip."

Mickey untangled his gangly limbs from out of the jumpsuit. It was surprising how awkward he felt inside his own body. And how uncomfortable he felt at Eden seeing him naked. She was right. She had *been* him for a month, she had seen every inch of his flesh. Still, once he was naked he would not meet her gaze. He dove onto the bed and yanked the covers up over both of them.

Eden threw the covers back off. "I have no qualms about you

seeing *me*." She slipped an arm around his hunched shoulders. "Mickey, we have gotten closer than any husband and wife ever possibly could. We have lived inside each other's skins. Relax."

Mickey relaxed a few muscles. "I know I'm being silly. We've already made love. It's just that we were in different bodies at the time."

"And now I want to know what it feels like for you to make love to me. Instead of me making love to me."

"You're right. This is much simpler." His tense frame eased a bit more. Until he looked toward the open doorway. "What about Carla?"

"Do you really think she wants to see her grandparents make love?" Mickey shook his head no violently. "She'll leave us alone." Eden reached down to stroke a tenseness of his that had not eased. "Does this feel as good to you as it did to me?"

"What do you think?"

"And this?" Her hand slid lower. "I remember this from Mickey Haiku sex ed one-oh-one."

Mickey sucked in half the air in the room. "Yes. Now for Eden sex ed one-oh-one."

"Forget that." She pulled his hand from her shoulder down to her breasts.

"I guess those hormones are raging right now."

Eden hugged Mickey tight. "You better believe it."

"I don't have any protection," Mickey protested. "Is there anything you can do?"

"Yes. Be pregnant."

"I've heard that old wives' tale before."

"It's no old wives' tale. Carla happened because our bodies were so jumbled up. We're back to normal now. I can't get pregnant."

Afterwards, Mickey and Eden, both clad in jumpsuits, joined Carla at the bridge. She scowled at their entrance. "I don't want to hear about it."

"Hear about what?" Mickey asked with a smarm.

"You two are glowing. Stay away from me."

"Mickey," Eden said, "children don't like to consider their elders' sex lives."

"She's older than we are." Mickey walked up to the captain's chair. "I just thought you'd like to know that everything is functioning correctly. Eden returned my body to me in good working condition."

"You didn't know what good condition was until you possessed my body."

"Get off the bridge if you two are going to carry on like this," Carla chided.

"Okay, granddaughter," Mickey said. "We'll behave ourselves."

"So what now?" Eden asked.

"Now you need to get everyone back to their proper places." Carla glared at Eden. "And everybody needs to stay there."

Mickey glanced at a pad of graph paper on the console before the monitor. It displayed a sketch of a shark the size of a grey whale. "That might be overkill. You want to intimidate Belos, not eliminate him."

"That's just a preliminary sketch." Carla tore off the page and wadded it.

"What's happened in my dimension during my absence?" Eden asked.

"Hostilities with the Morlox have ceased. The war ended in a stalemate."

Eden laughed. "I'm surprised Ralph settled for that."

"Ralph didn't," Carla said. "He was deposed. Mitchell is now in charge."

"He's no better than Ralph," Eden objected.

"I agree. It's only an interim appointment until elections can be held." Carla smiled. "How would you like to run for office?"

"Supreme Leader?" Eden backed away. "Me?"

"You would be perfect," Mickey urged. "Consider all the worldly knowledge you have recently acquired."

"I just want to get back to work."

"Your dimension needs you, Grandma. The world needs you."

"You could live in those beautiful gardens on the top floors," Mickey said.

Eden scowled. "Since traveling to the flora dimension I have developed a strong aversion to gardens."

"What about me?" Both females turned blank faces to Mickey. "Do I become a world leader in my dimension?"

"No. You *can* return to your blackboards." Carla stood. "Are you two ready to go back to the mountain top?"

"Yes," Mickey said. "George and Priscilla are probably sick with worry about us."

"I bet they are more concerned about their prospects of getting back to Chicago," Eden added. She studied him. "You don't seem too disappointed at not becoming President."

Mickey grinned. "I was afraid she'd say yes. I don't care about politics at all." He turned to Carla. "Me and the next Supreme Leader are ready to go."

2.

Mickey and Eden rode the updraft down to Lucy and Miriam's mountaintop. They leveled off beside the balcony. A little bump of air pitched them over the railing to drop them with a thud onto the stone floor. "Oww!" Eden cried out upon landing on her butt. She scowled over at Mickey, who was splayed out on the floor beside her. "I returned your body in good condition. You gave mine back with a broken butt."

"I never wanted to switch bodies in the first place. That was your idea." They both creaked up to their feet. "Besides, that wasn't bad, considering we dropped down from low Earth orbit."

"*Your* butt isn't aching."

Mickey scrambled back away from her. "You're not going to throw up, are you?"

"No, Mickey, that was *you* who always got sick."

George and Priscilla burst out onto the balcony. "Where did you go, Mickey?" Priscilla asked as they both rushed up to Eden.

Mickey raised his hand. "I'm over here now, guys."

George peered into Eden's face. "I don't think that's Mickey in there."

"Yeah," Priscilla agreed. "She looks too intelligent now." They both abandoned her for Mickey.

Eden rubbed her butt. "I'm glad you're concerned."

"It's just that we've known Mickey a lot longer," George explained.

"And he's from our dimension," Priscilla added. She peered into Mickey's eyes. "So you're back where you belong."

"Not yet. I belong in Chicago."

Eden limped over to the other three. "How are Stanley and Lori doing?"

"At first they were ready to toss us off the balcony," George said.

"But they settled down," Priscilla said. "I think my virus had a talk with them."

"So it's safe to go inside?" Mickey hugged himself. "It's freezing out here."

"Yes. We promised them we're leaving just as soon as you two got back." George looked hopefully at them. "Aren't we?"

"Carla said we could." Mickey headed for the door.

"How are Lucy and Miriam doing?" Eden asked.

George and Priscilla both laughed. "Wait till you see," Priscilla said.

When the four walked in off the balcony, they found Stanley and Lori sitting on the thrones bundled up in what looked like the hides of every animal that had ever lived on the mountaintop. A conflagration blazed in the fireplace, turning the throne room into an open blast furnace. Mickey smiled at the two. "Nice fire."

"We can't get warm," Stanley said through chattering teeth.

"Not without our plants," Lori added.

"How would you like to return to your dimension?" Mickey asked.

"And drown?" they both wailed.

"No. To return to your people."

"We can't," Stanley said.

"We'd kill everybody with the germs you've exposed us to," Lori said.

"*You're* not dead," Mickey said. That got their attention. "You've spent a lot of time exposed to our germs. Any ill effects?" They continued to glare. "Other than the cold. You can't blame our germs for that."

Eden stepped up to bat. "Our germs weren't lethal to you. So they won't be lethal to anyone else in your world. You can safely return home."

Mickey turned toward the fireplace. "Are we right, Pris?"

The Pris Virus appeared in the blazing fireplace. "I thought to install my people at the top of the mountain. They could have ruled all the dimensions."

"So *you* could rule all the dimensions. Stanley and Lori would merely have been your puppets." The Pris Virus voiced no denial. "But the dimensions aren't ruled from here. There is a dimension higher than this."

"I have become aware of this," the Pris Virus said with a frown. The blaze in the fireplace was dampened considerably.

"Since Stanley and Lori are so unhappy here why don't we all go home and leave this dimension to its previous rulers. I hope you didn't damage Lucy and Miriam too badly."

"Go see for yourself." The Pris Virus faded into the flames, and the fire blazed once again.

Mickey turned to Stanley and Lori. "Where are Lucy and Miriam?"

"Out in the cave," Stanley said.

"Doing their chores," Lori said.

Mickey ventured out into the cave. It was like stepping out of the Sahara into Siberia. He smiled upon finding Lucy polishing a large plaque depicting the standard model of particle physics. "I'm impressed, Lucy. I didn't think you knew the difference between a boson and a lepton."

She stopped polishing to give him a lusterless stare. "Mitchell explained that to me a long time ago."

Eden(Mickey) looked all around. "Mitchell's here?"

"No. That happened in another dimension."

Eden(Mickey) focused on her once again. "Are you doing okay?"

"I'm okay."

"You realize you never were controlling anything from up here on the mountaintop. Carla was doing that from a dimension above you."

"What was I controlling?" she asked.

It was growing clear to Mickey that Lucy hadn't recovered from the Pris Virus' assault on her brain. Perhaps she would, in time. "Never mind. Have you seen Miriam?"

"She and Ralph are off somewhere."

"Is she doing okay?"

"Yes. They seem happy together. Those two are inseparable."

Mickey chose not to delve too deeply into that relationship. "Everyone is getting ready to leave. You and Miriam will be on your own again. Will you two be okay?"

"I will be if Ralph quits grabbing my breasts. I've got the worst claw marks." Lucy pulled up her shirt to show him.

Mickey abruptly pivoted away. "I'll say something to Miriam." He rushed off.

Ralph jumped out at Mickey from behind a rock. "Bad monkey!" Mickey yelled. "Quit grabbing women!" Ralph flung poop at Mickey. He was ready this time and dodged it. Ralph scampered away.

"I'll trim his nails."

Mickey found Miriam sweeping the cave floor. "That's your solution? Trim his nails?"

"He hurts me, too." Miriam stopped sweeping to bare her clawed breasts.

Mickey averted his eyes. "I don't need to see, Miriam. Just train him better." Mickey hurried back to the other three awaiting him just outside the throne room.

"How are they?" Eden asked.

"A little slow-witted and apt to flash their breasts, but otherwise the same as always," Mickey said. "They'll be okay."

"Then can we go now?" Priscilla asked.

The door from the throne room opened. Stanley and Lori emerged with as many furs and hides wrapped around them as they could carry. "We're ready," Stanley said.

"Pris told us it was safe for us to return," Lori said.

"What's the plan, Mickey," George asked.

The Pris Virus shimmered out of the ice before Mickey. "You need to drive out of this dimension like you drove into it." She shimmered back into the ice.

"We're driving home," Mickey told them.

"Are you insane?!" Priscilla screeched.

Mickey headed toward the cave entrance without responding.

"Yes, he probably is by now." Eden followed him.

Stanley and Lori went next.

George shrugged at Priscilla, then followed, too.

"I'm coming!" Priscilla yelled, and chased after.

They found the car covered in snow. "It will never start," George said. "The engine is frozen."

Stanley and Lori began brushing the snow off. Underneath, piles of fur were revealed. "Pris had Lucy and Miriam wrap the engine to protect it," Stanley said. The other four joined in brushing off snow. Next, they removed the wraps and tossed them aside. With hard tugs all four doors opened.

"Mickey drives."

Mickey looked to see the Pris Virus standing before the car. "I don't know how to drive."

"It must be you." The Pris Virus faded away into the falling snowflakes.

George started to climb in behind the wheel, but Mickey grabbed his arm. "I'm driving."

"No way." George yanked his arm free.

"Pris said it has to be me." His three companions shook their heads no with determination. "Think about it. I'm the only one who can see when there is an opening between dimensions. Could any of you see the opening in the swimming pool back in Atlanta?" The three stared blank-faced, but they had quit shaking their heads no. "It's got to be me."

"I am not getting in that car if Mickey is driving," Priscilla said. "I don't care what my disease-self said."

"Then stay." Eden jumped in the front passenger seat.

Stanley and Lori piled into the back seat.

"I'm sitting next to you, Mickey." George climbed in the driver side and slid across to the middle of the seat, forcing Eden up against the passenger door. "I'll give you instructions."

Mickey climbed in behind the wheel with a smile. "You can be my driving instructor."

"Yes," George agreed with an insane smile, "and if you fail this driving test we all die."

"I'm not staying here with that pervert monkey," Priscilla yelled. "I'll die with the rest of you." She crammed herself into the back seat with Stanley and Lori and all their furs.

Mickey looked to George. "Now what?"

"God save us," Priscilla moaned from the back.

"Turn the key," George instructed.

Mickey did. The engine roared to life.

"Give it a little gas. Don't let the engine die. But don't flood it. The engine needs to warm up some."

Mickey frowned. "I have no idea what you are talking about."

From the backseat came, "Now I lay me down to sleep."

"Shut up, Priscilla," Eden said. "You're not helping."

"The engine sounds okay," George said. "Now see if you can shift into drive. Let's hope the transmission's not frozen."

"Lucy and Miriam wrapped the car really good," Stanley said.

"Nothing should be frozen," Lori said.

"Don't forget to release the emergency brake," George said. "And shift into neutral."

"One thing at a time! You are confusing me!"

"I pray the Lord my soul to keep," came from the back seat.

Mickey grinned back at Priscilla. "I know that one."

Eden reached around George to smack Mickey on the back of the head. "Focus, Mickey."

Mickey released the emergency. "Everybody buckled in?"

"No!" Priscilla screamed. She fumbled with the seat belt.

"You should have fastened your seat belt instead of praying," Eden chided.

"Okay," Priscilla said, breathless. "Seat belt buckled. Eyes closed. Prayers said. I'm ready to die."

"I'm not," Mickey said. "You'll have to wait until the rift opens."

"When it does, shift into drive and depress the gas pedal slowly," George said. "And hope the car can pull out of this snow bank."

While peering into the raging snow, Mickey gripped the wheel with his left hand. His right hand was on the gear shift. His right foot was on the gas. His left foot was on the brake. The car rocked, buffeted by the blasting wind. Before them a wilderness of white swirled like a snow globe shaken by an enraged infant. The other five in the car held their breaths. Except Priscilla, who muttered softly, "If I should die before I wake."

The snow parted before the car like a curtain drawn back. A sunny parking lot appeared before them. Mickey shifted into drive, took his left foot off the break, and eased the gas pedal down.

3.

Mickey jammed on the brake as the car skidded across dry pavement. The engine stalled out. A man jumped back away from the front of the lurching car and slapped the hood, yelling with a distinct New York accent, "Hey! I'm walking here! I'm walking here!"

"Switch places." George pulled Mickey out from behind the wheel across him into Eden's lap, then scooted over behind the wheel.

Mickey looked to George. "Did I pass the test?"

George was too busy trying to get the car started to answer, so Eden did as she helped Mickey settle into the middle of the front seat. "You did good, Mickey." She hugged and kissed him.

A crowd gathered before the only car in the lot that was covered in snow and ice. "Get us out of here, George," Priscilla urged. "Before people pull out their phones and we end up all over the Internet."

The engine roared to life. George picked his way through the throng of onlookers. Once out of the parking lot, George sped away down Pike's Peak.

"Where'd they go?" Priscilla screeched from the back seat. George peered into the rearview mirror, while Mickey and Eden turned around to see what Priscilla was talking about. Stanley and Lori were gone.

"Pris must have pulled them through the rift she created back into the dimension they belong in. Good." Mickey turned back around. "Only three more to go."

"What about me?" Eden asked.

Mickey fell silent. What about Eden?

The rest of the drive back to Chicago was uneventful. When the four walked into the alley outside Mickey and George's apartment, they saw Ralph and Miriam huddled beneath plastic. Ralph motioned them near. "Some girly said for you to come see me when you're ready to finish sorting everyone out."

"What did she tell you to do?" Priscilla asked. "Give us some cardboard?"

"No. Plastic."

"Sure, Ralph," Mickey answered. "We'll be back." He led the way into the apartment. Stan was sitting in the George and Martha chair watching a NASCAR race on a tablet.

"You're kidding," Mickey said.

Stan smiled at Mickey. "Your brother got me interested in

NASCAR. He said the Paulie team was his favorite, but they don't race in this dimension."

"I don't have a brother," Mickey said. "I'm an only child."

Stan frowned at Eden. "Just when I get this figured out. Did you two switch back?"

Eden walked up and kissed him. "Yes. And I am so happy to have my body back I could jump into bed with you."

Stan peered into her eyes. "That really is you in there, Eden? Mickey's not kissing me with your lips?"

Eden kissed Stan again, this time with passion Mickey could never muster for kissing a man.

Stan looked hopefully to Mickey. "Mick is passed out in George's bed."

"No!" Mickey surprised even himself with the vehemence of his refusal. "You two are not using my bed."

Eden hugged Mickey. "It was a joke, Mickey."

Stan frowned. "It was?"

"Have you heard from my brother?" Eden asked.

"No. He's still off with Edie." Stan cut the race off. "Can we go home now?"

"As soon as we get everyone together," Eden said. "Is Mick ready?"

"Yes. He's as anxious to get back as I am."

"That leaves George." Eden turned to Mickey. "Ready to go fetch him?"

Mickey's roommate George dropped Mickey and Eden off at Edie's apartment en route to turning in the rental car. Edie answered Mickey's knock from behind her locked door. "What do you want?"

"We need to speak with George," Mickey said.

"He's not going back, Eden!"

Eden shoved Mickey out of the way. "George! This is your sister talking. Not Mickey, your real sister. We have to return to our dimension!"

Edie opened the door. "He's not going anywhere."

Eden called beyond Edie into the apartment. "George? The world is coming apart at the seams. You can help save it."

George stepped up behind Edie. "Let them in." She turned away as the two entered, and George closed the door behind them. He peered into Eden's eyes. "Are you really my sister?"

Eden pinched his nipple.

"Oww!" He jumped back, rubbing it. "It's Eden, all right. She's done that to me ever since we were kids."

"And you were never allowed to pinch me back. Ha!"

"I don't want to go back, sis. I like it here. It's not crowded at all.

The cars here are nearly the same as the ones in our dimension. I could get a mechanic job here. Stay with Edie." He looked back at her standing across the room. "I know she looks like you. I've processed that fact. But she's not you. We could make a home here in Chicago."

"And raise a family?" Mickey asked. "Wouldn't you want a safe world for your children to grow up in? As long as you remain here the world will not be safe. The only way to make the world safe for your children and everyone else is by you returning to where you belong."

"The world is never safe," Edie said from across the room. "Dozens of people are shot every week in Chicago."

"You can't do anything about that," Mickey said. "This you can. This is on you two."

George dropped his head. "He's right, Edie. I have to go back." Once she began crying, he looked to his sister. "Give us one more night. I'll be back to the apartment tomorrow."

Without another word, Mickey and Eden walked out.

That evening back at the apartment Mickey and Eden were alone. His roommate and Priscilla had taken Stan and Mick out for the night so they could have the apartment to themselves. While Eden was in the shower, Mickey opened his laptop intending to listen to some Bicep. The OPEN ME NOW icon was on the screen. Mickey hesitated clicking on it. He didn't want George and Priscilla butting into his and Eden's last night together. But his curiosity got the better of him. When he clicked on the icon he was horrified to find only George on the screen. "Where's Priscilla?" Mickey asked, trying his best not to sound panicked.

"You are just Mickey now. Right? No need for both of us to be present while zooming with you. It's just us guys now?"

Mickey was so relieved he could hardly stutter. "Priscilla is okay?"

"Of course." George's visage clouded over. "Why are you concerned? Has something happened? Is something going to happen? To Priscilla?"

"I saw her get wiped out by a giant W boson."

"Oh, that." George laughed. "Happens all the time."

"She survived that?! It looked like a mortal injury!"

"It was." George stopped laughing. "Whenever something like that happens to one of us, the other merely skips back several seconds and pulls the about-to-be injured party out of the way. Whatever it was that was going to strike the one merely passes by. No harm, no foul."

"I've been worried sick."

"Nice of you to be so concerned."

"I've gotten attached to you two."

"Well, Priscilla is fine. I'm fine. The world will be fine as soon as you get everybody back where they belong. This is the last time I'll be contacting you."

"So this is just to say goodbye?"

"Actually, I was wondering something."

"No."

"Mickey, what would it hurt?"

"I'm not sure. But you don't need to know."

"I know someone higher up took over my and Priscilla's agenda. Who was it?"

"The less you know, the less damage you can do."

"I and Priscilla devoted the best years of our lives to this project. We deserve to know who commandeered our work."

"No, you don't. Tell Priscilla goodbye for me, George."

Eden walked in wrapped in a towel. "Who are you talking to?"

Mickey slapped the laptop closed. "Only you for the rest of the night."

4.

Later that night Mickey and Eden were cuddled up beneath the covers in Mickey's bed. He was sunk deep into a funk. "I know how Edie feels. This is our last night, too."

"We need to make the most of it." Eden said. She reached beneath the covers.

"Not yet," Mickey objected. "I can't. Again. How many times?"

"Who's counting?" Eden withdrew her hand. "What are you going to do when I leave?"

"I don't know." Mickey gazed off into the empty space between the atoms in his ceiling. "What could top what I've already accomplished?"

"What *we've* accomplished. You know you can never publish."

"Of course not. We can't make it easy for anyone else to do what we did."

"I'm sure you'll find something else to engage that amazing mind of yours. But that wasn't what I was talking about. What will you do without me?"

"I can't imagine, Eden. I haven't thought beyond you, yet."

"You should go back to Edie."

"She hates me."

"It's me she hates. I'm the one who tricked her."

"With my body."

"Which she seemed to enjoy. You two were a good fit. I think you ought to give it a shot." Eden smiled. "She's the next best thing to me."

"Why are you playing matchmaker?"

"I don't want you reverting to your old way of life. Of being totally cut off from the other sex."

"I *was* the other sex. How can I be alienated from women now? What about you? What are you going to do?"

"Carla says I'll be Supreme Leader."

"I'm talking about your personal life."

"I don't know. Mick is the father of Carl Friedrich. But Stan has stood by me through all this. He is a terrific person. And a great lover."

"You respect him." A frown crossed Mickey's face. "And it sounds like you enjoy him. But do you love him?" When Eden failed to answer, he pressed on. "My vote is for Mick. Not only is he the father of your child, but he is my twin in your dimension. It would be like we were still together."

"The same goes if you got together with Edie." Eden cuddled up to him. "Or rather got *back* together with her. You have already been with Edie. You just weren't there at the time."

Later that night Mickey awoke to electronica music. Andrew and Matt lounged on the floor at the foot of the bed, while Eden slept undisturbed. Mickey sat up. "Hi, guys."

"You should get Eden to design a sound studio before she leaves," Andrew said.

"Yeah, I love what she did with the Roman bath," Matt said.

"You saw that?"

"You didn't see us?" Andrew asked.

"We were relaxing next to that statue of the fiddler," Matt said. "Hero?"

"Nero," Mickey corrected.

"Nero is no hero," Andrew sang. "We could do something with that."

Mickey yawned, stretched. "What are you guys doing here?"

"We came to cheer you up," Matt said. "You and Eden worked hard to repair the dimensions. You deserve a better deal than to settle for each other's twins."

"What else can we do?"

"Insist on the real thing, not some pale copy," Andrew said. "Her ex-husband is a scumbag."

"While Edie is not a bad person, she's just not Eden," Matt added.

"As I said…"

"Bring the whole thing crashing down," Andrew said.

"You fixed it, you can nix it," Matt said. He started drumming on the side of the dresser. "Nero is no hero. You fixed it, you can nix it. Nero hero. Fix it nix it."

"You gave us some new material to work on, Mickey." Andrew joyfully slapped the floor with his hand.

"Owww!"

Mickey realized Andrew hadn't slapped the floor. Rather, Mickey had slapped Eden's butt. "Sorry. Bicep was here."

Eden raised up to look around. Although she saw no sign of anyone, she didn't doubt Mickey. "What did they want?"

"For us to be more assertive." There was a knock at the door. Mickey and Eden rearranged the covers more decorously upon themselves. "What?" Mickey barked.

"Eden's brother is here," Mickey's roommate George informed.

"We're coming." Eden peered into Mickey's eyes. "We knew this had to happen."

"Bicep said it doesn't. Matt and Andy say we could cause a lot of trouble. We fixed it, we can nix it." The two climbed out of bed and into some clothes, Mickey's from his closet and Eden's from her chip.

George was alone and downcast. "We already said our goodbyes," he answered Eden's questioning gaze. Stan and Mick stood expectantly by the front door, anxious to leave.

Mickey opened the door. "It's time to go see Ralph."

Ralph and Miriam were standing in the alley beside his makeshift home of cardboard and plastic. He seemed in a good mood. "Is this everybody, Haiku?"

"The last four. Can you handle them?"

"Yeah." He picked up a large sheet of plastic.

"I told you it's really roomy under it," Miriam said.

Mickey stared at the thin dirty sheet of plastic. "*That* can transport people between dimensions?"

"Just watch." Ralph pinched Miriam's breast to get her to move out of the way.

Miriam squealed, jumping back. She pulled her top out to look in at her breasts. "You have got to trim your nails, Ralph. I have got the worst scratches."

Mickey snapped up a forestalling hand. "You don't need to show them to me, Miriam." He turned to Ralph. "Where did you get the plastic?"

"From you. Like I get all my plastic." Ralph flapped the plastic open up into the air. It grew and grew as it spread out, encompassing Eden, her ex-husband Mick, her brother George, and Stan.

As it started to settle around the four, Mickey dashed underneath it.

5.

Mickey stood alone under the sheet of plastic. He started to pull it off.

"Don't do that, Mickey."

The male voice was familiar, but he couldn't place who it belonged to. The speaker was an indistinct blur on the other side of the dirty plastic. "Why not?"

"You'll die a horrible excruciating death."

"Good reason." Mickey released the plastic. "What happened to everyone else?"

"They returned to their proper dimension."

"Safely?"

"Of course safely. Have we harmed any of you in all your travels?"

"This place sounds pretty harmful." Mickey looked around, but couldn't make out much through the filthy plastic. "Where am I?"

"At the bottom of Shackleton Crater at the south pole of the Moon."

"Where it's minus one-hundred forty-seven degrees Celsius. How can this thin plastic protect me from that?"

"This material is keeping you from being fully in this dimension. It's like you are standing in an open doorway with a fierce blizzard before you and a roaring fireplace behind you."

Mickey was intrigued, of course. "I can't remain in this stasis for long."

"But you can. There is no air on the moon to transfer temperature."

"Why would you choose to live in such an inhospitable environment?"

"This is a science station. We're scientists. In this dimension this is the farthest outpost humans have established off-planet. It's exciting. There is ice down here in the bottom of the crater we can not only melt for water but also make oxygen out of, which we can both breathe and use for energy. We've dug out a comfortable abode for ourselves. If you move to your right several steps you will come to the entrance. Be careful to keep the plastic around you as you move. If you stuck a toe out from under it would instantly freeze."

Mickey shuffled along across the uneven rocky surface at a half-meter a minute speed. He dimly perceived an opening before him, and passed through.

"You can discard the plastic now."

Mickey stuck a toe out. Nothing happened. He extended his entire foot. Nothing. So he shed the plastic. To find himself in a small rocky cave in which several lights blazed, casting dark shadows all about. In the brilliant light just before him stood himself. "Is this a mirror?"

"No, it's me."

"My twin in this dimension?" Mickey looked around at the Spartan surroundings. "This is a higher dimension? Looks pretty crappy to me."

"We love it here."

Mickey continued to look all around. He could see nothing but rocky shadows. "You keep saying we. Who else is here?"

"Put this on and I'll show you." He handed Mickey a bodysuit similar to what he had donned upon entering the cave on the mountain-top for the first time. "Our space suits are much less bulkier than what you are used to seeing."

When Mickey pulled the ski-mask like hood over his head he saw the mouth was sealed and goggles were over the eye holes. "Where's the oxygen tank?"

"No need for one. There is enough oxygen stored in the ski mask for the short walk we're going on."

Mickey pulled on slim boots. "Were you in the tropical island dimension?

"Yes."

"So it was you who took my laptop from Priscilla."

"I had to get the laptop to George and Priscilla in the cave on the mountaintop so they could rescue you with Bicep's music."

"And it was you who gave that inter-dimensional plastic to Ralph?"

"Yes."

Once Mickey was fully dressed, his twin led him up out of Shackleton Crater. Stepping out onto the lunar surface, Mickey's attention was immediately seized by the blue-green globe hanging just above the horizon.

"Amazing sight, isn't it?" A familiar female voice said in his ears. "There is a transmitter in the ski mask. Talk normally and I'll hear you."

Mickey looked about until he located a similarly-dressed person, but with the ski mask on he couldn't see the face. Yet he recognized the curves of the skintight outfit. "I'd know that body anywhere, Eden. I used to walk around in it." Mickey turned his gaze back to the Earth. "How do you get anything done here? I would just stare."

"And what's wrong with just staring?" Eden bunny hopped across the surface. "Come on."

Mickey hopped after her. "I suppose you are the female who has been in contact with Ralph all this time?"

"Of course."

On his third hop Mickey crashed.

Eden hopped back to him. "Still clumsy as ever, runt."

"You have had a lot of experience doing this, I'm sure."

"I never fell flat on my face." She pulled him upright.

Mickey looked around, but didn't see his twin. "Where did he go?"

"Back inside. He wanted to give us some time alone." Eden took Mickey's hand, and they hopped away.

Mickey was getting the hang of bunny hopping on the moon by the time they arrived at a wooden park bench. To his amazement, Planck's Constant was emblazoned on it. "My bench! On the moon?"

"A replica." Eden sat. "It's a good place to watch earthrises and earthsets."

Mickey sat next to her. "I caught a glimpse of this once, a park bench on the moon, in the park in Evanston back in my dimension. But I didn't realize what I was seeing." Mickey gazed all around the heavens. "You know, there's a lot above you yet. Planets, stars, black holes, galaxies, galaxy clusters, super clusters, walls, voids. Where does it end?"

Eden shrugged. "What you just listed is only the four per cent of reality we can perceive. There could be additional dimensions in the dark matter and the dark energy. We don't know. We can't perceive what's above us any more than you could perceive Eden's dimension above you."

"In this mix of possibly infinite dimensions, what can it hurt for two people to remain together?"

"Consider a building constructed of bricks and wood intermingled with no rhyme or reason," Eden explained. "The wood would rot, causing the bricks to collapse. The lack of symmetry can't hold."

"Then why did you allow it to happen in the first place? I see now why Eden and I were chosen for this. Because you two were choosing your twins. The computations for inter-dimensional travel are incredibly difficult to craft. I know Eden is brilliant, but not that brilliant. She must have had help. From you, and I'm sure your Mickey must have helped me. So the question is, why?"

"Haven't you been told why?"

"I've heard all kinds of reasons. George and Priscilla told me it was to stop Eden's dimension from overwhelming mine and all the other dimensions. Others said it was to repair the damage our initial passage through the dimensions caused. Now tell me the real reason for our odyssey."

"The barriers between dimensions had become too impermeable.

Ideas need to flow from the higher dimensions down into the lower ones. That is how progress is made. The barriers needed to be aerated."

"That's all Eden and I were doing? Aerating? Like a lawn?"

"Didn't you ever wonder why we moved eight of you through the dimensions?"

"You mean you did that on purpose?"

"Of course. The eight of you were like tines on a garden rake. You all perforated the barriers as you moved up through the dimensions, then from your dimension you went back to repair from the other side where the perforating had been overdone. You and Eden did good, Mickey."

"So why are we being punished? I will find my way back to Eden. I now know it's possible for beings to pass from a lower dimension into a higher one. She's only one dimension above me. I will find a way to do it on my own. You can punish me all you want with migraine headaches, but I won't stop trying."

Eden had grown solemn during his tirade. "We are willing to compromise." That statement jerked Mickey's attention away from his contemplation of earth hanging in the black sky to the reason for his impetuous lunge beneath Ralph's plastic. "After all," Eden smiled, "you two are our twins. We don't want to make you too miserable." Eden laid her head on his shoulder.

Mickey slipped an arm around Eden. "*I* am Mickey Haiku. That's all I ever want to be."

"Mickey Haiku triumphant," Eden murmured. The couple relaxed into the park bench in silence to admire the beautiful Earth dominating the lunar sky.

6.

Eden sat at her desk before her computer in her office. Stan stood to her right with his hand on her shoulder. George stood to her left with his hand on her other shoulder. Standing behind her, Mick knocked Stan's hand off and replaced it with his.

Eden shot up out of her chair with a joyous shriek. "We're back!" She hugged George, kissed Mick, then embraced Stan with an ardent lip-lock.

"Eden," Mick objected. "I'm right here."

She released Stan and spun to Mick. "Oh, shut up." She kissed Mick again. "We're back." Eden raced around her desk for the door.

"Eden! Wait!" She spun once more, this time back to George. "When we left I was under arrest."

"And I had just committed a court martial offense," Stan added, "to save your brother."

"They're right." Mick stepped forward. "Maybe I should go out first to assess the situation."

Eden considered. For about one second. She flung open her office door. To find the entire floor devoid of people. The three men surged forward to look beyond her. "Where is everyone?" Mick craned his head over Eden's shoulder to look all around.

Stan brushed past Eden to take the forward position. "Maybe the Morlox have captured everybody."

Eden pushed Stan out of her way and strode toward the elevators. "I don't see any damage here, no signs of fighting. Besides, George and Priscilla said the fighting ended in a stalemate."

The three men rushed after her. "Perhaps we should report to Ralph," Stan suggested.

"Ralph's been deposed," Eden said without slowing her step. "Mitchell is in charge." She arrived at the elevators and pushed a button.

George blanched. "Eight-ninety-nine? Are you crazy?! Ralph, or Mitchell, or whoever's up there will throw me in prison."

Eden turned to Mick. "You're not in trouble, are you?" He shook his head no. "Then you come with me." She turned to the other two. "You two stay here until we find out what is going on."

Stan blocked the elevator door that had just opened. "No way am I letting you go up there without me."

George ran his hand through his hair. "Yeah, sis. We're all going.

Just see if you can bail me out."

Eden shoved Stan into the elevator. "Then let's go." Mick and George followed her in. Emerging from the elevator on the next to top floor, they were amazed to find it, too, was deserted. "No guards?" Stan marveled. He looked all around. "No soldiers at all?"

"Is everyone dead?" It was Mick who came up with this frightening possibility.

The notion rang Eden like a bell. Could she have caused this? With all her inter-dimensional travels? Was this the damage she had caused in *her* dimension? Mass extermination?

"Where are the bodies?" George asked. "If everyone is dead, then where are they?"

Stan rejoined the three from his search for soldiers. "The vultures could have flown them all off to the Pit."

"One point one billion people?" George wondered. "How many vultures are there? A thousand? Two? To collect over a billion corpses? No way."

"So maybe it's only the people in this building who died," Mick conjectured.

"We need to find out." Eden hopped over the guardrail and ran up the car ramp leading to the top floor.

Stan dashed ahead of her. "I'll scout it out." While the other two jogged behind.

Stan, then Eden, came to an abrupt halt at the top of the ramp. A wall of sandbags blocked their way. They were sodden, as was everything else in the rooftop garden. Puddles and pools stood everywhere. Drains swirled and gurgled. Leaves dripped rainwater as if from out of open spigots. Everything within sight was drenched.

"Eden?"

The four, for Mick and George had caught up with Eden and Stan, saw Lucy emerge from the greenery. She was easy to spot in bright yellow rain slicks.

Mick was nearly speechless. "Mom?" Lucy smiled at her son. "What are you doing here?"

"I'm living here now."

Eden looked around. "Where's Miriam?"

"She's gone. Along with Ralph."

"That's what I heard. So Mitchell is interim Supreme Leader?"

"Yes."

"And you are *his* special friend?"

"Mom!" Mick erupted.

"Don't be such a child," Lucy snapped at her son. "How do you think you rose to such a high position in the bureaucracy?"

"And here I thought it was because of me." Eden tossed a wicked laugh back at her ex-husband. "It sure wasn't because of your brains." She turned back to her mother-in-law. "What happened?"

"It stopped raining." Lucy stepped out from under dripping leaves to an open area where she could look up and see the sky.

Eden followed her gaze to see heavy clouds breaking up. "How long has it been raining?"

"Ever since you left." Lucy's amazed eyes turned back to Eden. "You return, and it stops."

"Where is everyone?"

"Trying to save the Morlox."

Stan climbed over the sandbags and advanced on Lucy. "We aren't fighting the Morlox?"

"The war stopped when the rain began. The water from the deluge flooded the underground. The Morlox who were trapped underground, which was most of them, were drowning. The Morlox who had fought their way to the surface stopped fighting to try and rescue their trapped people. At first we just worked to save our own soldiers who had been fighting underground. Ralph was okay with letting the Morlox drown. He was bitter about you leaving him behind. But nearly everyone else didn't go along with letting the Morlox die like drowned rats. Our soldiers, and then others, and then most everybody began helping the Morlox soldiers save their people. When Ralph tried to halt the rescue effort, he was deposed and Mitchell took over. So that's where everyone is. Trying to rescue the Morlox."

"It's been raining since I left this dimension?" Eden asked.

"It's been pouring. A second Rain Plague."

Stan stepped up to Miriam. "There are Morlox still alive underground? After all this time?"

"Yes. Most of them sealed themselves into water tight compartments. So they haven't all drowned. But the survivors are running out of food and air."

"What are people doing?"

"Running oxygen lines down to them. Manning pumps. Repairing the pumps when they break down. Manning hand pumps. Bailing with buckets. It's seemed like a lost cause. Everyone is exhausted." Miriam looked up at the clearing sky. "But now that it's stopped raining, people, and Morlox, will have hope again."

Stan dashed away. "I need to go help."

Lucy took Eden's hands. "You need to go, too, Eden. Everyone needs to see why the rain has stopped. The rain plague stopped when you returned. You returned to save us." She shoved Eden away. "Now go. Our city needs to see you. You will lift everyone's spirits."

Eden was in a daze. How had she caused this? How had she stopped this?

George took her by the arms. "Come on, sis. You won't have to bail me out of prison after all. Let's go bail water instead."

7.

Upon his return to Shackleton Crater, Mickey was escorted by his lunar twin to another nearby crater. By this time Mickey was becoming accomplished at bunny hopping in low gravity and made the trip without mishap. He was amazed to discover within this crater three parked Lunar Roving Vehicles. "Moon buggies!" he exclaimed with glee.

"The last three Apollo missions to the moon each brought one, and they were all left behind."

Mickey walked around the crater inspecting them. "Do they still run?"

"We've rebuilt them." Mickey's twin climbed in behind the wheel of one. "This is the latest model, from Apollo Seventeen."

Mickey climbed in beside him. "Where are we going?"

"Shoemaker."

It was a slow bumpy ride across the rocky lunar surface to Shoemaker Crater, but Mickey had never enjoyed himself more in a moving vehicle. He kept urging his twin to go slower so he could take in more of the sights. Also, so he could talk to him about Carla. "She is having difficulty designing a shark for a lower dimension."

His twin stared at him with concern. "Did you make any suggestions?"

"It was my idea."

"And she was okay with that?"

Mickey shrugged.

His twin shook his head. "We don't bludgeon people in the lower dimensions with what we think should be done. We don't practice mind control. We strive to be as unobtrusive as possible. We slip inspirations in during idle moments, or in dreams. Now she is likely to be resistant to any suggestions I or Eden might make."

"Sorry."

His twin smiled. "From now on, if you come up with an idea you believe would improve the situation in another dimension make a conscious effort to direct your thoughts up to me."

It was Mickey's turn to smile. "You mean, like pray?"

"Please don't call it that. It's just that I and Eden are focused on all our twins in all the lower dimensions. We will receive any thoughts you purposefully direct up to us."

To Mickey's great disappointment, they eventually arrived at

Shoemaker. The Lunar Roving Vehicle climbed up the lip and over into the depths. As they descended into the dark shadows, the illuminated read-out on the dash glowed brightly. Latitude and longitude coordinates flashed across the screen. Mickey realized he was being driven to a specific location within the crater. "What's in here?" he asked. "What are you heading for?"

Mickey never received an answer. Instead, he landed on his butt on the floor of the bridge of the space station in orbit above Earth. Carla screamed and leaped up from the captain's chair. "Where did you come from?"

Stunned, Mickey gazed all about. "The Moon." He rubbed his sore butt. "Shoemaker Crater, to be precise."

Carla holstered the gun she had drawn. "How did you get there?"

"A sheet of plastic." He creaked to his feet, still rubbing. "I thought I was rid of a sore butt when I gave Eden her body back."

"There haven't been any manned flights to the moon in generations."

"Not in your dimension."

"You came from a higher dimension? There are no higher dimensions."

"Why do people keep saying that? When all you know for sure consists of four percent of creation." He limped over to the monitor before the captain's chair. "Can you get me back down to Earth?"

Carla joined him at the monitor. "I can once our orbit passes over the portal above the Himalayan mountaintop the temple is on."

"The coordinates Mickey drove to in Shoemaker Crater must have been to the portal that sent me here."

"You met your twin in this higher dimension?"

"Mine and Eden's."

"Is it the highest dimension?"

"I seriously doubt it. Some string theorists postulate there could be twenty-six dimensions." He accessed an orbital chart on the monitor.

Carla slapped his hands off the controls. "Don't touch stuff!"

Mickey perused the chart anyway. "We'll be crossing above the Himalayas within the hour. Can you get me down there?"

Carla grinned. "To the mountaintop? That would do you no good. You need to go all the way down."

Mickey was aghast. "Down to Hellades?"

"If you want to get back to your own dimension. That's the only way. All the way to the bottom, then back up to your dimension."

"How will I get out of Hell? I don't have my laptop. Anyway, the inter-dimensional program was deleted."

Carla's grin broadened. "Then you'll have to make a deal with the Devil." Carla walked away. "We need to hurry. We'll be over the portal soon." Mickey hurried after. "By the way, there's a little chore I need for you to take care of."

"What now?"

"Elon got tired of them."

~ * ~

Mickey landed with a thud. There were two additional thuds, one on either side of him. By the heat, the dim light, and the lassitude he felt, Mickey knew he was back in Hellades. He also knew by the voice in his head. "Mickey!" the plant Laurie exclaimed. "Where are we?"

Mickey looked to one side. He saw Laurie's pot had landed upright. She screamed. "How can I see myself?"

Looking to his other side, Mickey saw Stan's pot was overturned, half of its dirt spilled out onto the rocky ground. "I'm in Hell. You two are in me. Settle down while I take care of Stan." Mickey brushed as much of the spilled dirt he could gather back into Stan's pot, then righted it.

Stan was a bit calmer than Laurie. "What's going on, Mickey?"

"Your consciousness has sought refuge in me, while your bodies are in a coma as a result of the low energy in this lowest dimension."

"We're safe?" the Laurie plant meekly asked.

"So far," Mickey answered.

"And we're inside you?" she purred, much less meek. "That's not so bad."

"Hey! Laurie! Get out of my amygdala!"

The Stan plant laughed. "She's sunk her roots into your nucleus accumbens. She's flooding it with dopamine."

Mickey sighed with pleasure. How were these two so much more comfortable inside his head than Priscilla, Edie and Carl Friedrich had been? How could Laurie take over control of the pleasure centers in his brain? Why should he care? Maybe he should just go with it.

Before Mickey could go any further with it, a bonfire blazed into existence before them. Even the Stan plant screamed inside his head this time, in unison with Laurie. The fierce visage of the Devil resolved within the conflagration. "Get up!"

Mickey scrambled to his feet with a moan for his aching butt. He had landed on the hard ground this time, instead of three soft bodies. "We seek passage up to the next dimension."

The vile flames burned even more malignant. "Why should I care what you seek?"

"Surface seeming flat/at moon's eclipse its shadow/argues otherwise."

Mickey was knocked backwards by a blast of hot air. "What is that?"

"Mathematical haiku, by Kevin Farey. 'Cosecant, you say/by the dawn's earliest light/is one over sine."

"Shut up!"

"'Suppose humankind/knew neither of pi's value/nor of winter's end'."

"SILENCE!!" Once silence was achieved, the Devil said, "I suppose you know more."

Mickey smiled. "We've got eternity, right?"

"No, we don't. You three don't belong here." Mickey and the two potted giant hibiscus were engulfed in flames.

When the flames subsided, Mickey found himself flat on his back in the middle of the living room of his apartment, with the two plants toppled over across his body. All three of them were smoldering. Mickey knocked the plants aside and sprang to his feet, slapping at his burning clothes. Giving up on this, he yanked off the scorched rags and stripped down to his undershorts, stomping on the smoldering pants and shirt.

Stan extended several stems down to the floor to leverage his pot upright. "What happened?" He helped a dazed Laurie upright.

"The devil kicked us out of Hellades up to my dimension." Mickey looked all around with a deep sigh. "I'm back home." He focused on the other two. "And you two are out of my head."

"But *we're* not home," the Laurie plant said.

"Damn," Mickey moaned. "What am I supposed to do with you two?"

"You could start by watering us," the Stan plant said. "Hellades dried us out."

"Sure." Mickey glared at the Laurie plant. "As long as you keep your petals to yourself."

"Oh, Mickey, all I ever wanted to do is give you pleasure."

Mickey laughed. "You can quit wasting pheromones, Laurie. You are half-burnt up. All I can smell are your ashes."

"It's a deal," the Stan plant insisted. "If you water us, we'll leave you alone. Besides, I'm tired of living in a pot. I'm ready to go home and get grafted back into our root system."

George and Priscilla, both in their underwear, emerged from George's room. "What's all the foot-stomping about?" George asked.

Priscilla yawned. "You woke us up." She wrinkled her nose. "I smell fire and brimstone. Did you three just come up from Hell?"

Mickey was perplexed. "You two don't seem surprised to find us here."

"What is there left to be surprised about?" George asked.

Mickey turned to Priscilla. "I see you are picking up bad habits from my roommate, going about in your underwear."

"Look who's talking," Priscilla said, pointing out the fact Mickey was standing there in his singed undershorts. As she walked away toward the bathroom, the seven dwarves wriggled across the seat of her yellow panties.

George attempted to draw Mickey's attention back to the problem at hand. "What are you going to do with the monster plants?"

Once Priscilla disappeared behind the bathroom door, Mickey looked back to the two giant hibiscus. "I have no idea." It was then he spied the folded sheet of plastic piled on the coffee table. "Where did that come from?"

"Ralph gave it to me. Said you would need it to do some gardening. Imagine, Ralph giving *us* plastic."

Mickey smiled as he headed for the kitchen. "As soon as I water you two, you are so out of here."

8.

Mickey sat at a table in the Evanston coffee shop across the street from the park. The Phun With Physics placard was on the table he shared with Lucy, Miriam, Albert, Stan, and Laurie. The open laptop before Mickey now displayed a new sticker on the lid—the surface of the moon with Earth just above the horizon, and two people seen from behind wearing bodysuits and ski masks standing side by side next to a wooden park bench tagged with Planck's constant while gazing up at the looming planet.

Lucy studied the sticker while nibbling on a cookie. "Interesting picture."

"What happened to Hypatia?" Miriam asked.

Mickey shrugged, looking through his notes for the meeting. "It was time for a change."

"Are those supposed to be aliens on the moon?" Stan asked.

"One of them is curvaceous, for an alien," Laurie said.

"Maybe they're people," Albert offered.

"If they are it's not very realistic," Stan said. "People would have space suits on, not pajamas."

"Did you put that together in Photoshop?" Miriam asked.

"No," Mickey answered, distracted.

"Somebody did. And they were good. It looks like it was taken on the moon."

Mickey grinned from above his laptop. "Maybe it was."

"How did you turn it into a sticker?" Lucy asked.

"There are sites that will do that for you."

"Send me a link to the site you used. I've got some number images from my book I'd like made into stickers."

"Always your book," Miriam harped. "You never let us forget you have a book."

Laurie continued to admire the sticker. "I like what you did with the female." She leered up at Mickey. "Maybe I can pose for you sometime, and you can put me on the moon." She turned her attention back to the sticker. "Only I don't have any pajamas like the woman is wearing. I sleep in the nude."

"She does," Stan confirmed. "Cuddling up to her bare butt is like cuddling up to a frozen turkey."

"I bet Mickey could warm it up." Laurie batted bedroom eyes at

Mickey.

Mickey ignored her. "Listen to this."

"You're not playing any Bicep, are you?" Miriam whined.

"Or reciting any mathematical haiku?" Lucy whined.

"No. These are sounds from space NASA posted. Remember the byline of the original 'Alien' movie? 'In space no one can hear you scream.' Turns out there is a lot to hear in space. This is plasma waves moving from Saturn to its moon Enceladus, recorded during the Cassini mission." Mickey played an audio file that sounded like a whooshing wind rushing by. He played another. "This is radio emissions the Galileo spacecraft gathered from Jupiter's largest moon, Ganymede." It sounded like the popping and crackling of AM radio static. He played another. "This is what the solar wind sounds like." This audio file sounded like a musical saw being played tunelessly. And another. "This is the flight of the Ingenuity Mars helicopter recorded by the Perseverance Rover. You can hear the humming of the blades above the Martian wind. Listen to the pitch change as it ascends and descends."

Seeing no one was suitably impressed, Mickey closed the laptop with a sigh. "It's been a while since our last meeting. Let's catch up." He turned toward Stan and Laurie. "First, I need to apologize for the way I acted toward you two. I was going through a crazy spell that last time we met in the alley. I'm sorry about that. Won't happen again, I promise."

Stan shrugged. "I've gone crazy at times, too. Especially right after I got back from Afghanistan. Apology accepted."

"I was hit harder than that puny little slap during basic training," Laurie said. "If that's the worst you ever do, you're a saint." A loose smile slid across her slippery face. "And I sure hope you aren't a candidate for sainthood."

Mickey hastily turned to the other three. "So what's new with the rest of you?"

"My daughter Edie is okay." Lucy glared at Albert. "She wasn't pregnant after all."

Anxious to change the subject, Albert spoke up. "I've got a birthday coming up."

"Wow, ninety," Mickey said with appropriate awe. "One decade shy of a century. That's impressive, Albert."

"I'm thinking about getting a pet," Miriam said.

Mickey nodded in agreement with the notion. "Pets make good companions for older people living on their own."

"I'm no longer living on my own. I've taken in a border."

Mickey raised both eyebrows. "Ralph?"

Lucy spewed laughter. "At your age?"

"*You* mock? Of all people?" Miriam turned to Mickey. "Ever wonder why Lucy is so interested in physics?"

"*I* am not living with anyone. Mitchell and I are merely dating."

"I and Ralph are not doing even that," Miriam sniffed. "We're sharing my apartment, not my bed."

"Why not?" Albert asked. "What could it hurt?"

Mickey attempted to change the subject. "What kind of pet are you getting, Miriam?"

"I've been looking at gibbons."

"No!" The other five stared in surprise at Mickey's outburst. "Not a good idea, Miriam. Gibbons are mean nasty animals. They pee on you and throw poop on you. And they grab at your private places."

Laurie laughed. "Miriam might enjoy all that, Mickey."

Mickey checked the time on his phone. "We need to get started with the meeting." He looked around to see if anyone was going to object. No one did. "Today I want to talk about what the world would be like if Apocalyptic rains flooded the Earth and drove everyone to higher ground to escape drowning."

"Like with Mitchell's ark?" Laurie asked.

Mickey nearly jumped out of his skin. "What did you say!?"

The other five stared back at him like he was having a relapse. "My wife said, 'like with Noah's ark'." Stan leaned forward in an unfriendly manner. "You're not going to slap Laurie again, are you?"

Mickey raised both arms in surrender. "No. Of course not." Mickey slumped in his chair. Where had that come from? He had heard Laurie say Mitchell's ark. Everyone else heard her say Noah's ark. Someone was messing with him.

Laurie restrained her husband. "The Bible promised that would never happen again."

Desperate to regain his composure, Mickey stuttered on. "Not in this dimension. But maybe in another. We need to consider other dimensions that might exist here on earth without our being aware of them."

One evening later that week Mickey sat at a desk in an empty classroom at Northwestern immersed in calculations on his laptop. He appeared well, and reasonably happy. There was a knock at the door. He was so lost in what he was doing he didn't respond. There was another knock. Then another. Still, Mickey did not look up. There was then a specific knocking that beat out a percussive rhythm. Mickey looked up at that. A young woman stood in the open doorway knocking out the beat with her knuckles. "Is that Bicep?"

She stopped knocking. "You know Bicep?"

"My favorite musicians. Know any mathematical haiku?"

"The Universe is/Chaos distilled to challenge/Till patterns emerge," she recited.

"Primeval silence/Broken, then pieced together/By a new language," Mickey followed up with.

"Both by Radu V. Craiu," the young woman said.

Mickey leaned back in his seat. "Who are you?"

"Freddie." She walked in. The young woman was short and trim, clad in baggy colorless clothes any self-respecting store mannequin would object to. "Mitchell sent me. He said Priscilla has been helping you, but she is too busy with work for him that she's gotten behind on. So I'm supposed to take over whatever she was doing for you."

"So we'll be working together." His grin grew wider. "Spending a lot of time together." Wider. "Getting to know each other." Even wider.

"If that's okay with you." Freddie seemed unbothered by his unhinged grin. She walked over to look at the laptop screen. "What are you working on?"

Mickey shrugged. "Life, the Universe, and everything."

9.

An exhausted bedraggled Eden limped into her brother's apartment and clapped her hands once. Her soaked filthy clothes holding several gallons of water disappeared. She no longer looked like a drowned rat; she looked like a drowned naked rat. She reached for a towel, but before she could pick one up she was clothed in Hypatia's robe. She jerked all around looking for the reason this happened.

Mickey stood next to the sleeping tubes. She had been so exhausted her threadbare eyes had failed to register his presence. His thin lips formed its customary crooked smile. "I didn't want you to expose yourself without knowing I was here."

Eden slapped her hands together in irritation. The robe once again disappeared. "Why would it bother me to be naked in front of you." She picked up the towel the unexpected appearance of Hypatia's robe had interrupted her reaching for, and began drying. "You lived inside my naked body. You saw me naked every day for a month. You saw me naked after you no longer possessed my body. So why would I think twice about you seeing me naked now." Her drying slowed, as her soggy, weary mind began to work its way out of its comatose condition. "How are you doing this, anyway? Did you copy and reproduce my chip while you had use of it?" Mickey stared at her blank-faced. "How are you here at all?" The drying stopped. "Unless you are not the Mickey I know." Eden tossed the towel down and the robe re-appeared on her. "What Mickey are you?"

"One you haven't met before." It was Eden's turn to stare blank-faced. "How are the rescue efforts going?"

Eden collapsed into a chair. It wasn't *her* Mickey standing before her, but it was *a* Mickey. All the twins in all the dimensions were like some weird extended family. At the moment she was too worn out to worry about such weirdness. "Better now that it's stopped raining. We've rescued a lot of Morlox. And we're making real headway draining the underground."

"You're a hero, Eden. You returned and the rain stopped. Those two events will be forever linked in people's minds. You have become a legend."

"Why did this second rain plague occur? Did I cause it?"

"Yes. But don't look so appalled. It stopped the war. Less people drowned than would have died in the war. You inadvertently saved a lot of lives." A smile appeared on his lips. "The people adore you so much you will become the next Supreme Leader. If you wish to."

"Who are you?"

Mickey spread his arms. "You know who I am."

"*Which* are you, then? Where do you come from?"

"The Moon. Shackleton Crater, to be specific."

"A dimension higher than the one that has a space station in orbit where a twin of my unborn daughter's daughter is restoring a damaged Earth?"

"Yes."

"Why didn't I make it to your dimension?"

Mickey barked an awkward laugh. "We didn't want you there."

Yes, Eden thought, *this sure seems like Mickey, dumb laugh and all.*

"We didn't want Mickey there either, but he came anyway."

That resurrected Eden's posture. "Mickey's been to your dimension on the Moon!"

"He forced his way in."

"How? Why?"

"How? Because we were careless. We never imagined he'd be so bold. While he was in you some of your brashness must have rubbed off on him. Why? He wanted to negotiate."

"Negotiate what?" When Mickey's smile grew so large it turned insulting, Eden stood and grabbed his shoulders. Or attempted to. Her hands went right through them. She stepped back. "You're not really here."

The smile diminished. "My holograms aren't as good as yours. Mine can't be felt."

"Can I come to the moon?" Eden begged. Then whined. "Mickey got to go."

"Sorry. Your inter-dimensional travels are over."

Eden sagged back down into the chair.

"Brace yourself. You're not going to like what I'm about to tell you."

That got her attention. She peered up at him with a mix of misery and injustice at what she feared she was about to hear.

"Mickey's travels aren't over. That's what he negotiated."

10.

Mickey lounged in the mouse chair with his open laptop on the coffee table blaring Bicep. The blackboard was surprisingly blank. For a change the room was clean as well as orderly.

The reason for the cleanliness became apparent when Edie entered the apartment bearing two cups of take-out coffee. For the first time since Mickey had known her, she was wearing a dress. She placed one cup on the table before Mickey. Glancing at the laptop, an expression that was a cross between a smile and a grimace congealed on her face. "I'm starting to like this music."

Mickey laughed. "You are a terrible liar."

Edie sipped her coffee. "Well, I don't dislike it as much as I did." She began pacing.

"Have a seat, Edie."

"I can't. I'm too nervous." The room being just a little over two meters by three meters, there wasn't much room for pacing. She stopped before the blackboard and picked up a fragment of chalk. She inscribed two vertical parallel lines, then crossed them with two horizontal parallel lines.

Mickey was intrigued. "What are you doing?"

"Playing tic tac toe solitaire." She quickly won a game, started another. "It passes the time."

There was a knock. "Come on in!" Mickey bellowed above the music.

Carl Friedrich and Freddie entered. Edie stood to greet them. "Would you like something to drink?"

"No," Carl Friedrich spat out. "Let's just get this over with."

Mickey turned off the music. "This isn't something to get over with."

"I know what this is." Carl Friedrich jabbed a thumb at Freddie. "This poor girl has no idea."

"You seem concerned for Freddie's well-being." Mickey hinted at a smile. "There's a reason for that."

Carl Friedrich stared at her. "I guess now you're going to tell me she's my aunt."

"No, your sister. In the dimension we're traveling to."

"Bullshit." Yet Carl Friedrich took a step back from Freddie. Apparently, he had been having un-sisterly thoughts about her.

Edie put the chalk down and stepped up to Freddie. "Don't listen to your brother. It's an amazing experience. There's nothing to be afraid of."

"Nothing to be afraid of?" Carl Friedrich screeched. "How about a giant ghoul with an axe wanting to chop you up and feed you to a monster in a box? How about a bunch of people on a tropical island weirder than Lost threatening to kill you? How about the Devil himself?"

"I thought you didn't believe in Hell," Mickey said.

"Don't be so hard on him, Mickey," Edie said. "He's like a lot of people. Do you know that Laura Nyro song 'And When I Die'? I love that one line. 'I can swear there ain't no Heaven but I pray there ain't no Hell'." She laughed. "That's so typical of people. I mean, if you're so sure there is no Heaven what's the point of praying?"

Carl Friedrich ignored her. He was watching Mickey close the laptop. "Don't you need that? I thought we needed that to travel between dimensions."

"Not anymore." Mickey walked into his bedroom.

"Is George here?" Carl Friedrich asked.

"He's at Priscilla's," Edie answered.

"Why aren't they going with us?"

Mickey walked back in with a folded sheet of plastic. "This is a family reunion."

"We're not family," Freddie protested.

Carl Friedrich pointed at Mickey. "This weirdo thinks I'm his son. I'm as old as he is. He would have to have been one when he sired me." He dropped the accusing finger. "And if he thinks you're my sister then that makes you his daughter."

"I never claimed you were my son," Mickey said. "I just carried you for a while." He smiled at Freddie. "A carried you for a while, also."

"See." Carl Friedrich turned back to Freddie. "Totally bonkers. He thinks he carried us in his womb. He doesn't even have a womb."

"Not anymore." Mickey began unfolding the plastic.

"Is that the same stinking plastic Ralph had out in the alley?" Carl Friedrich asked.

Mickey ignored him. "Now everyone step in close." Edie and Mickey eagerly stepped forward. Carl Friedrich and Freddie moved in with more reluctance. Mickey flapped the sheet of plastic up into the air above and it settled all around them to the floor.

When Mickey pulled the sheet of plastic off the foursome, he found himself standing in the lecture hall. Reimann was deep in discussion with Liebnitz. Ramanujan stood off to one side examining a book. Descartes and Newton were in a heated discussion, with Newton wagging an angry finger at Liebnitz. Pythagoras, Archimedes, and Euclid lounged on the floor in the middle of the room. Euler stood before a life-sized portrait of Hypatia on the steps of the Library of Alexandria. Gauss approached the new arrivals. "Do you know any good publishers?"

"If I did I would get *this* book published." Mickey took a step back and turned to the others. "Don't let Gauss get too close. When you get too close to Newton you get bopped on the head by an apple. No telling what other traps Eden has set in her hologram."

"I liked McDonalds better," Carl Friedrich said.

Freddie gaped all about. "Where are we?"

"A retirement community for old men, it looks like," Edie said.

"Ramanujan isn't that old." Mickey folded up the sheet of plastic.

"Then he probably works here," Edie replied.

"That's racist," Mickey said. "The only Asian in the group and you assume he's a menial."

Gauss extended his hand to Carl Friedrich. "I'm your Godfather."

Carl Friedrich looked to Mickey. "Is this one of Eden's traps?"

"You were named after Gauss. His first and middle names are also Carl Friedrich."

Carl Friedrich shook his hand. Then slung it loose, jumping back. He appeared distraught, while Gauss chuckled.

"What happened?" Mickey asked.

"I slid down this giant funnel."

"Did you slide inward or outward?"

"I don't know! What difference does it make?"

"I just wonder if his hand was a link to a hyperbolic non-Euclidean geometric space or an elliptic non-Euclidean geometric space."

Carl Friedrich's visage grew dark. "I hate you when you babble like that."

Edie tried to calm him. "He's not babbling. I'm starting to understand some of the things he says."

"Sure, Carl," Freddie had calmed enough to take part in the conversation. "Everybody knows the contributions Gauss made to non-Euclidean space."

Gauss nodded a smile to Freddie then walked away.

Mickey joined Freddie. "You were named after him, too. Eden must have really been impressed with Gauss."

The foursome were joined by another five. Eden entered bearing a baby swaddled in blue, her ex-husband Mick entered with a baby wrapped in a pink blanket, and her brother George entered empty-handed. He wasn't empty-handed for long. Edie ran up to hug and kiss him. The pair withdrew to a far corner of the lecture hall.

Mickey approached Eden. She had never appeared so beautiful. Her blue evening gown swept the floor. She glittered with jewelry. Her hair flowed down over her shoulders. An apparition of loveliness. "Your dress is pretty. Another hologram?"

"Yes, one you never wore," Eden replied.

"That's okay. I'd much rather admire you with it on, with my own eyes." Mickey didn't realize how boldly he was admiring her until Mick cleared his throat for the fifth time. Mickey pried his eyes off Eden to face him. "What happened to your beard?"

Mick shook his head. "Shaved it. And I started wearing these nerd glasses."

"They look like mine."

"They are just like yours. That's the idea."

Mickey was surprised. "And you're okay with that? Looking more like me?"

"How do you like my new haircut?"

Mickey burst into a grin. "It looks like mine."

"That was part of the deal," Eden said. "His expiation. Atonement for his affair with Laurie." She presented the baby she held to Mickey.

Mickey cradled the infant in his arms with glowing pride. "He really was inside me."

"Carl Friedrich was inside me the entire pregnancy. You were inside me for a month."

Mickey waved her away. "Mere semantics." He rocked the child, cooed. Then looked at adult Carl Friedrich. "Want to see what you looked like when you were a baby?"

Carl Friedrich approached brimming with doubt. "That's supposed to be me?"

"In this dimension."

"Is this who I think it is?"

Mickey turned to see that Eden was referring to Freddie. "Yes. Introduce her to her twin."

Eden drew Freddie over to Mick to show her baby Carla. She then called out to the far corner. "Edie! Want to see what the baby you and Mickey could make would look like?" There was no response from the dark corner.

"Leave her alone," Mickey said. "She's been a nervous wreck for days over seeing your brother again."

Eden handed baby Carla to Mick then took baby Carl Friedrich from Mickey. "So how is it going with you and Edie?"

"Okay. She doesn't hate me."

"That's all? The absence of hate?"

"She's in love with George."

"Who exists in a different dimension."

"So? There have been other long distance relationships."

Eden laughed. "None as long as this."

"Edie and I are friends."

"Any chance it will develop into something more?" Mickey shrugged, causing Eden to frown. "This is what I was dreading. You can't crawl back into your hole, Mickey."

"I haven't. I've got Carl Friedrich and Freddie. I'm still living with George, so I see a lot of Priscilla. And I negotiated this annual family reunion, didn't I?"

"I *am* impressed by that. So what am I like? In the dimension on the Moon? I met your moon twin. He showed up in George's apartment when I was getting ready to take a shower."

Mickey grinned. "And you told me you don't enjoy showing off your body."

"I thought it was you. It was you. A different you." Despite her best efforts, Eden flustered about. "Anyway, do our twins really reside in the uppermost dimension?"

"If Shackleton Crater is in the uppermost dimension." Mickey offered a finger to the baby Eden held. "How are you and Mick getting along?"

"Okay. He's a good father. He adores the babies."

"And he's good looking."

Eden laughed. "I've missed your deprecating humor."

Mickey frowned. "I said that with a straight face."

"There's nothing straight about your face. It's kind of a glob."

"We get to see each other once a year and all you want to do is insult me."

Eden stepped up to lay her head on his shoulder, cradling the baby between them. "What I want to do is drag you into my Roman bath."

Mickey petted her hair. "You wouldn't have to drag me." After a long content silence, they drew apart. "How are you and Stan?"

"It's over. I'm committed to Mick." She peered deep into Mickey's eyes. "I just wish you could find someone."

Mick, carrying baby Carla, and Freddie and Carl Friedrich joined them. "You two need to get a room," Carl Friedrich said.

Mickey stepped back with both hands raised. "No. Eden is a married woman. I respect the institution of marriage." He gazed from one baby to the other. "I respect families."

"That's good, because you are a member of this one." Eden looked toward the entrance door. "The food has arrived."

Carl Friedrich looked around. "I don't see anyone."

"The caterer sent a notification to my chip." Eden looked to the far corner. "George! Edie! Dinner is here. Come join us."

The pair reluctantly made their way across the lecture hall. Edie was crying, and George was somber. Seeing all the questioning looks, George spoke up. "We're breaking it off."

Through sniffles, Edie concurred. "Seeing each other just once a year won't work. I can't expect George to give up a chance at a happy marriage, at raising a family, for just that."

Eden shot an encouraging glance to Mickey, but he unobtrusively shook his head no. She clapped her hands four times. The lecture hall disappeared, replaced by the Library of Alexandria.

Mickey drew back to look around. The large room was empty, except for Hypatia seated in a distant corner studying a papyrus scroll.

Eden smiled at his surprise. "This is a trick you never learned. A hologram within a hologram. I wanted some time for just me and you."

Mickey was impressed, for about three seconds. Then he turned back to Eden. "I can't believe Mick went along with all that stuff you made him do. To make him look more like me."

"I also made him remove a tattoo." Mickey started laughing. "And you know that mole on your right shoulder?"

"You didn't."

"Plastic surgeons can put moles on as well as remove them."

"You are merciless."

"If I can't have you then I'll have the closest approximation possible."

"Is that fair? After all, you had an affair with Stan."

"It's not the same. That only happened after I left Mick because of his affair with Laurie. I never would have touched Stan otherwise." Eden kissed Mickey. "Enough about Mick and Stan." The kiss evolved into an embrace.

Mickey remained reluctant. "This isn't fair to Mick."

"Us being forced apart isn't fair. The world isn't fair." They kissed again, and Mickey's reluctance melted away.

Until his conscious jerked him back. "I can't do this."

Eden sagged against him. "I know. I could, but you can't. You're a better person than I am."

"No, I'm not. I'm just dumber than you."

Eden nodded her head resting on his chest in agreement. "Runt." She sighed half her soul away. "I don't know how you negotiated this family reunion, but I'm sure glad you did."

"I was negotiating with our twins. They were sympathetic to our plight, so it wasn't too difficult."

"It sounds like Edie is available now."

"Edie is a really nice woman. That's important to me."

"And she looks just like me."

"That's important, too."

"Your body will remember her. You two fit together very well." Receiving nothing but another slight nod, Eden pressed on. "Are you teaching her higher mathematics?"

"She learns quickly. She has a sharp mind. Like yours. It just was never trained."

"Same recipe cooked at different temperatures."

Mickey stroked her hair. "Your children are beautiful."

"Our children."

"Does Mick know Carla is mine?"

"I made sure he knew."

"And he's okay with that?"

"He'll be the husband of the next Supreme Leader. So he's okay with a lot of things." While Mickey chuckled, Eden continued. "Mick is more ambitious than you."

"So how was the delivery?"

"You missed the best part. It was hell."

Mickey's chuckle grew to a laugh. "I wish I could say I'm sorry it was you and not me."

"You louse. You aren't sorry at all."

"But the children are okay." Eden nodded. "You're okay?" She nodded. "That's good."

Eden stepped back. "Dinner is served."

Mickey looked around, but the Library was empty.

"Not here, runt. In the other hologram. They notified me on my chip." Eden took his hands. "I love you, Mickey Haiku."

Mickey squeezed her hands. "Eden Haiku triumphant."

They let go, and Eden clapped her hands four times. The Library of Alexandria disappeared. Mickey and Eden were back in the lecture hall. With everyone staring at them. "At least they still have their clothes on," Carl Friedrich quipped.

Mickey grew defensive. "We just talked."

Ignoring everyone, Eden clapped her hands three times, and all the scientists faded away. She clapped her hands twice, and the lecture hall faded away, to reveal they were standing in a small living room.

"You could clap one time," Carl Friedrich said.

"Carl Friedrich," Eden chided. "Is that any way to talk to your mother?"

"You are not my mother! If you try to hug me I'm throwing you off that balcony." Carl Friedrich scowled as he looked around. "You live here?"

"Me and Mick and the babies."

"It's not much bigger than my place. I thought you were Supreme Leader."

"Not yet," Mick said. "Mitchell is still interim Supreme Leader." He motioned toward the balcony door. "But we have moved up to the eight-hundred-sixtieth floor."

"Because of my accomplishments," Eden explained. "Not because of anything Mick has done."

"This high up means you get a car," Mickey said.

"Yes. I'll take you four for a drive after dinner."

Mick shook his head no. "You do not want to ride with her. She is worse than Ralph."

"I'm a better driver than Mickey. He nearly ran over a man in the parking lot at Pike's Peak." She looked to Mickey. "Have you gotten a license yet? Priscilla said she was going to make you get one."

"I've been too busy." Mickey followed Eden into the dining room. "Is any of it going to taste like stinky socks? Or armpit lick? Or dirty diaper."

"Speaking of dirty diaper." Mick held out baby Carla.

"Let me." Freddie took the baby from him. "Has anyone ever changed their twin's diaper before?"

"I'll help you." Edie accompanied Freddie to the changing table.

Eden leaned in to whisper to Mickey. "Looks like Edie likes babies."

Carl Friedrich scowled at the small dinner table in the cramped dining room. "We're all seven sitting here? And two babies?"

Mickey smacked him on the back of the head. "Where's your manners, son?"

Carl Friedrich glared at him. "On the floor. Where you are going to be if you hit me again."

And with that they sat down to eat.

11.

Mickey sat at the professor's desk at the front of a nearly empty college classroom. Before him Freddie and Edie, dressed for work, sat at students' desks. The three of them were finishing up a late night meal of vending machine food. The blackboard behind Mickey was filled with computations. Several desks around Freddie were covered with scattered piles of papers she was going over. Eden's cleaning cart was parked in a corner.

Edie looked up at the blackboard. "Do you think I'll ever understand any of that?"

Mickey looked up at her as if he had no idea what she was talking about.

"That," Freddie prompted, pointing to the blackboard.

Mickey swiveled to look, shrugged. "Mathematics is a language, like English or Spanish. You can learn it." He turned back around to face Edie. "It's just easier if you grew up speaking it. Like any language."

"I *was* growing up speaking it, until my father died." Finished, Edie began gathering her garbage.

Freddie jumped up to stop her. "You clean up eight hours a night." Freddie took over the garbage collection. "I've got this."

Edie sank back into her seat. "I've got tomorrow off. Do you want to come over for dinner with Mickey?"

Freddie snuck a smile to Mickey. "Sorry. I've already made plans." Gathering garbage from Mickey's desk, she kicked his chair. "I'm sure Mickey can make it."

He looked up from deep in the land of thought. "What? Dinner? At your apartment? Edie?"

Freddie smiled at Edie. "I'll remind him."

Edie stood. "I've got to get back to work." She grabbed her cleaning cart and left.

Freddie dumped the garbage she had collected then got in Mickey's face. "I wish you'd treat Edie better."

Mickey looked up aghast. "I don't mistreat her."

"I didn't say you did. But you could do a lot better."

"But Eden is in another dimension." Freddie gazed at Mickey at a complete loss. "You said I could do a lot better than Edie."

"I meant you could *treat* Edie a lot better." She turned away. "You are hopeless."

"Freddie, I *like* Edie."

Freddie began gathering up her stray papers. "I like her, too. She would make a good step-mother."

Mickey sighed. "It's late. You need to go home."

Freddie gave out an identical sigh. "I'll call to remind you Edie is expecting you for dinner tomorrow night. And text you. And email you. And direct message you. Watch out your window for smoke signals."

"Go home."

Freddie gathered up the last of her papers and left.

Mickey followed her to the door. After she walked away, he looked up and down the hall. No one was in sight. He glanced at a clock. Two a.m. He stepped back into the classroom and closed the door. With his back to it, he gazed into the middle of the empty room. "Pris. I know you are still infecting me. I can feel you inside me."

A disembodied voice replied. "What do you want, Mickey?"

"I want to see you."

The Pris Virus shimmered into existence in the middle of the classroom. As usual, she was clad in Priscilla's Arial nightgown.

"That trick you played at Phun With Physics wasn't funny." Silence. "I know it was you saying 'Mitchell' in my head when Laurie really said 'Noah'."

The Pris Virus remained solemn.

"You owe me, Pris."

A bottomless frown appeared. "For playing a little practical joke? Don't you think a virus can have a sense of humor?"

"I helped your Stanley and Lori gain control of the mountaintop dimension."

The Pris Virus snorted. "They didn't want control of it."

"I helped them nevertheless. And I rid them of those horrid plants."

The Pris Virus' image heaved with a sigh. "What do you want?"

"Eden."

"I can't bring Eden to you."

"I think you can." Braving her blank expression, he rushed on. "You are a virus. Your actual physical appearance is microscopic. The appearance you project is that of Priscilla, since you were fashioned from her. But I'm guessing it doesn't have to be Priscilla. Does it?"

The Pris Virus stared without responding.

"Could it be it's only an image in my head I'm seeing? I've seen that Little Mermaid nightgown you wear hanging in Priscilla's closet."

The Pris Virus scowled. "You couldn't expect me to wear that little flimsy pink nothing you like."

"Could you produce a different image from my memories?"

The Pris Virus faded away.

Mickey walked back to his desk and slumped into the seat. Maybe she couldn't do it, Mickey conceded to himself. Maybe she had to appear as Priscilla.

"Mickey."

Mickey shot up out of his seat at the sound of Eden's voice. He spun around to find Eden facing him at the closed door. He knew it wasn't really Eden, he knew it was a mirage, just an image of a memory, but that image was clad in his favorite hologram of hers—the little black dress. He walked toward her.

Eden(the Pris Virus) backed away. "You can't touch her."

"Of course not." Mickey halted. "There is nothing here for me to touch."

"Is this enough? Just to see her image?"

"And to hear her voice? I know it's not really her voice, it's your voice, Pris, but it sounds like her, it's like I'm really talking with Eden." Mickey smiled. "It's enough for now. We'll see where it leads."

"You realize this is your idealized memory of Eden I am drawing this image from. It's not how Eden looks now. She just gave birth to twins. She has stretch marks she hasn't got rid of yet."

"I'd love to see her stretch marks."

"You can't, because they are not part of your memories of her."

"So I'll always see Eden like this? Fifty years from now she will still look like this to me? I'm good with that." Mickey relaxed back against the side of his desk.

Eden(the Pris Virus) flared red, the angry image becoming a distorted amalgam of Eden and Priscilla. "Who said anything about doing this for fifty years?"

Mickey attempted to placate the virus. "I'm grateful for whatever you'll grant me."

The image settled back to one of Eden in her little black dress. But the frown deepened. "I don't know if I should tell you this." Mickey patiently waited. "This wasn't your idea."

Mickey rose up from the edge of his desk. "Of course it was."

"I have infected Eden, too. And she is in a higher dimension. She was able, with my help, to slip the idea to do this down into your mind."

"That sneaky little cur."

"I'd be careful what you say about her."

"Why's that?"

"Like I said, I have infected her, same as you. Right now an image of you from her memory is standing in front of her."

"Eden is seeing me like I am seeing her?" Eden(the Pris Virus) nodded yes. "What am I wearing?"

"That little green leaf."

Mickey barked a bitter laugh. "She is ruthless! Can she hear what I am saying?"

"No. But through me here the copy of the virus in your body can relay what you say to the copy of the virus in her body so the image of you it has produced can tell her."

"Like the time lapse on a live TV news broadcast between remote reporters?" Before his mind wandered any further, Mickey snapped back to the moment. "Then tell her I will never stop loving her."

The Pris Virus smiled with Eden's lips. "She already knew that, but I told her anyway."

"Well? Did she have anything to say in reply?"

"Yes. She said you can cherish your memory of her and love Edie at the same time. She says to go have a life."

12.

Mickey knocked on the door to Edie's apartment. He was wearing new jeans and an unwrinkled button-up long sleeve shirt of a subdued color. This was because Freddie had perp-walked him into a clothing store. She had also picked out a tie, but this he had balked at. Mickey bounced from foot to foot, as he did when nervous, humming a Bicep tune.

"Stop fidgeting."

The door opened to a pleasant sight. Edie wearing a dress.

"So you rate a dress, same as George. That's encouraging. Now say something nice."

"A dress? Another dress? What's the occasion?"

"I said something nice, runt, not something stupid. The occasion is you."

Edie smiled as she beckoned him to enter. "You saw the smoke signals?"

He entered and glanced around. "And got the text. And a phone call."

"Freddie is persistent." Edie closed the door. She motioned toward a covered dish on the coffee table. "Dinner is not quite ready yet. Have a snack."

Mickey walked over to lift the cover. A pair of dirty socks on a plate.

Edie couldn't contain her mirth. "Your favorite. Stinky socks."

Mickey replaced the cover. "I don't want to spoil my appetite."

"What would you like to drink?"

"Water is good. Just don't spit in it. Or pee in it."

Edie stared. "I suppose there is a story there."

"Belos had desalination spit. And urine. In his dimension."

"Glad I missed that one." Edie walked out to the kitchen.

Eden(the Pris Virus) appeared before Mickey. As before, she was wearing the little black dress. "Don't louse this up, runt."

"Are you going to be looking over my shoulder all evening? I'm nervous enough as it is."

Eden(the Pris Virus) laughed. "If you get too nervous to perform I'll help you out. I know what Edie likes."

Edie returned with a glass of water. "Nothing but water. Promise."

Mickey scowled past her at Eden(the Pris Virus). Edie had walked past her without noticing. Apparently, only he could see her.

Edie noticed the scowl. "Don't you trust me?"

"What? Oh, the water. Of course I trust you." To prove it, he drained the glass. "I'm just a little nervous."

"After what you've been through?" Edie took the glass from him. "Have a seat while I finish up in the kitchen." She turned toward her stereo. "Would you like some music? I don't have any Bicep."

Mickey sat on the couch. "How about some heavy metal?"

Edie reacted with surprise. "You like heavy metal?"

"No. I just wondered if you had any. Metal. That was heavy."

"I forgot what a silver-tongued devil you are." Eden(the Pris Virus) ladled out scorn. "You are not supposed to know she likes that kind of music. This is your first time in her apartment."

"Is this some of that double walker stuff?" Edie's surprise began morphing into apprehension. "But that's Eden who is supposed to be my ganger. What all did she tell you about me?"

"Nothing much," Mickey stammered.

Edie let it go. She turned on her stereo. "It's not heavy metal, but it's one of my favorites and we have to keep it down. The neighbors don't appreciate head-banging." 'The Sound of Silence' by Disturbed began playing. Edie walked into the kitchen.

Mickey collapsed on the couch. "This is going to be a long night."

Eden(the Pris Virus) sat next to him. "I sure hope so."

He frowned at her. "Are you going to be hanging around all night?"

Eden(the Pris Virus) smiled. "I'd like to. But I won't. I'll respect your privacy."

"What privacy? You know, this seemed like a good idea at the time."

"Of course it's a good idea. It was mine."

"Are you talking to yourself?"

Mickey threw a panicked look to Edie, who had walked in from the kitchen.

"That music needs to be louder," Eden(the Pris Virus) said.

Edie shook her head. "I know, you're a physicist. Allowances need to be made." She walked back into the kitchen.

"Will you two leave me alone?" Mickey managed to shout in a whisper.

"Good luck, Mickey," Eden(the Pris Virus) said. "Just remember I love you so much I need you to be happy." The image of Eden in the little black dress shimmered away.

Mickey heaved a sigh of relief.

"I'm still here, Mickey," the Pris Virus cooed in his ear. "I have infected you. I will always be here."

"I might go see Moderna about you."

"You wouldn't! You'd lose your link to Eden."

"Then give me some privacy."

His head grew silent. Mickey closed his eyes and sagged into the couch in relief.

"Are you tired?"

Mickey opened his eyes to find Edie staring at him from the kitchen doorway. "No. I've just got things in my mind."

Edie appeared puzzled. "Things *on* your mind?" Receiving only a blank stare, she shrugged. "Dinner is ready."

"We're ready." Mickey stood. "I mean I'm ready. To eat."

Mickey followed Edie into the kitchen. It was Italian night, with lasagna, garlic bread, and salad, with a glass of water and a glass of red wine. The small table all this was displayed upon had four chairs, but only two place settings. "Smells delicious."

"Mom gave me the recipe. She got it from Miriam. First time I've fixed it, so don't be too harsh."

"Harsh? You should see what I usually eat."

Eden(the Pris Virus) appeared behind Edie. "Garbage in, and you don't really want to talk about what comes out."

Mickey scowled his displeasure at the intrusion as he sat.

Edie noticed him looking beyond her, and turned around to see what he was looking at. She turned back to Mickey as she sat. "What?"

Mickey sighed. "I need to level with you. We've been through too much together not to be honest with each other."

Eden(the Pris Virus) grew alarmed. "What are you doing, Mickey?"

Mickey remained focused on Edie. "I've been infected. You probably have been, also. How are you feeling?"

Edie grew riveted. "Okay."

"It's the Pris Virus. I'm carrying her."

Edie heaved relief. "Oh. That."

Mickey's gast was flabbered. "You knew?"

"She's a virus. We were all exposed to her. I assumed I was infected."

"And you're okay with that?"

"Shouldn't I be? I mean, we carry all kinds of organisms in our bodies. They aren't all out to get us."

"Have you been hearing voices? Seeing things?"

"What are you hearing and seeing?"

Mickey looked beyond Edie. "Can you make yourself visible to Edie. I want her to know what's going on here."

A brilliant smile burst open upon Eden(the Pris Virus) as she stepped out from behind Edie.

Edie smiled up at her. "Hi, Eden. Hi, Pris."

Mickey's gob was smacked. "You're okay with this?"

"Are you okay with George?" Edie asked.

George(the Pris Virus) walked into the kitchen.

Mickey's bugged eyes darted from apparition to real body to apparition.

"He's speechless!" Eden(the Pris Virus) crowed. "He's not even spouting any mathematical haiku."

"You got him good, Edie," George(the Pris Virus) said.

"I had something to do with it," The Pris Virus' disembodied voice proclaimed.

Eden(the Pris Virus) sat at the table. "Eat, Mickey, before it gets cold."

George(the Pris Virus) sat in the empty chair across from the image of his sister. "Don't mind us."

Mickey looked at Edie. "You could see and hear Eden the whole time?"

Edie nodded, brimming with good humor.

"And you're okay with this?"

Edie beamed. "Why wouldn't I be? All three of my lovelies are here."

Mickey sagged with a sigh. "This is going to get complicated."

Edie sat across from him. "Mickey, you wouldn't want it any other way. You get bored when things are simple."

"She knows you well, runt," Eden(the Pris Virus) said. "And she considers you one of her lovelies. How sweet."

George(the Pris Virus) produced a deck of cards. "After you two finish dinner maybe we can play some Egyptian Rat Screw."

About the Author

Mike Sherer lives in West Chester in the Greater Cincinnati area of southwest Ohio. His screenplay 'Hamal_18' was produced in Los Angeles and released direct to DVD and is currently available on Amazon Prime. His paranormal/suspense novel 'A Cold Dish' was published by James Ward Kirk Fiction. His horror novella 'Under A Raging Moon' was published by World Castle Publishing. His Middle Grade novel 'Shadytown' was published by INtense Publications. His paranormal mystery novel 'Souls of Nod' was published by Breaking Rules Publishing. Mike has published 6 other novellas and 31 short stories. None of his works have been self-published other than his novella 'The Dead Sister', which is posted on Kindle Vella.

Links to Mike Sherer's published works are available on his web page: https://mikesherer.org where his travel blog 'American Locations' is also posted.

Check out these Books from WolfSinger Publications

Infinity – Ted Pennella

In the distant future, when peace between humanity and the artificial intelligences their ancestors created has been settled, Conrad Conner tries to live a quiet and unassuming life in orbit about Jupiter on the city-station *Socrates' Odyssey*. When Conner's attempt to create a prototypical communication artificial for use by the Sol-Humana Confederation's Stellar Fleet get derailed by attempted murder of the very artificial he's created, his life spirals into a mad flight back to Earth to try and save at least his sister's children, if not his sister herself. Past failures and heartaches resurface as seemingly unconnected dots become a plot by the First Admiral to steal not just power over the Confederation, but a secret Conner holds within himself. A secret not even Conner knows about.

Borne in the Blood – edited by Carol Hightshoe

Delve into the mysterious and powerful world of blood in "Borne in the Blood"

This collection of enthralling stories explores the multifaceted essence of blood—as a symbol of life, a medium of magic, and a bond of kinship. From the chilling tale of a minstrel haunted by a spectral king to the whimsical account of a vampire ice cream vendor, each story weaves a unique narrative around the theme of blood. Encounter a woman whose body bizarrely intertwines with metallic elements, and follow a girl's journey as she confronts her isolation due to her heritage. Feel chills as those who were wronged reach across the years to have their final revenge on the blood descendants of those who oppressed them.

Shifters, Vampires, Witches, and other ordinary and extraordinary folk—all bound together by that which they carry in their blood.

These tales will transport you through a spectrum of emotions, from the depths of fear to the heights of fantasy, as you unravel the mysteries and power that lie within the blood.

Proceeds from sales of Borne in the Blood will be donated to the Multiple Myeloma Research Foundation: themmrf.org/

Winter Emergence – Dana Bell

Kat has lived in the mountain her entire life. Going outside is allowed only to a select few, many of which never return, including her brother Ned. She doesn't want to believe he might be dead and tries every night to contact him via the coms. Silence is the only response.

Desperate to find an answer to his disappearance, Kat steals a snow cat and searches for her brother, putting the safety of everyone in jeopardy. She's joined by a cat who, for some reason, wants to come with her, and leaves once they reach the city, leaving her alone to face unknown challenges and threats for which she's not prepared.

In the city Word Warrior faces a new threat. A Striped One stalks the cats, wolves and snow ghosts killing any unfortunate enough to be caught as if they are rightful prey! He must find a way to stop the predator or all he has worked to accomplish might fail, forcing them to revert to the old laws of challenge and mate.

A new female appears bringing news of two legs, an enemy they all feared, who lived in a strange world where she had been forced to stay until she managed to escape. In fact, one was in the city and close by.

Faced with multiple threats, including worse snowstorms, Word Warrior faces the responsibility to protect their community from all dangers, knowing if he fails—they could all die.

Space Brides, LLC – edited by Dana Bell

Tired of those lonely dark nights? No one in your settlement suitable? We are here to help! We will help you find the bride or husband to keep you company, raise your children, and be your partner building a dream together. Contact us directly and give us your specifications. Success guaranteed.

In this collection of 15 testimonials read about the challenges and triumphs of some of our clients as they found love on the frontier of space.

From aliens to vampires, we brought these couples together and together they found acceptance and love—each in their own way.

A man with three kids finds an unexpected match in the brother of the woman he had contracted to marry when she runs away.

A woman running away from an abusive marriage finds acceptance and respect with a colony group that marries everyone to everyone in order to ensure they know they belong to a family.

A woman constantly rejected because of her skin color and origins finds acceptance and love with a wounded soldier.

Even though we encourage absolute honesty in your profile and correspondence with your potential spouse—many people don't. However, like some of the testimonials you'll read here; they still manage to expand their horizons—together.

Contact or walk into any of our offices 24/7. We are here to help you find that special someone and start a new future!

Other conditions apply.
Please ask for more information before contract is drawn up and signed.

The Dragon's Hoard – edited by Carol Hightshoe

Dragons are well known for their hoards—but not all hoards are created equal.

A young dragon starts his hoard with some very precious gifts.
One dragon shares her complaints about taxes with a friend as they wait for a lunch delivery.
Another dragon defends her most precious treasures against a group of greedy goblins.
And yet another may hold the solution to saving the Earth, after a devastating apocalypse, in his collection of bottled treasures.

In addition to the normal gold, silver and jewels here you will find dragons who collect many different treasures. 25 storytellers invite you to enter The Dragon's Hoard and share the treasures within.

The Dark See: Book Three of the MoleSkinCap – M.R. Williamson

As Helen Durkin's journey to find out about herself continues, she finally realizes that she needs the help of someone with more knowledge than dwarves, elves, or even dragons. But, just how do you approach the old Wizard Andsell Phagan?

As she tries to solve that problem, yet another dangerous situation presents itself. This mysterious person is not a friend of the Phagan family. Helen quickly finds herself on a collision course with a halfling who most refer to as Scar—one who dabbles in the dark side of magic.

With this added pressure, the effort to approach and perhaps train under Andsell Phagan intensifies. As time progresses, an old friend comes to her aid. Now, the race is on, and the old Dragon Pragamore takes the lead in Helen's plight.

Will Helen finally find out why the Faes are calling her Bright Helen?

What of Pragamore? Will his years keep him from helping?
And, who is Scar really after—Helen, the old wizard, or Pragamore?

The Steel Fist – Rob Jackson

The survivors of Recon 9 are needed in the Ozarks where some home-grown autocrats have taken over parts of Arkansas and parts of Missouri. They've looted National Guard armories and hoarded weapons, ammunition, and vital supplies, just waiting for the opportunity to take over the area. While most of their transport, armor, and aircraft are obsolete, they face people with no protection against such deadly equipment. And they're trying to get the local natural resources to gain control of weapons that even the military have no defense against.

Recon 9 has gained four new members and formed an alliance with locals, many of them veterans, against a common enemy. The locals have some grasp of tactics, an excellent knowledge of the hilly, forested countryside and a burning desire to be rid of the terrorists, who call themselves:

THE STEEL FIST

Crisis in Big-G City – S.D. Matley

Olympus, Inc., is locked in battle with climate change!

Athena's Secret Ops program steps in when bad boy and technological genius Hermes can't come up with a carbon-curbing solution. Undercover agents Cleo Petra and Pan are deployed in the mortal world to vanquish the notorious East brothers, chthonic fossil fuel magnates who pass as human and eat humans, too...

Two-month-old Pablo, the one-quarter chthonic infant son of two fathers formerly known as P.B., employs his extraordinary abilities of adult speech and intellect in pursuit of climate justice!

Meanwhile, David Bernstein, whose hot romance with Cleo Petra meets a rocky end, recovers the memory of his century-old love affair with a beautiful Spanish nurse. He time travels to 1918 to find her and encounters love, loss, and the City of Mount Olympus—a dark and sinister place where every inhabitant lives in fear of a volatile and destructive Zeus!

David's birth father and Hera's former fling, Saul Crispin, is outed as a mortal made immortal. Will Hera's high crime of granting Saul eternal life land her before a jury of her peers for judgment?

And what of baby-crazy Queen of the Underworld, Persephone, pregnant at last but not by Hades?

Intrigue, espionage, crimes of passion, secret babies and looming existential threats—everywhere you look there's a Crisis in Big-G City!

Tree of Bones – Book Two: A Familiar's Tale – Verna McKinnon

Two Curses

A curse of Darkness…Deep within the Thill forest, stands a tree made of human bones, crowned in black leaves and red thorns.

A curse of Light…Beneath the Wastelands of Skarros, a crystal imprisons a dark, immortal queen.

The Sorceress, Runa, is tormented by horrific images of this tree of bones in a distant, lifeless forest. Even as the visions debilitate her, Mellypip, her beloved familiar, also experiences these sinister dreams, bound by the same dream seer magic as his mistress. The tree of bones summons Runa, and she must risk madness and death as obsession drives her on. What she finds reveals a devastating truth.

Koll the Sorcerer awaits trial for his crimes. His familiar, Xabral, searches for allies to free him. Driven by his own dreams of dark prophecy, Koll seeks to free Obsydia, the Bloodstone Queen, from her prison. Determined to let nothing stop him, Koll will commit any evil to achieve his goal.

Runa and Mellypip's newest journey reveals truths behind ancient secrets, as Koll's obsessive hunt for a fallen queen threatens to doom the world forever. Runa and Koll, bound by opposing magical destinies of Light and Dark, will ultimately face frightening revelations and unimagined consequences.

Gate of Souls – Book One: A Familiar's Tale – Verna McKinnon

Familiars.

Magical animal companions of sorcerers.

Keepers of spells and secrets.

Most important, devoted friends for life.

When one such familiar, Mellypip, bonds with the young sorceress Runa, he shares in the wonders of magic. Together, Mellypip and Runa train under the tutelage of Runa's grandfather, Cathal, and his cantankerous mountain owl familiar, Belwyn. But secrets and spells do not make for good sorcery. Old friends begin to vanish even as enemies from Cathal's past return, threatening to reveal the truth of Runa's parents; a truth from which Cathal must protect his granddaughter at any cost. When Cathal is kidnapped, Runa and Mellypip rush against time to save their family and friends from dark sorcery that will not only destroy them, but shatter the Gate of

Souls and release demonic creatures of The Otherworld into the mortal realms.

And more – check out our books at
www.wolfsingerpubs.com